"A LIVELY PLOT . . . THE TEXAS ATMOSPHERE AGAINST WHICH THE STORY UNFOLDS IS SHARPLY DRAWN, REPLETE WITH TOUGH-TALKING JUDGES, COLORFUL DEFENSE ATTORNEYS, ALCOHOLIC DRIFTERS, AND HARD-WORKING NEW AMERICANS. . . . FUN . . . FAST-PACED AND SOLIDLY RESEARCHED."
—*The New York Times Book Review*

A TWISTING, RELENTLESS CONTEMPORARY COURTROOM THRILLER

TRIAL

CLIFFORD IRVING

"*TRIAL* IS LIKE A BIRCHBARK CANOE OR A SEVEN-LAYER CAKE: YOU CAN GO CRAZY TRYING TO FIGURE OUT HOW IT'S MADE, AND IT'S MADE BY A MASTER."
—*Los Angeles Times*

"JET-PROPELLED . . . COLORFUL, DOWN-AND-DIRTY CHARACTERS . . . THE LEGAL POINTS ARE ARTFULLY PRESENTED. . . . MOST READERS WILL WANT TO READ THIS AT ONE SITTING."
—*Library Journal*

"*A DECEPTIVELY LAID-BACK TALE OF A TEXAS DEFENDER'S NIGHTMARE . . . [AN] APPEALING HERO . . . SUSPENSEFUL AND CHARMING.*"
—*Kirkus Reviews*

"MASTERFUL . . . THE COURT PROCEEDINGS, STRATEGY, AND TESTIMONY ARE AUTHENTIC AND FIRST-RATE."
—*Publishers Weekly*

QUANTITY SALES

INDIVIDUAL SALES

TRIAL

CLIFFORD IRVING

A DELL BOOK

Published by
Dell Publishing
a division of
Bantam Doubleday Dell Publishing Group, Inc.
666 Fifth Avenue
New York, New York 10103

ISBN: 0-440-21017-8

Reprinted by arrangement with Summit Books, New York, New York

Printed in the United States of America

Published simultaneously in Canada

July 1991

10 9 8 7 6 5 4 3 2 1

OPM

To know and love another human being for nearly fifty years is a pleasure as deep as any the world has to offer. This book is dedicated to my dear friend Bernie Wohl, a hero of the city

THANKS

In Houston: especially to criminal defense attorneys Kent Schaffer and David Bires; and to Robert Turner, Deborah Gottlieb, and Edward Mallett of the same fraternity; and to Mike McSpadden, Tom Routt, and Norman Lanford, district court judges of Harris County, all of whom, for the purpose of this book, gave me access to their minds and the peculiar workings of the law. In Los Angeles: to Bob Lewin and Frank Cooper for their wise counsel. In Mexico: to my wife, Maureen Earl, for her good company and perceptions. In New York: to Jim Silberman for his calm guidance. And everywhere to Maurice Nessen for his passionate editing and attention to legal detail.

None are responsible for the ideas in this book, but all contributed, knowingly or not.

C.I.
San Miguel de Allende
June 1990

Justice, like lasting love, is rare but not impossible. Both depend on the courage and diligence of one enlightened person.

Jean le Malchanceux
A Crusader's Journal

In Houston, Texas, in the early winter of 1985, a petty thief named Virgil Freer devised a scheme to bilk the chain of Kmart stores. Using a bootleg electronic pricing gun, he drastically lowered the bar codes on such items as expensive fishing equipment and lawn mowers, bought the goods in one branch of Kmart and then returned them in other branches for a full refund. Like most crooks with a workable scam, Virgil Freer did it once too often. He was arrested, jailed.

Virgil was a small, wiry man with pale eyes and yellowed teeth, and skin that had the rubbery translucence of a jellyfish. He seemed beaten down by life, humbled, pitiable. A redneck who chewed tobacco, said "aw shucks" and "consarned," Virgil made inquiries around the Harris County Jail from the knowledgeable inmates.

"I need a real smart lawyer. A tough one. But I ain't got much money, so he'd better be on the young side. And a local boy's best."

He hired Warren Blackburn, twenty-nine years old, a criminal defense attorney toiling his way toward the top of his profession. Warren's father, the late Judge Eugene T. Blackburn, had been a protégé of Lyndon Johnson, and on the bench had been known as Maximum Gene, a tribute to the penalties he meted out to offenders foolish enough to give up their right under Texas law to be sentenced by a jury.

Virgil heard that Warren Blackburn was cut from different cloth—a friend to the friendless, a battler for clemency —but that he was stubborn and he got things done.

On a cool January morning the young, dark-haired lawyer, wearing a leather windbreaker and corduroys, sat opposite Virgil in one of the visitors' cubicles of the Harris County Jail. There was a persistent smell of meat loaf and disinfectant in the air. The jail housed more than thirty-five hundred men in tan jumpsuits and slippers without heels, and two hundred women in shapeless gray striped dresses, all either awaiting court proceedings or in a holding pattern prior to residence at the state prison complex up at Huntsville. The walls of the jail were painted yellow and some had claw marks in them.

Warren Blackburn said to Virgil, "If you're straight with me, Mr. Freer, I can help you. If you lie to me—well, hell, I've known enough liars so that one more won't crater me. It'll be your ass in the ditch, not mine."

Virgil liked this lawyer immediately. Confident, calm, wry in speech and keen of eye, he was not one of those fast-talking counselors who kept saying "Don't worry" and never quite bothered to explain the sharpened stakes and snares that lay ahead in the legal underbrush. A good ole boy, Virgil decided, with a college education. An honest man. *The man I need.*

"I swear I'll tell you God's truth about what-all you ask me," Virgil said. "But please, you got to spring me outa here right away or I'll go crazy. My wife's in the hospital with cancer. If I don't git back home, my kids'll starve."

Warren commiserated, probed, asked basic questions. "Virgil, do you have any prior convictions?"

Shamefacedly, Virgil admitted that some years ago up in Oklahoma he had been convicted for drunk driving and given six months' probation, and then later copped a plea for passing a few bad checks, with a sentence of ninety days in a county jail.

"That's just a little misdemeanor trash," Warren said, "so let's see what I can do."

They arranged a small fee.

Warren checked with Ben Taub Hospital and discovered that Freer had told the truth: his wife was about to be operated on for bone cancer. That saddened the young lawyer but it also made him feel he could trust his client's word. He put on a dark suit and went to the assistant district attorney who was prosecuting the case. The prosecutor slapped down on his metal desk a computer printout that listed the two prior convictions. He demanded $20,000 bail.

Warren shook his head mournfully. "Don't you want to be able to sleep nights? This is the man's first felony. His wife's in Ben Taub, he's got four little kids to support—you think he'll up and leave town? Give the poor bastard a break."

The prosecutor reluctantly agreed to $5000 bail. Using a bondsman who owed him a favor, Warren got Virgil Freer out of jail.

One windy evening Warren visited Freer outside of town, where the little man lived in a dilapidated mobile home with his four ragged, watery-eyed young children and several mongrel dogs. Virgil wore overalls and a red gimme cap with a CAT Diesel patch. He had a job as an auto mechanic; a buxom, slack-jawed young country woman named Belinda was taking care of the kids in the daytime. While the dogs snarled in the dust over some bones and the ragamuffin children whined and fought, Virgil pleaded with his new lawyer: "If I go to prison, there's no one to look after the little 'uns. The state'll throw them into one of them godawful homes! Mr. Blackburn, that'll kill my wife for sure. You're a married man, cain't you understand how I feel? You got to help me. I learned my lesson."

I've met a lot worse than Virgil, Warren decided. Using a pricing gun to steal from a Kmart was only a step above petty shoplifting and hardly rose to the level of armed robbery. Playing God, Warren decided that Virgil would never rape or kill anybody. He deserved a chance to go straight.

The case had fallen into Judge Louise Parker's 299th District Court. Lou Parker, as the judge called herself, was probably the most harsh and obdurate magistrate in the Harris County Courthouse. Warren kept plea-bargaining, delaying, hoping for a break. And he got one: Judge Parker's tough number-two prosecutor, who had been demanding seven years' pen time for Virgil Freer, suddenly jumped from the district attorney's office to private practice. He was replaced by a young black woman named Nancy Goodpaster, fresh out of Bates College of Law at the University of Houston. She was sincere and ambitious but overwhelmed by the crowded court docket.

In her small office piled high with papers and overflowing accordion files, Nancy Goodpaster and Warren began a fresh round of plea bargaining. "Freer's a first offender, isn't he?" the prosecutor inquired. She answered her own question: "I'm sure he is—I can't find any prior convictions in his file."

The computer printout citing Freer's Oklahoma misdemeanor convictions evidently was buried deep, perhaps lost. They didn't know!

A little startled, Warren changed the subject. "If we could come out of this with probation and a fine," he said, "we could live with it. The man's wife may die of cancer. He's got four little children to support. I'm not taking his word for it. I checked. He's never lied to me. Let me tell you, that's rare."

Nancy Goodpaster had heard around the courthouse that Warren was a scrupulous, trustworthy lawyer. She wilted, offering thirty days probated for a year, plus court costs and a $500 fine. A good deal.

Warren worried it over in his mind a while and then returned to Freer, who was biting his chipped fingernails on a back bench in the 299th.

His eyes were hard and stern. "Virgil, are you going to keep that job you've got?"

"Yes, sir."

"You going to get into trouble again?"

"Shoot, no!"

Warren looked as deep as he could into what he hoped was Virgil Freer's soul. In his three years of practice he had known his share of con men and criminals. Their gaze was either evasive or remarkably cool and straightforward. Freer's was neither; he had the harassed eyes of a simple, bedeviled man. Life had dealt him poor cards. An ugly little fellow, flawed but tenacious. And he had a good heart; he cared as well as he could for all those noisy bucktoothed children with their pale and violent eyes.

"You swear on the Bible and all that's holy, Virgil, and on the heads of your young 'uns, that you're going to stay out of trouble?"

"Yes, sir! I swear it!"

"Well, you better, because I'm putting *my* ass on the line for you." Warren explained the state's offer and said, "My advice is take it. Look after your kids and pray for your wife. Sign fast, Virgil, before I get religion and change my mind."

The paper to be signed was an affidavit in support of Virgil Freer's probation. Warren signed it too—or, as the law would have it, he knowingly executed the instrument. The affidavit stated that Freer had no prior convictions.

Warren's career proceeded along its steady upward track. He forgot about Virgil Freer until nine months later, one night on a highway north of the city, Freer was caught attempting to hijack a truckful of television sets. He was carrying a .38-caliber pistol. He exchanged six frenzied shots with the arresting officers before he was wounded in the leg and begged to surrender.

A zealous young Harris County assistant D.A. studied the full file and noticed there was something peculiar about Freer's last probation. He said to Virgil, "Look here, in this affidavit in the Kmart case last year, you swore you didn't have any priors. You lied, you scumbag."

"Yeah, but my lawyer told me to."

Warren, when he heard the charge, sank his head into the darkness of his cupped hands. He could bluff and say that Freer had never told him. But one more lie under such circumstances would be more than he could stomach.

That evening, at home, he told the tale to his wife, Charm, a young woman of slender grace and strong opinions. Under her maiden name, Charmian Kimball, she was a reporter for the local independent TV station. The Blackburns' house on Braes Bayou was a red brick rambler with a small backyard pool surrounded by banana trees. In the shadows, standing by the pool, Warren stared up at the silent and indifferent universe.

"I feel such a fool," he said. "I put my whole career in jeopardy for a man I knew I'd never see again."

"You thought he owed you something," his wife said quietly, with some reproach. "You forgot about human nature."

A few days later, from the district attorney's office, Warren learned that Virgil Freer's wife had died seven months ago. Large-breasted, slack-jawed Belinda had moved into the mobile home to share the lumpy bed. Virgil had sent his two oldest children to live with an alcoholic aunt in Fort Worth and committed the two youngest to a state-run institution that promised to arrange adoption.

Oh, my God, Warren thought. Where was my judgment? I've been around, I'm not a kid—how could I have been so wrong?

He was technically guilty of aggravated perjury, a felony, because the statement had been used in an official court proceeding. If convicted, he would be disbarred. But Maximum Gene had been popular with the gang over at 201 Fannin, the district attorney's office. Humiliated, disgusted with himself to a degree that no one at the courthouse fully realized, Warren arrived there with the pallid air of a penitent and managed to cut a deal: aggravated perjury reduced to a Class A misdemeanor, party to false swearing. The agreement was for one year's suspended sentence.

Wearing his most conservative gray suit, he pled before

Judge Lou Parker, since hers was the court where the offense had taken place. In her black robes of authority, Judge Parker sat upright in her big leather chair behind the judicial bench, eyeglasses dangling from a gold chain that she fondled with stubby fingers. She had a mannish voice, a deep South Texas accent. She called Warren "a disgrace to the legal profession and a blot on our memory of your father, a distinguished jurist."

In the windowless fluorescent-lit eighth-floor courtroom that always smelled of ammonia with a veneer of sweat, young Nancy Goodpaster was awarded the pleasure of prosecuting and spelling out the plea.

But Judge Parker intoned, "Mr. Blackburn, before I'll consider the state's recommendation, I want to hear in your own words what you think you did wrong, and just why you think I shouldn't drop three years of pen time on your bowed head. And I don't want any namby-pamby standard b.s. like y'all always throw up at me when you're pleading for some lowlife dog who sold cocaine to children. Make an effort, counselor. You're supposed to be an officer of the court."

Warren, throughout the proceedings, had been outwardly grave but his head was not bowed. He felt as many criminals feel: more furious for having been caught— through simplemindedness and childlike trust—than sorry for having broken a social contract.

To grovel now would compound the crime against his self-respect. He squared his shoulders and said, "I relaxed my ethical standards, your honor. Even if a lawyer's client is a lowlife dog who sold cocaine to children, we're supposed to do all we can to help him. I went too far. And I bought a sob story. I'm ashamed not only because I perjured myself as an officer of the court but because it was an extreme error of personal judgment—more than this court will ever know."

"You finished, counselor? That's it?"

"Yes, your honor. And it's a lot."

Scowling, Judge Parker honored the deal that Warren had made with the Office of the District Attorney. But she added on her own that he be suspended for one year from practicing law, and during that year keep his bloodied nose out of the Harris County Courthouse.

Despite Warren's dark mutterings of protest, his wife was in the courtroom when Lou Parker sentenced him to the year's exile. At home later, in their bedroom, Charm kicked off her shoes and said heatedly, "From what I hear —and my sources are pretty good—if every lawyer who signed a false affidavit got suspended for a year, and if every prosecutor who withheld evidence because it might damage his case got caught, they could turn the Harris County Courthouse into a goddam parking lot! And that self-righteous bitch of a judge is well aware of it."

Warren said, "Honey, I knew what I was doing. I paid the price."

"Too facile. I think maybe the reason you helped Freer was a little deeper than you realize."

Deeper? He had wanted to save a handful of human lives. He asked what she meant.

She said, "I guess all lawyers sometimes think, 'There but for the grace of God . . .' What I'm trying to say is, Warren, you were weak. You think it was an error of judgment, but you should never have been making a judgment in the first place. A lawyer has no right to ever set himself up as a judge or jury. You did it because you don't like the system. You find it painful that people go to prison."

"Not all of them," he grumbled. "Ship most of the bastards where they can't harm us anymore. Maybe a space station on the way to Mars, an extraterrestrial Australia." He realized that he was evading her point.

So did Charm. "I'm not talking about the evil ones," she said. "Most of your clients are just common sleazeballs. Nine times out of ten they did something either horribly wrong or unforgivably stupid. The law says if they're guilty they have to go to jail for a certain number of years.

You have to work within that law. If you don't like doing that, if you feel too sorry for them, maybe you weren't really cut out to be a criminal lawyer."

Warren had wanted to be lawyer not because his father had been a lawyer but because he believed he could be a better one. Even in law school he had understood that he didn't want to spend his life writing business contracts or becoming advisory partner to the battles of greedy men, although that way he might become rich. He wanted the challenge of litigative action. He knew that you couldn't thwart hurricanes or fight God's unfathomable will, but he believed that the law was meant to redress the imbalance wrought by human brute force, conniving, and wrongdoing. He had chosen criminal law.

"Jesus Christ," he muttered to his wife. "Lay off, will you? I feel like shit already. I don't need to be told I should quit practicing my profession."

"I didn't say that," she pointed out. But she backed off and let the matter drop.

During the twelve months of official disgrace he reported once a month to his probation officer. Damned if I'll vegetate, Warren decided. I'll use the time to do things I always said I wanted to do. He worked as an occasional part-time investigator for another lawyer, an old friend named Rick Levine. He joined a gym and pumped iron. He took a cordon bleu cooking class.

His office on Montrose was a single-story wood-frame white building, a converted residential cottage. Warren had started his career with a gang of young lawyers sharing a suite in a modern downtown building, but the sterility of the building outweighed the camaraderie. When he found the cottage, about a year before the Virgil Freer case, he moved in immediately. In that office, feet up on his desk, during the year of probation he read *One Hundred Years of Solitude,* most of Dostoyevski, some Faulkner, and books by Marilyn French and Betty Friedan in an effort to grasp how the world was changing. He studied *The Joy of Cook-*

ing and Julia Child and made notes on a legal pad. In the summer he drove down to Mexico for a month and took a course in intensive Spanish at a little school called Interidiomas in the mountain town of San Miguel de Allende.

Charm stole a week's vacation from reporting and flew down to join him. They stayed in a little inn on a narrow cobbled street where purple bougainvillea climbed over the balcony, with a view of a cathedral that some visionary eighteenth-century Indio architect had designed from postcards of Chartres. The town smelled of flowers and donkey shit. In the cool rainy afternoons they made love while cathedral bells clanged, mongrels barked. Warren remembered it as the best week of his marriage, even better than their honeymoon on Maui. Charm said, "You're a good man. When this is all over, honey, you'll be fine."

Banishment ended, he appeared at the courthouse to inform the world that he was again ready to practice law. Except for the judges and prosecutors, everyone was friendly, backslapping. But it was referrals he needed: clients, not lunch companions. An occasional misdemeanor or minor drug case came his way, but most of the time he sat in his office annotating his cookbooks and reading current volumes of the *American Criminal Law Review.*

Charm organized dinner parties for lawyers and their wives and husbands. Warren prepared escargots and coq au vin. The dinners were lively. Rick Levine—short, blackhaired, with a flaring mustache, sloping nose, and the beginnings of a paunch—gravely said, "Maybe you should open up a restaurant."

"If you didn't expect to fatten up on the cuff, I might just do it."

Warren and Rick had been schoolmates together at Lamarr High, then at UT-Austin, class of '77, then at South Texas College of Law in Houston. Rick had become a defense attorney specializing in drug cases, figuring his fees by the kilo: $500 for marijuana, $5,000 for cocaine. He owned four racehorses stabled nearby in Louisiana. Two

were named after his young children. Another was called
Acapulco Gold, another White Lady.

One night after dinner Warren drew Rick outside to the
terrace. "So I made a mistake once, but I'm still a damned
good lawyer. Don't people remember that?"

"I imagine," Rick said, "that prospective clients may
think that some of the judges are a little prejudiced against
you. And that might be true. Everyone wants an edge, not
a liability. I know it's bullshit, but that's how people are."

Warren realized that Rick had heard something. Maybe
he *would* be a liability to a client. The thought shocked
him a little.

Maybe I'm not tough enough: that, he realized, was
what Charm had been trying to say. It could be that in this
business you needed skin of leather and no heart. He remembered a Houston Oilers defensive tackle he had defended in a cocaine possession case some years ago. The
football player said, "There's these rookies, see, at training
camp? They show up on the field at seven in the morning
to run laps and they work out until seven in the evening.
Me, I show up at ten, leave at three. And they get cut, and
I stay. They can't ever figure it out. See what I'm saying?
They don't have it—whatever *it* is—and I do."

Warren came to question whether he had it, whatever it
was. But he also remembered William Faulkner's Nobel
Prize speech, where the old writer had said that our task
was not merely to survive, but to prevail.

I'll prevail, Warren vowed. And to prove to his peers
and betters that one lapse in judgment had diminished neither his skills nor his respect for the law, he began hustling
court appointments.

Houston, alone among major cities, employed no public
defender's office. If an accused claimed he was too poor to
hire counsel, the judge would appoint a lawyer and order a
legal fee paid out of public funds. Each morning at eight
o'clock, hungry defense attorneys left their business cards
on the bench at the judge's elbow, then crowded around

the desks of the court coordinators who helped dispense the cases. Some lawyers, fresh out of law school, officed out of the courthouse basement cafeteria where the overhead was the price of an overcooked hamburger and a cup of weak coffee; they sought court-appointed work in order to gain experience. Older lawyers hustled for it when their collars were frayed and they smelled of stale tobacco.

When he was younger, more brash, Warren likened the older lawyers to vultures waiting for dead meat. Now he was more forgiving. He was one of them.

He did court-appointed work for two years. It was survival. He never went to trial: all the cases were plea-bargained. Warren once overheard a journeyman lawyer tell a judge, "You can pay me $300 and I'll plead this guy guilty and move it through real smooth, or you can get some other guy for $150 who'll fuck up your docket. Up to you, your honor." Warren spent his days haggling like a merchant in a North African bazaar. He dealt with drunken drivers, vagrants, addicts and small-time crack dealers, the trash of the streets and ghettos. The court dockets were jammed—sentences were handed down swiftly, often by rote. Most of the judges' stone-faced speeches were generated by computers. The prosecutors were impatient, ambitious. The price of mercy was time. And no one had time.

Some days Warren wanted to smash his fists against the courtroom walls in frustration. I'm a trial lawyer, he thought bitterly, that's where I shine, that's what I love. For the sake of a son of a bitch like Virgil Freer I gave all that up. He grew depressed, moody. His face began to lose its youthful sparkle.

But still in his daydreams, like a lover whose indifferent mistress is far away, he embraced the shadowy belief that if he kept working at it and did his best, he could somehow claw his way back to where he had been before he lied to save his client who was now doing thirty years at Huntsville prison for armed robbery and attempted murder of a police officer, and whose scruffy, scrapping, shallow-eyed children, for whom Warren had felt such pity, were thrown away on the common garbage heap of life. If I live long enough, he thought with a renewed burst of outrage and shame, one day I'll be plea-bargaining for them too.

Rain beat on the roof, lightning crackled across the horizon. Behind each stroke the lightning left a wake of heated air that came to them as thunder. Charm Blackburn cried out softly and it woke Warren, who calmed her with whispers and touches until she subsided into uneasy sleep. The digital clock showed 3:30 A.M.: Friday, May 19, 1989. For a while Warren listened to the rain and the banshee wind.

The lawn sprinklers popped up at six o'clock, arcing their spray onto the soaked grass. Warren woke again, this time with an erection, which he attributed to his wife's presence on his side of the bed. Usually Charm hugged her down pillow and kept far to her own side, for the bony parts of Warren's body disturbed her sleep. But this morning she was behind him, breasts pressed against his shoulder blades, breath in his ear. He took that closeness to be a hangover from the storm and the unnamed fears it arouses in those of us whose roots are not strong.

Twisting toward her, he whispered her name. Charm opened her eyes to slits, but slid a hand from under the sheet to wag her finger briefly in front of Warren's nose. The wave was the same one she had learned to use down in San Miguel de Allende to fend off urchins who nagged for pesos. The kids backed off. Then Charm would say, "Oh, God, how could I have done that?" and chase after them to press coins in their hands.

"What time is it?" she whispered.

"Six-fifteen."

She turned away from him and pulled the comforter over her head.

The clouds rushed westward, birds chirped on the lawn.

Sliding out of bed, Warren embraced Oobie, his arthritic old golden retriever who slept on the carpet at the foot of the bed, and then slipped into his gray sweats. With Oobie joyfully limping and panting at his side he jogged for twenty minutes along Braes Bayou. At home again he showered, brewed coffee, and with it ate a bowl of Mueslix and a banana from the tree by the pool.

He dressed quietly, careful not to wake Charm. Looking down at what he could see of his wife—some strands of dark blond hair, a curve of ivory cheek, a familiar shape in a fetal curl under the covers—he whispered, "I love you."

A few minutes after seven he was in his BMW on the Southwest Freeway under a blue sky scrubbed by the night's rain. Under it you could dream of wranglers riding up from the Brazos and the old paddleboats churning foam on Buffalo Bayou. And indeed, Warren dreamed as he drove. But he dreamed that he was married to a woman who still adored him, that his office telephone never stopped ringing, that he was in control of his life. The wholeness of things held sway. He knew that he had to make a move or the center would fall apart.

From a telephone outside the basement cafeteria in the courthouse, he called his answering service. The only message of consequence was a request to call Scoot Shepard's office. Dropping another quarter into the slot, Warren returned the call. A secretary informed him that Mr. Shepard was in a pretrial hearing in the 342nd District Court.

"And what's happening in the 342nd?" Warren asked.

"A setting of bail in the Ott case," the secretary said.

"If I can't catch him there," Warren promised, "I'll call back."

Scoot Shepard was the dean of Houston criminal defense attorneys; he had been a friend of Warren's father. Few people are legends in their own time, but Scoot was one. In the trial of John R. Baker, the oil multimillionaire accused of poisoning his society wife, Scoot had hung the jury twice in a row until the case ultimately was dismissed. He had represented Martha Sachs, the sex doctor accused of murdering her woman lover in front of two witnesses, and won an acquittal. Scoot had defended major drug dealers and Mafia capos and got them off when there was little more than a hazy hope or a muttered Sicilian prayer. He had been profiled in *Time* and even *Vanity Fair,* and had been asked by a dozen New York publishers to write a book about his cases. Declining, he was quoted as saying, "Once I give away my secret, what advantage have I got?" But there was minimal honesty in that, Warren decided. Nobody could learn from a book what Scoot knew.

Warren took the elevator up to the fifth floor and the 342nd District Court. Under a lofty ceiling, its walnut-paneled walls were lined with oil portraits of robed judges from decades past. The current presiding resident of the 342nd, Judge Dwight Bingham, was one of Harris County's four black judges. His courtroom was the most spacious and dignified in the courthouse; he had earned it by seniority. "But what Dwight Bingham knows about the law," Warren's father had said, when Warren had just begun practicing, "you could stuff into a wetback's taco. He's too easy, too friendly. He doesn't like to send young niggers to prison on the theory that they get buttfucked and come out more violent than they went in. He's got what I suppose you and your hippie friends would call . . . compassion."

Warren liked and admired Judge Bingham. The law could be harsh. Good law became bad law if bad men administered it. The world was crueler than most people would admit, Warren believed, and it needed all the compassion available.

Ten days ago, in a familiar ritual, the clerk at the Office of the District Attorney had spun the birdcage that held colored Ping-Pong balls with the numbers of the twenty-six Harris County courts. The yellow ball with Judge Bingham's number had popped out; he had drawn the plum of the current season, the Ott murder case. The accused, the owner of a topless nightclub, had killed her lover, Dr. Clyde Ott, a multimillionaire gynecologist who owned drug detox clinics throughout Harris County. The State of Texas was charging willful murder; Scoot Shepard, on behalf of the defendant, had pled self-defense. For weeks the murder had been a lead story on the evening news. The trial was on the docket for late July, guaranteed to make headlines every day—the kind of trial a lawyer loved.

Nearing seventy years of age and ready to retire, Judge Bingham sat on the high walnut bench framed against the Great Seal of Texas. Although today's event was merely a routine application for reduction of bail for the defendant, there was no room in front of the bar on the courtroom bench reserved for lawyers. Warren squeezed into one of the spectators' pews, noting that more than a few defense attorneys and prosecutors were scattered among the crowd. They had come to hear Scoot Shepard, the maestro. Young lawyers learned from him, veterans simply enjoyed him.

Chunky, about five-ten, Scoot had a pale, domelike forehead, and his slightly bloodshot eyes were black disks set deep into his head. His nose was large and fleshy. Today he wore a wrinkled suit. Warren had always thought he could pass for an oil rig operator on holiday in Vegas.

Dim yellow lights gleamed from the high paneled ceiling onto Judge Bingham's bald brown head. He looked up from some papers and said gently, "All right now, Mr. Shepard, I've read this application on behalf of your client, Ms. Johnnie Faye Boudreau. You want me to reduce her bail from $300,000 to $50,000. I'm not sure I can do that."

Scoot Shepard scrambled awkwardly to his feet. "Your honor, my client's got the best reason a defendant can have. She's broke."

Judge Bingham looked across the courtroom at the frowning face of Assistant District Attorney Bob Altschuler, chief prosecutor in the 342nd. "I take it," the judge said, "that the State of Texas disagrees."

"Yes, your honor, and for the best reasons the state could have." Altschuler was already standing, feet planted wide apart like a wrestler's. A bulky, handsome man of forty-five, with snapping brown eyes and a full head of pepper-and-salt hair, he folded his arms in a truculent posture. "This is a murder charge. No question that the defendant, Ms. Boudreau, shot the victim, Dr. Ott, who wasn't armed. She's admitted it."

"No, no, no," Scoot Shepard murmured, barely audibly.

Judge Bingham said to the prosecutor, "Well, these papers claim that Ms. Boudreau surrendered voluntarily to the police. Says here that she lives in town, is gainfully employed, has roots in the community, and isn't going anywhere, even assuming she's got someplace to go. And she's showed up today." He peered down in a kindly manner at Bob Altschuler; they worked together nearly every day. "What's your contention, Mr. Prosecutor? Here today, gone tomorrow?"

"The state's contention," Altschuler said, "is that the defendant can afford the $300,000 bail set by this court before Mr. Scoot Shepard came on the scene. Especially if the defendant can afford to hire Mr. Shepard."

"Ah, but that's the point!" Scoot cried, taking a fencing step forward. "I don't come cheap! The amount of current bail might make it impossible for this lady to pay my fee! What if it comes down to a choice between me and bail? I know there are a lot of other good lawyers around town, and I'm not the spryest or the youngest, maybe not even the smartest." He spread his hands before the elderly judge. "But she wants me. What can we do about that, your honor?"

"Well, that might be a pity," the judge said. "We might be deprived of a fine trial."

Sitting on the bench in the rear, Warren smiled. He understood that Judge Bingham liked to perform for Scoot,

or with him, especially with reporters sitting in his courtroom.

The judge peered down now at the defendant, Johnnie
Faye Boudreau, sitting alone at the defense table. "Ma'am,
you claim you don't own that topless nightclub out on
Richmond that everybody says you own. What's it
called?" Adjusting the horn-rimmed bifocals on his fleshy
nose, he rustled the papers set before him. "Ecstasy! What
a provocative name. Is that right? Is that your contention?"

Scoot walked back and bent to whisper to his client.
Then he said to the court, "Your honor, Ms. Boudreau has
a slight sore throat, and this is a mighty cavernous courtroom. I don't want her to have to shout and aggravate her
condition. May we and Mr. Altschuler approach the bench
for this discussion?"

"Of course you may, Mr. Scoot," the judge said.

Johnnie Faye Boudreau rose slowly from her chair. This
May morning in the air-conditioned courtroom she wore a
white linen suit with high heels to match, one strand of
cultured pearls and an emerald ring. She had admitted she
was forty years old but could have passed for thirty. Two
decades ago she had been voted Miss Corpus Christi and
then runner-up in the Miss Texas pageant. Now there was
hardly a wrinkle on her face and her hands were as smooth
as vellum. She had high breasts, flaring hips, and a remarkably narrow waist. Her most remarkable feature, however,
was the color of her eyes. The left one was hazel, the right
one a cool gray-blue. Few people noticed that at first. They
just felt uncomfortable under her gaze.

She took several steps toward the judicial bench, then
turned and went back for her handbag. Zoologists would
have described her walk as that of a tiger in estrus. Even
Judge Bingham gazed at her swaying buttocks.

As she reversed course and approached the judge a second time, Warren Blackburn watched too from his seat on

the back bench. Look like a pair of boar shoats squirming around in a gunnysack, he thought.

The courtroom grew still. Everyone strained to hear.

"That's right, your honor," Johnnie Faye Boudreau said in a husky, relaxed voice. "I don't own Ecstasy. I just work there."

Scoot took over: "She's on salary, your honor—$40,000 a year, paid monthly. She borrowed the money from her employers to put up that high bond. Borrowed it at twelve percent interest. Her only current assets are a bank account with under two thousand dollars, some jewelry, and a car."

"Her car is a two-year-old Mercedes 450-SL," the judge pointed out.

"She's got good taste," Scoot said. "And we wouldn't take that car away, would we? How would she get to work?"

"Or to court, for her trial," Judge Bingham added.

Bob Altschuler, scowling, leaned his weight toward the defendant. "Ms. Boudreau, are you telling the State of Texas and this court that you have no stocks, bonds, savings accounts, mutual funds, CDs, money market accounts, or any other negotiable assets?"

Johnnie Faye Boudreau's wide mouth curved into a smile. "No, sir. Nothing except my checking account at Bank of America and the clothes on my back."

"And a few clothes in your closets at home, I'm sure."

"A few," Johnnie Faye said. "Do y'all want me to sell some of them?"

Perched on the edge of their seats, the reporters from the *Post* and the *Chronicle* scribbled in their notebooks. That was quotable.

Judge Bingham said, "Mr. Bob, these papers tell me that if the bail is reduced, Ms. Boudreau's employer—this corporation owned by some oil people over in Louisiana—is ready to lend the money back to Ms. Boudreau. Then she can pay Mr. Shepard and we can get on with this case.

Otherwise, Mr. Shepard isn't going to appear and you are going to be deprived of a worthy opponent. What do you say to that?"

Altschuler wheeled smartly on the defendant, as if to intimidate her with his bulk. "Ms. Boudreau, do you swear under oath that you have no controlling interest in this Louisiana corporation that owns Ecstasy? No shares at all?"

"No, sir. Neither. Just like the papers say."

The prosecutor glowered at the judge once again. "If she can't pay Mr. Shepard, that's too bad. There are plenty of defendants who would like to have him, but they have to settle for something less, or different. There's no constitutional right in the State of Texas to be represented by Mr. Shepard, your honor."

"That's true," Judge Bingham gently responded, "but I think this defendant ought to have the lawyer she wants. That's the American way. And you're not going to run away before or during the trial, are you, Ms. Boudreau?"

"No, sir," Johnnie Faye said firmly.

"You're going to show up every time we ask you to?"

"Yes, sir. I give you my word of honor."

"Well, then, I believe the request has merit. It's reasonable and certainly straightforward. I'm going to compromise. I'm going to reduce bail to $100,000." Judge Bingham tapped his big black mahogany gavel, a gift from Scoot Shepard ten years ago after the acquittal in the Martha Sachs case.

Warren Blackburn managed to intercept Scoot just outside the broad swinging doors of the courtroom. "Nice work," he said.

"Can't talk now," Scoot explained, dramatically placing a finger on his lips and gesturing at the gang of reporters about to corral him. "You available for lunch next week, young fellow?"

"Any day," Warren said.

"I'll call you after the weekend," Scoot said regally, "and tell you where."

A number of events that followed would mark Warren Blackburn's life, change it forever.

Late that same Friday afternoon Johnnie Faye Boudreau dug under the mattress in her guest room, stuffed $50,000 in hundred-dollar bills in her big ostrich-leather handbag, and went out on a spending spree. She knew from experience that it would raise her spirits. Despite the financial victory, she had not enjoyed her day in court. She was not used to begging or wheedling.

In Sakowitz, opposite the Galeria shopping mall, she bought a ruby brooch. Crossing the boulevard in 85-degree May heat, in the cool of Lord & Taylor she bought a Russian sable jacket, a T-shirt with a leopard motif, two lace bras, and makeup from Lancôme. And then in Neiman-Marcus she bought a gray shantung suit and a dark-blue silk dress she thought would be appropriate to wear in court for the Ott murder trial. She paid cash for everything.

At about the same hour a man named Dan Ho Trunh was repairing a pump and installing a pool timer in the backyard of a house off Memorial Parkway. A twenty-seven-year-old Vietnamese who carried a green card, Dan Ho had been in Houston for five years and would be eligible for citizenship in August. He was a journeyman electrician who worked cheap and liked to be paid in cash. His youth in Saigon allowed him to understand something that no United States government pamphlet or history book could ever teach: it was the right of human beings everywhere to avoid the payment of taxes.

With the job finished and three twenty-dollar bills in his wallet, he edged his old Ford Fairlane wagon into the thick traffic of the 610 Loop, then a mile later bore off on the Southwest Freeway in an easterly direction. Soaring glass facades of office buildings ricocheted light from a setting sun. Close to the Wesleyan exit, Dan Ho remembered that he had to pick up laundry and dry cleaning. With a quick glance into the rearview mirror, he flicked his directional signal, stepped on the gas and veered from the middle lane toward the exit ramp. This should not have been difficult. In his experience, Texans were courteous and forgiving drivers.

But the car to the right of him seemed to accelerate rather than slow to give him room. He felt a mild jolt, as if his rear bumper had grazed the other driver's front bumper.

It was not possible to stop. Cars were surging right and left. Dan Ho powered down the exit ramp. A minute later he swung the wagon off the road into the parking lot of a mini-mall, pulling up in front of the Wesleyan Terrace Laundry & Dry Cleaners. It was after eight o'clock and all the other shops but Crown Books had closed until morning. Except for a wino propped in a loose sitting position against an optician's facade, smiling at something that only a drunk could smile about, the parking lot was empty of people.

Through the plate-glass window of the dry cleaners Dan Ho Trunh saw the half-turned back of an Indian woman in a green and gold sari. She was stacking cardboard boxes.

Then he became aware that another car had pulled up parallel in the parking lot, and a woman in that car was in a rage and was shouting at him. She was cursing. He had no idea why. He rolled down his window.

"Hey, you! Speak Murkin?"

"What's the problem?" Dan Ho said quietly.

The woman snarled, "Don't get smartass with me, you yellow motherfucker, you scumbag slant-eyed sleazeball!"

He shook his head and said, "Lady, you're not only nasty, you're crazy."

"Who the fuck do you think you're talking to?"

Sighing, Dan Ho Trunh turned away, reaching into his

back pocket for his wallet, which contained his laundry ticket. From the car parked a few feet to his left, he heard a shriek. He looked up wearily and beheld a small black circle, the barrel of a pistol.

He felt a terrible pain. He went down backward on the seat, spurting bright blood on the dashboard.

The name of the smiling wino propped against the optician's shop in the mini-mall was James Thurgood Dandy —known back in his native Beeville, Texas, of course, as Jim Dandy. As the station wagon and then the second car pulled into the parking lot, Jim Dandy had clambered to his feet, yawned a couple of times, then felt an uncomfortable pressure in his groin which told him that his bladder was full. He turned against the side of the building and urinated. When he reached to zip up his fly, he heard a woman's scream followed by a sharp crack that could only be a gunshot.

Instinctively he ducked, cowering against the building, his fly still gaping. He turned his head toward the street. "Kitty Marie," he whimpered, "don't kill me. Whatever I done I didn't mean to. Please, Kitty Marie!"

But Kitty Marie was far away in Beeville, and no one killed Jim Dandy.

Finally he zipped up his fly and walked slowly over to the station wagon. The front window was wide open. He peered inside. Someone in that car looked awfully dead.

On the seat, the man's outstretched right hand clutched an open leather wallet. A laundry ticket protruded from it and a fat sheaf of wrinkled green was exposed in the billfold part. Jim Dandy reached into the car and took the wallet from the clawed hand. "Hot damn," he whispered.

He heard a sound, a gasp. From where, from whom, he didn't know. It might have come from the man he thought was dead. Clutching the wallet, he turned and ran.

* * *

An hour later, Hector Quintana, a homeless man, rolled his Safeway shopping cart down a concrete walkway, past the tennis courts and then between Buildings C and D of the Ravendale Apartments in the Braeswood district.

The Ravendale Apartments rented furnished apartments on a month-to-month basis to visiting yuppies and divorcées, who stayed until they went back home or found permanent living space elsewhere in Houston. The residents of Ravendale drank Bartles & Jaymes wine coolers and played volleyball in the pool on hot summer evenings. No one paid attention to strangers. They were nearly all strangers to each other.

Good Dumpsters here, Hector Quintana had learned. Gringos threw things out which back in El Palmito his people would battle to own. He once found a toaster oven; another time, New Balance running shoes with a hole in the toe. Fit him perfectly, aided by balled-up wads of newspaper. Peanut butter, a box of Wheat Thins, an unopened bottle of Mr. and Mrs. T's Bloody Mary Mix. He would never understand gringos.

Tonight he had even better luck. Rummaging in the Dumpster among the various garbage smells, he dug out a pair of dirty white tennis socks, a half-finished jar of Planters salted peanuts, and then a bottle of Old Crow about four inches full. He opened it, sniffing to make sure it was not kerosene. The aroma of bourbon filled his nostrils.

Pushing his luck, Hector dug farther. Amid lemon peels and coffee grounds, his brown hand closed on something cool and metallic: a pistol.

He looked at it and knew he had a prized possession, something which could change his life—if he could find the courage to use it correctly.

But where would that courage come from? To work that out, he sat down on the fresh-mowed grass next to the parking lot and ate the jar of peanuts, which he washed down with big swallows of Old Crow until the bottle was empty.

Before he parted from his wife and young children in his village of El Palmito, his father had taken him into the fields and said, "*Hijo mío,* when you get where you're going, don't forget Francisca and your children. Send money to them before you get drunk on Saturday night. And also don't forget, the reason opportunity is often missed is that it usually comes disguised as hard work. Go with God."

Suddenly Hector Quintana thought he understood what the old man had meant. Abandoning the shopping cart, he stuffed the little pistol into his back pocket.

He set out on foot in the warm May night, heading for the Circle K convenience store he had seen just up the block on Bissonet.

On the humid Monday morning following the reduction of bail for Johnnie Faye Boudreau, Warren Blackburn returned for the first time in two years to the 299th District Court, the scene of his crime. The sweat on his forehead slowly cooling, he stood for ten minutes in the anteroom of Judge Lou Parker's chambers. He had avoided her court assiduously until now, but now it was time. Can't duck her forever, he decided, and I've paid my dues.

Warren wore his best dark blue suit and his shoes had been shined by the bootblack in the courthouse basement. He watched Melissa Bourne-Smith, the new court coordinator of the 299th, bent over the computer at her government-issue metal desk. He had been introduced to her a few weeks ago in the cafeteria, and since then they had exchanged a few hellos in the elevators. He tried today to exude a mix of gravity and bonhomie, but he felt neither. In this court he felt like a burned-out failure of a lawyer.

Finally the court coordinator raised her Afro and shot him a radiantly false smile.

"Might have something good for you. The judge said she wants a young lawyer on this one." She glanced down at the docket sheet. "Defendant's name is Hector Quintana. An illegal alien. Capital murder, case number 388-6344. Can you come back at noon?"

Surprised, not quite believing what he had heard, Warren wrote quickly on his yellow legal pad.

Capital murder was top of the line, differing from ordinary murder in that there were aggravating circumstances: murder during the commission of another felony, murder of a police officer. A few veteran lawyers specialized in court-appointed capitals, since the fees averaged a decent

$750 for every day's appearance in court, even if it took only an hour's time to plea-bargain with whoever was the assistant district attorney on the case. But sometimes a judge gave an opportunity to a promising young lawyer. That Judge Lou Parker would do that for *him,* Warren thought, seemed unlikely.

"Who's the victim?" he asked Bourne-Smith.

"Some Vietnamese. Shot in the parking lot on Wesleyan. It's a nothing case, it'll go real fast. Just let me get the judge's okay."

"I'll be here at noon," Warren said. "Thank you."

Outside the 299th a chain gang of eight prisoners emerged from one of the courthouse elevators. All wore thin brown cotton jumpsuits with the words HARRIS COUNTY JAIL stenciled on the back. All were young, all but two were black. To a man they looked as if hope and freedom were dead issues. They were led by a woman deputy sheriff in tight taupe uniform, who said politely, "Gentlemen handcuffed by the right hand, place your hands over the chain like this. Now y'all follow me." The prisoners marched off in a file toward Judge Parker's holding cell. Warren wondered if Hector Quintana was among them.

Warren left the anteroom through the back door into the eighth-floor main hallway, then headed down the stairs to the fifth floor and the domain of Judge Bingham's 342nd District Court.

Three or four lawyers in ill-fitting suits and ties were lounging in Bingham's handsomely furnished jury box, guffawing and back-slapping at the latest courthouse gossip. They, like Warren, were waiting for the largess of the court coordinator.

"Morning, your honor. How's business?"

Judge Bingham glanced down from the bench, a shade startled. Then he said warmly, "Warren . . . you devil."

Warren sometimes wondered if Bingham confused him

with his father, or if there was a natural assumption about a chip off the old block.

"How's the wife, son? Saw her on the TV a few evenings ago. Looking peachy."

"She's fine, Judge. And how's your garden?"

The widowed judge, mocha-colored and slightly pink-eyed, looked preoccupied. "Can I do anything for you?"

"Whatever's available, Judge. My wife likes to shop at Neiman's."

"With what I imagine your wife makes, she can afford it. But you go see LuAnne. Tell her to give you next up."

Warren went back toward chambers to talk to LuAnne, Bingham's veteran court coordinator. A sign on her desk said: OLD AGE AND TREACHERY WILL OVERCOME YOUTH AND SKILL. Obeying the judge's order, LuAnne gave Warren the file folder for an escape case. The defendant, J. J. Gillis, had been under arrest for a DWI on the western edge of Harris County. When no one was looking he walked unmolested out of the local jail. He was picked up fifteen minutes later in a bar down the street.

Warren talked to Gillis, a black workingman of about forty with gnarled hands, one of them now shackled to a steel bolt on the bench outside Bingham's holding cell. Then he sought out Bob Altschuler, whose job required him to plea-bargain for escapes and DWIs as well as prosecute headline murders. Altschuler was talking quietly to the tall, curly-haired court reporter Maria Hahn. She stepped to one side when Warren nodded.

"The Gillis case, Bob. Man was still drunk when he walked out of the jail. You can't call that an escape. What kind of an offer will you make?"

Altschuler said sourly, "Intoxication doesn't negate the crime. A deuce," he said, meaning two years in TDC, the Texas Department of Corrections, in the Huntsville prison complex.

"I can do better in trial," Warren said.

Altschuler raised a bushy eyebrow. "Maybe you can,

but if you keep Bingham from a few afternoons tending his zinnias, you'll never get appointed in this court again except to sweep it."

Warren said, "How about thirty days jail time and five years probation?"

"No way. Six months and ten years."

Warren took the prosecutor's elbow and steered him firmly to the judge's bench, where he began to explain where they stood with Gillis.

The judge interrupted him. "Let's cut the baloney, I want to quit by two o'clock today. How about sixty days jail time and five years probated?"

Altschuler frowned. He hated to lose, even in something as minor as a DWI.

Elated, Warren went back to his client. He produced papers to sign: a waiver of indictment and of other constitutional rights. Gillis scrawled his name and then, without a word, turned his head away.

It was 9:35. At the court coordinator's desk, Warren filled in a voucher for his $150 fee. What he had done would make no headlines. He could do it ten times a week, if he was lucky enough to get that many appointments, and it would never make him rich. But he had helped a man—there was something to be said for that. He wished Gillis had thanked him.

Any sense of accomplishment vanished an hour later. He had a sentencing in another court, this time by a judge who had hitherto been a dedicated prosecutor. Warren's current client, with two prior misdemeanors for possession of marijuana, had been indicted for molesting a minor. He was black, nineteen, a high-school dropout who could barely read or write more than his own name.

Warren had entered a plea of nolo contendere. Now he made his closing speech. "Your honor, this youngster with an eighth grade education is mentally incompetent. We can't unscramble the egg. Of what benefit to society is incarceration? He has a family that's willing to take care of him and get him a simple job. I submit that to place him in confinement is neither just nor compassionate, and it isn't productive for the community."

The judge gave the boy eight years.

One for every year of his schooling, Warren realized. He left the courtroom feeling whipped. These were his days: win some, lose some—a bit of triumph here, a bit of failure there. Troubled dreams, scattered lives he would never touch again. He dealt with young men who were bewildered, or vicious, or grossly ignorant, or beaten down by life. If you were a lawyer, man could be an unlovely species. There was no glory here.

Glory, with all its attendant penalties, had first come to Warren when he was twelve years old. The Blackburn family had lived on a street called Bellefontaine that deadended on the Shamrock Hilton Hotel, then the center of the city's social activity. In summer, together with other professional families, the Blackburns rented a lanai room around the huge hotel pool with its ten- and twenty-meter diving boards. What every boy wanted was to become brave and strong enough to dive off the twenty-meter board, but all were forbidden until they reached sixteen.

At the age of twelve, Warren said to his friends, "Watch this. . . ." He climbed the metal ladder to stare down at the green surface, thinking that it hadn't looked nearly that high from poolside. His knees were trembling, but he launched himself out in a belly whopper, careened through the air, hit the water, and split his cheek so badly that it required five stitches.

Maximum Gene grounded him for two weeks.

After school Warren and Rick Levine would climb on their bikes and pedal down to the Shamrock for the conventions. At the funeral directors' convention Warren lay down in four different coffins. He begged one of the directors to embalm him: "Y' know, just to see what it'd be like . . ."

Air France stewardesses sunbathed topless at the Shamrock pool. The Frenchwomen liked those Texas boys who were not afraid to come up and say, "Hi, y'all, *comment allez-vous?*" There was a kind of glory there too, Warren found.

He was a curious mixture of sophistication and country ways. His paternal grandfather, a snuff-dipping shoe store owner, had always rolled his own cigarettes from bags of Duke's Mixture. When the weekend came, Maximum Gene himself drove about town in a Ford pickup that dangled furry dice from the rearview mirror. The judge's favorite home-cooked meal was deep-fried turtle and buttermilk biscuits. All women were called gals. He was cordial to black lawyers but at home he referred to the man who mowed the lawn as a nigger. Warren winced. Still, like his father, he chewed toothpicks after lunch, whistled through his teeth when he called the dog, got out of bed before daylight, said "ma'am" to any woman over thirty he didn't know, and when he went out to a picnic in the hill country he pulled on his oldest cowhide boots, rolled up his sleeves and jammed a gimme cap over his black hair.

But as a prelaw student at UT he had taken elective courses in music and philosophy, he could quote Shakespeare and Emerson, and he played Verdi on his tape deck more often than Merle Haggard. Backpacking around Europe the summer after college graduation, he stood in line for the opera at Covent Garden and in Paris had an affair with a young Dutch painter who guided him through the Louvre until his feet ached. Back in Houston for law school, he bought a subscription to the Alley Theater, and in 1980, in his first year of law practice, took on two pro bono cases for the NAACP and the Animal Rights League.

He met Charmian Ellen Kimball by the side of the Shamrock Hilton pool one September Sunday afternoon in his twenty-sixth year. He was wearing aviator glasses and cutoff Levi's, and five minutes later he struck a match with his thumbnail. Charm had just been graduated from the University of Pennsylvania as a journalism major—a willowy, blond young woman with serious blue eyes and a strong, clear voice. Her stepfather, a Boston stockbroker, had brought the family to Houston when a branch of his firm opened in the Galeria mall. She fought for the right to go back East to college, and then to spend her junior year in Paris. No idea was more foreign to her than that of marrying a Texan.

Warren took her to dinner that evening at a good French restaurant and announced, "Not bad. But if God hadn't meant us to eat grits with every meal, then why'd He give us red-eye gravy?"

"For God's sake," Charm cried, "how can you be a lawyer and a redneck?"

"Hey, I drove a Harley at UT, and I know where Johnnie Cash served time—but so does my father and he's a judge."

There was a solidity about Warren, a usefulness. He could make Charm Kimball laugh, and he touched a yearning spot deep inside her. She came from a broken marriage, whereas Warren's parents had been married for thirty-five years. He lived in a bachelor studio apartment on the edge of Hermann Park; it was there, a few weeks after they met, that he and Charm became lovers. She was in her first season as a television reporter. "It may seem glamorous," she explained one December evening, curled against him in his bed, "but a few days ago I interviewed a woman who poured gasoline on her two kids and lit a match. . . ." Charm shook her head furiously to clear the image. "You have to look so goddam serious while you're chirping away into the microphone like a dingbat. There's no time to know what people really *feel*."

"You care," Warren said forcefully. "And when I see you on the tube, it shows."

"Am I good, or is it surface bullshit?"

"You're good. You're so personal."

He hugged her while she cried a little, for she realized that, for Warren, to love meant to help and appreciate. She felt a weight to his love that she could lean on. By then Warren's two sisters had settled with their husbands and babies in Southern California, Maximum Gene was dead from a heart attack, and Warren's mother had remarried and moved to Dallas. He took Charm with him on a skiing holiday to Aspen. He had a visceral need for a mate, and they were married a year after they had met: married at the Shamrock.

Throughout the summer before their wedding they debated about where to live. "I miss the East," Charm said wistfully, meaning concerned Bostonians, abrasive New Yorkers, wit that didn't depend on country metaphor. Houston was friendly, laid-back, dumb. Warren shrugged and said, "Maybe. But the first thing I notice when I land at JFK is the sour look on people's faces. That has to rub off on you."

They agreed to stay in Houston, where he was making a name for himself as a young criminal defense attorney, and they pooled their money for the house on Braes Bayou. He gave up his bachelor habit of leaving crusted dishes in the sink. He quit smoking because Charm didn't smoke and it worried her that he did. He cherished his young wife for her rummaging intelligence, her drive toward womanhood.

Charm graduated to co-anchor on the evening news. Warren chose their few investments and took care of the mortgage from a joint account. He picked up the tab for their skiing holidays, their occasional trips to New York and Europe, all their nights out in restaurants. But after Virgil Freer's confession and the year of suspension handed to him by Lou Parker, there was no more Europe, and he flinched at the rising prices of lift tickets on the slopes. He had to ask his wife for money. After his suspension was lifted he was going over the credit card statements one month, when he saw $1200 for Marshall Field and $1600 for Lord & Taylor. He asked her what it was for.

"I bought two new suits," Charm said.

"That's a hell of a lot for just a couple of suits. I haven't bought a suit in two years. And if I was feeling flush and went to Brooks Brothers, it might cost me five hundred."

He knew right away he'd blundered. Women's clothes were a subject that men rarely understood.

Charm's eyes grew hooded. "You can't afford a suit," she said, "and I can. I need good clothes for my job, which is what's supporting us these days. You really piss me off, Warren."

"You want to tell me why?"

"Because you've given up on your life. I don't think you even realize what's happening to you."

They were in the den, where the TV was hidden behind a built-in walnut cabinet. One wall was lined with books and the other featured Currier & Ives prints and photographs of both their families. Oobie lay on her mat, watching them carefully with wet eyes. Warren stood framed in the arched doorway, his hands stuffed in the pockets of his jeans.

He hated these discussions. He wanted this part of his life to be harmonious, even if the rest of it year by year had degenerated. He slid his hands from his pockets and folded his arms across his chest, mirroring Charm.

"I don't want you to cook," Charm said. "I appreciate it when you do, but I think it's just a way of avoiding more important things. You're doing that court-appointed stuff all the time. You think it's demeaning but you still do it. You hate the people you have to deal with. You're not fighting hard enough, Warren. You're bright, probably a lot brighter than you want people to know. You've got a mind that cuts right to the heart of a problem. But you've let that drift away from you. You're only thirty-three, and you've lost your zest."

The truth of all this was so obvious that he became inwardly furious. But he tried to keep it in check.

"Zest for what?"

"For everything . . . including me. When you want to make love to me it's usually in the morning, but you know I'm only half-alive then and I'm a lousy lay. At night, when I'm in the mood, you're too tired. Somehow we manage to do it twice a week, never more, sometimes less. I get the feeling you mark it on a calendar and say to yourself, 'Well, the old lady's due for another bang, better give it to her so she doesn't get antsy and go elsewhere for it.' And I'll tell you something else. We used to have great sex. We don't anymore. It's by rote."

All this, except for his marking a calendar, was so on the money that he felt appalled. And maybe, mentally, he did mark a calendar.

Charm was not finished. "We used to talk about having children when I was thirty and my biological cuckoo clock began to act up. Let me tell you, it's chirping now—really loud."

"Are you saying you're ready to have a baby?"

"Don't you see I'm saying the opposite? Warren, I don't want children if our marriage is going down the drain. I love you, but your life's so screwed up you can't find the energy to love me back. I don't know if I want your kids. You're not doing the work you want to do. You're poor and you don't like being poor. You talk to your dog more than to anyone else. You're depressed, you're irritable, you snap at people. What kind of a father would you be? Get your act together. *Do* something about it."

No one had ever hurt him more deeply. He hadn't been able to reply. He walked out of the room into the kitchen and poured a glassful of whiskey, which he drank in five minutes. And then another.

Warren believed this about most women: they were not as logical as men but therefore wiser. They reached conclusions by a route that few men could take—intuitively, often dogmatically. Rarely could they explain that journey to a man, for there were few if any detours on the way to the conclusion, the kind of detours that men loved and that made them feel they had intelligently rejected all alternatives. Women could do this because by their biochemical nature they knew what they wanted. Not many men did—most appeared to live as if they did, but there was a stubborn ruinous denial of truth at the heart of the human male ego. The complexity of men's desires did not allow much honest communication. The forest was often impenetrable.

And so Warren did not reject his wife's accusations. He did not argue. He asked himself what he had done wrong. Had he been kidding himself all his life? It's possible, he thought grimly, that I wooed her too well, made her think I was of substance when I was nothing.

He went into joint therapy with Charm and at one weekly session realized aloud to the therapist, "If I was willing to work at learning to cook and at picking up Spanish down in Mexico, I should be willing to work at making a good marriage. It's the basic human challenge when you pass beyond maintenance."

Their sex life improved for a time. In the evenings, he seduced her. On some weekend mornings, when he came back from running with Oobie, Charm was propped against the pillows, face freshly washed, waiting for him.

But that did not last. The rest of his life, his life as a lawyer, continued to puzzle and defeat him.

There is a winding-down in an unhappy marriage, a struggle to define what's wrong, a reluctance to relinquish what's right—and a need, if need be, to bow the head and accept the probability that protestations of love, so glorified by and dear to the human imagination, may not be enough for sustenance.

Another year passed, and Hilton sold the Shamrock to the Texas Medical Center to turn into a ten-story parking lot. His marriage, Warren realized, seemed to have gone the same route: from elegance and passionate gaiety to the drab business of getting on with things.

A faded glory, he thought, like his love affair with the law.

But then, one Friday in May, he listened to Scoot Shepard plead for reduction of bail for Johnnie Faye Boudreau, and the following week a court coordinator he hardly knew asked him to defend a homeless man named Hector Quintana against a charge of capital murder.

He called Scoot Shepard's secretary, who told him that the lunch date was set for Thursday. "Mr. Shepard will be in trial in the 181st. If you could pick him up there around twelve-thirty, he'd appreciate it."

"I'll be there," Warren promised.

He would have time for a cup of coffee before his noon meeting with Judge Lou Parker. He maneuvered around a pack of waiting jurors into the elevator. When it stopped on the fourth floor, Rick Levine darted inside, his brown eyes shining with good humor. In the late nineteenth century Rick's great-grandfather had emigrated from Kiev on a ship bound for New York, but the immigration authorities at Ellis Island, overburdened with paperwork, rerouted the ship to Galveston Island in the Gulf of Mexico, thus helping to establish the first Jewish community in Texas.

Rick threw an arm around Warren. "How are you, pal?"

"Just took it up the *culo* in the 416th," Warren said. "Eight years for a kid who dry-humped a fourteen-year-old girl in a high school playground."

"He should have fucked her instead—she might have liked it and never complained." Rick asked, "Did you tell him that for future reference?"

Bob Altschuler stepped aboard the elevator. Although he usually had the shaggy solemnity of a woolly mammoth, the prosecutor looked pleased with himself. He nodded at the defense attorneys.

"How come you're so happy now?" Warren asked. "You must have fucked somebody over really good."

Altschuler's smile faded and he muttered something the two other lawyers failed to catch. He got off the elevator at the second floor.

"Can't stand that man," Warren said.

"I have a feeling he noticed."

"There's a guy enjoys putting people behind bars for as long as the law will allow. Probably jacks off every night thinking about it."

"You're in an interesting mood today," Rick said.

In the basement cafeteria, under fluorescent lighting that washed out all shadows from faces, they sipped coffee from plastic cups. Rick said, "I'm in the 252nd with a client who delivered five kilos of crack cocaine. So I try to crank up a plea but the state won't go for less than thirty years. My client says, 'Fuck y'all, let's go to trial.' I couldn't convince him you can't trust your fate to twelve people too stupid to get out of jury duty."

Warren had barely listened. "Lou Parker's got a new court coordinator," he said, "who doesn't seem to know what happened between me and the judge three years ago. Parker's looking for a young lawyer, she claims, to appoint to a capital—a wetback shot some Vietnamese. Didn't know I qualified as young anymore, but I walked in at the right time. Or maybe the wrong time."

Rick's olive-colored face split into a frown. "Parker won't give a capital to you."

"That's what I think. But if I can get it, I want it."

"You ready to put on the gloves again with the lady hyena?"

"It's not my heart's desire, but I'll handle it."

A bleak look, a vexation of the spirit, showed on Rick's face. "Listen to your old buddy," he said. "Parker has a sign on her desk: THE LORD IS MY SHEPHERDESS—I SHALL NOT WANT. She smokes on the bench but she won't allow anyone else to smoke in her courtroom. Won't allow women lawyers to wear open-toed shoes. I took an old black janitor before her once on some chickenshit possession charge. She kept calling him 'boy'—that man will go his grave remembering that. If you go to trial in the 299th and the jury awards probation, Lou Parker automatically gives your client thirty days in jail as a condition of it. She's telling you, 'Dare to waste my time, I'll teach you a lesson.' It's court rental."

Both lawyers laughed thinly.

"See, we're laughing," Rick said, "but that's cruel."

Warren checked the time on the wall clock. He drained the last sip of coffee. "I have to go."

"Watch yourself," Rick counseled. "She's got a long memory. If there's a way the bitch can hurt you, she'll dig a tunnel to find it."

The court coordinator slyly said, "Judge has been waiting on you for ten minutes, Mr. Blackburn."

Warren knocked on the oak door of Judge Parker's chambers, then twisted the brass knob and walked in. The room was spacious, its windows facing westward: framed against a vehemently hot blue sky were the rotunda of the civil courthouse and the gothic rise of the Republic Bank Building. On the wall, flanking her diplomas, Judge Parker displayed oversized framed photographs of George Bush and John Wayne. The bookshelves were lined with volumes of the South Western Reporter Texas Cases and the Harvard Classics. Warren didn't remember any such hint of literacy, but then he recalled that on his last visit, three years ago, he had been blind to everything but dishonor.

Lou Parker sat behind her cluttered desk, square-faced, frowning, chewing on the eraser at the end of a pencil, and holding a long filter cigarette in one hand. She waved Warren into a leather armchair.

With no preamble, she asked, "You want this capital?"

Warren stayed silent a moment. Why would he *not* want it? It was a way to begin to crawl back from the basement of criminal law into the high-rent district. He wondered what Parker had in mind, and then the answer occurred to him. She might well need a lawyer who would do what he was told, someone she could step on. It had been known to happen. Some judges were less than impartial.

But he would have to take that risk. "I want it," he replied.

"What do you really know about me?" Judge Parker asked.

He wondered again what she meant. He knew that she

was divorced with grown children, had been one of the first women defense attorneys in the county, ran the 299th like a German railway station. And doesn't like me.

But he quickly realized that he had been asked a rhetorical question.

"In '53," Lou Parker said, "I graduated SMU with a degree in Accounting. Got married, started raising children. Woke up one morning and said, Hey, this is unskilled labor, any redneck woman from the back bayou can do this. So I went downtown to an oil company I heard had an opening in Accounting. You want to know what happened?"

Warren understood it was his job to move his head briefly in either a vertical or horizontal direction, and it didn't matter which.

"They turned me down because I was a woman. Guy told me that to my face. Real sorry, he said, but also real proud he was being so honest. So I said, 'Fuck you, fuck your dog, and fuck the horse you rode in on.' I walked out of there and enrolled in law school. Twenty years a defense attorney. Got my court seven years ago when your daddy passed away."

Judge Parker stubbed out her cigarette in an ashtray already overflowing.

"I'm not popular like Dwight Bingham and I don't give a shit. I do as I please, I say what I please. You defense attorneys complain about me because I don't let you get away with the stuff you're used to getting away with. I run a tough courtroom. I get things done and I know what I'm doing. Unlike some others whose names I won't mention."

There was a certain amount of truth to that, Warren knew. Texas judges were elected—the only requisites were party backing and five years as a member of the bar. On his first day in office, a certain judge, a one-time insurance adjuster, had walked into his new chambers as the preceding judge was clearing out his law books. With some anxiety the new judge asked his law clerk, "Do I have to buy those books too?"

"The D.A.'s office doesn't much care for me," Parker rasped, "because I don't take crap from them. This is *my* courtroom—you better get that straight. No speeches for the peanut gallery. No tricks. Hint of a stunt like you pulled four years ago, you're out on your ass. You can fish in the bayou for a living."

Judge Parker waited, but this time Warren did not nod his head.

"I'm giving you this capital," she said, "because you finally had the guts to walk in and ask for a case, and I suppose every son of a bitch on this earth deserves a second chance. It's no great shakes, because it's a whale in a barrel for the state, but it's better than you've had in a long time. Just move it along. I'm not saying the defendant's guilty—I'm not allowed to say that. But I'm telling you that all the prosecutor has to do in this case is take aim and squeeze the trigger. So don't waste my time, understand? I expect you to plead it out for whatever you can get."

There it was. It could not have been clearer.

Lou Parker's dark eyes glinted. She blew cigarette smoke in the general direction of his face. "Now go see your client."

In the park opposite the eight-story ugly granite monolith of the courthouse, Warren found a quiet bench under an oak tree. He bought a hot dog from a vendor and ate it while he studied the *Quintana* file. Some mustard dripped onto the pages. Warren wiped it off with his breast pocket handkerchief.

An hour later he settled into a steel-backed chair in a Harris County Jail visitor's cubicle, as he once had with Virgil Freer. A modern facility, a massive cube twelve stories high—air-conditioned, computerized, with closed-circuit TV—the jail was never silent. Men yelled, women wept, telephones jangled, doors clanged. Warren sat at a shiny bare metal desk under fluorescent lighting so garishly bright that it made his eyes ache. He talked to Hector Quintana through a metal grill.

Quintana had smooth skin, black hair, an uncomplicated face. Warren guessed they were about the same age.

"Mr. Quintana, do you understand English?"

Quintana nodded, but Warren saw the uncertainty in the man's brown eyes.

He kept his speech simple. "My name is Warren Blackburn, and I'm a lawyer appointed by the court to represent your interests because you don't have the money to hire your own lawyer. The State of Texas will pay my fee, but I don't want you to think for one minute that means I work for them. I work for you now, Mr. Quintana, unless you have any objections to me. If you do, you'll have to explain them to Judge Parker. There's nothing you tell me about this case that I'll ever repeat to another living soul unless I have your permission. I'm bound by a solemn oath—what we lawyers call confidentiality and lawyer-client privilege. You understand what I'm saying?"

"Sir," Quintana said, "I didn't do what they say I did."

Warren ignored that. He would never ask Quintana if he had done it. That was the first rule of a criminal defense attorney, carved into his mind from the day he began practicing.

"Do you trust me?" Warren said.

"Yes, sir."

"Let's get rolling."

Warren formally told Hector Quintana that he had been accused of murdering, on or about the night of May 19, 1989, in Harris County, a man named Dan Ho Trunh, an electrician by trade, twenty-seven years old, married, the father of two children—

"I doan know this man," Quintana said.

"Let me finish, please."

Slowly, now and then using some of the Spanish he had

learned in San Miguel de Allende, Warren explained that the indictment returned by the grand jury was for capital murder, because it was believed that the offense took place during the course of a robbery—Dan Ho Trunh's wallet had not been found on his person or in his car. Texas law mandated that if Hector Quintana stood trial and was found guilty of capital murder, or instead pled guilty to the court, there were only two possible penalties: life in prison or death by injection.

Quintana gasped. "But I doan kill this man. I doan know him. I try to rob a store, *nada más.*"

Warren was used to this sequence. Few lawyers had ever introduced themselves to an accused murderer who said, "Glad to meet you, counselor. Sure I killed the sleazebag, and if you gave me the chance I'd do it again."

That came later, down a long road filled with rocky detours.

"Hector, suppose you tell me your version of what happened on the evening of May 19."

"I was *borrachito,*" Quintana said. A little drunk.

"Where do you live?"

With friends near the stables in Hermann Park. In the evenings, behind a shed, they fried pork cracklings in a pot of deep fat. Sometimes they cooked *menudo,* a kind of tripe soup that was wonderful for a hangover. When he first came here he had pumped gas at a Mobil station. He had lost the job because he showed up one time *borrachito* and then hadn't shown up another time because of, he seemed to remember, the same reason. Later he worked as a handyman in a convenience store, a 7-Eleven. The 7-Eleven was a good job, but the franchise had been sold to a Vietnamese who paid Hector a week's wages and let him go because a brother-in-law wanted the job.

"Did that upset you?" Warren asked.

"I had no work. It wasn't fair."

Bad, Warren thought. If the D.A.'s office didn't know it now, they would surely find out. *"And you were angry at being fired, weren't you, Mr. Quintana? And isn't it a fact that after you were fired you harbored a grudge against all Vietnamese people?"*

Since February he had lived by doing odd jobs—cutting wood, knocking on people's doors and offering to wash cars for two dollars—but in April he gave up his bed in a barrio roominghouse in order to save the rent and send money back to Francisca. That was when he began to sleep with his friends Pedro and Armando in the park by the stables. The *policía* didn't bother them if they were quiet. A few times he was asked to help clean up horseshit, and given five dollars for a morning's shoveling.

He found a shopping cart one day from the Safeway—

"Found? Where did you find it, Hector?"

"In the street, I doan remember . . ." But Quintana flushed, looked ashamed.

Warren didn't care. You had to batter at them a bit, make them see that it made no sense to tell petty lies. Big lies like *"I didn't do it"* were all right for a time. But the little lies blazed like neon. They could cost more than they were worth.

"You stole the shopping cart from the Safeway parking lot, isn't that so?"

"I found it. Maybe someone else stole it. *Yo no*—not I."

A stubborn man. But maybe it was true. You never knew. In theory, never quite translated into practice, you were innocent until proved guilty.

Quintana related to Warren the various treasures and staples he had inherited from apartment house Dumpsters and his wonder that they had been discarded while they still had a useful life. He went often to Ravendale and it was there, on that night, that he had found what was left of a bottle of whiskey. And *la pistola.*

After finishing the last swallow of Old Crow, Hector Quintana said, he decided to change his luck and rob the Circle K up on Bissonet. He shrugged, as if to say to War-

ren: this was no big deal. These are hard times. A man
grows weary and relaxes his principles. The pistol was not
loaded, and he was glad of that. But he believed that if he
pointed it at the clerk in the store and ordered him to hand
over what was in the cash register, the clerk would be
frightened enough to do so without any fuss.

"There is something I wish you to understand," Quintana said, seeming to change course, looking at his lawyer
with a clear gaze. "If I had not been a little drunk, I would
not have done this thing."

Or not have been able to do it, Warren thought. He
remembered what Altschuler had said that morning: intoxication does not negate the crime.

The clerk in the Circle K claimed he couldn't get the
cash register open. It often jammed like this, there was
nothing to do except bang away. He said, Hector recalled,
"Please don't shoot me, I'm doing my best." Finally the
drawer crashed open, whereupon, in slow motion, he
handed Hector a little over $120 in small bills and loose
change.

"I was so happy," Hector told Warren, "that I thanked
him. I went out into the street. But by then the police were
there. They were so quick! I couldn't believe it. . . ."

Two HPD cops leaped from a blue-and-white, revolvers
drawn. *"Police!* Freeze, asshole! Drop the weapon at your
feet! Kick it away from you!"

Hector had seen this scene so many times on TV that it
seemed unreal, and yet at the same time he knew exactly
what was required of him. Without being asked, he turned
to lean against a nearby car so that they could frisk him
and cuff him.

"Did they tell you that you had the right to remain
silent, the right to a lawyer, and so forth?"

"Yes, it was the same as on TV."

Only late the next day, here in jail, did the matter of
murder arise. He couldn't believe they were serious. He

told them they had the wrong man. But it was clear that they didn't believe him.

Warren asked him where he had been earlier on the evening of May 19, before he arrived at Ravendale.

Walking around, just thinking about Francisca and his children. He was from El Palmito, a village near the city of San Luis Potosí in north-central Mexico. He had married at the age of twenty. He was given a scrawny milk cow as a gift from his in-laws, a sway-backed burro from his father, and a patch of bare land on the bank of a stream where warm mineral water flowed. Still, in the end, with the rising prices, it was not enough to live on.

"And in those hours before you found the gun in the Dumpster, did you talk to anyone? Did you meet anyone you knew?"

He had knocked on a few doors, Quintana recalled, to ask if anyone wanted their car washed. No one had wanted.

Warren thought diligently for a minute. "Let's focus on *la pistola,* Hector. It's the same one that was used to murder a Vietnamese man earlier that evening, and the fact that you had it in your possession is very bad. You understand that, don't you?"

"There were no bullets in it," Quintana said. "I tole you."

"Did you ever show that pistol to anyone? To any of your friends at the stables?"

"How could that be?" Quintana asked, puzzled.

"It would be foolish of you to lie to me about the pistol. If you do that, I can't help you. I'll get my ass caught in a wringer and so will you. And it'll hurt you a lot more than me."

Quintana looked him in the eye. It was a look he had not shown before: it was slightly menacing.

"If you think," he said in Spanish, "that you can make me say I killed a man, or ever fired that pistol, you are betting on a lame cock. Perhaps, as you say, I must ask the judge for another lawyer."

"Don't get your feathers ruffled," Warren said sternly, gathering up his papers. "I'll be back."

Maximum Gene had told Warren a story of an old mountaineer who said of his pancakes, "No matter how thin I mix 'em, there's always two sides."

Warren would have to find out the other side of Hector Quintana's pancakes. Unfortunately, the best person to ask under these circumstances was the prosecutor. That was Assistant District Attorney Nancy Goodpaster, to whom Warren had lied four years ago about Virgil Freer's prior convictions.

When he reached the seventh floor and entered the windowless 299th District Court, Judge Lou Parker was calling the roll of defendants and attorneys. "No talking in court," the judge said in her spikiest tone to some women on the rear bench.

Warren caught Nancy Goodpaster's eye and walked back with her to her cool little office next to Parker's chambers. It was crowded with case files and a computer terminal. The desk was neat, and he noticed a photograph of a gray-haired black couple that he assumed were Goodpaster's parents. Their smiles shone proudly in the direction of a four-volume set of the *Texas Prosecutor's Trial Manual.*

"The judge is not in a good mood today," Warren said.

Settling herself behind the desk in a steel-backed swivel chair, Goodpaster looked at him calmly. "The judge is in the mood she's always in. We all live with it."

There was an unspoken coda: and unless you're a fool, you'll live with it too.

"She gets things done," Goodpaster added, with what Warren took as a grudging note of apology. "In the 299th we move right along." But again she was also saying: and you'd better move right along with us.

When Goodpaster had been fresh out of law school and had missed Virgil Freer's priors in the case file, she had been soft-faced and fluttery. She had picked the skin off her thumb whenever he talked to her, and the grave air she had projected Warren had taken as a cover-up for her gratitude that she was suddenly being taken seriously as an attorney. Now she was a veteran at the age of thirty, the ranking prosecutor in the 299th. A slim and delicate young woman, she wore her short black hair in a pageboy. She no longer affected the severely tailored suits and oversized bow ties that young female lawyers wear in order to look more like young male lawyers. Today she was dressed in a loose skirt and black blouse and casual light tan jacket. No tie, no rings or jewelry. Her thin hands were steady on the sheaf of papers in front of her. She didn't pick at her thumbs anymore.

"Mr. Blackburn," she said, "I'm looking to settle this case. So let's get down to it."

Five years with Lou Parker and the State of Texas, he thought, and she's a gunfighter.

He nodded at the file on her government metal desk. "What have you got?"

What she had, she said flatly, was a good case. She had motive, opportunity, and possession of the murder weapon.

"Any *Brady* material?" Warren asked.

Brady material was evidence that might help a defendant or impeach the credibility of a prosecution witness— so named because of *Brady v. Maryland,* wherein the Supreme Court reversed a conviction because the prosecutor had withheld information that might have proved the defendant innocent. You could squeeze more juice from a week-old cut lemon than *Brady* material from the Harris County district attorney's office. Their attitude was: you find it. There were lies of commission and lies of omission, Warren thought. And the state protects its minions.

"Not a thing," Goodpaster said.

The motive for the murder was money. The victim's family would testify that when he left the house that morning, Dan Ho Trunh had more than fifty dollars in his wallet, and it had been established that during the course of that day he had been paid at least ninety dollars in cash for electrical repair work he had done. His wallet had not been found.

As for opportunity, an hour after the murder Hector Quintana had been picked up within a mile of the crime scene. If he had an alibi, it had not yet surfaced.

Warren coughed, said nothing.

Ballistics confirmed that the murder weapon was the same .32-caliber Diamondback Colt clutched in Hector Quintana's hand when he ran out of the Circle K on Bissonet. They had traced the gun and discovered its most recent recorded purchase was five years ago, from a pawn shop in Dallas. The buyer had given phony I.D.

"And when Quintana walked into the Circle K the gun was empty, right?"

Goodpaster nodded. "He was drunk, the police offense report says. Maybe too drunk to think of reloading."

"They gave him a Breathalyzer test?"

"They could smell the booze on him." For the first time since Warren had been in the office, Goodpaster allowed herself to look other than solemn. She said smugly, "Whether Quintana was drunk or not, I could care less. He's not under indictment for D&D or armed robbery of a convenience store. This is capital murder."

Warren leaned back in the wooden chair, making a steeple of his hands. "But you have no witnesses."

"What makes you think so? We have a witness who saw him at the crime scene, and two days later she picked him out of a lineup. Sorry, Mr. Blackburn."

He did not reply, but his face answered her. Goodpaster

reached into the file and plucked out a stapled sheaf of papers. She tossed them across the desk to the unhappy defense attorney.

A few days later, once again, Hector Quintana glared at Warren through the metal mesh. The rich brown Indio eyes were eloquent with anger and desolation, but the dark flesh had begun to take on some of the pastiness common to men who saw the sky through sealed grilled windows and breathed artificially chilled air night and day. The eyes would change next: any liveliness would blur. The desolation would remain, but the anger would turn to ennui.

He was doing okay, Hector said. He was working in the kitchen as a dishwasher.

"Don't talk to anyone about the case," Warren warned him. "Jails are full of snitches."

"No one asks me why I'm here." Quintana sounded a little bewildered at that.

"That's jail etiquette. You didn't tell me," he said quietly, "that you'd been in a lineup."

"What is a lineup?"

"The police make you stand with a bunch of other guys facing a mirror. Then they make you stand in profile. Each of you holds up a number."

"Oh," Quintana said wearily, unconcerned. "That happened. I held up Number Five. I didn't know what it meant."

"I thought you said you'd watched a lot of TV."

Quintana glared at him again.

"What happens in a lineup," Warren explained, giving his client the benefit of the doubt, "is that there are people on the other side of the mirror. They can see you but you can't see them. In this instance, there was an Indian woman named Siva Singh on the other side of the glass, and she picked you out. She said, 'That's him.'"

Him meant the man whom Siva Singh had seen running away from the shopping complex on Wesleyan. Singh had been in the back of the Wesleyan Terrace Laundry & Dry Cleaners, slipping suits and dresses into plastic sheaths. She had heard what she later realized was a gunshot. Coming up to the front of the store a minute or two later, she had noticed a man standing by a station wagon parked in the lot. And the next minute: "My goodness, he was running away very fast."

She rarely went outside in the summer heat unless it was necessary. She went about her business and a few minutes later a customer came in to drop off some dry cleaning. The police offense report noted the customer's name as Rona Morrison, forty-five, a white divorced female, mother of two, who worked as a clerk at Better Buy Motors on Bissonet.

On her way back to her car, Morrison glanced in the window of the station wagon.

Siva Singh heard a scream. She hurried outside and found Morrison on her knees in the parking lot, gagging. Singh then peered inside the station wagon and saw the dead man. She brought Morrison into the store, settled her on a chair, and telephoned 911.

When the HPD squad car arrived, Singh was interviewed by homicide sergeants Hollis Thiel and Craig Douglas. That was when she described the man she had seen running away as "about five feet nine or five feet ten inches tall, with long black hair, and he wore just a pair of trousers with a shirt. He wore no jacket. He looked, if I may say so, to be poor and homeless. He was white, not colored. I thought he might have been Hispanic." She had never seen him before in her life.

Downtown at Harris County Jail the next morning she picked Hector Quintana out of a lineup of six men. "It is most certainly number five."

Warren related most of this to Quintana, whose hair was black and could be described as long.

"What were you wearing that night, Hector, when you held up the Circle K?"

"A shirt and pants."

"No jacket?"

"Was a hot night. My jacket was in my shopping cart."

"Where was the shopping cart?"

"I left it under a stairway near where I found the gun. I was going to return there and get it."

"This is not good." Warren shook his head gloomily. "The Indian woman says it was you she saw running away. Can you explain to me how that's possible? And please think a minute before you answer."

"I doan have to think a minute," Quintana grumbled. "She saw someone else. *Yo no.*"

"That's your story? That you were never near that station wagon, that dry cleaners? That you never ran away from the shopping center? Understand, I'm not asking if you shot and killed this man—I'm just asking if you ran away from there or any other place. No crime in running away."

The glare intensified. "If you doan believe me—"

"I know, I know. I'm betting on a lame cock." Warren grinned to establish some camaraderie, then let the expression wither. The tough part came now. The dialogue between lawyer and accused client was a process of discovery, a voyage through jagged shoals in stormy weather, often a voyage from obscurity to painful light. The fact of Quintana's denial of guilt was beside the point. Men had been known to deny guilt until the very moment they stepped into the courtroom and saw the grim faces of the jury. Texas juries killed. That was part of their heritage.

"Hector, I hear everything you're telling me. I believe you. But I'm a lawyer, not your mother. I have to look at the evidence, because that's what a jury is going to look at. So . . . I'm not saying it's true or not, but here's this Indian woman who's going to get on the witness stand and point a finger in your face and state that she saw you running away from the scene of the crime. And the HPD ballistics expert is going to say that the gun you had in your hand an hour after the murder was the gun that killed this Vietnamese man. That's bad, very bad. Do you see all that, Hector?"

Quintana nodded gravely.

"Now, what have I, as your defense lawyer, got to tell the jury? I can't tell them you were somewhere else when the murder was committed, because I can't produce a single live body who can verify it. I can't say you're a peace-loving citizen, because in the first place you're not a citizen, which is neither here nor there, but in the second place you were caught robbing a convenience store with a gun. Not a peace-loving act. You were drunk, but that won't help you. Hector, what I'm trying to tell you is— you are in deep shit. *Mierda profunda,*" he added, translating literally.

This was usually the moment when the defendant lowered his head, gripped the metal mesh until his knuckles turned white, and then said, with immense and bitter effort —because the world was pressing in on him and he finally understood the terrifying price he had to pay for his sins and no doubt his stupidity—"What can you do for me if I plead guilty?"

That Hector Quintana was guilty of murdering Dan Ho Trunh, Warren had almost no doubt. The qualifier was there not only because he liked Quintana—he was all too wary now of the consequences that might arise from liking a client—but because he thought he saw in the man's face a kind of peaceable gravity he had seen on the faces of many poor men in Mexico. Men who might get pissy-eyed drunk on Saturday night and lie down in the cobbled streets and bay at the moon, but not men who would kill unless they were seriously insulted or had a vision that some fool was making a public pass at their woman. No psychotic Mexican climbed to the top of a university tower with a high-powered rifle and sprayed random bullets.

None butchered his wife and children and then slit his own throat. There were plenty of murders down there in the drug trade, but usually if men robbed you it was because they were poor—they took your money and split to go home to their Rosa or Carmencita or get drunk with their compañeros. The conquistadors and then the hacienda owners had whipped most of them into a state of subservience. Machismo, which they'd lapped up with their mother's milk, didn't equate with violence.

But there must be exceptions, Warren thought, and maybe Quintana was one of them. The evidence certainly suggested it. As a lawyer, and with the best interests of his client in mind, Warren had to deal with the evidence.

He had one more idea, sprung from his thoughts about the men he had sometimes seen sprawled in the early hours of Sunday morning outside the *cantinas* of San Miguel de Allende.

"Hector, I know that when men get drunk they do things they wouldn't do otherwise. They get crazy. I'm not saying it's true, but maybe you bumped into this Vietnamese guy in that parking lot. Maybe he was a stupid son of a bitch, and he insulted you—said something nasty to you about your being a Mexican, a wetback. Is that possible?" Warren felt his cheeks warm up with enthusiasm. "If it is, then I can get up there and explain a lot of things to the judge"—a picture of Lou Parker on the bench popped into his mind, and quickly he amended that—"or to the jury, because if we plead guilty we have the right to ask for a jury to do the sentencing. And if you're straight with me, and I'm straight with them, the jury will understand why what happened happened . . ." Realizing that his client was barely listening, he shrugged. ". . . if it happened."

Quintana said in his soft voice, "There will be a trial?"

Warren ground his teeth. This was some stubborn bastard.

"There can be a trial by jury. Twelve men and women. Your peers. Plain people."

"Can I speak to the jury?"

"You have that right. It will be testimony under oath."

"Then I will tell the jury that it's not true, that this woman makes a mistake, and that I doan ever know this man and doan kill him."

Warren cleared his throat to hold back his impatience, leaning forward to the mesh. "If there's a trial," he said quietly, "and you testify and they find you guilty, the jury will sentence you either to death by cyanide injection or to life in the penitentiary. That's the law. The jury can't deviate."

"But I will tell them, and they will believe me even if you don't. I will tell them," Quintana repeated desperately.

Warren walked at a slow pace through the twisting underground tunnel that connected the Harris County Jail with the courthouse, where he bumped into Myron Moore, a burly fifty-year-old lawyer who always reminded him of Idi Amin. Around the courthouse Moore was called Dr. Doom. He made heavy contributions each year to the campaign funds of nearly all the judges, and if there was a capital murder involving an indigent defendant, Moore was at the top of nearly every judge's list—he would plead anyone guilty and if he was forced to go before a jury he guaranteed the quickest trial possible. The lawyers joked that the Texas Department of Corrections was considering opening a Myron Moore Unit just to house his clients.

Moore stopped him in the tunnel. "I hear you cut me out of a capital in Lou Parker's court. You need any help over there?"

"Not yet, Myron."

"Who's prosecuting?"

"Nancy Goodpaster."

"Play her tough," Moore said. "Don't give her nothing. She's just another dumb ole Texas nigger gal."

Warren frowned but decided not to comment. "What's Scoot Shepard doing in the 181st, Myron?"

"A DWI trial. The mighty have fallen."

"I doubt it. Must be a good fee."

Continuing through the tunnel to the courthouse, thinking about Hector Quintana, Warren felt a barbed pain in the upper part of his back. No fucking wonder. It was a hopeless case. The judge had been clear: *"Don't waste my time. I expect you to plead it out for whatever you can get."* This sorry Mexican is giving me a hard time, Warren thought. And I like the man. I don't want him to die.

It occurred to him then that Hector Quintana had never asked what would happen if he were willing to plead guilty.

Warren would have said, "I can plea-bargain, Hector. The charge that the murder was committed during the course of a robbery is what turns it into capital murder. The prosecutor's not particularly vicious—believe me, there are worse. If you wanted to plead guilty, I could try to get her to reduce the charge to plain murder. Vanilla murder. She'd probably go for it—she knows the judge doesn't want to tie up the court with a long trial. You can get hit with five years probation up to life in prison. The prosecutor will make a recommendation and the judge will buy it. That's the system, that's how it works. I'd try for thirty years. The prisons upstate are crowded, they're fighting for space. You could be out in fifteen years."

If Quintana agreed, that would be a minor blessing for everybody. Warren would be in Lou Parker's good graces. Word would spread. A small start, but still a start. And Quintana would stay alive and one day see his Francisca again.

But if Warren took the case to a jury and they gave his man death, which seemed an excellent possibility, he would be worse off than when he started. They would say he had thrown away a defendant's life for the chance to play to the crowd. Not easy to live with. A lawyer's responsibility in a capital case with powerful state's evidence was to see that the client came out of it alive.

And I can't take it to trial, he thought, reaching the end of the gloomily lit tunnel, pausing at the door to the court-house. That's the deal with Lou Parker.

He took the elevator up to the 181st on the third floor, passed the bar and squeezed onto the front bench reserved for lawyers. Again, with Scoot Shepard at work, the courtroom was crowded. The defendant, a thirty-five-year-old bank vice-president with a handlebar mustache, looking debonair but concerned, sat next to Scoot at the defense table. Warren had been right: there was a good fee.

Scoot was in the midst of cross-examining a young police officer with an alert expression on his face. The bank vice-president had been pulled over one night for weaving back and forth on the freeway at an erratic rate of speed. The police officer had asked him to recite the alphabet and the banker had failed to do so accurately.

Scoot asked the officer if *he* knew how to recite the alphabet.

"Yes, I do."

"Would you do it, please, for the benefit of the jury? And may I approach the witness, your honor? I'm just a tad hard of hearing, and I want to make sure I catch every little letter."

With the defense attorney only a few feet away from him and staring intently in his face, the young cop tried his luck. "A-b-c-d-e-f-g-h-i-j-k-l-m-n-o-p-r . . . ah . . . p-q-r-s . . ." Predictably, he blushed. "No, wait a minute, let me start over."

"You must be drunk," Scoot said.

The officer laughed uneasily. "No, sir, I'm not drunk, I'm just temporarily confused."

"And didn't it appear to you on the night of March 5 that my client might also have been confused?"

The officer boldly said, "I'm not confused, I'm nervous. Because you're standing very close to me, sir."

"And weren't you standing close to my client on the night of March 5? And are you nervous the same way someone might be nervous who's stopped at one o'clock in the morning by two Houston police officers who accuse him of being intoxicated when he knows he's not?"

The police officer said, "Your client had no reason to be nervous. But I do."

"Why? You're not going to jail."

"But you're a famous lawyer, and I don't want people to think you can make a monkey out of me. And I *do* know the alphabet."

The judge laughed. The jury laughed. Even the prosecutor grinned.

"I'm sure you know the alphabet. You're a bright man. Pass the witness," Scoot said.

The judge declared a two-hour break for lunch. Scoot immediately came up to Warren, squeezed his hand and said, "Let's trot over to my office. I'll have Brenda send out for sandwiches. These goddam restaurants around here, air-conditioning's so high I get icicles on my nuts."

But five minutes later when they reached Scoot's office on the sixteenth floor of the Republic Bank Building, Warren said, "For God's sake, Scoot, it's five degrees colder here than my refrigerator."

"I'll lend you a shawl, I've got plenty." Marching down the long carpeted corridor, Scoot offered a cheery hello to one of his law clerks. In his office he pulled two cans of Lone Star beer from a diminished six-pack in the little refrigerator behind his desk. The rosewood desk was bare except for a yellow legal pad, a jar of pencils, and several stacked volumes of *Reversible Errors in Texas Criminal Cases.* Brenda was dispatched into the heat for turkey sandwiches and another six-pack. Scoot lit a cigarette, popped the beer can, and dropped with a sigh into his leather armchair.

Scoot had wanted a drink, Warren realized, and not in public. An old tale.

Sixth child of a rag-dealer father and an alcoholic mother, Scoot (born Joseph Howard Shepard) had grown up in Houston's Fourth Ward. A street kid, a carouser, he had put himself through college by running numbers—his nickname came from his speed in delivery—and then law school at the University of Houston. Some years before Warren's father died, Warren had asked him: what *is* Scoot's secret, the one he'll never tell?

"It's no secret at all," Judge Blackburn said. "He just lives by it better than most people. Lawyering is acting, a con game. Assuming his case has some merit, if a lawyer gets a jury to like him and then trust him more than the son of a bitch who's arguing against him, he's home free. Beyond that, Scoot's prepared. And he can size up a witness after he listens to him for five minutes. Knows what it'll take to cozy up to him or get him so mad he'll spit blood. Most people lie on the witness stand, because the greatest human illusion is that we can remember anything accurately. But if Scoot decides a person's basically telling the truth, he can figure out a way to make him doubt what he believes . . . sometimes doubt what he actually saw. In my court once in a rape case, he kept a poor woman on the stand for a solid week. When she got off, she was destroyed. It was the most masterful job I'd ever seen, because this woman had described the rape in minute detail. And to this day I believe she was telling the truth."

Young Warren had frowned. "Then why'd you let him go on at her for a whole week?"

"Because I was fascinated by what he was doing! He brought three briefcases into court—he knew everything there was to know about this woman's life from the day she was born until the day she took the stand. And he knew everything there was to know about the law on sexual assault. I kept saying, 'Stay away from that, Mr. Shepard, it's not relevant,' and five minutes later he'd be back.

I'd interrupt, and he'd come back some other clever way. The prosecutor tried for a while to stop him, then he just sat there and took it up the *culo.* I wouldn't have given old Scoot a cut dog's chance in this case—and by God, he won an acquittal!"

His father's vision of the trial process made Warren uncomfortable. A battle, a joust between opposing counsel, where each victory is sweet and each defeat adds zest to the next challenge. In law school Warren had understood that most trial lawyers yearned to win—and so did he. Cross-examination was the ultimate confrontation, the gunfight that left either lawyer or witness bleeding in the dust. The great trial lawyer Racehorse Haynes had once said, "I continue to dream of the day when I am examining a witness and my questions are so probing and so brilliant that the fellow blurts out that he, not my defendant, committed the foul murder. Then he will pitch forward into my arms, dead of a heart attack."

But there had to be more, Warren thought. More than adversaries and great actors, lawyers should be the standard-bearers of what was decent and fair. Should be, but rarely were: for they were born and shaped as human before they could be turned into lawyers.

The whites of Scoot's huge black eyes seemed more bloodshot than ever and beneath them were dark yellowish circles where the skin was drawn tight, as if he might have liver trouble or had undergone cosmetic surgery. He was probably sixty-five years old, but his hair was still full and black. Transplanted and dyed, Warren figured, but with flair, leaving small silver-gray wings above the ears.

Scoot lowered the can of Lone Star. "What do you know about the Dr. Ott case? And my client, Johnnie Faye Boudreau?"

Warren wondered for a moment why Scoot would want to discuss it with him. But he said, "Whatever I read in the *Chronicle,* and I was there in court when she pled poverty and you got the bail reduced to a hundred grand. And of course I remember the Underhill murder."

Between pulls at the can of beer and puffs on his cigarette, Scoot gave him a synopsis.

The victim, Clyde Ott, had been a successful Houston gynecologist. In his early thirties he had married one of his patients, Sharon Underhill, the forty-year-old widow of an oil-and-gas baron and the mother of two teenaged children. With Sharon's money Dr. Ott built the Houston Woman's Clinic, the Ott Clinic for alcoholics, the Underhill Clinic for drug addicts, and then a series of expensive retirement homes with small medical units attached. There was a waiting list to get into all of them.

"I knew Clyde Ott," Scoot said. "We met now and then at dinner parties, and one of my nephews spent some time in the Underhill Clinic to get rid of a little cocaine habit. Before Clyde married Sharon he'd fucked more women in Harris County than the whole Houston Astro infield put together. Marriage didn't stop him. When he got to be a wealthy entrepreneur he still kept up his gynecological practice—he liked pussy and that was the fastest way to meet it. But his main squeeze in recent years was Johnnie Faye Boudreau. You saw her in the courtroom. Quite a woman. She runs a topless bar out on the strip behind the Galeria. Maybe she owns it, maybe she doesn't—who really knows? Won a couple of beauty contests when she was younger, then became a model, then a dancer. Couple of brothers got killed in Vietnam—she talks about them all the time. Married twice, no kids. First husband, musician of some kind, she divorced on grounds of nonsupport. Second husband was a drug dealer and ex-con. She divorced him after he got sentenced to a thirty-year bit over in Austin. That was just after she took up with Clyde Ott."

Almost two years ago, on a sunny October morning, Clyde's wife, Sharon Underhill Ott, was shot down in a parking lot on her way to an aerobics class. A high-powered rifle had done the killing. A man in a black Lincoln town car was seen speeding away from the scene. Clyde Ott was in San Diego at the time, at a medical convention. Johnnie Faye Boudreau was visiting her mother down in Corpus Christi. Airtight alibis.

"Johnnie Faye had another part-time boyfriend then," Scoot said, "called Dink, because his real name was David Inkman. He was an assistant manager at her club, an ex-Marine. Did some time up at Huntsville for assault and battery. Dink drove a black Lincoln town car. Naturally, considering the close relationship between Clyde and Johnnie Faye, Dink fell under suspicion. But he had an alibi too. A couple of hookers swore he'd got drunk with them the night before, slept over at their house and stayed till noon. They swore his Lincoln was parked in their garage. HPD never could pick up a tire tread in the parking lot to match Dink's white-walls, and they never did find the murder weapon. Case closed."

Warren remembered photographs in all the papers of the grieving widower. After he had inherited the bulk of Sharon's $35 million estate Dr. Clyde Ott had donated $5 million of it to the Texas Medical Center.

Scoot popped another can of Lone Star.

"Dink—Inkman—had a little rundown wood frame house in Montrose. About three months after Sharon Ott was killed, Dink was shotgunned to death in the driveway of his home from a passing pickup. They had to scrape him off the concrete with a fucking trowel."

Warren blew out his breath. "You're saying—"

"Not me. Others did. Said that Johnnie Faye was behind it all, that she wanted to marry Clyde Ott, and the first thing she had to do was get rid of her husband, which was easy—there was a story made the rounds that she'd told the law where he was picking up the dope in Austin—and then Clyde's wife, which was hard. And then after Dink had done that for her out of the blackness of his loyal heart, she had to get rid of Dink too. They said there were a lot of ex-cons she'd done favors for. The theory was she'd hump these guys and supply them with dope, and then when she had them under her thumb she'd ask them for a little favor. Promise to pay them something, and payment would come later, if there was a later. Around the time of the Inkman murder there was another guy she was dicking around with, a guy named Bobbie Ronzini who also worked for her at the club. Ronzini fell under suspicion but the cops couldn't prove anything. Then he vanished. Maybe into a hole in the ground. No one knows. I'm just giving you some background," Scoot said graciously.

"I never heard about the Inkman murder," Warren admitted.

"Why would you? After Washington, D.C., and Detroit, Houston's the murder capital of the western world. May even beat out Beirut. The newspapers can pick and choose."

And they did. Dan Ho Trunh's death had merited half a paragraph on a back page of the *Post,* and the *Chronicle* had completely ignored it.

"So now we come to the Ott case," Scoot resumed. "But here we know that Johnnie Faye Boudreau pulled the trigger. She admitted it. Called HPD to tell them. Of course, Clyde's stepdaughter was in the house when it happened, so it would have been a tricky business for Johnnie Faye to cut and run."

She had shot Clyde Ott twice with a .22-caliber pistol, her own gun, which she normally carried in her handbag. She had a permit; at her club, Ecstasy, she had to deal with some bad people.

"Now, I can see in your face that you want to know how come I'm talking to you." Scoot Shepard leaned back in his tall leather chair, while cigarette smoke spiraled lazily toward the air-conditioning vents. It was a high-profile case, Scoot said. Seemingly straightforward, like most self-defense cases, but it had its pitfalls. Bob Altschuler, the prosecutor, was a first-rate trial lawyer and a skilled headline-grabber. He had won forty-nine cases in a row and had a particular interest in making it fifty; he wanted to run for judge next fall. The D.A.'s office had manpower and the full resources of a bureaucracy. Against that, Scoot couldn't handle the case alone. There was law to research, potential witnesses to be hunted down and interviewed. The two younger lawyers working in his office, who would normally assist him, were tied up for months with major litigation—an antitrust case: trials in state and federal courts with hundreds of witnesses.

"You had a bad break," Scoot said to Warren. "Lou Parker screwed you. You've been doing a lot of shit since then, but I've been watching you for years and I think you're a damned fine lawyer. If you're free, I'm asking you to sit second chair with me in *Boudreau.*" Scoot lit a fresh Camel from the butt end of the old one. "I knew your father, but you're smart enough to realize this isn't charity —I can't afford to be charitable when I need good help. Johnnie Faye's given me a retainer of $75,000 and I'm billing her monthly at $350 an hour. I'll pay you twenty grand up front against your hourly rate, whatever it is. Trial's set for July 24. I'll give you one or two witnesses to handle. You might have fun. You might learn something. How about it? Is that a deal?"

Warren never hesitated.

The media would clamor to talk to Scoot, not the lawyer who sat second chair. But if Scoot trusted him, others would; if Scoot praised him, the world would listen; and if Scoot won, some of the glory would rub off. It was a real step to a comeback, to work with style, in the right company. Significantly better than struggling for a homeless Mexican who refused to see that he was doomed.

"Deal," Warren said, and extended his hand across the desk. Scoot shook it firmly.

A woman had probably killed her lover's wife and then at least one hired assassin, and now had admitted to doing in her lover in self-defense. It wasn't capital murder because it hadn't been committed in the course of another felony and there were no other special circumstances. The law required that she have legal counsel and further required that her counsel do the utmost to have her acquitted. Failing that, to plead with a jury for leniency. There were no scruples involved—it didn't matter whether she was guilty or not. It was an adversary system: the state would try to put her away for life, the defense would fight to walk her out of the courtroom. Without a competent and enthusiastic defense, the state would have its way whether she was guilty or not. The system would collapse.

Warren asked, "What's the theory of the defense?"

Scoot said, "You know the story of the Harvard graduate comes to Texas a while back and says to his rancher uncle, 'Unk, how come you can get heavier punishment here for stealing a cow than for killing a man?' Unk says, 'Look out the window. See those cows out to pasture? See any of them look like they need stealing?' "

Warren smiled, even though he knew the story.

"The defense is the oldest in Texas," Scoot said. "*The son of a bitch needed killing.* A little hard to do these days now that so many Yankees moved down here, but you can still try it to a jury. *I'd* listen."

Warren set down his can of Lone Star. "Kind of depends on what they think of our client, doesn't it?"

Scoot nodded appreciatively. "And you saw her, didn't you? You want to keep that can of beer real cold, you can't do better than lay it right next to Johnnie Faye Boudreau's heart. So there's a little work we have to do. Take this home and read it."

He handed Warren a copy of the thick file marked *Texas v. Boudreau.*

A gray scum of clouds floated above the city. In his cottage office Warren turned the air-conditioning up a notch against the afternoon heat, settled down behind his desk and opened the file.

On Sunday evening, May 7 (according to the secretary's

transcript of Johnnie Faye Boudreau's first interviews with
Scoot Shepard), the defendant had been invited by Dr.
Clyde Ott to dinner at the Hacienda, a Tex-Mex restaurant
just off I-10. It was one of Johnnie Faye's favorites, a big
place with several dining rooms and two-foot-thick adobe
walls. There were strolling mariachis.

"I love Mexican music by candlelight," she told Scoot.
"And I love a good spicy guacamole and then beef fajitas
with onions all sizzling and golden brown. If my breath
smells, I usually say, 'Sweetie, I'll make it up to you some
other way.' "

She whistled the musicians to their table and had them
play "Las Mañanitas" and "No Vale Nada La Vida," her
favorite Mexican song. She tipped them well. Before dinner Clyde had a couple of drinks, and during dinner a few
more, and there was no telling what he'd sipped before he
got there.

"Mixing booze and dope will hasten you to an early
grave," Johnnie Faye explained. "One way or the other
. . . as it turned out."

Clyde drank, she said, and he sniffed cocaine, which he
usually possessed in extravagant quantities. He was the
sort of drunk who never fell down or slurred his words; he
just got mean. Last Christmas he had hit her with a
clenched fist, a right cross to the schnozz. She had been
sitting on the leather sofa in his TV room, trying to talk to
him and sort out the mess of their lives, and somehow he
had taken offense at whatever she'd said, and crossed the
room in that bearlike waddle of his and let fly before she
knew what was happening. Pow! There was blood all over
her silk blouse.

Was he contrite?

"If you ask that, Mr. Shepard, you didn't know Clyde."

He kept on yelling and threatening to kill her. She had
to muscle her way out of his house and get to the emergency room at Hermann Hospital. She thought her nose
was broken, but it turned out there was a hairline fracture

of the cheekbone. Still a tiny depression there, where before it had been perfectly round and smooth.

Clyde had beat up on his wife, Sharon, too and one of his other girlfriends, a cocktail waitress at the Grand Hotel. Knocked out three of her teeth, had to pay her $25,000 plus the dental bill just to shut her up. And he'd threatened Johnnie Faye more than once. Raised his fist and said, in front of two friends they were having dinner with, "You bitch, I could kill you."

She wanted to marry him, that was a fact. Love is a funny thing—you don't always pick the most upstanding person to lavish it on. His being that rich had nothing to do with it, although she wouldn't pretend that his money stood in the way of her affection. "But I'm a working gal," she told her lawyer. "Always have been. I've got enough money of my own. My independence is very dear to me."

She and Clyde had begun their affair when he was still married; that was no secret. Clyde and Sharon slept in separate bedrooms in their twenty-five-room house in River Oaks. If he could get a divorce and not lose his clinics in the process, absolutely, he'd marry Johnnie Faye. He was crazy about her. She was terrific in bed, she indulged all his fantasies the way no one had ever done, she was the most exciting woman he had ever known. He said that often, when he was sober.

Then Sharon was shot down outside her aerobics class in her brand-new pink designer sweatsuit. Shot down by some mad killer, the kind that seems to pop up every season in the Sunbelt. Maybe he mistook her for someone else. We'll never find out.

Clyde didn't mourn her. He was a louse but no hypocrite. He was shocked, of course, and he stayed out of public places for a month or so and gave all that money to the Texas Medical Center to help cure cancer. Then he went skiing in Tahoe, and when he came back he stepped out into the world again. Now he could marry Johnnie Faye.

But he didn't.

"It upset me. I can't lie about that—it goddam upset me."

She didn't mean that he shouldn't go through some kind of decent social mourning period. Although, as she often said, get the gusto while you can. She put it to him: "Are we or aren't we going to do it, and when?"

"Well . . ."

" 'Well' is not an answer, Clyde."

"I need some time."

"Time to make the decision or time before we get married?"

"Both, I guess, sweetheart."

That pissed her off. She never could get Clyde to tell her what really was the problem, because he was naturally closemouthed like men tend to be, afraid to reveal his deep self (as if she wouldn't be sympathetic, wouldn't stroke him and guide him toward the light), and because most of the time his brain wasn't functioning properly as the cells were being destroyed at a prodigious rate by single-malt scotch and Colombian coke.

"Let's have a quiet dinner," she said. "No friends. And we'll talk about getting married. We'll make a timetable we can live with."

That was the purpose of their dinner at the Hacienda on the evening of May 7. They arrived about nine o'clock. But Clyde got drunk and nasty. Accusations flew across the table over the fajitas and sizzling onions. "Take me home," she said, before the espresso came.

By home she meant her apartment, but Clyde had other ideas. Drunk or stoned or sober, he couldn't get enough of her, although in the first two instances his capability seldom matched his desire. She drove and they made it to the house on River Oaks Boulevard without incident. Parked the Porsche in the garage. Went up to the bedroom.

Why did she go, Scoot asked, if he'd turned mean?

Well, sometimes sex was a way of resolving problems, of

purging the hate. Or whatever it was that made him mean. And she was a little drunk too, not thinking straight.

But when he couldn't get it up, when she had tried every trick she knew and he bellowed with frustration and then began calling her names again, she climbed out of bed and got dressed. "I can't take this anymore, Clyde. I'm not here on this earth to be your target. I'm leaving you."

Usually when she said that he became contrite, begged her to give him yet another chance. But not that night. He yelled, "I'm sick and tired of your threats!" and slapped her in the face.

In his black silk pajama bottoms he followed her downstairs to the living room. He was a big man, six feet tall and two hundred twenty pounds, with thick shoulders and a gut. At Texas Christian he had been a wrestler in the light-heavyweight class. He waddled when he walked, but he was quick enough. In the living room he maneuvered himself between Johnnie Faye and the hallway that led to the front door. His eyes were bloodshot. He was gasping: for a moment she thought he was going to have some kind of fit. He raised his fist and she backed across the carpet toward the fireplace.

Resting against one of the andirons was a poker; Johnnie Faye snatched it up to defend herself. Clyde twisted it out of her hand like a twig. Stumbling across the room, she positioned herself behind a white Italian sofa, with bookcases at her back. She kept screaming at him, "In God's name, what have I done?" She hoped her screaming would wake his stepdaughter, Lorna, visiting from Dallas and occupying one of the guest suites. But the house was huge, the walls were double-insulated brick.

In her handbag she had the compact .22 she always carried. Never had fired it except years ago on a range north of town. She fumbled among the keys and loose Kleenexes and makeup, then pointed the pistol at him. Not aiming, just pointing.

He started to amble across the room.

"Clyde," she said clearly, "if you come near me, I'll shoot you."

His response was to lift the poker like a baseball bat. She yelled, *"Don't!"*— but the drunken fool kept coming. And in her panic she pulled the trigger. The .22, when it was manufactured in 1928, had been a semiautomatic pistol, automatically ejecting the cartridge case of a fired round and loading the next cartridge from the magazine into the chamber. But long ago some previous owner had filed down the sear, the pivoted internal piece that held the hammer cocked, thus making the pistol fully automatic. She'd forgotten about that, she said. That was the tragic part. She couldn't stop it from firing three shots.

Believe it or not, he still took a swing at her with the poker. When she raised her head cautiously she saw him tumbling onto the white sofa. He was probably dead when he took the swing, because although one bullet missed, one of the other two had hit him between the eyes and the other in the chest.

There was an old saying in Texas: *God made men, Smith & Wesson made them equal.*

Scoot asked, What about the safety?

She must have released it without thinking when she grabbed the gun out of her handbag.

And did she know it was illegal to file down that sear?

"I didn't do it," she explained.

She didn't scream. Clyde lay on his knees, head pillowed on the sofa, one arm dangling to the carpet. She never touched the body. She became aware that the TV was on in the next room. Probably Lorna had left it on. She walked in there and turned it off in the middle of a Johnny Carson monologue.

From the telephone in the TV room she dialed 911, gave her name and the address in River Oaks, and said, "I just killed a man. He was about to assault me, and I shot him. Please come and help. . . ."

She told a briefer version of that tale to the Homicide

detectives when they arrived at the house. A copy of her statement was in the file. She was always consistent in the details. If there's no one to contradict her, Warren thought, we'll win this case. Can't lose unless Scoot goes to sleep in the courtroom, and that had never happened.

At home that evening he warmed up last night's chicken gumbo in the microwave, fed Oobie a mix of Purina Chow and raw ground chuck and corn oil, then spread the papers on the living room couch. He read the file a second time, until midnight, then went to bed. Charm hadn't come home: of late she had her own social life, a gang of friends from the TV station, a separate schedule.

She was there in the morning, asleep beside him, blond hair tangled on the pillow. He studied her face. He had loved it for eight years and knew it down to the tiny scar where the branch of a blueberry bush had hooked the corner of her mouth when she was thirteen. Warren understood that at first we love the illusion of perfection. Later we come to love imperfections, because they signal vulnerability: and what we love, we yearn to protect.

He wanted to talk to her. The oath of confidentiality, he believed, did not extend to man and wife. And she had always helped him to see more clearly. She looked pale, puffy around the eyes. But she treasured her sleep in the morning, and he didn't wake her.

Running with Oobie along the bayou, heels pounding the concrete in stoic rhythm, he came to a decision. Working with Scoot on the Ott case was the major leagues, and he had earned the chance without even realizing it. He had lost self-esteem, had toiled like a humble peasant in the fields of the law, and finally it had paid off. He was going to do a good job. Going to prevail.

But he couldn't live a divided life. Two murder trials were one too many. Get rid of *Quintana*, he concluded. Be an intelligent lawyer and face facts. Stop being sorry for the poor bastard—he's guilty. Plead him out, fast.

The next day in Judge Bingham's court, Warren was registered as co-attorney of record for the defendant in *The State of Texas v. Johnnie Faye Boudreau.* He shook hands with a dark-suited Bob Altschuler, whose grip was like that of a heavyweight wrestler trying for an armlock.

"Congratulations," the prosecutor rumbled. "Let's sit down and cut a deal. You know this woman's a fucking mad serial killer—you *know* that, for Christ's sake, don't you? She's out of her tree! I gather you think I'm a cross between Pontius Pilate and Attila the Hun, but, my boy, I know what I'm talking about here. She's got the morals of a rat. She's a cannibal, a homicidal maniac!" He refused to let go of Warren's hand; he needed a captive audience. "She owns that nightclub—this corporation in Louisiana is just a shell with some fucking Cajun second cousin fronting for her. It won't come up in court, but she knocked off Ott's wife and the guy who did it for her and the guy who knocked off *that* guy, and we think that back in '82 just on the spur of the moment she offed some Korean kid who worked in her club as a chef's assistant and gave her some back talk when she wouldn't give him a raise—told her she was crazy. You think I'm kidding? I *know*. And God alone knows who else before that. With this broad, murder is a way of working out problems and settling scores. You want to do a service to society, help me put her away, at least until she's too old to do more damage. Tell your partner I'll settle for fifty years."

Warren sighed. "Are you finished? Can I go?"

"You think I'd lie to you?"

"You might have a tendency to exaggerate."

"You don't believe any of it?"

"It's not for me to believe or disbelieve," Warren said. "It's for you to prove it. Do your job and stop wasting my time." He managed to shake his hand loose from Altschuler's, but his fingers were bright red and the bones ached.

He walked briskly up the stairs to Judge Parker's court. The jury box was full of lawyers waiting for appointments. Three days ago, Warren thought, I'd have been with them.

He drew Nancy Goodpaster off into a private corner of the hallway. Deals were cut everywhere, some even in the courthouse toilets.

"Cards on the table, Nancy. What will you give if Hector Quintana pleads out?"

"Is that what he wants?"

"He says he didn't do it. Whether it's true or not, I need something to offer him."

"What do *you* want, Warren?"

Now that she thinks she can whip the case through the docket and get a pat on the back from Lou Parker, she calls me by my first name. He pretended to think for a while.

"Reduce the charge to vanilla murder. Twenty years. Drop the charges of armed robbery and possession of a weapon."

"You're wasting my time, counselor." Nancy Goodpaster looked at her gold wristwatch. But Warren knew she had nowhere more important to go.

"The Siva Singh I.D. won't stand up."

"I think it will."

"It was dark in that parking lot outside the dry cleaners. I checked it out. No decent street light. There are a thousand guys who have black hair and wear shirts and trousers on a summer night. I don't think Singh really saw the man's face."

"She claims she did."

"Nancy, what makes it a capital is the assumption of robbery. So tell me—what did Quintana do with the hundred and fifty bucks from Trunh's wallet? He didn't have it on him when he robbed the Circle K. Even if he threw the wallet into a trash can, he didn't throw the money away with it, did he? Who'd believe that? You can't make capital murder stick." He waited a moment. "You want to settle this, don't you?"

"Naturally."

"Then give a little. Give with a good heart."

"Fifty years."

"My man will never buy it. He has no record. He's had jobs, he's not a vagrant. He's a simple Mexican *campesino.* A wife and kids back home—his father gave him a donkey for a wedding present. He's not a murderer."

"He killed, that makes him a murderer."

"You know what I'm talking about."

"And it doesn't make any difference. Murderers have wives and kids. I knew one used to rescue lame dogs from the pound. I remember one who raised pet squirrels. So now I know one who has a donkey. Jesus, Warren . . ." She sighed. "You feel sorry for him, that's all. Another poor slob, like that guy in the Kmart case. Well, maybe if he were my client, I'd feel sorry for him too."

Good. He was getting somewhere. She had a heart. He liked her for it.

"And if Quintana gets up there on the witness stand," Warren said, "the jury's going to feel sorry for him too. He's not surly, he's not mean, he's not a bad man. He's got pride and dignity and it all shows. A jury will never go for the capital. And if they find him guilty of the lesser offense, they'll give him considerably less than life."

"Forty years," Goodpaster said. "My final offer."

"You're a hard woman."

"No, I'm doing my job. Like you're doing yours." She seemed upset at the accusation.

"You'll drop the charge of armed robbery?"

"I'll think about it, Warren. Now I have to go. Have a nice weekend."

Warren sighed. He hoped he was masking his feeling of triumph. He was saving a man's life.

In his office late the following Monday afternoon, Scoot Shepard asked, "You know the statute on self-defense?"

Warren nodded, frowning. "And I know there was a provision engrafted in the penal code back in '74 that calls for 'the duty to retreat.' "

"You're on target." In one hand Scoot held a cigarette, in the other a glass of bourbon on the rocks. Whenever the sun threatened to dip below the yardarm, Scoot switched from Lone Star to Wild Turkey.

"Seems to me," Warren said, "that one question a prosecutor might ask a jury to focus on is this: if Clyde Ott was drunk and abusive that night, why did Johnnie Faye Boudreau even enter the house with him? Why did she go upstairs? And when she first came downstairs from the bedroom, why didn't she just go out the door before he blocked her path? Did she retreat *sufficiently?* And if Clyde had fractured her cheekbone once before and she believed him to be violent—why was she still seeing him? If her story's true, he once said in front of two witnesses that he would kill her. That's superficially good for us, but it's got a flip side. The state will say that's why she carried the gun in her handbag on a dinner date. They'll call it premeditation."

"True, true." Scoot smiled delicately. "Of course that all depends on how the lady tells it when she testifies. It boils down to credibility. Don't fret too much about 'the duty to retreat.' All those Yankee lawyers come to practice here when oil was up at thirty-five dollars a barrel, they rammed that down the throat of the state legislature. They were looking to bring Texas into the twentieth century, so to speak, juristically. Pissing against the wind. This is still Texas. People pack guns and everybody thinks he's the fucking second cousin of Wyatt Earp. Bravery and loyalty and honor and duty—we're eaten up with that stuff. No man has to back down in the face of a threat. That's the basis of self-defense, regardless of what the law says about a goddam duty to retreat."

Warren remembered that Texas had the longest history of frontier warfare of any state in the Union. Its citizens were tied to guns and blood and the Alamo, backs always against the wall. He also remembered the Texas paramour statute that held it was not an offense to kill your wife's lover. It had been stricken from the books about twenty years ago, but the law still stated that if you heard from a reliable source that somebody was out to get you, you had the right to arm yourself, go forth, and seek an explanation.

"Let me tell you a story," Scoot continued. "My first murder case, nearly forty years ago. My client, a guy named Whitey Garcia, walked in and shot his wife and her boyfriend to death while they sat calmly drinking a beer in a bar in the Third Ward. Purely intentionally. He walked up to them and asked his wife what she was doing. The other guy, whose name was Ramos, butted in and said, 'She ain't doin' nothin'.' Whitey whipped out a nine-millimeter pistol and shot him in the stomach. His wife jumped up, screamed, ran across the bar. He shot her in the back. Then he shot Mr. Ramos again in the head. Stuck the gun back in his belt and marched out of the bar.

"The state was offering Whitey Garcia sixty years in prison to a plea of guilty of the murder of his wife. They didn't care about Ramos. We turned it down and I tried the case to a jury. They found Whitey guilty. Gave him ten years pen time, came over and shook his hand and told him they'd done the best they could for him, and if he just hadn't gone so danged far as to kill his wife, they'd have let him go."

Scoot refilled his glass from the quart bottle of Wild Turkey.

"What I'm saying is, you have no duty to retreat. Now, some great advances have been made in recent years regarding the rights of the fairer sex. Equal opportunity, equal wages, no goosing in the office, and so forth. My theory of defense is this: in our enlightened age, why should a Texas woman have to retreat any more than a man should? Especially when the son of a bitch needed killing. I want to sell that theory to the jury and walk my client right out of Dwight Bingham's courtroom, just like Whitey Garcia walked out of the bar."

A women's rights case. *Dear Jesus, hear my plea.* Warren clucked his tongue. If anyone could do it, Scoot could.

He said to the older lawyer, "You think Johnnie Faye's story is true?"

"Hard to say. So far it's all I've got to work with. I want you to talk to her, then go nosing around and talk to anyone else you have to. And then talk to her again until she's sick of the sound of your voice. Find out where we can be hurt. When I go before that jury, I don't want any unpleasant surprises."

"When do I meet her?"

Scoot looked at his Rolex. "In about two hours. We're all going to the Dome for the Astro game—you and me and Johnnie Faye and her new boyfriend. Her idea, her treat. Baseball bores the crap out of me. But between innings, you can get to know the lady."

Warren reached for the telephone. "I just have to make a phone call and break a dinner date." While he punched out the number he said, "Scoot, if we pick any Spanish-speaking people for the jury, I wouldn't have Johnnie Faye get up there and tell them her favorite Mexican song."

"Why, what is it?"

"According to the file, 'No Vale Nada La Vida.' "

Scoot looked puzzled.

Warren laughed coldly. "You don't know what that means?"

"Can't say as I do."

"It means, life is worth nothing."

* * *

Driving home to change, Warren avoided the crowded freeway and took a route along Main Street and Holcombe past the old site of the Shamrock. He would be at Braes Bayou by seven-fifteen, at the Astrodome by eight. When he turned the corner into the cul-de-sac leading to his house, he saw Charm's Mazda RX-7 in the driveway. It meant she had driven home immediately after work. She was not expecting him; he had told her he was meeting the Levines for dinner. Charm was invited too. "I doubt I can make it," she had said, "but if I can, I'll call Shepard's office."

In the hazy evening heat Warren saw that Charm and a man he didn't know were standing by a car parked farther up the street on the same side as the house. Charm's back was to him, her legs spread slightly, her skirt taut. She wore a pale blue suit—the $1600 one from Lord & Taylor, he recalled. The door of the car was open and the man was leaning on it, gesturing emphatically. Warren touched the brake of the BMW.

The man put his hand on Charm's shoulder, seemed to squeeze it. Then he placed his palm on her cheek and kept it there a few moments. Charm bowed her head slightly.

In their gestures there was an eloquence which Warren understood at once.

Slowly he braked to a stop next to another car about fifty feet away from them. The cul-de-sac prevented him from driving past—his house was near the end of it. He could make a U-turn and leave, or back up to the avenue, but they would notice that. And he couldn't bring himself to embarrass them by wheeling the car into the driveway. He waited, the air-conditioning vibrating gently, until finally the man stopped talking, bent to kiss Charm briefly on the lips, and ducked into his car.

He drove past Warren with not even a glance. Hands tight on the wheel, Warren stared at him as the car moved by. He saw a suntanned man of about forty with a mustache. The word *paramour* formed in his mind. He was aware that his lips, dry as bone, had pulled back over his teeth in a grimace.

Charm turned and walked quickly, heels clicking down the driveway, into the house. From his car Warren saw but didn't hear the front door close behind her. Yet he could imagine the sound as clearly as if he had heard it: the sounds of doors closing in your own home are so familiar, so personal.

Farther up the block, children shouted at each other. Roller skates rasped on concrete. Warren parked at the outer edge of his driveway.

Go in? Slink away? Go out and get drunk?

He wanted to shout in anger. He had a sudden yen for a cigarette and realized he had never lost the craving. He felt disgusted with himself. The heat of the moribund evening pressed against his forehead.

It was still his home. His clothes were there, and he needed them. He slipped his keys out of the ignition, got out of the car, unlocked his front door, and stepped into the cool hallway that led to the living room. Oobie stumbled up to him, wagging her tail violently.

I wish you could talk, Oobie. I'd ask you a lot of questions.

Charm was seated in a rocker at the pine kitchen table, drinking a glass of cold white wine. The creaking of the rocker was the only sound as she looked up with blurred eyes. There was a certain wild look too, and an anger equal to his. Anger masks fear, he realized.

"I saw you out there," he said. "I was in my car."

She stared at him in silence.

Warren's heart fluttered but everything else felt numb. "Can we talk in the bedroom, Charm? I have to change."

With what Warren perceived as counterfeit obedience, she followed him, carrying her glass of wine, and Oobie trailed behind, tail tucked hard between her legs. Oobie knew. Charm sat on the edge of the king-size bed while Warren took off his suit and folded the edges of his trousers properly into the press of the wooden hanger. The numbness was gone but now there was a ringing in his ears. *I don't know what to say or do,* he thought. *It's up to her.*

"Okay," Charm said at last, sighing.

"What's okay?"

He began the hunt for his baseball cap, stuffed somewhere among sweats and old tennis shoes and torn T-shirts with various logos.

"He's a man I've been seeing," she said quietly.

"Seeing?"

"Having an affair with."

He found the black Astro cap and decided to put it on his head right then and there. Each of his hands felt like twenty-five-pound weights, and he kept fumbling stupidly with the brim, aware that he was breathing as in a workout at the gym.

When he turned around, Charm said, "You look silly."

He was wearing a white shirt, red Jockey shorts, and the Astro cap.

"That's because I feel silly," he explained, while he felt the blood hum through his veins.

"What are you going to do?" Charm asked. "What's the traditional response down here when you find out your wife's having an affair? Do you beat her up? Stomp on her with your cowboy boots? Yell and walk out the door in what y'all call a mother huff?"

Her eyes had misted with tears.

"We do that sometimes," Warren said, "and sometimes we go out and hunt the son of a bitch down and shoot him between the eyes."

"Wonderful," Charm muttered.

"Just tell me about it."

Was she relieved that he wasn't yelling? That he seemed in control of himself? He couldn't tell. She didn't seem quite there.

"You want to know his name? All the salacious details?

How long, how often? You want to know if he's better or worse than you in bed? Is that it?"

"Please, Charm."

After a silence she said, "Just what is it that you want to know?"

That forced him to think and clarified something, and he said gently, "How you feel. What you're going to do now."

She cried for about five minutes.

He was used to that; she was a woman with deep emotions and a short fuse on her tear ducts, and sometimes she couldn't stop: like when the sewage had backed up and overflowed the downstairs toilet into the living room, or the time her immediate boss down at the station tried to take away her interview segment. Her father was a cold fish and had never really loved her—that was a recurrent theme. She hated Houston weather, the humidity of the five-month-long summer was unbearable. She was pre-period. Men didn't understand women and never would. Her oldest sister needed a mastectomy. These and other traumas brought riverine tears. The sobs made her throat hoarse.

Warren's usual reaction was to hug her and whisper to her, massage her back the way he'd seen mothers do to babies who hadn't burped. She summed it up once: "I'm insecure. It's common among kids from divorced families —I'm going to do a good documentary on that someday. My real father jerked us up and down the whole East Coast until I was ten years old. By the time I was twelve I'd gone to five different schools. I never could keep a friend. And then I got hauled out here. I have no roots."

"You do," Warren would reply. "You have them here. Now, with me."

But now in the bedroom in the fading light he didn't comfort her with his hands or soothe her with his words. He no longer knew how.

She went to the bathroom to wash her face. During that time Warren put on a pair of freshly washed jeans, a clean white shirt, and his cotton windbreaker. Promises to keep, miles to go before I sleep, as the poet said. He sat on the floor and worked his feet into the old cowhide boots.

When she came out, he repeated, "Tell me about it."

"That won't help."

He understood she was referring to herself. There was a terrible meaning to the words.

"Maybe it will help *me,* Charm."

She was thoughtful for a while, perched once more on the bed, a box of Kleenex at her side.

"All right. Maybe it will."

He was a lawyer—civil, not criminal. A partner in a big firm. Which one? Never mind. He was from New York. His name? Beside the point. A few months ago he'd had some business at the station, some potential libel suit, and he had come over from his hotel and questioned her. They had a margarita, then dinner.

"We liked each other. He was bright, and funny. So we decided to be friends. I never told you because, frankly, you and I have been leading pretty separate lives this last year."

"Not my choice," Warren pointed out.

"Are you going to argue and interrupt? If so—"

"Go ahead, Charm."

The man had returned to New York, but he'd called several times and then come again for a week on the law-suit business. She had seen him, and they had started an affair. He was in love with her, he claimed. She wasn't sure how she felt about him. She might have been in love with him too.

"Have been, or are?"

"I don't know the answer to that."

In love with. He wanted to tell her that was chemistry and lust, nature's way of getting the species to propagate. Nature's dirty trick. Chemistry was unstable. Lust ebbed and flowed. She loved *him,* she was his wife. They were partners, companions. That had substance, richness, longevity.

But none of this could he squeeze into acceptable words. He tried to make his thoughts show in his eyes and propel themselves across to where she sat hunched on the edge of the bed.

Her lover kept calling her from New York. He took two weeks off and flew out a third time. He was separated from his wife back in Manhattan, awaiting a final divorce decree. He had three children. He hadn't been looking for something like this to happen to him so soon after the breakup of his marriage, but it had happened.

"Three children. Jesus," Warren muttered.

"Is that meant to be a snide comment?"

"It just slipped out. How do you feel about all this?"

"Confused."

"I can imagine. And what about our marriage?"

That was at the root of everything, wasn't it? She wouldn't have begun the affair if the marriage wasn't failing her in some fundamental way. She had lost faith in Warren—she saw him as a man going nowhere, a man, as she'd said a while ago, with no zest left in him. Their sex life had improved, then waned. He didn't communicate with her; hadn't for a year, not since their try at therapy. What was going on inside him, behind the shell? She had no idea. All their dinner parties were with lawyer couples, and the only subject was what went on at the courthouse: the endless sarcastic analysis of cases, judges, prosecutors —lousy legal gossip. Outside of work, her life was dull. Unfulfilled. He bored her. Probably, doing all this court-appointed stuff, and putting on his chef's cap to make his cordon bleu, and using the remote to flip through the forty-seven TV channels after dinner while he sat mired in his easy chair, he bored himself. That was the impression he gave. Maybe she wasn't in love with him anymore.

" 'In love' is an irrational state. But you love me," he said doggedly. "There's a difference."

"Don't treat me like an adolescent. I understand the difference. Yes, I do love you. I care for you. And the last few years I've felt sorry for you."

No more than I've felt for myself, he thought. But it wasn't like that anymore. He wanted to tell her that, but the words felt pretentious and silly, and wouldn't come.

"Do you want to leave me and marry this guy?"

"He puts a lot of pressure on me."

"That's not an answer, Charm."

"I don't know what I want to do."

He glanced at his watch. It was ten minutes to eight. "I'm sorry," he said. "More than you know. I guess I've been letting you down. Maybe you've been letting me down too. I want to talk to you about all that. And I'm also sorry that I have to go. We'll talk when I get back. Or else tomorrow."

Charm's blurry eyes took on some heat. "You're going? Now? Where?"

He was already headed to the bedroom door, reaching for his car keys in the pocket of his jeans.

"To the ball game, with Scoot Shepard and a client."

"Are you serious? To the ball game, when our lives are falling apart?"

"I have to go. It's business." He hated the words even as he said them.

She jumped off the bed and hurried after him, barefoot, through the hall and the living room to the vestibule. When his hand was on the front doorknob, he turned to face her.

"Fuck you!" she shouted.

He put a hand out to touch her shoulder, but she jerked back from him. He said softly, "Charm, listen carefully. I still love you, and I won't let you go."

He opened the door and stepped outside into the thick evening warmth. It had grown nearly dark. Then he turned and said more strongly, "As for this New York lawyer with the wife and three kids—his story is as sorry as a two-dollar watch. I'll bet he drinks martinis before dinner and wears shirts with alligators on the pocket. If I ever catch him hanging around my house again, it's him I'll stomp on."

But saying all that didn't make him feel any better. Driving to the Astrodome he felt a fool, a cuckold, a homeless man. As homeless as Hector Quintana. In the car, he cried.

The Astros took an early lead on a home run by Glenn Davis with two aboard, and the crowd in the air-conditioned Dome grew boisterous. From the box seats behind third base, Warren cheered and hooted. Ordinarily he was not a great fan of the Houston team, but he had a particular rooting interest tonight against the New York Mets.

"Pile it on!" he yelled, after the home run. "Let's go!"

Mike Scott was pitching for the Astros. "Show 'em the spitter, Mike! No mercy!"

At his side, Johnnie Faye Boudreau gave a snort of laughter. "You sure are having a good time, Mr. Blackburn. I appreciate that kind of enthusiasm."

Scoot drank Wild Turkey from a silver flask. Warren and Johnnie Faye and a man named Frank Sawyer, who said he was from Alabama, drank beer from plastic cups. Sawyer was clean-shaven, about thirty, with light blue eyes and close-cropped fair hair. He seldom spoke, and forced a reluctant half-smile whenever Warren looked over at him. Military, Warren decided. He seemed to be both bodyguard and stud. A bouncer at her club, Johnnie Faye said. I'd like to hire him, Warren thought, to bounce that fucking New York lawyer.

And you wouldn't want Sawyer to bounce you. He had the lean nasty look of certain southern deputy sheriffs, his black T-shirt revealed a weight lifter's biceps and shoulders, and he was tattooed on both arms: a blue-and-red spitting dragon on one, an anchor and the word "Rosie" on the other. Warren wondered if he had done time like the dead Dink and the vanished Ronzini. Whenever he traveled up to Huntsville to visit one of his clients, he noticed how many inmates had their life stories inscribed on their arms and chests. Virgil Freer had flexed a naked dancing girl on his left deltoid.

Warren chatted idly with Johnnie Faye, but images of Charm kept invading his mind like mosquitoes swarming through a torn screen. In the bottom half of the fourth inning, Johnnie Faye asked him if they should be talking about the case.

"This isn't exactly the right time and place," Warren said, as cordially as he could. "But why don't you tell me about yourself?" He could see her eyes flicker with appreciation; he had opened the door to everyone's favorite subject. "Scoot told me you were a beauty queen," he prompted.

"One of the high points of my life." She smiled. "Tried to take Texas women with me into the twentieth century."

She had been brought up in Odem, she said, a little town west of Corpus Christi, with her beloved twin brother, Garrett, her older brother, Clinton, and a younger sister, Jerene, who still lived in Odem and was married to a pharmacist. Daddy was a part-time Baptist preacher who ran the filling station there. A sign outside read: ED'S EXXON AND HOUSE OF PRAYER. *JESUS IS COMING SOON!* COLD BEER TO GO. It was the kind of small town where you dialed a wrong number and talked for fifteen minutes anyway. When she got out of high school along came Vietnam, which, in Johnnie Faye's book, we should never have got involved with in the first place. That was not so much a political opinion as a personal one engendered by tragedy: her brother Clinton had been blown up by a mine at Da Nang, sent home to Texas in a body bag. And now the goddam gooks were *here,* buying up everything from shrimp boats to convenience stores, and their black-haired deadpan kids were nailing down all the scholarships that real Murkin kids couldn't get anymore.

"*I* wanted to go to college," she told Warren, "but I couldn't afford it. Biggest regret I've got."

She pumped gas until she'd saved enough money to

move to Corpus Christi, where she waitressed at an International House of Pancakes, fooled around with boys, survived a coat-hanger abortion, wasted time. By then she'd realized Corpus was a backwater, best epitomized by a guy who came into the coffee shop and asked for a piece of pie and when she asked what kind, said, "Tater pie, gal! What the hell you think pie's made of?"

She considered herself an authority on guitar picking and rattlesnake killing but not much else. For a few semesters she took night courses at Del Mar College. She wanted to make something of her life. Then she met a couple of local women who were burning their bras on Ocean Drive and holding parking lot rallies about women's rights. One of them was a lesbian. Johnnie Faye tried it. Didn't hate it, but preferred men. She burned her bra outside the pancake house. ("Made no difference," she confided to Warren. "I had boobs like rocks.") She joined the movement, which had its state headquarters in Dallas and was called SPIT, Society for Protesting Injustice in Texas. "I guess I needed friends."

In the fifth inning, with two out, the Mets scratched together a run on a walk, an error, a bloop single. The mosquitoes came back, swarming, stinging. Was Charm with her New York lawyer? What was she doing at this precise instant? Warren sifted through his memory of her words, frowning.

"We'll win," Johnnie Faye said. "Don't you fret about it." She turned to Sawyer. "You eavesdropping on my autobiography, Frankie, or you watching the ball game?"

"Which y'all want me to be doin'?" Sawyer drawled.

"Whatever pleases you, big boy." She patted the dragon tattoo on his biceps, then continued her tale.

A few women from Dallas SPIT came down to Corpus Christi to give a pep talk. Johnnie Faye was twenty-one years old, but with presence, a ripe body, a sweetness in her lips not quite extinguished by the downpour of experience yet to come. The annual Miss Texas Pageant was coming up in Austin, and before that there would be local qualifying contests all over the state. The SPIT women were militant and imaginative. They asked, "Can you sing, honey?"

She gave them a colorful rendition of one of her favorites: "Bobby Joe, Your Wife Is Cheatin' on Us Again."

They bought her a modestly cut black one-piece bathing suit, an expensive white glitter gown, a push-up bra from Frederick's of Hollywood. One of the women, a hairdresser, dyed Johnnie Faye's hair to a pale gold color and stationed her under a sunlamp.

Johnnie Faye won Miss Corpus Christi, and with the title came a prize of $1500. The only reason the judges hesitated, they explained, was that they thought her a bit too sexy, "and maybe too assertive."

With that in mind, the women tutored her. Before the Miss Texas Pageant she dieted, did three hours of exercise every day in a gym. She practiced demure, took singing lessons, read *Seventeen*.

There was one problem: in the local gym she met a curly-haired young fiddler with a country music band—his name was Bubba Rutherford. He reminded her a lot of poor Clinton. She hopped into bed with Bubba and decided she loved him more than her current boyfriend. Bubba promised her the world, and two weeks later she married him at the Corpus city hall.

Up in Austin she lived in a household with SPIT women but spent her nights with Bubba in his RV at a nearby trailer park. Her SPIT friends, when they found out, warned her to shut up about it. All Miss Texas contestants had to be single.

After the preliminary rounds the pageant officials again instructed her to tone down her personality, be more dainty, and lose a few more pounds. Most of the other contestants were on speed to keep their weight down; others were bulimic, pigging out and then stuffing their fingers down their throats to vomit it back. "They lifted their boobs with duct tape and sprayed their derrieres with Pro-Grip. They were a bunch of flakes and hysterics. I felt sorry for them."

Johnnie Faye made it to the final eight, and in the talent portion of the finals, when she sang in her down-home voice "He's Gone, and He Took Everything but the Blame," she won the second-place silver trophy.

If she had won the gold, the plan was to keep buttoned up until the Miss America pageant. But that wasn't the case, so she stood at the microphone, flashed her white teeth at the TV cameras, and said, "Folks, I'm about to tell you now what this contest is all about. . . ." The pageant officials tried to cut her off but the TV people loved it. She went on to describe the daily lives of her vitamin-deficient, anorexic, duct-taped, emotionally battered fellow contestants. The response was so enthusiastic that she veered from the prepared script and revealed to the world that she was really Mrs. Bubba Rutherford, but she'd had to keep that under her hat: "Virginal meat is the only kind the male chauvinist pigs will let you show off in this circus."

The SPIT women carried her out of the auditorium in triumph.

She was stripped of her runner-up title, which she had expected, and picked up some modeling offers from a Houston advertising agency, which she hadn't expected. Soon she became bored with SPIT and bored with Bubba. Forever wasn't nearly as long as they'd planned on.

"So I got a divorce and stayed on here. Meanwhile my brother Garrett showed up and moved in with me. I supported him. He had nightmares and he was a junkie. The war did that to him. I used to tell him, 'Garrett, you did what you had to do. You can't be sorry for wasting those yellow fuckers—they deserved it.' But he went off one weekend with some of his so-called buddies and o.d.'d on heroin. I loved that kid, and that was the worst thing ever happened to me, even worse than when my daddy passed away. I was dancing by then and I was worn out. Found a backer for Ecstasy a few years down the pike, and the rest is history. You want to hear that part too?"

Scoot had excused himself and left in the sixth inning. Now, in the eighth, the Mets had nibbled away at the Astros' lead and tied the score.

The buzzing refused to leave Warren's head; he kept having visions of Charm and her New York lover. And to try to exorcise them, he cheered even more vigorously than before for the Astros. Johnnie Faye told him how she redecorated and restaffed the club, married a guy who turned out to be a no-good drug dealer—"got caught delivering twenty keys, so I divorced him." The game went into the tenth. Strawberry clubbed a home run for the Mets and in their half of the inning the Astros couldn't get the ball out of the infield.

"I still go down to Odem three times a year to see my mama, and I'm loyal to anyone's loyal to me. That's my creed," Johnnie Faye concluded.

They filed up the ramp toward the exit. At the hot dog concession, Johnnie Faye dug her heels into concrete and leveled a finger at his chest. "Good buddy, I've got a beef, and it's also my creed to speak what's on my mind. Since the fucking seventh inning you haven't heard a word I said. I'm divulging my entire life story, which you asked for, and you're sitting there worrying whether some peckerhead's gonna get ball four or strike three!"

"That's not it," Warren said.

"Then what is? You're supposed to be my lawyer along with Mr. Shepard. He told me to talk to you and tell the truth, the whole truth and nothing but, which I did. But I don't know if I want a lawyer who can't bother to listen. I won't raise any more sand, but you owe me an explanation."

Warren took a shaky breath and said, "My wife just told me she's having an affair. She might leave me. That's what was on my mind. Not the game."

Johnnie Faye's face bloomed like a pink rose. The darkness left her bicolored eyes. "You should have told me that before, Warren," she said, while the crowd ebbed around her. Her voice softened: "Nothing in this world I don't know about what goes on between men and women. I've been around that block so many times I could write a guidebook."

She hauled Frank Sawyer close to her and kissed him on his bony cheek.

"You go on back to the club, honey. I'm taking my new friend to a bar and listen to *his* story. The lawyer man needs help."

She gave Sawyer a push, then slipped her arm through Warren's. "You give her half a chance, there's a kind of woman will tear your heart out and stomp the sucker flat. Is your wife like that?"

"No," Warren said, "she's not."

"Then maybe I can help you." She propelled him toward the parking lot.

In the Astrodome Sports Bar, over their third round of bourbon on the rocks, Johnnie Faye laid a hand on his arm.

"Good lawyer buddy, are you ready to listen?"

Nearly midnight after a hard day, and Warren nodded wearily.

"No matter what she tells you to the contrary, what a woman wants in a man is for him to take command. I personally never found one I'd let boss me around for more than five minutes, but I certainly don't give up trying. Maybe, like you say, your wife loves you. I like to think that's true—you're a good-looking fellow, and you're intelligent, and you've got what I call quality. But your little wife is confused. Life's confusing enough and people don't make it any clearer the way they carry on. Aside from life, you're the main reason for her confusion, not this other dude. Why? *Because you ain't been in command!* That's what it's all about, believe me. So you got to set up now and growl. Not like a puppy dog. You ever watch those *National Geographic* specials? I love 'em. You see these lions over there in Africa, and the females go out and do the killing so they can all eat, and then the male lion comes up and lets out a growl—*grrrr*—soft, but believe me, they get the message, and they all back off so he can dive in and get the best cut of dinner. But he's got to growl first, to let 'em know he's still king of the beasts. You get all doe-eyed and sad, your wife'll feel sorry for you a while, but sooner or later she'll say, 'Don't cry on me, Warren baby, you might rust my spurs.' Got to give her a little sweetness too, but mostly you got to give her the feeling that you're in charge, just like you'd do in the jungle or in a courtroom. Understand? The good Lord is like a judge, sittin' high up there, and the good Lord hates a muddle the way a judge hates a hung jury. The good Lord says, 'Mr. Man, Mr. Lawyer, you can walk, you can run, or you can lie down, but don't ever wobble.' "

Warren, drunk, listened to the parade of metaphor. Be a lion. Growl. Be a lawyer. Be in command. Please the good Lord, the biggest judge of all.

Could you take marital advice from a woman who had possibly arranged to murder her lover's wife and the man who had done the killing for her, and then pulled the trigger on another lover?

You probably could if you were drunk enough. And down enough. And feeling sorry for yourself.

That last barb upset him. There were men and women sleeping in alleys, people in hospitals with I.V.s in their veins, kids starving over in Africa and overdosing right here and being stabbed with cigarettes in houses from coast to coast. And he was bleeding inside because a woman didn't love him anymore.

But I'm inside this skin, and it's all I've got, and it hurts.

"I have to go, Johnnie Faye," he said finally, throwing down some cash on the bar and rising from the wobbly stool. "I have work to do tomorrow."

Warren arrived at the house of the late Dan Ho Trunh at nine o'clock in the morning, hung over from drinking in the Astrodome Sports Bar. Charm had been asleep when he got back home at 1 A.M. In the darkness he slid silently into the bed, keeping to his side, listening for a while to her steady, quiet breathing. She seemed at peace. All her words rushed back at him like blows. He crushed the edges of the pillow with his fingers and pain pressed against his eyelids. None of this is true. I'll wake up in the morning and it will all be gone.

He was awakened by a polluting sadness. He dressed and went through his morning rituals and left the house without even looking at his wife.

The Trunhs lived south of the Loop in Blueridge, on a street with small neat brick houses. A small Chevrolet was parked in the driveway and Warren peered inside. No gum wrappers on the floor, not even a smudge of dust on the dashboard.

The house was immaculate too: brocade curtains, doilies on the kitchen table, lace patches on the arms of the living room chairs, photographs of dignified older Asian men and women on the wall above the TV. Dan Ho Trunh's tiny young widow and mother were dressed in black blouses and black jeans, and some kids played quietly in another room. Warren offered his business card and explained that he was the lawyer appointed by the State of Texas to defend the man accused of killing their husband and son.

Not easy to say.

They seemed to understand. The younger Mrs. Trunh, the widow, who looked to be about twenty-five, invited Warren to have a glass of grapefruit juice or a Diet Coke.

Her dark eyes were grave but she kept smiling at him. How could they help?

"By telling me everything that happened the night before Dan Ho left the house. And that morning too."

They told him nothing he didn't know already, except which TV programs the family had watched.

He focused on the widow, who spoke better English than her mother-in-law. "You stated to the police that your husband was carrying his wallet that day. Did you see him pick up his wallet when he left home, Mrs. Trunh?"

"No, but he always carried it. His money and many different cards were in it."

"Credit cards?"

Mrs. Trunh shook her head. No credit cards. He paid by cash and check.

Warren said, "I'm terribly sorry to impose this way. I know how you both must feel."

The two Mrs. Trunhs nodded again with forgiveness.

"How do you know that he had more than fifty dollars in the wallet that morning?"

"He always did," the widow said.

"Did your husband have any enemies, Mrs. Trunh? Anyone who had a grudge against him?"

The widow said no.

Warren swallowed the rest of his grapefruit juice and asked questions about the family and Dan Ho's friends. Seventy percent of homicides were committed by friends or family of the victim.

Everyone liked Dan Ho. No one had ever threatened him.

This was going nowhere but downhill. Warren scratched his head. He asked if the police still had the car her husband drove that night. No, the widow said, it had been returned. It was in the garage out in back.

"May I see it?"

The women in their matching mourning jeans led him

through the kitchen into the garage, where tools and paints were stacked neatly on plywood shelves. The old blue Fairlane wagon looked as if it had been recently washed and waxed; the paintwork, a particularly garish shade of blue, gleamed in the shadows. Warren opened the driver's door. Heat poured out. The inside had been vacuumed—it was as neat as the Chevy in the driveway. If there had been bloodstains, there were none now.

His mind wandered. In the heat of the garage he remembered the first time he had kissed Charm in the front seat of his old Trans Am. How the kiss had gone on and on until he had floated off into another world, and how later, at least once a year, she'd said wistfully, "Will you ever kiss me like that again?"

He opened the glove compartment. Empty, except for the registration and insurance papers held together by a paper clip. When he stepped behind the car to write down the license plate number on his legal pad, the women murmured in their soft language. He looked up and tried to smile reassuringly.

"Lawyers write down a thousand things that are never of any use. Please don't worry."

He saw that the right rear bumper had been torn away a few inches, and there was a cream-colored rip along the shiny blue metal in front of it. While he was looking at that, his mind elsewhere, the mother-in-law chattered more loudly. She seemed angry.

"She is not angry at you," the widow said. "She is angry at the police for damaging the car."

Warren asked what it was the police had done.

"What you were just looking at. The bumper and that big scratch—they were not there when my husband left that morning. The police did that when they returned the car to us."

"Oh," Warren said. The mother was still talking in Vietnamese, using her hands now to emphasize her point.

The widow said, "Naturally they say, 'No, we didn't do

that. It was there already.' And so it is we who must pay for it to be fixed. These things are very expensive."

A man, a husband and son and father, was dead. It was amazing what people flew into a lather about.

"Yes, they're ridiculously expensive," Warren said, while out of habit he made a note on his legal pad about the damage.

He drove from the Trunhs' to Hermann Park and the stables. Before he got out of the car he took off his jacket and rolled up his sleeves.

Behind the shed where Hector Quintana had once lived, Warren found a blackened pot where someone had fried pork cracklings—in the afternoon sun you could smell the grease. A rolled-up rag of a plaid blanket lay on the earth. But there was no one around. A nearby dressage ring, with gates and fallen triple bars, was also deserted. The heat rolled over the ground in waves. A horse whinnied in the stables.

Inside the stables the air was shadowed and pungent. He saw that a mare had been led from one of the stalls and tied to the cantle of an English saddle lying on some straw. Inside the empty stall a man shoveled horseshit into a bucket, splashing the dirt with water from another bucket.

"Armando?"

The man turned, wiping sweat from his forehead. He was thin and dark and wore baggy, stained trousers.

"Armando is not here," the man said.

"Then you must be Pedro."

The man nodded. He was neither suspicious nor hopeful. He just looked tired.

"So how y'all doin'?" Warren said. "Hard work—*mucho trabajo, sí?*"

"Not so much," Pedro said.

"Well, you sure look worn out. And I'll bet you're hungrier'n a stray dog. You finish up, I'll buy you a bunch of chicken tacos and a beer. I'm a friend of Hector's."

At the taco stand Warren brought the plastic plates back to his car, where he had left the motor running and the air-conditioning on. To his amazement—although as soon as he thought about it, it made sense—Pedro hadn't known that Hector was in jail. Hector had just vanished. Pedro and his friend Armando had shrugged. Maybe Hector would turn up, maybe he wouldn't.

"Nobody from the D.A.'s office came to talk to you?"

No one had come, Pedro said, layering the salsa deep into the taco. Warren couldn't do that—it would rip the top off his palate and leave his tongue numb.

"Hector suppose' to have kill a man?" Pedro didn't stop chewing, but he shook his head strongly. "I doan believe that."

"Neither do I, Pedro, but they say he did. With that *pistola* he carried around in his shopping cart."

"He din' have no pistol," Pedro said, apparently surprised.

"You never saw it?"

"Saw what?"

"The pistol Hector bought, or borrowed."

"Never saw no pistol, I swear to you. Who he can borrow it from? We doan know anyone has a pistol."

"When did you and Armando last see Hector?"

On the day Hector had vanished, in the early afternoon. Pedro was positive.

"Maybe he bought the pistol after he left you," Warren said.

"He din' have no money for buy a pistol."

"How can you be so sure?"

"He borrow three dollars from me that day. I trust him —I borrow him before, he always pay back. I borrow from him too when I doan got nothing."

"Would you get up in court and testify to all that?"

Pedro looked unhappy.

"I can't pay you to testify," Warren said, "that's against the law. But I can give you some money to eat for a few days. I can buy you some clothes." He slid two twenty-dollar bills from his wallet, slipping them into Pedro's dirty shirt pocket. "You can't get hurt, not if you get up there and tell the truth. Do you understand what I'm saying? Hector's your amigo."

With his fingers Pedro scooped up some chicken that had fallen out of the taco.

"Pedro, if they find him guilty, they could kill him."

"Shoot him? You got the firing squad?"

"No, that's inhuman—those guys can miss and they gutshoot you. You hang a man, that knot can slip and he can strangle. Electric chair, he sizzles, been known to catch fire. Gas chamber, he pukes and yells. Texas is more modern. Here we drug a man, then inject cyanide into a vein. They say it doesn't hurt. No one's ever come back to say yea or nay."

Pedro still said nothing. Warren realized he hadn't understood.

"Look, you get up there in court, you talk, you leave. They won't kick you out of the country for having no papers, I promise you. If I can arrange that, will you do it?"

"Okay," Pedro said. But it was not heartfelt.

Warren drove the Mexican back to the stables, gave him one of his business cards, made sure it was tucked away in a pocket with the forty dollars, and let him out of the car.

"Don't leave the city. Don't even leave Hermann Park without calling and letting me know where you are. You can call collect. Don't let me down, Pedro. Don't let Hector down! *Viva México!*"

Pedro nodded his head and then, as Warren drove away waving, waved back in that odd Latin way, with cupped fingers, as if he were beckoning.

Later in the afternoon Warren went to see Siva Singh at the dry cleaning establishment. The Indian lady politely informed him that the district attorney had told her not to speak to anyone about the case. Cute, Warren thought.

"Nancy Goodpaster told you that? The woman prosecutor?"

"Goodness me, sir, please don't be angry. I have her card right here." Taking off her glasses, she dipped into her pocketbook.

"She has no right to tell you that, Ms. Singh," Warren explained. "I think you may have misunderstood her. You certainly have the right to talk to me. And if you want to be fair, you should."

Singh still refused to talk to him. He put in a call to Goodpaster but couldn't reach her.

He spent the next morning, a Wednesday, at Ravendale, knocking on doors of the apartment buildings near the west parking lot, which he judged to be the one where Hector had sat down in the darkness and made his decision to rob the Circle K.

The few people who were home stared at him in astonishment. "In the Dumpster? Three weeks ago? Do I remember throwing out a half-empty bottle of Old Crow or a pair of tennis socks? Are you kidding me?"

Warren offered his business card, so no one thought he was entirely a madman. But no one could remember seeing a man rummaging in the Dumpster or sitting in the parking lot. But not everyone had been home. People were out playing tennis or swimming or destroying their skin in the sun by the pool.

In the main building Warren waited his turn behind two other people, then showed his card to a pretty woman at the reception desk. She wore a lapel tag that said "Janice." He asked her if they had a bulletin board where he might post a notice. No, Janice said, the bulletin board was strictly for tenant convenience.

"Well, I wonder, ma'am, if I had a little flyer printed up,

could you do me a favor and put a copy in everyone's letter box?"

"Mail is delivered to the door."

"What are those letter boxes for?"

"Spare keys, bills and notices from the management. You can't put an advertisement in there."

It wasn't an advertisement, Warren explained patiently. It was a request for information that might help a man perhaps falsely accused of a crime.

"I'm sorry," she said, "and I'm busy." She turned away toward a desk.

"Just a minute, Janice." Reluctantly, she swung around, and he said, "I'm an attorney, and my client faces the death penalty for something he says he didn't do. I realize this may be a hard day for you, but I need your help. If not, I'm sure I can find someone in this office who'll do what's proper and do it courteously as well."

He hadn't raised his voice at all.

"I'm so sorry," Janice said. "I have a terrible migraine headache. If you knew what goes on around here, you'd understand. You don't want to use the bulletin board—no one ever looks at it. If you bring me the flyer, I'll put it in the boxes."

"Thank you, ma'am. I'll send a note to the management expressing my thanks for your kindness."

At HPD headquarters downtown on Reisner Street, Warren picked up a visitor's plastic I.D. card at the desk downstairs and then took the elevator up to Homicide on the third floor. After speaking that morning to Nancy Goodpaster, he had called Sergeants Hollis Thiel and Craig Douglas to find out when they were on duty. They were the arresting officers in the case and Thiel had filed the affidavit of complaint that the D.A.'s office had taken to the grand jury in order to secure the indictment. It read, in part: ". . . *that Hector Quintana de Luna, on or about May 19, 1989, intentionally and knowingly caused the*

*death of Dan Ho Trunh by shooting the Complainant with a
gun, and committed the murder while in the course of com-
mitting a robbery, AGAINST THE PEACE AND DIGNITY OF
THE STATE."*

The peace and dignity of the state. Fuck them both,
Warren decided. They don't exist.

Homicide overlooked a parking lot for blue-and-whites
and a tangle of concrete freeway ramps. It had acoustic tile
ceilings and government-metal furniture. Besides cigar
smoke, Warren always believed he could smell a mix of old
sweat and recent fear. If you weren't a cop, the faces that
peered at you from the maze of glassed-in offices tended to
be unfriendly. Maybe you hadn't murdered anyone yet,
but you were probably thinking about it. You were certainly capable.

Douglas was tall, in his thirties, and looked like a ca-
daver. Thiel looked like an older Porky Pig. Warren's private opinion was that Thiel was a bitter, honest, hard-
working homicide detective, and Douglas was a lowlife
mongrel who would lie on the witness stand to make himself look good and to secure a conviction. But both hated
defense attorneys with equal vigor.

"Goodpaster call you?" Warren asked.

Thiel nodded. "She said we could tell you a few things."

"She say anything about showing me the offense report?"

"We can't do that," Douglas said. "Witnesses talk to us
in confidence."

Thiel said, "We'd like to, but we can't."

Warren laughed with less than amusement. "Mutt and
Jeff. You guys are some comedy act."

"You lawyers come in here," Thiel said, "and expect us
to roll out the fucking red carpet. And then we get up on
the witness stand and y'all try to make us look like lying
scumbags."

Warren shrugged. "That's my job."

"And you know what ours is," Douglas murmured.

"Just tell me about Quintana in your own choice words."

That they would do. Thiel repeated the story of the arrest, which was much as Hector had told it. The clerk in the Circle K had pushed a button with his foot. An alarm had flashed in the nearest police station. The next day Ballistics had called Homicide to tell them that the caliber and rifling in the barrel of Hector's gun matched the bullet that had been found in Dan Ho Trunh's brain. Since Thiel and Douglas were the detectives who had made the crime scene at the Trunh murder, Hector had been brought over to their office in Homicide and read his rights a second time.

"He was sitting right where you're sitting now, counselor," Douglas said. Meaning, we wish it was you.

"And did he look at your smiling face and say, 'I did it, I confess'?"

Thiel laughed shrilly.

"Did he ask for a lawyer?"

"Too fuckin' dumb to do that," Douglas said. "Just sat there and babbled, 'I doan know what you talkin' about.' "

"You ask him where he got the gun?"

Thiel stroked his jowls. "He had some story, I can't remember what it was."

"Did he say he found it in a Dumpster?"

"That was it."

"Any other prints on the gun?"

"Smudges."

"Y'all examine the car where the victim's body was found?" Warren asked.

"Nothing in it. Nancy said to give you a set of photographs." Thiel slid open a file drawer and plucked out a manila folder.

"What about the crime scene unit?" That was the special unit that went over every homicide site with vacuum and tweezers, and dug under the victim's fingernails.

"Zilch." Thiel slid the folder across the desk. "The victim was shot in his car through an open window on the driver's side. Ballistics says maybe five, six feet. Your guy must've just reached in and took the wallet after he wasted him."

Warren glanced down at his notes. "By the way, who drove the car away from the crime scene? It was a Ford wagon, right?"

"I did," Douglas muttered.

"You sideswipe any lampposts going back to the HPD garage?"

"Hey, I already had this out with the gook's old lady." Douglas unclipped the manila folder and spilled the color 8 x 10s out on the desktop. Under the bone-white glare of fluorescent light that flooded down from the ceiling, Warren stared at a slumped body on the car seat, the face masked by blood.

"This one," Douglas said, tapping a photograph he slid from the pile. "See it? That fuckin' bumper was ripped up when we got there. I told her that." He laughed hoarsely. "You going into civil law, counselor? Represent the victim's wife and sue the poh-lice for vee-hicular damage?"

"Thanks, guys." Warren stood up, shaking out creases in his seersucker jacket. He put the photograph file into his briefcase. "Tommy Ruiz in the shop?"

Ruiz was the homicide sergeant who had arrested Johnnie Faye Boudreau on the night of Clyde Ott's murder. He had to be dealt with too.

"I think so," Thiel said. "Let me buzz."

Tar on the pavement was beginning to melt. Warren eased the BMW into the low-priced parking lot behind the jail on Austin Street, stuffing two one-dollar bills and a quarter into the slot that matched the number of his stall, hoping he would remember the number, which on several occasions had not been the case. But so far his car had never been towed. Small favors from an otherwise unbenevolent fate.

Two silent bums strolled by on their way to the mission, a few blocks past the courthouse and the complex of modern office buildings. The midday Gulf Coast heat surged violently down on Warren's bare head. He unknotted his tie.

Another image intruded, cast down by the afternoon sun. He was back in Mexico, that week with Charm. They were walking through the mountains to a rock pool. Crouched down in a field of violet wildflowers, Charm had dropped her pants to pee. He had screwed on the telephoto lens to snap a photograph. She threw an arm across her face and shook the other fist in indignation. Warren was laughing.

Ten minutes later he again sat opposite Hector Quintana in one of the visitor's cubicles at the jail. The sweat was drying on Warren's forehead and his back was cold where the air-conditioning blew on the damp patches.

"Hector, we have to make a decision. And certain things have to be said."

"What more can I tell you?" Quintana asked, glowering.

"It's what I can tell *you*. The D.A.'s made you an offer."

"Who is the D.A.?"

"The D.A. is a guy you'll never meet—he just makes

policy. I'm talking about an assistant district attorney, Nancy Goodpaster, whom you will definitely meet and probably grow to hate. She wants to put you in jail for life or get the State of Texas to inject you with cyanide. That's her job. And she thinks she's got a good case. Problem is, in that respect I agree with her."

Quintana took some harsh breaths. Warren raised his hand to forestall what he thought was coming.

"I'm trying to be objective. That's part of *my* job. But it's not quite so bad as I'm painting it. Relax."

Quintana's breathing eased a little but not much.

"The courts are crowded. So Nancy Goodpaster is willing to compromise. She'll reduce the charge from capital murder to plain murder. She's offered you forty years."

Softly, Quintana repeated the number.

"I know forty years sounds like a lot," Warren said, seeing the man's horror in his brown eyes, feeling a small part of it begin to take root in his own heart. This was the nasty part, bargaining away the consecutive seasons of a man's life. Maybe you could get used to it, but you could never learn to like it.

"And it *is* a lot," he went on, "although with time off for good behavior you'll do only half of whatever they give you. But I want to point something out to you. You can't do half of death."

Quintana groaned.

"I know, Hector. I know. You say you're innocent. I might be able to get them to offer less than forty. Maybe thirty-five, but I can't make any promises on that. And the decision is yours."

Quintana clenched his fists.

"Let me ask you something," Warren said. "And think before you answer. You've been here a couple of weeks now. You like the life?"

After he had thought about it, Quintana replied, "I have a couple of friends. Other Mexican guys."

"That's good. You'll make more. Some you can trust,

some you can't. But try to answer my question. Do you like the life?"

Warren knew that prison could become a normal existence. Jailing, the cons called it. Three meals a day, a bed to sleep in, a TV to watch. No rent to pay, no worry about meeting the bills. You could read, take correspondence courses, and once they sent you up to TDC at Huntsville you could laze around in the sunshine, play ball, lift weights, run around the track. With the right connections you could get booze and dope. You couldn't have a woman but a lot of men secretly or not-so-secretly didn't mind: they'd had far more heartbreak than joy from the women in their lives. You had a job to help pass the time—making furniture or license plates, washing dishes. If you were fired, there was always another job waiting. No one to yell at you that you'd fucked up, because you *had* fucked up, that was a given, but so had everyone else around you. Some thrived on jailing or at least accepted it as a solution to an otherwise unsatisfactory existence. Some did life on the installment plan. A few years ago a client of Warren's had got out of Huntsville after completing five years on a ten-year bank robbery bit. He had taken the bus to the town of Bryan thirty miles away, walked into the First National Bank of Bryan and held it up with his fist stuffed inside a paper bag to simulate a gun. He never made it out of the bank. In a few weeks he was back in Huntsville. Warren asked why he had done it. He said, "I got scared. I wanted to go home."

Now Warren waited for an answer to his question.

"No," Quintana said. "I doan like it here. I want to go back to El Palmito."

"That may not happen, Hector."

Quintana quietly began to cry.

Warren coolly tried to figure out why. There were several possibilities. Because Hector missed his Francisca, because he'd killed a man and now had to pay the price, or because he hadn't killed a man and this process was beyond comprehension. Any one of those or a combination would do. You poor son of a bitch.

"Forty years . . ." Quintana murmured. "Twenty, you said, if I behave."

Numbers for me, Warren thought. Years for him. Three hundred and sixty-five days and nights to each one.

"What should I do, Mr. Blackburn?"

"Don't dump that on me, Hector. You've got to tell me."

"Mr. Blackburn, listen to me. I doan ask you about the evidence. You tell me all that, and I think I understand. I ask you if you believe I killed this man I never even know. In El Palmito I have trouble killing even a pig. People laugh at me, think I'm foolish. Do you think I did such a thing as kill a human being who never harm me, never speak a word to me?"

Warren looked into Quintana's liquid eyes. There was no fright there and suddenly no desperation. There was only yearning and a simple plea. A feeling welled up from somewhere in the most profound part of Warren, and it touched his heart, which gave a lurch for this man. He had never had a feeling like this before. He had felt sorry for Virgil Freer—for Hector Quintana he felt a different emotion. He couldn't explain it. Maybe to Charm, but to no one else. It was a feeling akin to love. If you loved someone, you believed them. You trusted them. However irrational, in that moment the feeling seemed indisputable.

Pedro had said that Hector didn't own a pistol, had no money to buy one. Words with the ring of truth. Pedro hadn't known that Hector had been arrested; hadn't had time, before Warren's appearance at the stables, to rationalize and figure out a way to help his amigo if the opportunity arose. *Res gestae,* the law said—words spoken in the unguarded heat of the moment. Lawyers learned to trust such words. In trial they were exempt from the hearsay rule: you could quote them if you were on the witness stand.

As for Siva Singh, Warren saw her as a sincere woman who believed in law and order and wanted to help the police. Eyewitnesses were always so sure of what they had seen. Once they had committed themselves to a story, they had a vested interest in keeping to it. Most eyewitnesses don't have time to tell red from green or short from tall. They make it up later, without realizing it.

Everyone seemed to know that except juries.

Hector's story was a simple one. He never deviated, never contradicted, never blushed except when talking about the Safeway shopping cart. Maybe that was true too, maybe he'd found it somewhere, knew he should return it to the supermarket but hadn't done so, and was ashamed. I believe him. This is not a man who would kill.

Warren linked his fingers together behind his head, leaned back and cracked the vertebrae of his spine. This was crazy. He had an understanding with Lou Parker. He had the Boudreau trial looming. The most important trial of his life. If he could win with Scoot, if he could impress Scoot, he would be more than back on track. But he couldn't back away from Hector Quintana. He would have been ashamed.

He had gambled on Virgil Freer and lost. Maybe life owed him one. Or maybe not; maybe he was making the same mistake all over again. The thought was terrifying.

But with a stubborn rush of certainty, he thrust it away. He was not the same man he had been four years ago.

"No, Hector, I don't believe you did it."

"You don't?"

There were fresh tears in Hector's eyes. From pain or joy, Warren didn't know.

"No, I really don't. I would never lie to you."

"Then why should I go to prison for twenty years?"

"I can't think of a single fucking reason," Warren said.

Hector nodded slowly.

Warren's cheeks grew flushed. "Now listen to me. I'm going to break the rules, I'm going to tell you what I

would do if I were in your shoes. If I were innocent—I
mean, if I weren't bullshitting my lawyer and hoping for a
miracle that will never happen—I'd pray a lot, and I'd go
to trial. If I were *really* innocent. But it's your life, not
mine. The odds against you are big. Gigantic. Stupendous.
Their case looks airtight. I'm not pushing you one inch in
any direction. I'm just telling you how I feel."

"All right." Quintana spoke softly.

"All right *what?*"

"I go to trial."

"You want to do that? Take the chance?"

"Yes."

"You understand what happens if you lose?"

"Yes. They will kill me, put me to sleep. Maybe that's
not so bad as twenty years in prison. I don't know. I don't
care. I am innocent."

A *nothing case, it'll go fast.* What the hell am I doing?
Tinkering with another man's life and death? But you
can't plead a man guilty and take twenty whole years out
of his life, not if he says he's innocent and you believe him.
That's not what being a lawyer means. It's not what being
a human being means. The feeling of certainty that
Quintana was innocent moved through him again. If I believe that, Warren thought, I have less choice than he does.
And if they kill him I'll have to live with it longer than he
will.

There was no way to shake hands through the mesh or
the slot at the bottom of it for the passage of documents.
Warren pressed his palm against the cool metal. Quintana
pressed back.

Warren gathered up his papers. "I'll do what I can," he
promised. "We'll give these bastards a run for their money.
But for God's sake, if you change your mind, let me
know."

Judge Parker ordered Warren into her chambers after he
had spoken to Nancy Goodpaster. Goodpaster looked un-

happy. She said to Warren, "I think you're making a mistake. You and Quintana both."

Once again Warren remembered his youthful vision: the law as protector, lawyers as the standard-bearers of decency and fairness. And he remembered Hector saying, "I don't know. I don't care. I am innocent."

He sat on the couch in front of the bookcase full of Harvard Classics, facing the judge's desk. The full strength of the afternoon sun burned through the windows behind him onto his neck. On the desk, behind a Tibetan statuette of a horse, was the bronze plaque that Rick had mentioned, invoking guidance from the deity and promising Her indulgence. Warren hadn't seen it before now. He wondered if the judge set it out there only for special occasions.

Lou Parker pinched her cigarette between her thumb and index finger and pointed it at him as if it were a dart she was about to throw. Right between his eyes.

"Let me get this straight, Mr. Blackburn. Less than a week ago you asked the prosecutor if she'd cut a deal with you."

"That's correct, your honor."

"Nancy agreed to forty years. That was a pretty good deal."

"But my client won't go for it, your honor."

"If a guy comes to me for sentencing on a capital, I drop fifty to sixty on him."

If you're in a good mood, Warren thought.

"My client is a stubborn man," he said. "He says he's innocent. And I happen to believe him."

Parker rasped, "Then you're a fool. My memory is that you and I sat right here one day not so long ago and got our signals straight. I'm not supposed to know the facts of a case until it comes to trial, but I ain't deaf or blind. I told you this was a whale in the barrel for the prosecution. I told you to plead this guy out and not waste my court time. You think I've forgotten? You do this to me, and I promise you'll never get an appointment in my court again."

"So let Nancy take her best shot," Warren said, ignoring the threat. "What difference does it make if my client insists on going to trial?"

Parker raised her voice: "I'll tell you what difference it makes. You're supposed to represent this man's best interests. If he pleads not guilty and doesn't stand a chance to win, and you've got an offer on the table that will save his miserable life, you've got a responsibility to try and talk him into taking that offer. *Even if you think he's innocent!* That's elementary, but I have a bad feeling in my colon that certain elementary things may escape you from time to time, like they did once before."

Warren frowned, drumming his fingers nervously on the arm of the couch. The barb had drawn blood.

The judge leaned forward, like a hound pointed toward a quarry. "Have you talked straight with this man Quintana?"

"I did my best," Warren said, wondering if that was true.

"How come I don't quite believe you? How come I think you're aiming to use up two valuable weeks of my courtroom time playing to the crowd? And picking up a fat fee for every day you're in court?"

"I don't know, your honor," Warren said, letting his annoyance show. The back of his neck felt toasted from the sun slanting through the window. "Why don't you tell me how come?"

"Don't sass me, counselor!"

"Then, Judge Parker, don't question my doing what I think is best for my client, whom you never met, and who, I remind you, claims he's innocent."

"And don't they all," said Parker, "until you give them the facts of life. We're not talking about shock probation or ninety-day jail therapy here. We're talking about a needle in the arm. *Buenas noches, José.*"

"He knows all that."

In the face of his firmness, her exasperation ripened. Her face grew florid. "Just how do you plan to benefit, counselor? You won't work in my court again. This case isn't going to make any headlines—this is a dumbshit ignorant wetback supposed to have blown away a Vietnamese handyman. So what's on your so-called mind? How do you justify this farce?"

There was a quality to her voice, Warren thought, that would have made a rake scraping across a concrete sidewalk sound appealing. His back muscles tensed. His fingers kept drumming and he tapped one shoe steadily on the carpet. Quintana's defense would be flimsy even in a fair trial with a dispassionate judge. Now that he had pissed Parker off to this extent, the concept of dispassionate judicial rulings seemed about as likely as the chance of snow on the day of trial.

And I might be wrong, Warren thought. Jesus, I might be wrong again. I can't afford that. That won't just kill my career, it will kill all the faith I ever had.

He felt a growing dismay but he knew he would not, could not, budge. When she realized he had no intention of answering her, Judge Parker clenched her teeth and snatched her court calendar. She leafed through it rapidly, then turned to Nancy Goodpaster.

"Madam Prosecutor, is the state ready for arraignment?"

"Yes, your honor." Those were Goodpaster's first words in chambers.

"The court will take a plea this coming Monday, June 12, at 9 A.M. Defense motions next Friday, June 16. State has a week to respond. How about a trial date? State ready?"

"The state can be ready in seven days," Goodpaster said.

"Too soon. But I have an open date on the docket for Wednesday, July 5, right after the holiday weekend. On

July 21, that's a Friday, I go on vacation to Hawaii. That's the deal."

Warren jumped to his feet.

Voir dire—the questioning and selection of jurors—normally was done in groups of forty or sixty citizens at a time, depending upon the size of the courtroom. But in a capital murder trial, because the possibility of the death penalty existed, each juror was questioned individually. The process could take weeks.

"Judge Parker," he pleaded, "that's a gun to my head. Including voir dire, you're allowing less than three weeks for the whole case. And I've got only three weeks to prepare! In a capital murder case, that's nothing!"

"You're talking Chinese to a pack mule, counselor. My docket's full right through Thanksgiving. See for yourself." She tossed her open calendar book to his side of the desk. "You want a trial, voir dire begins on July 5. That's it."

Warren made himself calm down. He tried another tack. "Scoot Shepard and I are trying *Boudreau* on July 24. With all due deference, can't we do *Quintana* when you come back from your vacation?"

The judge stubbed out her cigarette and leaned back in her armchair. "Never mind that due deference bullshit. You don't defer to me at all, and you can be sure I won't to you. You're a goddam fool. I feel sorry for you."

She flicked her hand toward the door.

In Goodpaster's office—after she had settled behind her desk and dealt with an insistently ringing telephone, and after Warren had reflected for some minutes on the awful prospects ahead, for himself as well as for his client—he said, "You have a good memory, Madam Prosecutor?"

Her eyes narrowed. Sunlight filtering through the venetian blinds accentuated her cheekbones. "I don't forget court appearances, if that's what you mean."

"I want you to remember everything that happened in there today. Make some notes if you have to."

"Why?"

"Just for the hell of it, Nancy," he said. "Just in case in the heat of battle I forget. Did you tell Mrs. Singh she shouldn't talk to me?"

"I wouldn't do a thing like that. I just told her she didn't have to if she didn't want to."

"Can I see the offense report now?"

"No."

"Didn't Parker tell you this was a whale in a barrel? What are you scared of?"

"I'm just keeping to the rules. I could have showed you the file if you were going to plead out. But you're not, so I can't. You know that. It's war now, not a game."

"I wonder what made me think it was a game," he said. "Fuck you."

Goodpaster managed a small smile. She was a prosecutor—she had heard those words often from defense attorneys. After the trial, prosecutor and defense attorney usually had a drink together and apologized for any expletives uttered in the heat of combat. And they always shook hands.

Warren rose to leave, then stopped at the door, turning again to face her. "You intend to do this for the rest of your life?"

"That might be a little tiring," Goodpaster said.

"You mean one day you'd like to be a defense attorney and make those big bucks. Be another Scoot Shepard."

Goodpaster shrugged. "I suppose so. That's the light at the end of the tunnel. Although sometimes, as you should know, the light at the end of the tunnel may be a train."

"That's good. Is that original?"

"I might have heard it somewhere, I can't remember."

"Work on your memory, Nancy," Warren said.

* * *

That evening, about an hour before Warren drove home, Scoot Shepard left his office in the Republic Bank Building and headed toward the Houstonian Club. On balance he was in a good mood—the jury had found his banker client not guilty of driving while intoxicated. As was his habit, Scoot had spent about ten minutes alone with the twelve men and women in the jury room to find out what had motivated their decision. "We didn't trust the police officer's judgment," the jury foreman explained, "after he made a mistake reciting the alphabet."

Scoot was meeting some cronies for an early session of bourbon and draw poker. Behind him, downtown office buildings were reflected in the mirrors of yet other facades. Ahead of him a veil of cirrus cloud was touched with the fire of a setting sun. He reached into the glove compartment of his Cadillac for a bottle of Maalox tablets. All day he'd been chewing, but his indigestion refused to go away. Neither would the headache at the base of his skull.

He had passed Allen Park and Buffalo Bayou and was on Memorial Drive heading west. Without warning—if you discounted the last two years of headaches and dizzy spells, and the admonitions of his wife and the nagging of his doctor—his eyesight blurred. The road went severely out of focus. Scoot felt only a jarring pain in his left temple, as if someone had jabbed him with a knuckle. He had suffered a slight stroke, caused by the occlusion of a blood vessel in the brain.

He was on a winding part of the drive flanked by colonial homes with clipped lawns, and at that moment the road changed from a right curve to a left curve. Scoot failed to see that. Just as the Cadillac hopped the curb, his instincts were good enough to force his foot onto the brake pedal, or he would have plowed up a lawn, knocked down the cast-iron statue of a black boy in hunting regalia, and smashed at forty miles an hour into the side of a two-story brick house.

The Cadillac veered, but there was still a leafy old pin

oak in his path. Just as his bumper struck with a thunder-
clap and the grillwork wrapped itself around the trunk of
the tree and the steering column began to fracture his
chest, Scoot cried out desperately, *"Oh, shit! They got
me. . . ."*

What "they"? What furies? What avenging demons
from courtrooms past? No one would ever know. No one
would even know he said the words.

Driving home on the freeway, seeking out the lanes where
traffic seemed to flow less jerkily, disconsolate over what
had happened in Judge Parker's office and what it foretold
for his client's trial, Warren felt a new refrain pounding in
his head. *I want my wife back.* I need her, I need someone
to talk to. I may be going off the deep end. There was no
blame in his heart now, only soreness. He speculated yet
again as to why she had been in tears when he came into
the house. Had her New York lawyer given an ultimatum?
Was she mourning her marriage? Was she feeling sorry for
me? He had ached to ask but hadn't dared. She might have
answered truthfully.

I want her back. I'm a country boy. We mate for life.

Alone at home, he mixed a vodka tonic at the wet bar.
Six thirty-two on the wall clock. He switched on the TV in
the family room.

There was Charm, ripening in color, blue eyes leveled at
him, lips moving soundlessly, slim hands clasped together
on the desk in front of the skyline backdrop. He punched
up the volume a few clicks.

". . . when we come back, we'll have the tragic story of
a Sugar Land woman who gave birth to her second set of
deformed triplets, and the weather, and sports, including
the latest about the Astros from our ever-optimistic Don
Benson. Please stay with us, friends."

Nice touches. She always seemed to mean what she said.
He had understood Johnnie Faye in the Sports Bar. But it
was Charm's choice, not his. He would have to listen and

grasp and unburden. He couldn't keep all his depression of the last years locked out of sight. In the end, all he could do was tell her he loved her and forgave her, and wanted to try to be closer to her. He wondered if the New York lawyer was still in town. He tried to keep vulgar images from his mind, and of course the moment he fought against them they forced their way in. Think of anything but an elephant . . . that was a game they had played as kids by the Shamrock pool. And you saw elephants every-where.

He untied his slim file on the *Quintana* case.

Voir dire in three weeks. Lou Parker was within her rights: the law held that you had to be ready for trial thirty days after indictment, or ten days after the court took your plea. Usually the dockets were so crowded that the judges granted continuances even more automatically than they marched through their sentencing speeches. Once a date was set you could demand a postponement only if there was a missing witness who was crucial to the case. But you had to prove it. And he had no such witness.

He studied his notes from the visit to the Trunhs. Good-paster in final argument would make the point that if robbery hadn't been the motive, what sense did the murder make? No one claimed that the murderer and the victim knew each other. My best chance, he thought, is to knock out the special circumstances—the theft of the wallet. If I can do that, then the jury might ask themselves why Hector would want to murder a man he didn't know. Not that a jury was required to consider motive—they were judges only of the facts: did Hector Quintana willingly and knowingly kill Dan Ho Trunh? But juries were not always rational, did not always follow the judge's orders. Maybe, if they believed there was no robbery, one or two of them would be uneasy on the question of motive. It took only one or two to hang up a jury. Or maybe they would find Hector guilty and then, when they had to decide on punishment, be lenient.

Two maybes. A human life depended on them.

Maybe Hector had done it. Drunk, unable to remember, blocking out the horror now because he couldn't believe it was possible. The thought was like a block of ice pressed unremittingly against Warren's spine.

On the TV screen he saw Scoot Shepard, doused in brilliant white halogen light, talking to reporters outside some courtroom. Smiling liberally yet elfishly, as Scoot always smiled. Surprised, Warren leaned forward from the couch. Had the state dropped the charge against Johnnie Faye for lack of evidence? But he quickly deduced that it was an old clip from the news file. Scoot was younger. Looked healthier.

Warren hit the mute button to regain the sound.

Voice-over, in her gravest tones, Charm said: ". . . so at the age of sixty-four, a great Texas lawyer is dead. The man who successfully defended sex doctor Martha Sachs, oil billionaire John R. Baker, and Mafia overlord Nick 'the Horse' Fellino could not defend himself against the twisting curves and late-afternoon sun of Memorial Drive. A preliminary medical report indicates that Mr. Shepard was driving while intoxicated and suffered a minor cerebral stroke just prior to the fatal accident. We'll have an update on Channel 26 Eleven O'Clock News. Don?"

"Tonight at the Astrodome," Don Benson said, "the stumbling Houston Astros will go with hard-luck pitcher Jim Clancy in an effort to salvage a win in the final game of the series with the New York Mets. . . ."

Hard to believe, even harder to digest and accept. Warren punched over to the networks, but they also were doing weather and sports. He turned off the TV. The silence of the house fell like thunder about his ears.

Warren paced the room. Scoot, you poor bastard. He moaned aloud, surprising himself.

He hadn't spent enough time with Scoot to mourn him. But he had known him, respected him, even liked him. Death was so elusive: in the courthouse you dealt with the details and consequences of death but not the fact itself. As a boy Warren had wondered: if I die, what will I feel? But there won't be an *I* anymore. Nothing to feel. No point of view. As a man he wondered too. No answer came. He heard Scoot's drawling voice. No more, other than in memory.

And now the Ott case . . . the best shot of my life, gone. Gone with Scoot. He finished his drink and poured another one.

Johnnie Faye Boudreau would have to pick a new lawyer. One of the old dogs with plenty of experience and clout, although none of it would equal Scoot's. The chances of that lawyer's asking Warren to sit second chair were zero. They all had people they worked with. If Scoot's boys hadn't been tied up on the antitrust case, Warren thought, he never would have asked me in the first place.

When he was first starting out as a lawyer Warren had pinned two hand-lettered notes to the bulletin board above his desk. One said: *Never assume.* The other said: *If you prepare, what you're worrying about won't happen—but something else always will.* Over the years the sun had faded the slogans and finally he had crumpled them and thrown them out. I should have tattooed them on my wrists, he thought.

He waited up for Charm. In all his life, not since the first day his mother had left him at the schoolyard, he couldn't remember feeling this abandoned. He didn't eat, just drank more vodka tonics and finished what was left of a jar of salted peanuts. At midnight, a little dazed and brain-weary, he went to bed. He was almost asleep when the telephone rang. He snatched the receiver from the cradle and said, "Charm? Are you okay?"

But it was Johnnie Faye Boudreau. She sounded frightened; she was blubbering. Warren had trouble understanding her words. Finally he realized that she was at the club, and someone had been listening to the late news on a car radio and had just told her of the tragedy.

Warren heard laughter in the background. Johnnie Faye's voice rose in pitch. "What am I going to do?"

"You're going to calm down," Warren said firmly, "and in the next few days you're going to find a new lawyer to take the case. The judge will grant a postponement of the trial date, the new lawyer will have plenty of time to prepare. It will work out just fine. You have a good case. Any decent lawyer can win it, I promise you."

"I want Mr. Shepard!" she cried.

"That will be a little difficult," Warren said.

"Can I see you? Can I talk to you? I need your advice."

"Yes, of course."

"I mean *now*."

"I'll be at the club in twenty minutes."

In a garden restaurant near the courthouse, Warren lunched with Judge Dwight Bingham. Wandering through the heat, a breeze brought to their nostrils the fragrance of dog roses and star jasmine. Warren had come back from the Ecstasy club at three o'clock in the morning and had risen at six-thirty. He had gone to his office, where he read through the *Boudreau* case file and pored over law books and then called the court at 8 A.M., just a few minutes before the judge began his docket.

Bingham lifted a forkful of blackened catfish to his mouth. He had been born on a plantation near Texarkana and had worked ten years as a bailiff before he finished putting himself through law school. A long journey, and he had seen a great deal happen.

"It's you I'm worried about, young Warren. Bob Altschuler's an awfully good prosecutor. He'll run for judge in November. This is a big case, maybe his last big one. He'll fight like hell to win it."

"So will I," Warren said flatly.

"If you lose, you'll look bad. Especially after that affidavit thing that happened with you and Lou Parker."

"Old hat," Warren said.

But he knew it wasn't. He had ordered a creole fish salad, but he had no appetite. Nevertheless he toyed with the food, pretending to be involved with it.

"I can handle it," he said at last. "Scoot and I had three or four meetings and I have a copy of the full file. I'll try it just about the way he would. Look, Judge, the Boudreau woman thinks she wants me. That's what matters."

He hadn't asked her. He hadn't pressured. Last night at Ecstasy she had said at least four times, "I don't know what to do," and Warren had kept repeating that she didn't need to make a snap decision. She could ask around town—any lawyer would take the case. It was a good case, he stressed. She would only have to testify to the truth. Only a fool could lose such a case.

"You have faith in me?" Johnnie Faye asked.

Did he have faith in *her*? What an odd way to put it.

"If you told the truth to Scoot," Warren answered carefully, "and you keep on telling the truth to whomever you pick as your new lawyer, I have faith in your defense."

"Could you win my case?"

"Yes, I could."

"*Would* you win it?"

"Yes."

"Mr. Shepard was the smartest lawyer in town," Johnnie Faye said, "may he rest in peace. He picked you to work with him, so you have to be good too. He told me more or less what happened to you a few years ago—he said you'd do anything for a client but you just went too far that time. He said you were one of the best young lawyers he knew of. Real smart, real quick, and you worked hard. I think you're smart too, except maybe in your love life. But I've noticed that a lot of very bright people aren't too bright when it comes to all that emotional stuff. Maybe they don't have time to think things through. If I asked you to take the case, would you?"

"Yes," Warren said.

"I want to get this over with. I don't want the trial postponed, it's hanging over my goddam head like a sword. I can't sleep nights. So let me think it over. I'm tired now. I don't know what to do."

"You'll do the right thing," Warren told her.

In the garden restaurant, Judge Bingham frowned and touched a cold glass of iced tea to his sagging cheeks. "Why don't you tell her to get someone like Myron Moore, and you sit second chair to Myron?"

"Because Myron is lazy. I can run rings around him. Come on, Judge. You *know* that."

"When will Ms. Boudreau give you an answer?"

"I'm meeting her again tonight at Ecstasy."

"I want to tell you something, Warren. Off the record." The old judge let out a soft sigh. His face seemed compounded of shiny brown lumps and sallow slack folds. "You quote me on this, I'll call you a liar. You were there that day in court, the hearing for reduction of Ms. Boudreau's bail. All that business about the Louisiana corporation owning that club, her having no money, that was bullshit. I knew it, couldn't prove it, didn't want to be bothered. That's a clever woman. Gets what she wants, twists people around. You watch yourself, son. Don't do anything I wouldn't do."

"I haven't in years," Warren said truthfully.

He paid the bill over the judge's protests and left the restaurant. To defend Johnnie Faye Boudreau was literally the chance of a lifetime, like Rocky Balboa getting a shot at the heavyweight crown. But if Johnnie Faye said yes, Warren realized, he would be trying two murder cases back to back. The pressure would never let up, he would be spreading himself so thin that he might tear. He could win it all . . . or break even . . . or lose it all. Stand there, stricken, and bravely tell his more stricken clients, "Well, I did my best. . . ."

If in fact that was true.

The lobby of the Harris County Courthouse, and even the halls outside the courtrooms, seemed to be under a hush, as if Scoot Shepard's death had momentarily checked the bustle and clamor of apparent justice. But inside the courtrooms, where the flags of Texas had been placed at half-mast, the process moved along.

Warren called Rick Levine's office and found out that Rick was conducting a pretrial examination of a cop who had made the collar in a drug case. Several defendants were lumped together in the indictment and Rick was working with Edith Broyer, one of the lawyers with whom he shared his suite of offices.

In the courtroom, when the judge declared a recess, Warren grabbed Rick by the sleeve of his jacket. "Got a minute?"

They walked outside to the stairwell, where drywall brushed off white on both their suits. The floor was rotting and there were open pipes on the ceiling. All over the courthouse, doors banged and echoed.

"Poor Scoot," Rick said. "He bought the farm a little before his time, didn't he? But he was asking for it, the dumb fuck. Where does that leave you with *Boudreau*?"

Warren related his discussions with Johnnie Faye and Dwight Bingham. "If she says yes, what I need is a good lawyer to sit second chair. Not just a good lawyer—a *very* good lawyer. Will you do it with me?"

Doors continued to bang. Somewhere, far off, a woman was crying. Rick stroked his mustache thoughtfully. "I'm doing enough charity work now. Is there any money in it? I need to support my racehorses."

"Whatever I get I'll split with you."

"That may not even pay for oats. What's the plea?"

"Self-defense. Clyde Ott threatened to kill her—there are people who heard him say it. And before she blew him away, he picked up a poker from the fireplace."

"Did she provoke him? If she did, she can't claim self-defense."

"She claims she didn't," Warren said. "There are no witnesses to contradict her."

"I have a lot on my plate in July." Rick frowned, scratched his head. "I'd have to get Edith to fill in for me on this drug case. I'd have to trade her x for y and a player to be named later."

Warren waited, said nothing.

"Fuck, sure I'll do it," Rick said, banging him on the shoulder. "It's a good case. Plenty of TV coverage. Let me do the cross on a couple of the witnesses. The cops—I'm terrific with the cops."

"You're going to love our client," Warren said. "If she becomes our client."

Warren and Johnnie Faye Boudreau sat at a small round table near the horseshoe bar in Ecstasy. Frank Sawyer leaned against the bar, drinking a 7-Up, scanning the Friday-night crowd. Young women were moving among the customers as waitresses and couch dancers. They wore high heels and thongs and yellow ribbons in their hair, and a few pairs of their bared breasts might have won contests. The dancers straddled some of the men, writhing to the disco beat without actually touching them, expecting a ten- or twenty-dollar bill to be slipped into their thong as reward. The music was relentless and cigarette smoke swirled in the beams of the overhead spotlights. Warren's eyes itched.

He inclined his head toward one of the dancers, who looked no more than eighteen. "Where do you get them?"

Johnnie Faye seemed to have recovered from last night's trauma; her laugh was merry. "From all over Texas. Small-town gals, usually run away from a mean daddy. Got a couple from England too, one from Sweden. You interested? Take your mind off your trouble at home?"

"It wouldn't quite do that," Warren said. "Well, are we in business or not? If we are, I have to go back and Xerox a copy of the file for Rick Levine."

"I asked around about you since yesterday. You've got a lot of people who think an awful lot of you. Maybe you didn't know that. That's all well and good, but what I need from a lawyer is to hear that I can't lose."

Warren said, "Any lawyer who tells you that you can't lose is a fool."

"Mr. Shepard said it."

"I don't believe that. You may have misunderstood him.

It's a very good case. It's winnable. Not quite what they call a whale in a barrel, but close."

"Do better than that, counselor." Both Johnnie Faye's blue-gray eye and her hazel eye had clouded. He understood: they all wanted absolute commitment, certainty. It didn't exist anywhere else in the world—then why between client and lawyer in a major criminal case? Because nowhere else was your life so nakedly on the line.

"Trials aren't simple," he said. "Some witnesses lie. Some truthful witnesses appear to the jury to be lying. Some lying witnesses appear to be telling the truth. Other witnesses forget. Others become confused. Some jurors fall asleep or don't listen. Lawyers can make mistakes. So can judges. The jury's always right, whether it is or not. Bearing that in mind, we'll represent you as well or better than anyone else in town."

"You see," she said, "you're a good talker when you get wound up. That's what I wanted to hear. You'll walk me out of there. I like you, counselor. Go for it—you and Mr. Levine. He's a Jew, right?"

Warren nodded, wondering what would come next.

"Can't lose with a Jew and a good ole boy on my side, can I?"

Warren smiled softly.

While he was working out the details of the fee, one of the dancers, a blonde in her early twenties, worked her own way through the tables. She began to gyrate her hips in Warren's direction. She was high-bosomed, with swollen rouged nipples that seemed like miniature breasts placed in the center of the principal ones. What the world has always got plenty of, Warren thought, is flesh. Moving within six inches of him, she twisted her torso to the bass beat of the music. He looked at her coolly.

"Scat," Johnnie Faye ordered. The blonde danced away.

"You're hurting, good buddy," Johnnie Faye said. "I know the cure. Want to come party with me?"

"Not tonight. I'm spending this weekend with a law book."

"You're so square," she said. "I like that."

At Scoot's funeral on Saturday, with several hundred lawyers, judges, and former clients in attendance, Warren stood off to one side in the heat, sweating, barely listening to the eulogy. He heard other voices. He carried on conversations in his head. He was in command; his eyes and tone conveyed knowledge. "This makes sense. This is a marriage. *That's* an infatuation . . . at best." Tenderly enfolding his wife, he whispered in her ear, "It's going to be all right. Have faith in me." He played a younger Cary Grant, and Charm became pliant in his arms. She would stay, give up the New York lawyer. She saw the light and it wasn't a train. In his fantasies he was astute and wise. The worst he imagined was that one moment she murmured, "I need time." He said, "Take all you need, my darling."

Johnnie Faye was there at the funeral, wearing black silk, carrying a black parasol to ward off the afternoon sun. "How are you?" she asked.

"Fine. Rick and I are meeting tomorrow."

"I have faith," she said.

When he reached home that evening, Charm's car was parked in the driveway. He had hardly seen his wife since Monday, the day he had found her outside the house with her lover. Since that day, everything in Warren's life had changed. He walked through to the bedroom with Oobie clawing at his pants leg. Charm was in the shower, washing her hair. She came out with a thick brown towel wrapped around her head, another one draped around her body like a sarong.

She didn't seem surprised to see him. Or was she just indifferent? He was not wise enough to know. This was reality, not fantasy. Like the years that could pile up for Hector Quintana.

"You going to the ball game tonight?" she asked, as she

began to dress. Opening the big closet door, she stepped behind it. To deny him the sight of her body. Just as well— he might have pictured it elsewhere.

"That was with a client in a murder case."

"Aren't you out of it now that Scoot's gone?"

"I'm trying the case. Rick is sitting second chair."

Charm came out from behind the closet door, wearing panties and a black silk blouse that she was buttoning over her bra. Her pale eyebrows were raised. "How'd you manage that?"

He told her about his meetings.

"And Rick's willing? No glory in that for him."

"There's enough to go around if we win. And we're both being paid."

"That's good for you, Warren. That's very positive. Is it a good case? Will you win?"

"You never know, do you?" Ordinarily he would have offered her details. "Charm, can we talk?"

"I think that's a good idea."

But the talk didn't resemble his daydreams in the car. Perhaps he had rehearsed too much. Yes, of course she wanted time . . . not for him to win her back, but to figure out what to do with the rest of her life. She had hired an agent in Chicago, a man named Bluestein. He was going to try and get her an anchor job in a top market: Chicago, Los Angeles, Boston, New York.

"But our life's here."

"Your life is here, Warren. Not mine. You know I always wanted something better."

"And what about us?"

The pain of the other night bloomed again in Charm's eyes. He wanted to hold her. She raised a hand to keep him back. He saw her fingers trembling.

"Warren, this is hard for me to say. I want a divorce."

It was like his worst nightmare. He took a rapid turn around the room to get control of himself. But he wasn't in control. Why the hell should he be in control? Growl like a lion. He wasn't a lion. He was a man.

"So you can marry this other lawyer and move to New York?"

"I'll decide that when I'm ready to decide it. I don't want to be rushed."

"Good," he said bitterly.

No, it wasn't good. It was awful. *Good:* the sole word he could manage to describe the destruction in his heart.

"I thought of moving out," Charm said. "But I'm self-ish, I don't really want to do that. You know how I hate apartments. I thought we could share the house for a while. I just don't think we should share the bed. It's a little painful for us both."

Feel pain. Feel it the way I feel it.

"So who vacates?" He waved a hand at the room.

"That's up to you, Warren. I don't have the right to kick you out. But the guest room closets are so small. I have so much more stuff than you do. Would you mind awfully?"

After a minute he said, "I would mind a lot."

Sighing, she unwound the towel from her hair, shaking loose the wet blond strands. He followed her toward the bathroom, where she plugged in the dryer.

"Charm, are you going out?"

"Yes." The word was spoken calmly but carried weight enough to hit him in the chest like a large stone. "What about you?" Her finger poised at the switch on the hair dryer.

"I have work to do."

"Maybe we'll become friends, Warren."

"I very much doubt it." He walked out of the room before tears misted his eyes.

In the kitchen he patted Oobie, who hadn't been fed. In the recesses of the house he heard the dryer whir. It re-minded him that he had to do his laundry; he was running out of underwear. He poured out the chow and mixed it in the bowl with some chunks of Alpo and then let hot water drip in to make gravy.

He watched Oobie eat. Yes, I mind a lot.

He sat down in the living room and put his head in his hands. He couldn't stay in the same house with her.

Charm left ten minutes later, calling a muffled goodbye. He heard her high heels hurrying on the walkway.

He went out for dinner at a nearby fast-food chicken house, then came back and worked on the *Quintana* file for an hour. After that he turned his attention to the *Boudreau* file, but his eyes began to tire. The two cases blurred, became one. I'm not seeing things clearly, he realized. Can't concentrate. The lives of two people are in my hands, and my fucking hands are shaking.

He watched the last part of *Casablanca* on the late movie; he knew the airport scene almost word for word. Switching off the TV, he turned down the covers on one of the twin beds in the guest room and read the new García Márquez novel for half an hour, then switched off the bedside lamp at 2 A.M.

He woke at daybreak on Sunday morning. The short sleep had not refreshed him. On his way to the kitchen he noticed that the door to the master bedroom was ajar. He knocked softly, then went in: maybe they could talk. The bed had not been slept in. Charm had not come home.

"Fuck her," he said softly. And thought, I'll get on with my life. Using the kitchen telephone, he called Ravendale and made arrangements to rent an apartment. By ten o'clock he had moved himself in, with his dog for company.

Late on Monday afternoon in Judge Bingham's court, Warren M. Blackburn and Richard C. Levine were registered by the deputy district clerk as co-attorneys of record in *Texas v. Johnnie Faye Boudreau*.

Warren had Xeroxed a copy of Scoot's file. "I'll read it by the weekend," Rick promised.

Rocky came up from nowhere, Warren remembered, to whip Apollo Creed. If a tongue-tied palooka from Philadelphia can do it, so can I.

Toward the end of June, on a rainy afternoon with chocolate-brown skies crowding in from the Gulf, Judge Lou Parker called Warren and Nancy Goodpaster into her chambers. She directed her flinty gaze at the man who stood between Hector Quintana and death.

"How about clothes for your dude? I don't want this beaner sitting there with scuffs on his feet and a Harris County jumpsuit and making us all look bad. Does he have anything? If not, buy it for him. The county will reimburse. I don't mean for you to get him a five-hundred-dollar suit from Hart Schaffner & Marx. Find out his size and hike your ass down the block to Kuppenheimer. They've got a sale on." Without waiting for a thank-you she turned on Goodpaster, wagging her stubby forefinger at the prosecutor the way a father does at an errant child. "I don't believe in trial by ambush. I've told you this before, Nancy—if you've got anything smells a whiff of *Brady,* cough it up. If you can't give the defense all the information you've got and still get death, then it's not a capital case."

Get death. It was an abstraction, not a fact of a human life ending and a family drained by grief. The law stated that death was a proper penalty—*lex talionis,* slaying by legal sanction. Penalty: as in, you made a mistake and this is what you must pay. Fifteen yards for unnecessary roughness; throw dirt at the umpire and you get kicked out of the game. Knowing the criminal population as intimately as he did, Warren believed there should be stiffer sentences for violent crimes committed for profit: any man who carried a loaded weapon during the commission of a felony was prepared to use it. Give him a fair trial, then separate him from peaceful society for as long as the law allowed. The death penalty, however, was no deterrent and a dangerous balm. Primitive man hanging tough.

Nancy Goodpaster repeated to Judge Parker that she had nothing to reveal.

"Jury selection starts a week from Wednesday," the judge advised, "and I can goddam well guarantee that I'm not going to spend more than eight days picking a jury. I limit voir dire to thirty minutes a side for each juror. I keep a chess clock on my desk. When it goes *ping,* you've had it. No exceptions. Get yourselves organized."

She stared at Warren somberly. "You better think hard about all this. You want to cut a deal and plead your guy out at the eleventh hour, I won't be overjoyed you waited so long. But I sure as hell won't stop you. That clear?"

"Clear," Warren said.

Her scowl deepened. "I'll see you both for voir dire, a week from Wednesday at nine sharp."

Proper voir dires in Texas capitals had been known to last more than a month. Not in Lou Parker's court. The chess clock ticked.

"Which is fucking unconstitutional," Rick Levine said, when Warren told him. "Not to mention disgusting. You could challenge her on it, you know. File a motion citing higher court rulings against any limitations. If she overrules, it's built-in error for a reversal."

"I'd just as soon save the point," Warren said. "It may be the only thing I'll have on appeal."

In the evenings, in his apartment at Ravendale, he watched movies on a rented VCR. He rented a package of pots and pans and other kitchen paraphernalia, a clock-radio, some prints of racing sailboats and snow-covered mountains, and he stocked his refrigerator with cold cuts and frozen Stouffer's dinners, pepperoni pizzas, a quart of Polish vodka in the freezing compartment. No more cooking—that had been in another life. He finished the García Márquez book and began one on the Reagan presidency. Sometimes, at high volume, he played Bach and Verdi and Gordon Lightfoot on his ghetto blaster, until the neighbors complained. He never made the bed and he washed the dishes every third day. The furniture in the apartment was ordinary beige motel-style, but he could leave a mug of hot coffee on the coffee table without anyone telling him to put a coaster under it. The rings on the table grew and overlapped.

He and Rick met several times with Johnnie Faye to hear her story and prepare a trial notebook. Warren gave her a definition: "Self-defense is where you use deadly force to thwart the immediate anticipation that you're about to be killed or suffer serious bodily injury, and you have no opportunity to retreat. It's what we call an affirmative defense. The jury is charged to view all of the circumstances from your point of view." Johnnie Faye's testimony was the key: if the jury believed her she would be acquitted, if they doubted her she would be found guilty. "This goes in three stages," Warren explained. "First you tell us exactly what happened. Then we interview other possible witnesses. Then we woodshed you—prepare you for direct examination and cross-examination under oath. For now, don't leave anything out, no matter how trivial you think it is. Don't put anything in that isn't a fact. Tell us the minute-by-minute truth. We're your lawyers. We're here to help you, not to judge you."

But her tale of the events never varied. The lawyers took notes. Rick then brought the notes back to his office for his secretary, Bernadette Loo, to transcribe into computer memory. Small-boned, round-faced, heavy-lidded, pure Chinese in appearance, Bernadette Loo was third-generation Texan in speech and attitude. She favored cheongsams and jade jewelry, was divorced from a Houston fireman and dated a seemingly endless string of men. She said things like, "He ain't much to see, but he looks real good through the bottom of a glass."

"Good case," Rick said, the first time Johnnie Faye was gone from the office. "Checks out all the way so far. If she's telling the truth, your dog could defend her and win this case. So why did you need me?"

"You bark prettier," Warren said.

The district attorney's office in the person of Bob Altschuler had given them a copy of parts of the HPD offense report. The print division had picked up enough ridges and valleys on the fireplace poker to match the fingers of both Clyde Ott's right and left hand. The poker had been found lying on the living room carpet, directly in front of the sofa that had become Clyde's penultimate resting place. Johnnie Faye's prints were on it too, but that matched her story. Altschuler had also provided Warren with a set of photographs of the living room, a floor plan of the mansion on River Oaks Drive, a transcript of what Johnnie Faye had said over the telephone to the 911 dispatcher, and a copy of Sgt. Ruiz's notes after he had reached the Ott place and heard the confession. *Brady* material, all of it, or the pages would have remained locked in the file at 201 Fannin.

Warren wished his client had kept her mouth shut until she had seen a lawyer. When he asked her why she hadn't, Johnnie Faye said, "Because that would have made me look like I was hiding something. I wanted those peckerheads to know right away that I was sorry for what I did, but I sure as hell wasn't ashamed."

Warren went to the library of the *Chronicle* and Xeroxed the clips on the murders of Sharon Underhill Ott and David Inkman. Any reference to them was barred from coming up in trial, but the defense team needed to know the background. Altschuler would have done the same thing, and you could never tell in what way it would be important to know what the prosecutor knew.

Late the same afternoon Warren drove out I-10 to meet with the personnel at the Hacienda restaurant.

Both the waiter and the maitre d' remembered Dr. Ott

and Johnnie Faye dining there, and the management provided a copy of the bill that showed they had consumed ten frozen margaritas. The waiter remembered an argument at the dinner table. No, he couldn't remember what the lady and gentleman had said. So many people had arguments in restaurants.

Two of the musicians wandered in. Stolid and soft-voiced, they carried guitars in scarred black cases. Yes, they had sung for Johnnie Faye, and she had tipped them. An argument? Who knows? So long ago.

Not too good, but not bad either. Warren put all the names down on a witness list for possible subpoenas.

On a different evening he visited the couple who Johnnie Faye had said heard Clyde threaten to kill her. Dr. and Mrs. Gordon Butterfield, a cosmetic surgeon and his wife, lived on Memorial Drive in a house filled with Swedish Biedermeier and Art Deco furniture. They characterized Johnnie Faye as flashy, amoral. They had been friends of Clyde's, they emphasized. They had said to him, "She's out for your money. Get rid of her before it's too late." Prophetic words.

But they recalled that particular evening a year or so ago—it had been a charity dinner for the homeless, held at the Houston Racquet Club.

Dr. Gordon Butterfield said, "They were arguing, as usual, about the money Clyde spent on his stepchildren. The boy is what I'd call a ne'er-do-well, and the girl is twice-divorced and has several children. They inherited from Sharon, of course, but not quite enough for their needs. Clyde's considerable fortune had come from Sharon, as surely you know. Clyde was a generous man—he had faults, he was human, but he was definitely generous. He subsidized the stepchildren, and the Boudreau woman disapproved. So what happened was, in the midst of this argument, which we tried to halt because, frankly, we were bored with it, the Boudreau woman threw a drink in his face. Ran down over his dinner jacket and soaked his bow tie. Uncalled for, in my opinion. And Clyde said, 'You bitch, I could happily kill you for that.' Which I assure you I didn't take as a genuine threat. It's just the sort of thing you say when you're angry and you've been humiliated in front of friends. Quite innocent in intent.''

Lila Butterfield said, "She'd been insulting poor Sharon too. I went to college with poor Sharon."

Warren said, "Do you recall Ms. Boudreau's exact words, Mrs. Butterfield?"

"If my husband says she said what he said she said," Lila Butterfield explained, "then that's exactly what she said. He has an excellent memory for trivia."

"You didn't hear the remark?"

"With half an ear. It was all so vulgar. So inappropriate to a charity dinner. One doesn't necessarily listen."

Warren finished his scotch and left. He said later to Rick, "The woman drank half a bottle of sherry while I was there. We may have to use the husband, but he was Clyde's pal and hates our client, and he's a pompous ass. I asked if Clyde ever beat up on Sharon, and he screeches, 'No way, don't even *suggest* such a thing!' I tried to find out if Clyde ever snorted cocaine in their presence. His wife gasps like I'd asked if he screwed ten-year-olds. Gordon sits up straight in his wing chair and says, 'Clyde was an esteemed member of the medical profession, Mr. Blackburn. That's my answer to you, and it will not vary.' I managed to get the names of the other people who were with them at this charity dinner. Let's find them. Let's cover all the bases."

But when Rick did so, no one else who had been at the table remembered a thing other than that a drink may have been spilled.

Warren had better luck at Hermann Hospital, where he secured a copy of the Emergency Room report on the night of December 22, 1988. PATIENT'S INITIAL COMPLAINT: *suspected fracture, nasal bone. (Some swelling observed in dorsum.)* DIAGNOSIS: *hairline fracture of left zygo-*

maticofacial foramen. TREATMENT:*none.* PRESCRIPTIONS: *Tylenol III.* The young doctor who had treated Johnnie Faye agreed to testify. Yes, she'd told him her boyfriend had hit her. Wasn't shy at all about admitting that. And they usually are, the doctor said.

Rick dropped by the bar at the Grand Hotel, but Cathy Lewis—the cocktail waitress to whom Clyde had supposedly paid the $25,000 for knocking out three of her front teeth—hadn't worked there for eighteen months. No one knew where she had gone. There were six listings for C Lewis in the Harris County telephone books, but the only one named Catherine sounded at least seventy years old. "Call all the hotel bars," Warren told his partner, "and try your people at social security and the DMV. We need her. You find her and she's your witness."

The defense team decided that Warren would do the woodshedding. At their last two meetings Johnnie Faye had directed almost all of her statements to him. Sometimes, when Rick broke in, she cast him a look of irritation bordering on anger. Rick concluded, with an airy wave, "She doesn't like me. That's rare but I've known it to happen. You're the one Scoot picked, you're her blankee to chew on. I'm just a fast-talking Yid. I mean, she's not dumb—she respects my superior intelligence and my knowledge of law, but I get the feeling she doesn't relate to my humor or my nose. So you do the woodshedding. I'll shut up and look biblically wise."

"She's right," Warren said. "You don't like her."

"She's got a great body, but she'd have your nuts in a paper bag if you gave her thirty seconds and a pair of scissors."

"Maybe that's a feeling you project to her."

"Think I'm wrong?"

Warren said, "Right or wrong, she's our client."

Every morning he ran along Braes Bayou with Oobie. Oobie was in the apartment illegally: no pets were allowed.

He gave the two handymen each a ten-dollar bill, told them if they heard a dog barking in his apartment during the day it was a tape he played to scare away burglars. On Saturdays he had a maid come in to clean, an enormous black woman from Barbados named Theodosia, which she told him meant God-given. Theodosia sang calypso songs while she vacuumed and scrubbed the accumulating dirt from the oven, and one morning Warren joined with her in duets of "Brown-skinned Gal" and "Day-O," the only such lyrics he knew. He looked forward to Theodosia's visits. He was lonely.

He went to court when it was required, and met with Hector Quintana in the jail visiting room, and with Rick and Johnnie Faye Boudreau in Rick's office or his own, and with potential witnesses. He drew up witness plans and a theory of defense for both cases. One was simple. The other, for *Quintana,* made him clench his teeth and groan. Veering back and forth as he did between the two cases put him on edge, gave him dreams that were nightmarish in their confusion. "You've got a responsibility to try and talk him into taking that offer," Lou Parker had said, *"even if you think he's innocent."* Warren dreamed the words into the mouth of Dwight Bingham, and saw himself, in slow motion, in Bingham's court, pleading Johnnie Faye Boudreau guilty. Afterward Johnnie Faye screamed at him, "How could you do that? You *knew* I was innocent!" He fell at her feet, groveling.

Then he awoke, his pillow damp with sweat. The air-conditioning in the building had broken during the night. He got up, showered in cold water, then turned on the tape deck and listened to a Mozart flute quartet, trying to calm down.

If he was back in his apartment by six o'clock he avoided Channel 26 and watched the local news on one of the networks. He had left a message on Charm's answering machine to tell her where he was, and in the last two weeks she had called twice and so had he. Routine matters: a

disputed bill from Blue Cross; by any chance had he taken
her manicure kit with him? No, he hadn't. He asked her if
he could come by on Saturday morning and get his spare
pair of sweats and some Reeboks which he'd left in the
dryer. No problem, she would be away for the weekend.

Twice she inquired if he was all right, and each time he
said, "I'm fine, Charm. How about you?" The first time
she replied, "I'm doing well," and the second time, "I'm
doing okay."

But he didn't focus on subtleties. He was giving her the
time she needed to do whatever it was she elected to do,
and he didn't want details or apologies or arguments. He
kept the conversations short. He was heartsore, but that
was none of her business now.

And his heart wasn't consistently sore; there were hours
when he didn't think of Charm at all. Some June evenings
he went to the weight room in the main building at
Ravendale, pumped iron and tugged at pulleys, worked up
a sweat, then went out to the pool. There was usually a
water-volleyball game in progress and a few times he
joined in, splashing and yelling. A young black-haired
woman on his team told him her name was Mary Beth and
she'd just moved here from Michigan, where it was so cold
in winter it'd freeze the you-know-whats off a brass monkey. And what was his name? And where was he from?
And what did he do? He was polite to her, then he slipped
away.

Janice, behind the desk, regularly bared her teeth in an
engaging smile whenever he came round to ask if there
were any responses to the flyer he'd had printed and
stuffed into every mailbox. In her eyes he recognized the
veiled beacon of invitation he had hunted for so assiduously in the years when he and his pals traipsed around
town to parties or hung out at the Shamrock pool.

Not what he needed, not yet. No entanglements, no hit-
and-run. Focus on the Boudreau woman's testimony and
suffering Hector Quintana. Get a good heart pump going

in the weight room. Take good care of Oobie, because she loves you and depends on you.

One evening he forgot to feed her. The next morning, on the freeway, en route to interview a witness, he remembered. He turned off at a downtown exit and drove all the way back to Ravendale, where her tail wagged with joy. He hugged her fiercely. A dumb and hungry dog was all he had.

Casually, at an easy moment in conversation, by poolside and in the front office, he said to both Mary Beth and Janice, "I'm separated from my wife. I miss her. Still trying to figure out what-all went wrong." Exactly the same words each time. And he gave both of them an arm's-length smile.

But women seemed to smell his availability, if that's what it was. Courthouse gossip was rife, swift as sound if not light. One morning in Judge Bingham's court when he was setting up a date to hand in his subpoenas in *Boudreau,* Maria Hahn, the court reporter, nudged his elbow.

Maria was in her late thirties, with an illegitimate eight-year-old son, a fact that discouraged most of the bachelor lawyers. Tall and leggy, she had short brown hair in a frizzy permanent wave, bright blue eyes, a neck like a Modigliani portrait. The married lawyers hit on her regularly, but Maria laughed at all of them except for Bob Altschuler. They were supposed to have had an affair, now history. Rumor had it that she ditched him. Altschuler, a married man of forty-five, was still in pain. You could see it in his eyes when he gazed across at Maria behind her steno machine, red-tipped fingers flying.

She was always telling off-color jokes and she giggled a lot with Dwight Bingham, who called a break in court proceedings whenever he thought she was tired. "Break for the beautiful Maria," he would say, and more often than not, Maria, smiling up at the bench, transcribed it into the record. Bingham didn't care.

She asked Warren how he was doing, and he said fine.

"Warren, I belong to this club, called, would you ever believe it, the Towering Texans of Houston. Monday's the legal holiday—there's a big Fourth of July party Sunday night. I don't want to go alone, and I really don't care for any of these giant geeks. Want to come with me?"

"Sounds good," Warren said, after a moment. He liked Maria; she was a cheerful woman. "Exactly how tall are you?"

"Five-foot-eleven. You?"

"Six-one. Maybe shy a quarter inch."

"Well, you can't join the team. Men members have to be six-two. But I'm allowed to bring along a short guy." She squeezed his arm, and a chortling sound issued from her bountiful chest. "Want to hear a real disgusting joke?"

"Do I have any choice?"

"It's a riddle. Why do women have cunts?"

"I can't imagine."

"So that men will talk to them."

Maria howled with laughter like a benevolent witch. Warren rocked back and forth on his heels, thinking it over.

Maria's laughter ebbed. "More truth than poetry, right?"

He wondered if Charm would laugh at that joke.

"Give me your new number," Maria said. "I'll hoot to tell you when and where."

His new number. The words rang with melancholy and promise. Was a new number like a new life?

Wearing shorts and a safari shirt from Banana Republic, Rick Levine arrived at Warren's cottage office. It was the Saturday afternoon of the long Fourth of July weekend. This time Rick brought Bernadette Loo; she had been sick with the flu and had fallen behind in the transcription of their notes. Today she appeared glum. Just kissed another boyfriend goodbye, she explained. "How come I get mixed up with so many jerks?"

"You keep turning *me* down," Rick said, "and your Chinese God, not to mention Jehovah, is punishing you."

There was no truth to that: Rick was one of the few men Warren knew, other than himself, who was faithful to his wife. "Got no time to fool around" was Rick's explanation. But Warren doubted that too. Rick had his family, his racehorses, his friends, his practice, and was loyal to them all. His wife grumbled, "When he's in trial, he comes home in the evening, I talk to him, he's not even there. Drives me *crazy*." But Warren had noticed that when Rick and Liz were together they laughed often, touched each other, were never cruel. He had envied them that simplicity.

The two lawyers were going over the list of witnesses. Johnnie Faye was due to arrive at four o'clock and they would continue to woodshed her for cross-examination. Bernadette set herself up at a desk in the corner alcove where Warren kept his computer and printer. The *Boudreau* file already filled half a cabinet drawer and spilled over from two briefcases.

"Got a question before we begin," Rick said. "Been thinking about it . . . something's bothering me."

"Fire away."

Rick unrolled the simplified drawing (provided by Bob

Altschuler) of the downstairs of Clyde Ott's house on River Oaks Drive. The dimensions of the house were on a grand scale. You entered into a large Italian marble vestibule and directly ahead, in southern style, was a broad marble staircase leading to the two upper floors. To the right was the family room and media center with oversized television, Dolby Surround audio/video system and pool table; to the left, through an archway, a vast living room with Oriental carpets and, for the most part, white Italian leather and dark rosewood furniture by Chippendale. Opposite the fireplace, quite a distance away, an alcove on one wall contained a built-in bookcase in front of which stood the leather sofa on which Clyde Ott had died.

Rick's finger pointed at the outline of the sofa. "Suppose, like our client keeps telling us, Clyde was waving the poker over his head in a threatening manner, and she shot him just as he took a swing at her. Then how come, when he fell, the momentum of his arm didn't sling the poker over the sofa against the bookcase? Or at least onto the sofa? How come the poker wound up two feet *this* side of it, on the carpet?"

Behind them Bernadette Loo tapped away at the computer keyboard, occasionally sipping a cold longneck Bud that she had pilfered from Warren's little fridge in the hallway.

"Think about it," Warren said. He already had done so.

Rick shrugged. "I'd like to, but two of my horses are running at Derby Downs tomorrow, and Liz and I are flying to New Orleans tonight. So you enlighten me."

"It's possible," Warren said, "that Clyde swung the poker in such a way—like, right around his body, strike three—that it wound up behind his body on the carpet. However . . ." Warren clamped his lips into a tight smile.

Rick nodded. "It's also possible that the poker hit the bookcase and wound up behind the sofa, and she moved it after she killed him because it looked more obvious as to what had happened. And that way the cops wouldn't miss it."

"They wouldn't have missed it in any case."

"She might not have realized that," Rick speculated.

Right, Warren thought, if you bought the premise of that scenario. The other murders came to mind: Sharon Ott, Dink, possibly Bobbie Ronzini, and the unknown chef's assistant Altschuler had mentioned. If she had set up any of those killings and stepped away unindicted, she would think all homicide cops were morons.

"Of course, there's one more possibility," Warren said. "An entirely different set of facts."

"Yeah, the poker story is a fucking fairy tale. Clyde never picked up the poker and swung at her with it. She shot him, then put the poker in his hand to fix the prints. And then she laid it down on the carpet in what she figured was the most visible spot, so the schmucky cops wouldn't miss it. And made up that cockamamie story."

"You've got it," Warren said.

"You think that sweet little pussycat from Odem did such a heinous thing?"

"Anything's possible, however unlikely. But I'm not about to ask her."

"Bob Altschuler is. If we figured it out, he'll figure it out. He'll have some sort of expert on moving objects, whatever that science is called. A fucking *physicist*! Or maybe Glenn Davis of the Astros—come to think of it, that's more Bob's style. You sure you want to put this black widow up on the witness stand?"

"What have we got without her? If the jury believes her, she walks. And why shouldn't they believe her? Who has the state got to contradict her? There are no surprise witnesses in this case. Altschuler's only prosecuting because he's pissed off about what he thinks she got away with in the past. He's hoping for a miracle. We're here to make sure there *is* no miracle." Warren thought a bit. "But I'll have to woodshed her on the duty to retreat."

"You told me Scoot said not to worry about the duty to retreat."

"He ain't trying this case," Warren said.

Johnnie Faye Boudreau arrived at Warren's office at five o'clock in the afternoon. She left her Mercedes in the concrete parking area out in front, next to Warren's BMW and Rick's Saab and Bernadette's Plymouth two-door. When she swept in, wearing a Guatemalan silk blouse and tight white Dior slacks, all swiveling hips and ear-to-ear smile, she cried, "How're y'all? How's my team? Are we gonna win, or are we gonna kick ass?"

Warren introduced her to Bernadette, who was typing a fresh set of Rick's notes. After about ten minutes, when Warren began to review her story about the tussle with Clyde and the poker, Johnnie Faye's smiles faded. She wriggled in her chair. She kept crossing and uncrossing her legs. Her eyes grew flat and cold. She began picking under a fingernail, then glanced up from under dark penciled brows with a definitely theatrical frown.

"Could I talk to you gentlemen alone for a minute?"

"Bernie," Rick said, "go see if you can find an extra six-pack and some potato chips."

A ten-dollar bill appeared in his hand. Bernadette left the cottage.

Johnnie Faye let out a soprano-sized sigh. "Okay, guys, what's she doing here?"

"She's Rick's secretary," Warren said.

"I know that. I've seen her in his office. I don't like it. I trust y'all. Not her."

Warren explained that client confidentiality extended to lawyers' secretaries and clerks. A lawyer would be disbarred for breaking his oath; a secretary would not only be fired and never work again in the legal profession but might face criminal charges. And be horsewhipped. And they needed the notes they had taken in previous sessions. Bernadette would type them up beautifully.

"Listen, I've been around a lot longer than you. I don't trust them."

"Legal secretaries?"

"No, you dumb shit. Don't you know what I'm talking about?"

Rick coughed gently. "Ms. Loo has been with me for three years. Her great-granddaddy was a coolie came over from Foo-chow, or one of them Chink cities, with a contract to lay railroad ties for the Southern Pacific. Bernadette graduated U of H. She may look like Charlie Chan's sister but she can't read or write or speak Chink. She drinks Bud and Miller Lite. She is a trustworthy one hunnert percent Murkin."

It was hard to say if Johnnie Faye realized he was mocking her. Her eyes darted all over the room. She rocketed into a tirade.

Slopes were no fucking good. The Japs were taking over our banking industry, buying up all the stocks in the Fortune 500 and half of the high-priced real estate, while Toyota was killing Ford and Chevy. The Chinks were all commies, sent over like a fifth column. The Vietnamese were the worst—she made the speech Warren had already heard about the Texas shrimpers who'd been driven out of the business, and the 7-Elevens that looked like whole families of slanteyes camped there. They had their own Mafia here. Drugs? They invented them. We tried to save their ass over in 'Nam, had a hundred thousand boys killed or their privates blown off or turned into addicts like Garrett, and did those smug dirtballs show any gratitude? "You think I'm exaggerating," she said, "but most people don't have the guts to say how they really feel except maybe when the Japs buy up another TV station. Well, I do. Send 'em all back where they came from, before it's too late. If I had my way—"

Her face was scarlet, her breasts rising and falling under the Guatemalan silk. She was out of breath. Warren and Rick looked at each other.

"Anyway," Johnnie Faye finished, in a quieter tone, "in case you didn't get my drift, what I'm trying to say is, I don't trust them."

"We got your drift," Rick said.

"So when your little friend comes back, I'd appreciate it if you told her we don't need her. Nothing personal, of course."

A few minutes later, when Bernadette popped open the screen door and set a cold six-pack of Bud down on the desk, Rick said, "We're finished, my dear. You can go home. Or," he added, with hardly a change of expression, "go over to the Bamboo Garden or Fu's and get a good meal. My treat."

"God, you know I can't abide that stuff," Bernadette said, gathering up her things.

"I forgot," Rick said.

The lawyers went back to work on Johnnie Faye: the layout of Clyde's living room, the poker, her knowledge of how the .22 worked. In an hour the telephone rang. It was Charm. She was sorry to bother Warren, but she was in the neighborhood—could she come over for a few minutes? Could they talk?

Her voice startled him, and for a moment he didn't answer.

"Is this a bad time for you, Warren?"

"Hang on a minute—" He put a palm over the mouthpiece and spoke to Rick, who said, "Okay with me, we've wrapped it up for today. I'll catch an early plane and tell my horses a bedtime story."

"I'd like to meet your wife," Johnnie Faye said sweetly. "Mind if I stay? Just to say hello and how's tricks."

"His wife doesn't take on tricks anymore," Rick said.

"You think you're some kind of stand-up comic," Johnnie Faye snarled, "but the man's in pain. That kind of talk is uncalled for."

"I apologize," Rick said to Warren, and dared to wink.

But in some way Warren was glad that Johnnie Faye would be there when Charm arrived. He didn't want to guess at what she wanted, and yet the possibilities ballooned in his mind. A divorce . . . or getting back together. No doubt it was neither of those. Probably something utterly trivial.

Rick banged out the door, and Johnnie Faye excused herself to the rest room to fix her makeup and brush her hair. Warren ran the tape back to the beginning and busied himself watching the spools fly, the one diminishing, the other augmenting. Like future and past.

Johnnie Faye came back looking clear-eyed. Warren said, "We have a few minutes. Let's go through this business with the gun once more."

"I've got it."

"Run it by me. Use different words this time. On cross the prosecutor will peck at you, and if you keep using the same phrases by rote, it makes a bad impression on the jury. Focus on the truth, but see it from different angles. Literally, see yourself from different angles of the living room. Can you do that?"

One of the troubling questions was: did she reflexively shoot Clyde, or did she shoot him because she meant to kill him? And the lead-in to that was: did she cock the action on the pistol, or, not being really familiar with it, did she just pull the trigger and discharge the weapon? So far she had given several answers. She had cocked the action, she had not cocked the action; she had meant to shoot *at* him but not kill him. Often she said, "It went so fast. I don't really remember it too well."

Warren had decided not to ask her any of that on direct examination. Let Altschuler do it. Let him sound as though he were bullying her or going off on what lawyers called a fishing expedition.

Warren had never told her to make up facts and never made up any for her. That would have been not merely against the canons of legal ethics but against his own self-interest. You never knew what a defendant would blurt out if a prosecutor as good as Altschuler got her on the run in a mile-a-minute cross and demanded, "Did Mr. Blackburn tell you to say that, Ms. Boudreau?" Or what kind of statement she would make if a jury found her guilty. Warren remembered Virgil Freer's betrayal. Until now in the woodshedding, he had tried to convey his feelings about Johnnie Faye's answers by means of encouraging smiles or, when she went off-line, frowns. Let her pick up on it. Let her get comfortable with the most helpful vision of the truth.

She hadn't answered him. He said again, "Can you do that?"

"What happens if I fib a little?"

"Beg your pardon?"

"Look, you're my lawyer. It's all in confidence, right? So I'm asking you—what happens if I really don't remember something? Or what if I remember it in a way that might put my tit in a wringer, and so instead I get up there and tell it in a way that's good for me?"

He considered for a moment. Not that he was in doubt about the basic answer. Only how to express it to her so that she got it and wouldn't forget it.

"What could happen if you lie, Johnnie Faye, are two things. You could get away with it. Or if the prosecutor wears you down and gets you confused, or if there's a witness to contradict you or hard evidence that says otherwise, or you told someone else the truth and that person testifies to what we call your 'prior inconsistent statement' —you could get hurt. Mangled, probably." He paused with as much significance as he could muster. "And there's one thing more. If I put you on the witness stand I'm vouching for the probity of what you say. If I know you're going to lie, I can't put you up there. Those are the rules."

"Funny game, counselor," Johnnie Faye said.

Just then he heard the familiar sound of Charm's Mazda

rolling into the little concrete parking area. A car door slammed, characteristically hard.

"That's my wife," Warren said. "I'll be a few minutes. We'll finish up after she goes. Think about what I told you."

He brushed potato chips from his lap, stood up and went to the fridge for a beer. After a minute, while he imagined her touching up her lipstick, Charm's quick footsteps approached the door. Sounds like she's wearing her Nikes. He shook his head, perplexed. I know so much about her.

Charm, dressed in faded jeans and a Greenpeace T-shirt, also wore a certain quizzical expression, and her eyes shot darts at the woman seated by the desk. Warren introduced them.

"I'm real proud to meet you," Johnnie Faye said. "Can't say I watch the news a lot, but when I do, you're right up there with that fella whose name I can never remember."

Charm offered a tepid smile, turned back to Warren and said, "I thought—"

"You told me just a few minutes. I start trial this week. If you want privacy, we can go outside."

It had grown a little cooler, down to 85 degrees, moving on toward evening. As he guided her into the parking lot, Warren said, "We can sit in my car. I'll turn on the A/C."

"I don't mind the heat as long as it's dry. I may even miss it when I go."

"You're odd," Warren said.

With Charm facing him, he leaned his buttocks against the hood of Johnnie Faye's cream-colored Mercedes. "So what can I do for you?"

"I think we should start taking steps toward a divorce. I wanted to tell you face-to-face. It just didn't seem right to write a letter or say it on the telephone."

Not trivial at all. Wrong again.

"I've talked to a lawyer. Here in town," she added

quickly. "His name's Arthur Franklin. He'll be in touch with you."

Warren nodded grimly. "Don't know him," he muttered.

"It'll be simple," Charm said. "No alimony. We sell the house and split the money down the middle. Unless you want to keep the place and move back in, in which case we get the bank to assess current value and you pay me half. Same with all our investments, such as they are. Is that fair?"

"What about child support?"

"What?"

"Just joking."

"I don't think it's so funny."

"Oh, lighten up, Charm. It's all your idea, isn't it?"

"I suppose it is."

"Suppose?"

"Don't be so lawyerly. This isn't as easy for me as you may think."

"Not for me either," Warren said.

"You're the one who makes jokes. You seem in a pretty good mood."

What was happening with Charm seemed like a dream sequence in a movie, or one of the soap operas he'd watched on the office TV when the phone wasn't ringing and he was in the dumps these past few years. A good mood? The moment he allowed himself to think about the little balcony in San Miguel de Allende, the mood would flee like a burglar.

"Are you going to remarry? Be a stepmother to this guy's three kids?"

She tossed her head, her blond hair flaring into a temporary mane. "I don't want to discuss that, Warren. Give me a break."

So she was in pain too. But over what? Over leaving him or over whatever was going on with her beau from New York?

"I want to tell you a quick joke, Charm. Get your opinion on it. A woman told it to me." He repeated Maria Hahn's riddle as to why women have cunts. "So is that funny," he asked, "or insightful, or just downright sexist? What's your opinion, Charm? Analyze it."

Her mouth had curved up briefly and uncertainly—then she had clicked the bare smile off like a camera shutter. "Is this some sort of a message to me?"

He had no idea what she meant. Did she think he was commenting on her new relationship? Maybe he was. Otherwise, he wondered, why would I have thought of that?

But he said, "I'm asking your opinion. You're an enlightened woman."

"You're getting a little crazy, Warren, did you know that?"

That may have been true.

"Anything else you want to tell me?" he asked.

"I don't think so. Not today. Are you eating well? You look thin."

Old habits of caring died hard, he realized. "I work out," he said. "I've given up serious cooking for the time being, so I may have lost weight."

"How's Oobie?"

"Hip bothers her, but she's frisky."

"I take it that's your client in the Ott case." Charm nodded toward the window of the cottage. "Formidable-looking lady."

With his palms, Warren hoisted himself up to a sitting position on the hood of the car, boots dangling. The metal gave a bit under his weight.

"You always sit on your clients' Mercedes?" Charm asked, curling her lip.

She was implying a certain intimacy. He said nothing, just shrugged with nonchalance.

"Well, I'm sure she won't mind," Charm said. "I can see she's a careless driver."

Again there was an implication. But this time he bit. "What makes you say that, Charm?"

"The bumper. And the fender." Charm's reporter's eye flicked toward the front of the car.

He jumped down lightly from the hood and turned in the direction of her glance, where he saw that the bumper had separated from the grillwork. There was a small dent, with a nickel-sized spot of bright blue paint ground into the cream-colored paint of the fender. You could easily have missed it if you didn't look closely in good light.

He kept staring at it, at first not knowing why. And then, not instantly—more like mud oozing up from a fault in the earth, sluggishly assuming shape, primordial meaning—he remembered where he had first seen that combination of blue and cream. Strange coincidence. He had told Johnnie Faye he was working on another case that would go to trial before hers, but she had waved it aside, asked few questions about it. Clients needed to preserve the illusion that you were concentrated on them alone.

But how many cars in Houston were painted that peculiarly bright shade of blue? And how many collisions could those blue cars have had with other cream-colored cars? The breath almost left Warren's body.

After Charm had gone he walked back inside to where Johnnie Faye waited. I can't deal with this now, he thought. This is for later, when I'm alone. Be careful, and assume nothing. Johnnie Faye was drinking a beer and browsing through a three-month-old copy of the *Law Journal.* Warren apologized for the delay.

"You look upset," Johnnie Faye said.

"I am," he admitted. "But I don't want to talk about it." A canny idea picked at his mind. "I need to work more with you. Are you tired?"

No, she said, she wasn't tired. Her eyes grew bright, as they always did when he focused on her. She treated it like a game, a play where she was the star. "Let's do some more cross-examination," Warren said. "You're on the witness stand, under oath. I'm Bob Altschuler. I'll start off with the murder weapon, but I may skip around to different topics, because that's what he'll do. You ready?"

Johnnie Faye nodded.

"Ms. Boudreau, you shot Dr. Ott with a .22-caliber pistol, is that correct?"

"Yes."

"Did you always carry that .22 in your handbag?"

"Yes, I needed it for protection."

"No," Warren said, "don't justify. Just answer his question firmly and clearly. If you add an explanation it makes you sound defensive. And he can ask the judge to make you stop. Understand?"

She nodded.

"Ms. Boudreau, is that .22 the only pistol you own?"

"No."

He digested that and said carefully, "Describe the other pistol, please."

"It's a .45. I keep it in my desk drawer at the club, under lock and key."

"You're sure it's a .45, not some other caliber?"

She looked at him oddly. "Yes."

Get off it, Warren thought, or she might catch on. "Was the .22 that you carried in your handbag always loaded?"

"Yes."

"Safety in the On position?"

"Yes."

"Did you know it was in your handbag that evening you went with Dr. Ott to the Hacienda restaurant?"

"Well, I knew, but I wasn't thinking about it."

"Just yes or no," Warren cautioned.

She frowned. "Yes."

"Was Dr. Ott aware that you were carrying a gun that evening?"

"I don't know."

"Good," Warren said. "That's the right answer. Matter

of fact, Altschuler probably wouldn't ask that, and if he did I'd object. You don't know what Clyde knew or didn't know, and make sure you don't get trapped into speculating. Okay—did you tell Dr. Ott you were carrying the gun that evening?"

"No."

"In the Hacienda restaurant, where you and Dr. Ott dined, you argued, didn't you?"

"He argued."

"Was he abusive to you?"

"Yes."

"And were you abusive to him?"

"No, I just shut up and listened."

"Was Dr. Ott drunk when you both reached his house that night, after dinner?"

"Yes."

"Were you drunk?"

"Yes, but not as drunk as he was."

"You had your Mercedes parked at his house, didn't you?"

"Yes."

He considered what he could ask about the Mercedes. *Is that your only car? Does anyone else drive it? Have you had any accidents with it lately?* No, don't be a fool. Stay away. She was waiting. He could feel her mind ticking.

"So when you got back from the Hacienda to his house, you could have gone home then, right away, in your car, to your apartment, if you wanted to?"

"Well . . . yes, I suppose so."

"But you didn't, did you?"

"No. Wait," she said to Warren. "Can't I explain why I didn't go home?"

"Not unless he asks you, and he won't. He won't ask any questions that begin with 'why.' And he won't ever ask you, 'How do you account for such-and-such,' because that's also a *why* question. But I'll ask you plenty of that on direct examination, and you can talk as much as you like—so you'll already have explained why you didn't go home right away. Okay, let's keep going. We'll skip forward a bit. Ms. Boudreau, later, after you came downstairs with Dr. Ott, where did you go?"

"Into the hallway, what he called the vestibule."

"The hallway by the front door?"

"Yes."

"Dr. Ott was drunk and abusive and threatening?"

"Yes. All three."

"Were you still drunk?"

"Yes."

"You could have gone directly out the front door, couldn't you?"

"No."

"He blocked your path?"

"Yes."

"You came down the stairs first, and he followed you, but still he managed to block your path out the door?"

"Yes, he caught up with me in the vestibule."

"Well," Warren said, "I didn't ask you that, but it's okay. That's a natural response. Now, Ms. Boudreau, how did you get from the vestibule into the living room?"

"He shoved me in there."

Warren stopped to make some notes.

"All right," he said, "then you picked up the poker to defend yourself and he took it away from you. He cursed at you, threatened to kill you. Where were you standing, Ms. Boudreau?"

"Behind the sofa."

"And you already had your gun leveled at him?"

"No."

"When did you take the gun out of your handbag?"

"When he raised the poker like he was going to hit me with it."

"And he came running at you with the poker over his head?"

"Yes."

"And then you shot him?"

"Yes."

"He was running at you when you shot him?"

"Yes."

"He never hesitated at all? Never stopped?"

"No."

"You aimed at his head and pulled the trigger?"

"No, I didn't aim at all. I was petrified."

"You pulled the trigger three times, didn't you?"

"No, just once."

"But three bullets were fired, isn't that a fact?"

"Yes."

"You cocked the action when you took the gun out of your handbag, didn't you?"

"I don't remember."

"Did you know the sear had been filed down on this gun?"

"I'm still not even sure what a sear is."

"You've practiced with that pistol, haven't you?"

"Once, five years ago, when I bought it. I don't even think I hit the target more than two or three times."

"All right," Warren said, after he had made some more notes. "That's enough for today. How do you feel?"

"Fine," Johnnie Faye said, her eyes sparkling.

"Well, I'm bushed. Let's go through it again sometime next week. I'm starting my other trial on Wednesday, picking a jury. I'll call you."

Through the parted blinds at the window Warren watched the Mercedes bump over the curb, turn up Montrose and vanish in the long shadows of early evening in the direction of the University of St. Thomas.

He dropped into his swivel chair, tilted it back and swung his boots up on the desk. He locked his hands behind his head.

Coincidence. It had to be coincidence.

From his desk he took out the *Quintana* file and the

manila envelope with the packet of photographs that the two homicide sergeants had given him. He stared at the photograph of Dan Ho Trunh's blue station wagon, at the cream-colored rip in the metal on the right side just ahead of the rear bumper. That rip, Mrs. Trunh swore, hadn't been there when her husband left the house on the morning of his death.

All right. It could have happened anytime that day. Trunh could have sideswiped any number of cream-colored cars.

But there was one cream-colored car with that shade of blue paint ground into its front left fender. The blue paint was garish, distinctive—probably hand-painted. And the nature of the owner of the cream-colored Mercedes was also distinctive. *"Slopes are no fucking good. . . . If I had my way . . ."*

He remembered Bob Altschuler casually telling him that unproved tale: *"We think that on the spur of the moment she offed some Korean kid who worked in her club and gave her some back talk when she wouldn't give him a raise. You think I'm kidding? I know."*

It can't be, Warren thought. It made no sense. There was no connection. If Johnnie Faye Boudreau was a murderer in the past, she murdered out of clear motive. Sharon Ott, in order to make Clyde free. Dink, because he knew too much and was dangerous. Ronzini (if he was indeed dead), for the same reason. Clyde Ott, in self-defense—if she was telling the truth. If she's lying, then she had no reason other than ungovernable rage.

If that's what had happened with Clyde, and with whoever had worked in her kitchen, why couldn't it have happened with Dan Ho Trunh?

Because there's no connection. None except the blue spot on the car.

He spent nearly all day Monday in his office, preparing an opening statement for *Quintana,* blocking out the witnesses in his trial notebook and worrying over a theory of defense. The test for such a theory was not legal relevance; it was persuasive relevance. There wasn't much. After the state had presented its case Hector would stand before the jury and tell his story: "I didn't do it." Wonderfully relevant, yet hardly persuasive.

In the late afternoon Warren visited Hector to make sure he had the proper clothing and to tell him how to conduct himself in the courtroom. Hector was grave and courteous. Now and then he tried to make polite conversation about life in jail, but it was an effort. Warren left there feeling depressed. *This man could not have done it. He's innocent. And I have no way of proving it.*

He went back to the office and again put his boots up on the desk. He stared at a blank part of the white wall, forcing his brain to work as hard as it could. He tried to make simple connections. He flew through the alternatives, then began again, working his way through them more deliberately, coldly, in mental slow motion. Silently the first time; then aloud, his voice barely above a whisper vibrating in his throat, as if it came from elsewhere. He stood up to look at himself in a mirror. His eyes looked calmly back at him in the fading light. They were not the eyes of a lunatic.

He sat down again at the desk, leaned his elbows on the comforting wood. Dusk fell. He stared at the HPD photograph. The second hand of his watch moved around and around the face, wearing away human time. If he hadn't made a glaring error of observation, if he hadn't thwarted logic in discarding the alternatives, if he dared to believe her car had collided with Dan Ho Trunh's Ford and there was some causal relationship between that event and his death—there still remained the questions of *why* and *how.*

No connection, other than the rage she had shown in the office, and her nature, and Altschuler's accusation. And her brothers. But that was too farfetched.

Can I ask her? Cutely probe? Find out where she was that day, that evening? I have no reason to ask. But if she's innocent she won't know what I'm getting at and she'll tell me where she was—so I risk nothing. If she did it, she'll be evasive, maybe furious. I'll see it, I'll know the truth. And she'll see that I know. And that risks everything. I'll be finished as her lawyer and I won't have a nickel's worth of proof.

He looked at his watch: it was nearly eight o'clock. He gathered up his things and locked the office and drove back to Ravendale to change for the party with Maria Hahn.

A bearded man at least six-and-a-half feet tall clapped Warren on the shoulder, yelling above the din, "So, little buddy, how come you're improperly dressed for this patriotic occasion?"

"Didn't know it was a costume party," Warren admitted.

"What?"

Warren yelled up, "I said, my sarong shrunk in the dryer!"

The bearded giant guffawed, then headed for the swimming pool on the lawn behind the house. Warren followed, en route snatching a piña colada off the bar.

It was his fourth since he and Maria Hahn had arrived at the Towering Texans' Fourth of July party, which was taking place in the home of a couple whose combined length stretched end to end, Warren had calculated, would be twelve feet five inches. The fifty large guests seemed to threaten the proportions of the house. Most of them had drifted to the back lawn and its limitless ceiling of starred July sky, where they could stretch their limbs and twirl their hips to the disco beat without fear of punching a hole in drywall.

Many of the tall people carried their drinks into the pool. No need to change clothes since the announced theme of the fiesta—bannered across the patio in computerized script (the host was a programmer for Compaq, but could not have worked on their speller utility)—was SOUTH SEAS INDEPENDENSE.

"Fuck," Maria exclaimed, when she and Warren arrived and saw that everyone was wearing thongs, muu-muus, feathers, and garlands of shells, "how come I forgot all about that?"

"Denial," Warren said. "I know a lot about that."

"We'll get sloshed," Maria proposed, "and then we can strip down to our whatevers and jump into the pool and no one will give a damn, least of all you and me."

Warren reminded her that one of them still had to negotiate his car homeward over thirty minutes of freeway on a holiday night.

Maria laughed. "Relax, counselor. I'll make sure you get back in one piece."

Was that stodgy of him? To want to arrive at his bed alive? He didn't think so. Maria was an oddball, a quiet adventurer. Contemplating that thought, his mind lay open and unguarded for a moment, and an idea invaded him. He hesitated, but being a hair more drunk than he realized, he passed in a matter of moments from hesitation to determination. There was something he had to do. Not only could he do it tonight, he *had* to do it tonight: the necessity of it punished him like iodine on an open wound. Tomorrow might be too late. How had he missed it? Not grasped that urgency?

The buzz in his head was wonderfully liberating, yet he knew that if he downed one more of the frosted rum drinks he would be inoperative. He roused the hard edge of his mind. Make the call, then go. He set the drink down on a patio table and turned back to the house. His watch said 11:25 P.M.

There was a pink wall telephone in the bathroom. Sitting on the closed toilet seat, Warren punched out the number of Ecstasy, the club that Johnnie Faye claimed not to own. It rang five times before he heard the blare of sound and then the announced name of the club.

"MCI operator. Person-to-person from Corpus Christi for Johnnie Faye Boudreau, ma'am."

The five-second wait was shorter than he had predicted. She must have been in the back office.

"Yes? Mama, is it you? What's wrong?"

Warren broke the connection by jabbing the # button a few times and then depressing the wall hookup, hoping to simulate an operator cutoff.

Maria's wiggling feet and shapely calves dangled in the water of the pool; she was talking with two women in muu-muus. Warren caught her eye, and she excused herself to come flowing over to him. He had never really noticed how graceful she was. Other things were more obvious: that witchlike laugh, the barrage of scatology.

"I'm having a fine time," he said, "but I have to go somewhere else. Take care of something. I should have told you about it before. And I might need some help."

"Boy, you *are* mysterious," she exclaimed, as if she had suspected it before and now he had confirmed it.

"I need a lookout. And a witness. No questions asked."

"Just one, my weirdo friend, if you don't mind. You going to rob a bank?"

"Photograph a car."

Maria didn't cross-examine, seeming to prefer the poetry of the unknown to prosaic reality. That was fine with Warren. She was Dwight Bingham's court reporter.

Down the darkened street from the party house he unlocked the door to the BMW. "You have your camera with you?" she asked.

"No, I'll have to . . . oh, shit!" he howled. "Charm has the fucking camera!"

Maria quickly touched his forearm with the tips of cool fingers. "Take it easy. I have a camera. And a flash. And film. Just stop off at my place and I'll get it, and then we'll go wherever you need to go, do whatever you have to do."

Half an hour later, Maria had changed into thonged sandals and a loose cotton dress with a sash of multicolored Thai silk. She snapped open the back of her Pentax and slipped in a fresh roll of Kodacolor 200. It was twenty minutes past midnight. Warren headed west for the Richmond strip.

She closed her eyes and was silent until they were nearly there. He thought that she was asleep.

"Want to hear a joke?" Before he could reply, Maria said, "Why do politicians have one more brain cell than horses do?"

Riddles were her favorites, he guessed. He said that he didn't know why.

"So they won't shit on the street during parades."

He laughed politely, then spotted the lights of Ecstasy. Outside the club, the glow from overhead street lamps cut the shadows of the night that lay upon the parking lot. Warren eased the BMW into a slot on the outer concrete edge, in darkness, not far from a fast-food chicken franchise. In the illuminated doorway of the club under flickering red neon script, silhouettes appeared: black figures scissored from tin. A hum of laughter followed by a salvo of music broke from the door into the night. Then the door squeezed pneumatically shut. The laughter and music ebbed away to silence.

"This car you want to photograph—"

"I see it."

He had worried that the Mercedes would be parked too close to the front door of the club. But the car was in the second row, about six spaces from the front door. Johnnie Faye must have arrived late.

"You want to tell me now what it's all about?" Maria asked.

"I really don't."

She laughed. "What can I say? Okay. Anything I can do to help?"

"Show me how this flash works, sit tight, and keep the motor running."

"Jeez, this is like an old movie."

Warren smiled automatically, but his heart clenched and suddenly picked up cadence. He remembered those old movies she referred to, where, in the getaway scene, something always went wrong.

He knew where Johnnie Faye lived, although he had never visited her apartment. He could have gotten his photo there the next morning when surely she would be asleep. Not surely: probably. And the high-rise had a locked underground garage, so he would need an electronic clicker to get in or else gain access through the building. And there might be an attendant. Too risky. But tonight, he realized, was riskier. He would need more than the photograph, maybe even a chemical analysis. Be smart: hire a private investigator to do the job. He hesitated, impaled by a thin needle of intelligence.

"I like you, Mr. Blackburn," Maria said.

"How come?"

"I'm trying to figure that out. I suppose it's mostly chemistry. Look"—taking the camera from his hands, she seated the flash in the sprocket—"you set it for distance here. When you push this button and the red light shows, all systems are go." She tested it and there was a fast bright glow. "Now you can click away. Just make sure the little red mother goes back on."

"I've got it," he said, but his resolve was buckling.

If I wait for another day or hire someone else to do it, the car's liable to be repainted by then. That was how things happened. You knew you had to do something but you put it off for what seemed such a good reason—and then, with no warning, opportunity slithered away, other cautions intervened: it was too late.

Make a beginning. Do it now.

"Maria, I may need you to verify what I'm going to do. Watch me."

"My son yells that when he jumps off the diving board into the neighbor's pool."

Warren walked through the warm night air toward Ecstasy. Nothing furtive, he decided. Do this fast.

Maria saw it all. Saw Warren crouch and raise the

Pentax as he reached the front of the light-colored Mercedes on the driver's side. Saw the thin little black man at the door of the club whose head swiveled toward Warren. Saw the man stare, then vanish. Heard the bass rock beat, then silence again.

Warren's back was to the club. He flicked the switch on the flash attachment and the red light popped on. Other cars blocked the gauzy glow of the parking-lot lamp. Peering through the camera's viewfinder, he found it more difficult than he had anticipated to focus the bull's-eye on the small blue scratch adorning the Mercedes' fender. He was sweating.

He clicked off one shot, noted with satisfaction the swift flood of white light, then moved left a pace and did it again.

How can I prove it was this car? *Her* car?

Back off, get all of it in frame. Then one more of the front license plate and the fender. An irrefutable sequence.

Maria heard the lunatic thump of music as the front door of the club opened and the thin black man and a taller white companion stepped out, bumping shoulders in their haste. Maria reached across to the driver's door and shoved it open. Twice, and loudly, she yelled Warren's name.

At fifteen feet Warren focused manually. He had nearly the whole car in frame, including the fender and the front plate. He pressed his eye once more against the viewfinder. The car went suddenly dark, obscured. Something tugged at the camera.

"What is this?"

Frank Sawyer, in the same black T-shirt and chinos that he had worn to the Astrodome, had one hand clamped around the Pentax lens. Lean and feral like a coyote, he confronted Warren. The dragon tattoo was flexing.

"The fuck you up to, counselor?"

The little black man had edged away. Trouble was for Sawyer to take care of. Sawyer stepped into the glow of the overhead lamp, his cold blue eyes austere, accusing, impeaching all possible innocence.

"Just doing my job, soldier," Warren said, and thought, that was pathetic. He had no excuses prepared. This was a job where if you failed, you failed utterly.

Muttering, Sawyer tried to yank the camera away, but the strap around Warren's neck prevented it. Warren felt himself being pulled forward awkwardly, and to stop that he shoved Sawyer in the center of the chest with a flat palm.

Dropping into a crouch, Sawyer hit Warren hard with a boxer's left hand, high on the face, between the cheekbone and ear. The knuckles drove deep into the nerve. The strap around his neck and Sawyer's grip on the lens kept Warren from falling to the concrete. But the world was darkening; he believed he was sinking to lightless depths a mile below the last glimmer of sun, drowning in an ooze of stupidity.

Frank Sawyer lowered him until he was prone, then tore the camera off his neck and smashed it onto the ground. He did that several times until the camera was reduced to junk.

Warren knew nothing of this: he heard distant crunches and spectral voices. His next awareness was of someone dragging him by the elbows. He was being lifted. There was an aroma of fruity perfume. He was crawling up into a soft seat. The seat was in his BMW. Maria's voice came from a hundred yards away in a mist.

". . . it's okay, it's okay. For God's sake, take it easy. . . ."

His mind and eyesight began to clear. Cool air washed over his cheeks. Maria Hahn was driving. They were on a boulevard, not a freeway. His head throbbed as if a drummer were using it for a martial beat. He made a major effort of will and stopped groaning.

"Where are we going?"

"To a hospital."

"I don't need a hospital. An ice pack would do the job."

"I yelled," Maria said. "You didn't hear me." The camera was gone, she told him. She didn't know what Sawyer had done with it. He had just walked away, back into the club.

"He took the camera? That's rotten. I owe you a camera." Warren raised his head a little from the seat, saw streetlights whip by and at the same time felt raw pain. He wanted to tell her something that seemed important. It was amazing how the past intruded on the present, but usually too late to take advantage.

"When I was a little kid," he said, finding the words with difficulty, "my father took me to a farm in Fort Bend County where there was this mule. I ran up to it, thought it was a horse, wanted to ride it. My father pulled me away and said, 'Watch out, son, it's dangerous.' But this old farmer boy said to me, 'Boy, that mule t'weren't gone hurt you. You never could have got close enough to it.' "

He bedded down on Maria's living room couch, an insulated bag of ice pressed to the right side of his face. Maybe his cheekbone was broken, but he knew from his visit to Hermann Hospital that you couldn't set a cheekbone. The pain kept him awake, but the wakefulness allowed him to stumble to the kitchen and change the ice every hour or so. He had swallowed two Empirin with codeine and knocked back several shots of Stolichnaya.

At 4 A.M. he took the icy vodka bottle to bed with him as a companion, pressing it against his forehead when he was not tilting it to his lips.

His dreams were not pleasant. He was the wheel man in a get away car in front of a bank. It was all in black and white. His pals came running out with the loot. He turned the key, and the engine wouldn't start. In another dream, this one in color, the mule kicked him. In another, an airport scene, Charm was smirking at him. Then she turned her back and walked away through the dusk toward a private plane that was taking her to New York and out of his life forever.

A small boy stood over him, watching, as Warren opened one glued eye. The living room was shadowed, the blinds drawn, but clearly it was morning. The boy had freckles and curly brown hair and an interested expression.

He heard Maria Hahn's voice: "Randy, don't bother him. Let him sleep. . . ."

The boy's face disappeared. Warren's eye closed.

He awoke again at ten in the morning. In Maria's bathroom mirror he observed that the right side of his face was swollen. With each step or each movement of his head came jolts of affliction. Shadows had bloomed under his eyes and the eyes were pink. The bruise on his cheek was a shiny green edged with purple, the coloring of certain large, vicious Texas bottle flies.

He walked slowly out of the bathroom. Maria's neck tilted gracefully from a navy blue terry cloth bathrobe. She was barefoot on the kitchen floor.

"How you feeling?"

"I've felt better."

"Looked it too. You hungry?"

"Yes, please." Coming to terms with what his body was telling him, he decided to abdicate any pretense at control and settle into a natural state of helplessness.

At the breakfast table she stirred eggs and fried some bacon. The smell made his stomach queasy. He asked, "Where's your son?"

"Gone over to a friend's house. Will you tell me what this was all about? I think I need to know."

"I can't do that," he said.

"Can't, or won't?"

"Can't. Believe me. I'm sorry."

Maria took a turn around the kitchen, leaving the bacon to sputter, while she worked at accepting that answer.

"Okay," she said, "for now. What's your plan?"

He felt cobwebbed, heavy-legged. He had no plan. He had plenty of misgivings and regrets but no plan. But he tried to focus on one.

The Fourth of July party had been held yesterday, on Monday. All offices and the Harris County courts were closed today. Jury selection for *Quintana* would start tomorrow. Doggedly, with suffering brain cells, Warren recalled that he had two tasks scheduled for today. Go to Hermann Park and twist old Pedro's arm to ensure his testimony on Hector Quintana's behalf the following week. Have the photographs of the Mercedes developed, printed, and enlarged.

That was no longer on the docket. By now Frank Sawyer was probably under orders to grab a wad of sandpaper and bucket of paint and do the job on the car.

Sorry, Hector, I tried.

Not good enough. Johnnie Faye Boudreau would dump him as her lawyer. She would go before Judge Bingham tomorrow and tell him she'd lost faith, hadn't realized that her lawyer was so inexperienced. Bingham would grant a continuance until she could find someone else. The story would spread. Warren's grand comeback would be a downfall.

"My plan," he said to Maria Hahn, "is to dig a cool hole and crawl into it."

"You can do better than that," Maria said.

He probably could. And should. And would. He was grateful to Maria. Why was she being so kind to him? He wasn't used to that lately.

"Just as soon as I finish these eggs. They're delicious. They're wonderful. They're the best eggs I've ever eaten."

Maria laughed and looked at him with friendly blue eyes.

At noon, with the July heat building, he drove to the stables at Hermann Park. The shed was empty. The pot with fried crackling grease was gone. A black man was hard at work cleaning a stall in the stables.

"There were two men here," Warren said. "Two Mexicans."

"They gone."

"When?"

"Day before I came."

"When was that?"

"That was Thursday, Friday."

"I don't believe this. Where did they go? Does anyone know?"

The man shrugged.

Gone. Vanished, like Hector had once vanished, like the scar on the fender of the Mercedes would vanish. Like the case for Hector's defense, already so shitty, would vanish if he couldn't find Pedro. He stamped the turf with frustration. I should have gone last week—should have gone there twice a week to keep Pedro in line. Should have set the Mexican up in a hotel room. Should have given him more money. Should have gone to Johnnie Faye's garage instead of the club, or hired a professional to do the job.

With sudden malignance, the blood throbbed through the vessels in Warren's head. He felt dizzy and stumbled toward shade, a tree dappled by light, where he leaned against the rough bark for several minutes.

He drove back to his office on Montrose for the solace of a cold beer and a darkened room and penitent silence. The red light on his message machine was blinking. The first calm voice was that of Arthur Franklin, Charm's divorce lawyer, who asked Warren to return the call at his earliest convenience.

Okay, Arthur Franklin. Will do.

The second voice was Johnnie Faye Boudreau's. Call me back today, she commanded. I want to see you. We have a lot to talk about, lawyer buddy.

* * *

Her apartment was on the eighteenth floor of a new-mint brick building overlooking the Texas Medical Center, with a sweeping view of downtown Houston: mirrors of glass and steel backlit by sun. Warren had expected modern decor, but Johnnie Faye's living room was an old lady's, crowded with memorabilia and fussy furniture. Gold-framed photographs stared gloomily from every wall: her mother, father, brothers, other family, herself when young and innocent. Surfaces were covered with knickknacks and bowls, jars, vases, porcelain statuary. There was an antique grandfather clock and one oil painting of a western sunset. The mahogany sideboard and credenza both had bowlegs. The carpet was faded Shiraz, the drapes mauve damask, the TV a big RCA console. A glassed-in bookcase was crammed with more eclectic junk.

"You can see," Johnnie Faye said, "that I'm a collector."

She wore gold tasseled slippers and a glittering gold pantsuit that highlighted creamy cleavage and her narrow waist. Settling into an ornate Queen Anne chair, she put her feet up on a hassock. A pitcher of iced tea, two glasses, and a bowl of sliced lemons stood on the little coffee table.

"Minute I got that phone call supposed to be from Corpus, I knew something was out of line. You got to respect my sixth sense, counselor. And if it wasn't my mama, which I found out quick enough it wasn't, who was it? Somebody wanted to make sure I was there at the club, and deviltry was afoot. But why? That's what I asked myself. . . ." She raised her glass of iced tea in what amounted to a toast to her acuity. "So I sent a guy back here to guard the fort at home, and I told Frankie to keep an eye peeled at the club in case anything odd went down. And it sure did. You look like stepped-on dogshit. But you got what you deserved, you can't complain."

"Do you have any Bufferin?"

"I have Bayer and Tylenol and Excedrin and Midol.

And I have some good Sonora grass and some real good coke."

She was a consumer as well as a collector.

She fetched a tray of assorted medication, and Warren swallowed two aspirin with an iced-tea chaser. Johnnie Faye opened a pretty little green Kashmiri papier-mâché box; in it were half a dozen neatly rolled joints and a little cellophane bag of white powder. She took a joint from the pile and got it going with a gold Ronson. When she offered it, he thought, what the hell. This was so crazy anyway.

The hot smoke tore at his lungs. His fingertips tingled.

"You're my lawyer," Johnnie Faye said, "and I'm supposed to level with you. But it's a two-way street. So I think I've got a right to know just what there is about my car that makes you want it in your scrapbook. But," she said slyly, "I'm not about to ask you, because you'd lie. And that would piss me off considerably. So keep quiet, counselor, and listen to me."

It was all so civilized and polite. He was sitting with a woman who had probably murdered three people—three that he knew of. She was serving him afternoon tea and aspirin and he was sharing a joint with her. That's what it meant to be a lawyer. But where did it end?

"You're still my lawyer," she said, as if she had read his mind. "And I need your advice. If I committed another crime, could they bring that up when I go to trial for what happened to Clyde? Could they ask me if I did it?"

Warren grew wary, but he was obliged to answer honestly.

"They can ask you in cross-examination," he replied, like a man on the edge of a chasm, "if they have a reasonable ground to believe you did it. But they're bound by your answer. They can't contradict you or then bring in proof that you committed the other crime."

"Even a murder?"

"Yes, even a murder."

"Even if it's the murder of that Vietnamese guy you think I killed?"

He felt himself growing pale. So it was true. "Yes," he said.

"Well, I did it. In self-defense. I had to."

Warren's heart began to beat out of rhythm. But he said carefully, "You shot him in the Wesleyan Terrace parking lot outside the dry cleaners. You used a .32, and then you shoved it in a Dumpster in some apartment complex."

Saying nothing, Johnnie Faye took a deep drag, then passed him the joint. Warren shook his head in refusal.

"Why?" he asked, dumbfounded.

She told him—

Heading back home that day from Lord & Taylor and Neiman's, with her booty and cash to spare, she had a choice of battling the red lights on Westheimer or the traffic on the Southwest Freeway. Johnnie Faye chose the freeway.

Cars were backed up ahead of her as far as she could see. An accident, she decided, or some beaner's rattly pickup run out of oil in the fast lane. Creeping along at fifteen miles an hour in her Mercedes, she turned up the air-conditioning a notch, lit a Marlboro, and punched in a tape of Led Zeppelin.

That was when the Ford Fairlane wagon tried to get off the freeway. She didn't blame him for that—it was on her mind too. But he didn't signal, and he clipped her bumper, powered into the right lane in front of a braking semi, and headed for the exit ramp to Wesleyan.

She cut off two vehicles to catch up to him, but she peeled no paint. At the first red light on Wesleyan she drew parallel and leaned on the horn.

She yelled, "Hey, pull over, motherfucker! I want to talk to you!"

Her window was shut and he couldn't hear her. Now she saw him clearly for the first time and realized even if he'd heard her he probably wouldn't have understood a word, because he was a slope: the usual black hair and threatening deadpan look.

The light flicked to green and he was off again. She hit the accelerator and drilled after him and then, serendipitously, he popped the wagon into the parking lot in front of the dry cleaners. Even as she buzzed down her window Johnnie Faye saw the Indian woman stacking cardboard boxes. This place, she thought, used to be the United States of America. Now it's an Asian dumping ground.

She began yelling, giving him what-for. Dan Ho Trunh didn't reply, just gazed at her as if she were a freak. His face twisted a little, although still there was no real expression. But she had seen *Platoon* and *Full Metal Jacket,* she knew what these people were capable of. Her brothers had died for these foreign dirtballs.

He cursed back at her, she told Warren, hissed through his protruding white teeth and reached back toward his pants pocket to take something out of it. Johnnie Faye felt a surge of terror. This was the way your life could end, in a parking lot you didn't know, at the hands of an alien stranger. She twisted the knob of the glove compartment and snatched the .32-caliber Diamondback Colt that lay among the stack of cassette tapes. In one practiced motion she snapped the safety to the Off position.

The Vietnamese straightened up, and there was something dark in his right hand and it was pointed at her.

"I guess I screamed," she said to Warren. "But I did to him before he could do to me. The Golden Rule."

Breathing rapidly, jerkily, heart pounding, thanking the Lord above that she'd been spared, and congratulating herself on having been ready, willing, and able to defend her life, Johnnie Faye burned rubber.

The Diamondback Colt lay on the seat next to her. Loved that little gun, she thought sadly. But it has to go.

* * *

Warren believed that she believed what she was telling him. You had to see it from her point of view, as a jury would be instructed to do. *"Murder is a way of working out problems and settling scores,"* Altschuler had said. An obvious, instant, primitive solution. Only when it was done did her sophisticated self take over to muddy the trail. Warren had never known anyone like this, but he had known such mutants existed.

He asked, "Did you ever hear of a man named Hector Quintana?"

"You can't be serious," Johnnie Faye said, frowning. "You must think I came in with the first load of watermelon. Hector Quintana's the name of the guy you're defending in that other case, isn't it? The one where you were appointed by some woman judge?"

Warren nodded, but he was bewildered at her knowledge. Clearly there was a logical connection that he had missed. Staring at her, he asked, "And what about Quintana?"

"He didn't do it, which we both know now. So you'll get him off, same way you'll get me off for shooting Clyde in self-defense."

Simple as that. She was a woman of immense faith. Blood throbbed in Warren's temples.

"And let's get something real clear between us," Johnnie Faye said strongly. She had allowed the joint to expire in an ashtray. She sipped at her iced tea, then set it down on a cork coaster. She leaned forward across the table, fixing him with her thoughtful bicolored eyes. "You're still my lawyer. I'm keeping you on."

He stared at her, unbelieving. He had thought this was the kiss-off.

"You want to know why? Because I know you better than you think. Maybe in some ways better than your wife does. That's called intuition. Comes from experience, and I've got it." She smiled at him with her lips but not with her eyes; they were still probing and cold.

"You don't know me," Warren said.

"I do. You may not like that, but it's true. You're square, like I told you the other night. Straight. Boy Scout rules. You won't let me down. If you're my lawyer, you'll do the best you can. Maybe even better now that you know what you know. Because you'll be afraid not to."

"What makes you think," Warren asked, "that I still want to be your lawyer?"

"Don't you?" She seemed amused by the question. "I thought this was a big deal for you."

"If they still had hanging in this state," Warren said hoarsely, "I'd knot the noose, and not too tight. I'd put the fucking needle in your arm myself."

"Sure," Johnnie Faye said, "sure, in your fantasies. That's natural. But not in reality. See? I do know you. Why quit my case? What do you gain by quitting? You can't go to the D.A. You're my lawyer now, and you were yesterday and the week before and the week before that. Everything I told you is secret between us, even if you quit me. Now and forever, no exceptions. I checked the law, I have friends who understand these things. *Confidential* is the word, right? You can help me win, and you and that wisecracking Jewboy are going to do that. *But you can't tell anyone what I told you.* Isn't that so, counselor?"

He failed to halt a groan. "Why did Scoot pick *me*?"

"Why did—?" Johnnie Faye's eyes widened. "You think it's a coincidence, right? Just bad luck, what you might call irony, that you're Quintana's lawyer and my lawyer too?"

Seeing his expression, she slapped her own cheek in mock astonishment. "You still don't get it!"

"I guess not," Warren said quietly, dreading what was to come.

Leaning forward almost eagerly across the little table, Johnnie Faye explained, "I read in the *Chronicle* that the Quintana guy had been arrested for killing the slope, and I was a little bit interested, you might say, in how things would work out. Then Mr. Shepard calls me in and informs me he needs some help in my case: 'There are a few good lawyers I can pick from, but it's your money, so I'll tell you a bit about each one and you can give me some input.' Your name's on the list. Mr. Shepard tells me what you did way back when, and he says, 'But now this fella's on the comeback trail, and he's real sharp. He was just appointed to defend some illegal alien shot a Vietnamese.' "

A few minutes later Johnnie Faye concluded that "Warren Blackburn sounds like the right man."

Keep Blackburn close. Keep an eye on him. Learn what he knows.

Warren shook his head in numbed wonder. By taking him on as her lawyer, she ensured his silence if he discovered anything that implicated her in the death of Dan Ho Trunh. Did that mean that from the outset she had imagined the day would come when, gleefully, and with freedom from harm, she would confess?

I don't believe I want to know the answer to that, Warren thought. The muscles of his legs pressed hard on the floor. His fists clenched at his sides. His breaths had grown shallow.

"Why do you believe," he asked, "that if I defended you in court on the Ott murder, I wouldn't throw you to the dogs? I could fuck it up so badly the jury wouldn't even have to leave the courtroom to hand down a guilty verdict."

"I thought about that," Johnny Faye said. "I lost a lot of sleep over that. You can't do that. You fuck up, they'll see it. You'll be out on your ass again. I'll get a new trial, I'll get someone else to defend me." She patted his sleeve. "And you won't do any of that. I know you. You'll do your best. You'll do your job. That's the way you are, counselor. That's why I like you. And I like the idea of having you around me, so I can still keep an eye on you." She yawned, reached for a cigarette. "Sleep on it. Get used to the idea. You'll see I'm right."

"What if Hector Quintana's convicted?" Warren asked, his mind gray with helplessness. "What if I can't save him? What if he gets death, or life in prison?"

"A sad song don't care whose heart it breaks," Johnnie Faye Boudreau said. "You of all people should know that."

"All rise!" the bailiff cried, as Judge Lou Parker swept into the courtroom to take her seat behind the high oak bench for the capital murder trial of Hector Quintana.

Her gaze flicked like a bullwhip from counsel tables to jury box to the dozen or so Vietnamese spectators. In her flowing black robes, her brown hair with steel-gray streaks swept into a bun at the back of her powerful neck, she was a force as irresistible as a high wind, as implacable as a boulder. Most other judges, on the engraved plaque nailed to the face of the judicial bench, had an announcement that proclaimed: *Hon. So-and-So* (with full name, including middle initial), *District Judge, 299th Circuit Court.* But the plaque on Louise Ann Parker's bench said: *Lou Parker, Judge.* The message escaped only the dull-witted or the hopeful.

On this day, courtesy of the State of Texas, Hector Quintana wore a reasonably well fitting blue suit, white shirt and dark blue tie, black shoes and socks. Standing next to his client at the defense table as the judge entered, Warren placed a hand on Hector's arm and squeezed it quickly.

For courage.

Goodpaster was seasoned and swift. In her opening statement to the jury she said repeatedly, "The evidence will show . . ." and all the while she made eye contact with the jurors. Warren watched them nod as they looked at her. They saw a bright young black woman, not too pretty as to make them envious, not too didactic to make them feel she condescended. She wore a mustard-colored blouse under a cheap serge suit that was exactly the same shade of blue as Hector's. Maybe, Warren thought, she had hiked her ass down to Kuppenheimer's.

"The evidence will show," Goodpaster concluded, "that the defendant"—she faced him squarely and jabbed a finger at Hector exactly the way they taught it at prosecutors' seminars, on the theory that if you don't do it the jury will believe your heart is not in it—"set out deliberately not merely to rob Dan Ho Trunh but to murder him. Ladies and gentlemen, the evidence will show that the murder was not the result of any struggle. There was no threat to the assailant and no resistance. The evidence will show that Hector Quintana intended from the very beginning to kill Dan Ho Trunh in order to steal a sum of less than $150. The evidence will show cold-blooded, premeditated murder of an unarmed human being."

Seated now, Hector Quintana threw his shaking hands up in the air. He groaned loudly—the wail of a tortured soul.

The piteous cry echoed through the courtroom. Every eye swung in his direction. Nancy Goodpaster's mouth fell open. For three full seconds the room was preternaturally silent, so that Warren could hear the thump of his own heart. Could a guilty man emit such a ravaged sound? Would the jury not grasp the truth?

Judge Parker cracked the silence: "*Counselor, don't let that happen again!* No more outbursts! I want his hands on the table or I'll have them cuffed!"

Warren whispered in Hector's ear, "Don't do that again." He added, more softly, "Not today."

When Goodpaster sat down, the judge waved a pale, many-ringed hand at the defense attorney.

The whole right side of Warren's face ached, but the headache was gone. The bottle-fly bruise was turning from black-green to purple. His story was that at two o'clock in the morning, coming back from the tall people's party, he had blown a tire on the freeway. He had changed it himself; the jack had slipped. Warren had no idea whether anyone believed him.

He had prepared a short opening speech, but now he changed his mind. He cleared his throat and stood to face the jury.

Warren said, "Hector Quintana is innocent. He's innocent of everything he's been charged with. Not just 'not guilty' under the law, but truly innocent. The defense will show that he wasn't there. The defense will show that he didn't kill Dan Ho Trunh, and that this entire case is a frightening miscarriage of justice. And we will prove it to you beyond a reasonable doubt."

That was as far as he dared go.

The night after his meeting with Johnnie Faye Boudreau he had paced the carpet in his apartment, stared sightlessly at images on the TV, thumbed through law books and tomes on legal ethics. A great deal had been written about attorney-client privilege and the duty to keep or disclose client confidences. The lawyer as whistle-blower was a favorite topic for Bar Association symposiums. Debate was heated.

Warren had gone out to the balcony, where he gazed at a few stars glowing faintly between massed clouds. The heat pressed against his temples. He let cups of coffee grow cold.

One thing was clear. A trial was ostensibly a search for truth, but the test for truth was relevance and conformity to statute. No witness who swore to tell "the truth, the whole truth, and nothing but the truth" would be permitted to do so. The mantle of innocence was flung over the defendant to such an extent that he—or she—was safeguarded by rules of evidence which often barred revelation of that total truth. A defendant had the rights of counsel, trial by jury, due process, and the privilege against self-incrimination. To tell a secret to a lawyer believing that it was inviolate, and then have that lawyer reveal the secret, was a form of self-incrimination. The Code of Professional Responsibility and its fourth canon said: no matter how heinous the secret, to reveal it is forbidden.

Surely in this instance, Warren thought, there are overriding concerns, graver duties. What about his obligation to Hector Quintana?

Frantically he checked federal and Texas case law, just as Johnnie Faye Boudreau must have done. This too was stunningly clear: a client's confession about an unrelated crime must not be disclosed. The canon read: "A lawyer shall not knowingly use a confidence or secret of his client for the advantage of himself or of a third person unless the client consents after full disclosure." Confidentiality was sacred. And privileged communication did not lose its privileged status by reason of terminating the relationship. Even if Warren quit her in the Ott case, he was bound by the bond of silence. He was priest, she was penitent—forever.

No, he thought, this can't be. Whatever the penalty, I've still got to do it. If the law is an ass, so be it, but I am a human being.

The canons allowed him, since he had not been instructed otherwise, to share his knowledge with co-counsel. Late the next afternoon he went to Rick Levine's office. As afternoon cooled toward evening they walked together through Tranquility Park on the edge of the hard silver center of the city.

"You dumb son of a bitch," Rick said, "if you hadn't gone to her and given her that chance to throw a noose around your neck, you could have run right over to the D.A.'s office!"

"And told him that I suspected her? That I saw her car with a blue scratch on it? What good would that have done? I had no fucking *proof*!"

"There must be exceptions to the privilege rule," Rick said gloomily.

"Yeah, there are four exceptions. If your client gives you

permission, if a client tells you about a crime planned for the future, if it's the only way you can collect your fee, or if it's to defend yourself against a false accusation of wrongful conduct."

"Well, she's paid us, so that won't work. You don't think it would be wrongful conduct to let this guy Quintana go to jail for a murder that the dragon lady committed?"

"I do, but there's no accusation against me. That could only be if Quintana is convicted. And so what happens if I speak up then? I still have no proof! I can't nail Johnnie Faye to the wall, and if I can't do that I can't save Quintana."

They sat under a magnolia tree near a small pond and some beds of golden poppies. Lovely, Warren thought. The world is lovely. Humans are all that's corrupt.

Rick shrugged. "Then go to the D.A. now and tell him that you saw the scratches on the two cars. You figured it out all on your own. You never talked to her, she never confessed, and you're not violating confidentiality. Dump that in the D.A.'s lap and let him run with it."

Warren laughed bitterly. "I thought of that too. So they'll investigate her, but they can't prove anything. And then she brings charges against me before the judicial committee. She says, 'This guy lied four years ago in the Freer case, didn't he? He's doing it again. He hates me, and he's doing this to me to save another client's ass.' The D.A. may insist I take a polygraph. And I won't pass the test because I'll be lying about the lack of the confession. Then I'm disbarred."

"Go to Nancy Goodpaster or Lou Parker. You have a duty to try and save Hector's ass."

Warren slammed a fist on the grass. "Don't you think I know that? Parker would have a fucking orgasm if she thought she could get me disbarred for violating privilege. Nancy will say, 'That's all well and good, counselor, but how do I know you're telling the truth? Where's your proof? What am I supposed to do, Mr. Blackburn, drop a case because you say someone other than your client is guilty? The facts indicate otherwise. There's possession of the gun. There's positive I.D. by an eyewitness. Nice try, counselor.' "

Warren sniffed at the scent of roses brought by an early evening breeze. It brought no pleasure. "I'm going to withdraw from *Quintana*," he said, standing pale in the last sunlight.

"And you think Hector's going to understand what you're telling him, and why you're bowing out right in the middle of voir dire?"

"No, he won't," Warren said.

"Parker will appoint someone like Myron Moore. Myron will plead your guy out for forty years before you can say jackshit. Can you live with that?"

"I can't live with any of it," Warren groaned.

"I don't know what to tell you, except not to let Johnnie Faye know you talked to me. She'll freak out. We don't need that."

Warren left the park no wiser than when he had entered it.

That evening in his apartment he thought, my obligation is not only to my client Hector Quintana, and to my client Johnnie Faye Boudreau, and to the canons of ethics and to the rule of law—above all, it's to my conscience. An agnostic on the question of where ultimate truth lay, Warren nevertheless felt himself committed to a process untainted by false or incomplete disclosure. Once again he remembered the Freer case. He had thought, until now, that he had learned his lesson. With Virgil Freer he had broken the rules and countenanced fraud by lying. Here, if he *obeyed* the rules, he would countenance fraud by silence.

That struck him as mildly insane.

I can violate confidentiality, he decided. I can go to Charm, and if she can't do anything, to the rest of the media—I can disclose what I know. *I'm giving up my practice. I wouldn't do that if I weren't telling you the truth.*

Help this man! And they might headline it, exploit it as juicy news.

But how would that help Hector? The jury had taken an oath to decide Hector's guilt or innocence based on the evidence alone. That oath would not change.

The law, Warren thought bitterly, protects us from barbarism, and in its place gives us the barbarism of the law.

I can violate confidentiality, yes, and I will . . . *if there's a purpose.* If there's no purpose, there's no sense. I can't desert Hector Quintana now. I know things that no other lawyer could ever know. There's no answer to this, no decent solution. Day to day. Stick with it. Stick with both cases. Wait, like a lion in the brush, for the prey to show itself and make a mistake. Stick close to her, for the same reason she wants to stick close to me, and see what happens.

In the Dark Ages, guilt or innocence was often resolved by having the accused walk barefoot and blindfolded over nine red-hot plowshares laid lengthwise at unequal distances. If he was burned, he was declared guilty.

Not much had changed, Warren thought.

Less than twenty-four hours after he knew who had murdered Dan Ho Trunh, he and Nancy Goodpaster had begun to pick the jury that would decide the life or death of Hector Quintana. He had little faith that you could predict what any individual juror would do. You could eliminate a few obvious killers, the devout Lutherans and the thin-lipped retirees who assumed, no matter how the judge lectured them, that the defendant was guilty until proved innocent. The prosecutor would strike the obvious bleeding hearts. Beyond that, Warren operated on a simple principle: if you don't like a juror's face, chances are he doesn't like yours—better get rid of him. If they keep smiling at you, take them. He often asked, "If you were the accused, would you want someone like yourself on this jury?" It usually worked: before his years of court-appointed plea bargaining he had won more than his fair share of trials. He was a little rusty now, but it would all come back.

Defense and prosecution were each allotted a set number of peremptory strikes—disqualification of jurors with no reason given. Goodpaster used most of her strikes to eliminate Hispanics. On his part Warren had made up his mind not to let any Asians on the jury, but none were in the panel. He wanted young jurors. He theorized that the young ones would have more sympathy for an illegal alien, a member of the new legion of homeless. If sympathy mattered, if sympathy could overpower evidence, if it wasn't a matter of a blind man dodging red-hot plowshares.

On the first morning Warren took Hector to the rear of Judge Parker's courtroom and said, "Listen carefully. Lawyers don't usually give a rat's ass if a client is guilty or not guilty. We just do the best we can. It's actually better if you believe your client did it. If the jury convicts him, you think, well, so what? The rotten son of a bitch got what he deserved."

He didn't add that if you believe your man is innocent, it tears your heart out when the jury doesn't believe you.

Hector blinked a few times.

"I *know* you didn't do it," Warren said.

Hector nodded in silence. Cold comfort, Warren realized, on your way to prison or death row. But it was all that Warren could offer.

In the midst of voir dire he had taken Maria Hahn to an Italian restaurant for dinner. "I haven't done anything about replacing the camera, but I will. I promise. I'm not quite with it these days. I'm feeling a little crazy."

Maria waved her hand in dismissal, rosy fingernails glittering in candlelight. Later, outside the restaurant, Warren kissed her on the cheek fraternally and said good night.

Two days after that, at noon, he bumped into her in a crowded courthouse elevator. She clasped his arm. "You look awful," she whispered. "I'll buy you lunch. Cheer you up."

Nothing dark or desperate or depressing about lovely Maria Hahn. She could pick her affairs, if that's how she wanted to play the game. Then what did she want from him? Friendship? Company? What he wanted too. A perfect match for this macabre season of his thirty-fifth year. If his loins stirred, he had that under control. But he sensed a naivete in his thinking. "Independence," Charm had once said, "is an unnatural state for any woman with intelligence and normal DNA."

A day at a time in this too. Don't say anything you don't mean. If you don't know what you mean, then shut up. That seemed a decent enough formula for survival when your wife was divorcing you and you were swimming upstream to save the life of a client you knew beyond all doubt was innocent.

He reached for the check at lunch. "I invited you," Maria reminded him.

"Too late."

"I want my Pentax."

"Give me until Friday night."

"It's a date—I'll take you to dinner. And leave your money at home."

The *Quintana* jury was picked and sworn by Thursday. It comprised seven men and five women: seven were white, five were black, half were under thirty. Warren was guardedly pleased, but he knew that from the moment a jury is sworn it becomes a new creature with its own separate life.

Judge Parker instructed the jurors not to discuss the case among themselves or even with family, and to be in court by 8:30 A.M. Monday.

The next day Warren stopped at a discount camera store and bought the Pentax, then lugged his heavy briefcase up to Arthur Franklin's law firm on the thirtieth floor of the Texas Commerce Tower. Charm's lawyer was in his sixties, a man with a smooth face and clear eyes, dressed in a gray suit, blue chalk-striped shirt, red power tie: a Texan who had gone to Harvard. His office smelled of wood polish, Havana cigars, and tax-free bonds. Maybe, Warren thought, I should have gone into civil law. I'd be bored, but I wouldn't lose so fucking much sleep. I wouldn't have to deal with murderers and scumbags and accused innocent men.

"You're an attorney, Mr. Blackburn. You know these matters are never pleasant, but they needn't be acrimonious." Arthur Franklin followed with the short form of the standard divorce lawyer's speech. In the end Warren agreed to all of Charm's terms. There was nothing to argue about. But he felt rotten all over again. A part of his life was ending. Had ended. In the elevator he shook his head, bewildered. A woman in the elevator looked at him, then took a defensive step backward. Warren realized he had clenched his fists and his lips were drawn back in a silent snarl.

No fucking wonder.

He went home to shower and feed Oobie, and at eight o'clock he met Maria Hahn at a French restaurant in River Oaks. Warren looked at the menu and said, "Do you mind if I ask you something gauche? Can you afford this?"

"Sure," Maria said. "Not all the time, but life is short."

She was paid a salary for her normal day in Judge Bingham's court, she explained, but by the page for extra work. She did best when there were appeals that required the entire record, or big cases with well-heeled clients like drug dealers whose lawyers requested day-by-day expedited transcripts of testimony. She had a second stenograph machine at home in her spare bedroom. Sometimes she worked until midnight. "The kid has to go to college one day. He says he wants to be a doctor, and you know what that costs since Reagan fucked up the scholarship program. Randy's a smart boy. I was thinking of the Ivy League. Penn or Cornell."

"A little early for that, isn't it?"

"You have to plan ahead."

"My wife went to Penn," Warren said.

Maria smiled easily. "Good for her."

After espresso, the restaurant offered a snifter of Remy Martin to honor the 200th anniversary of Bastille Day. Warren lifted his glass. "To independence."

Maria paid the bill with a Visa card and said, "Let's have the other half at my house. I own a whole bottle of Courvoisier. We'll celebrate the revolution the way the French do."

She lived nearby in an English Tudor condo tucked behind Westheimer, just inside the Loop. Following her there in his car, Warren came to the conclusion that it would have been churlish and unfriendly to say no. Just one drink. All the way there he thought about Hector Quintana and Johnnie Faye Boudreau.

Maria's son was spending a month with his grandparents over in Austin. Maria put some Spanish guitar music on the tape deck, turned the volume low, kicked off her shoes, then dropped down next to Warren on the living room sofa. The room was cool and lighted with the discreet glow of two table lamps. The drink warmed him, the sofa was soft; like any stray, his response to these comforts was instantaneous. Extracting the half-finished glass of cognac from his hands, Maria set it on the coffee table. Her lower lip was slightly heavy and slack. She leaned toward him and kissed him. He was taken by surprise—but not really. He had seen it coming. Just one kiss.

But the kiss continued and Warren enjoyed it beyond expectation. She was a beautiful woman, he believed. He had always admired her oddly tilted Modigliani neck. The veins of its slender arch pulsed under his fingertips. He began to kiss it, running his lips from top to bottom and then up again, touching all its quadrants while she shuddered against him. She wore no bra, and he could feel that her breasts were round, soft but growing firmer against his chest. From beyond expectation he moved to beyond reason. Still . . .

"Maria—"

"Oh, shut up," she said quietly. "I promise it won't hurt. Let's just do it."

Warren left her condo at six o'clock on Saturday morning and drove to Ravendale, where he fetched his briefcase and Oobie and a sack of dog food. He drove back quickly on the empty freeway. From beyond reason he had passed to a state that was beyond control. Maria's bed was queen-sized, with half a dozen plump down pillows in frilled, peach-colored pillowcases. He had wondered if he would have a problem, if Charm would intrude. He had wondered too if Maria had wondered.

"Let's just fuck till we're dead," Maria said.

Stop wondering. This woman is accommodating, and her body is warm. She's lighthearted and alive. And today, for a change, so am I.

They stayed in bed most of the day with the blinds drawn, the cool air blowing. He could not remember when he had made love with this kind of energy and uncomplicated wantonness. He gave the credit to Maria, but he was pleased with himself. What traps life springs on us. And what pleasure it offers when we don't think too much, don't deny and don't lie.

In the late afternoon, when he took Oobie for a run, Maria went out to rent videos of *Jean de Florette* and *Manon of the Spring*. Warren had never seen either movie. For Maria it was the third time. Nevertheless, tears sprang to her eyes on and off during the four hours.

"Let's not go out again," she decided. "Let's hide our watches and the clock."

She called a nearby mall to order a pizza and two cold six-packs. During the night she slept against his back, leaving a cool layer of sweat from shoulder blades to thighs. There were pizza crumbs under the pillows.

On Sunday morning she brought trays of eggs benedict and cappuccino to the bed. "My culinary specialty," she said.

"I know what your real specialty is, Hahn."

"No, Blackburn, you don't."

In mid-morning, when he propped himself up against the pillows and tried to work his way yet again through the *Quintana* file, she showed him. Later he asked, "Have you got anything to read?" She admitted she was in the middle of a novel by Jackie Collins—it lay on the carpet beside the bed. While she clutched it to her flushed face, heaving cries that made Oobie rush in from the kitchen in alarm, as if firecrackers had gone off, Warren returned the favor.

When it began to grow dark he slipped out from under the sheet and pulled his watch from the bureau drawer. Feeling wonderfully decadent, drained, boneless, he dressed slowly. Maria announced that she was going to stay there in bed. Sleep till morning.

"Thank you," he said.

"For what?"

She had resurrected his cock, he explained. He had thought all desire, all sense of pleasure, was dead.

"Are you telling me," she said, "that the cock leads the man?"

"No, but it's nice to have it along on the journey."

"Get out, you lawyer." She waved at him as he moved toward the door.

At home he studied the state's order of proof in *Quintana,* then his own witness list. The time with Maria faded from his mind. It had been a dream. He was back into the nightmare. And on the following morning, a hazy day with some thunderheads lurking on the horizon toward the Gulf of Mexico, and with the temperature registering 94 degrees on the thermometer outside the courthouse, he began the first trial.

The bailiff led Hector Quintana out of the holding cell. On one of its azure-painted walls a prisoner had scrawled "The Blue Room of Doom," and in another handwriting someone had printed "Parker's Court of Western Justice." Judge Lou Parker refused to allow the graffiti to be scrubbed off.

Wearing the austere jet-black robes of absolute authority, her hair glittering more iron-gray than brown in the light of banked fluorescent tubes, Judge Parker peered down from the height of the judicial bench. She nodded in the direction of Nancy Goodpaster. "You may call your first witness, Madam Prosecutor."

"The state calls Khuong Nguyen."

A slightly built man in his fifties seated himself in the witness chair. He was dressed in a pale gray silk sport jacket, white shirt, Countess Mara black tie with red polka dots, and perfectly creased dark gray trousers. He could have been a Saigon banker or a professor of Oriental philosophy at Rice University. He identified himself, however, as the owner of the 7-Eleven near the corner of Westheimer and Kirby in River Oaks. He had contracted for the franchise last November upon arriving in Houston. When he took over the 7-Eleven, the defendant, Hector Quintana, had been employed for about three months by the previous owner as stock clerk and general handyman.

Goodpaster asked, "Did the previous owner make any recommendation to you regarding Mr. Quintana, sir?"

"Objection," Warren said. "Calls for hearsay."

"Sustained. Try rephrasing the question, Madam Prosecutor."

"Thank you, your honor. Mr. Nguyen, what was your

feeling about the defendant after you'd spoken to the previous owner?"

"I still object," Warren said. "The answer will depend on hearsay, on a statement made out of court. The previous owner's not here to say yea or nay."

"Don't explain hearsay to me, Mr. Blackburn!" Judge Parker glared down, then shifted her gaze to Goodpaster. "Well?"

"Your honor," Goodpaster said, "it goes to Mr. Nguyen's state of mind at the time. We're not claiming any truth to what the other owner may have said. We're leading up to show motive."

Warren said stubbornly, "It's not relevant, it's prejudicial, and it's not admissible."

"I'll allow the witness to answer." Parker turned to the jury. "You're not to believe or disbelieve any remarks attributed to the previous owner. Just pay attention to the reaction of the witness at the time."

In a cultured voice with a slightly French accent, Mr. Nguyen said, "I was told that Hector Quintana was a good worker but, shall we say, not entirely reliable. That on several occasions, during working hours, he had perhaps been intoxicated."

Goodpaster asked, "And as a result of being told that, Mr. Nguyen, what did you do?"

"I was forced to let him go."

Warren jumped to his feet. "Your honor, I object to this entire line of questioning. What's it got to do directly with the crime? It's leading to an attempt to prejudice the jury. I ask that all of it be stricken and the jury instructed to disregard."

"Overruled," Judge Parker said, "and sit down, Mr. Blackburn. Objections don't carry any more weight if you make them standing up. I told you a long time ago not to play to the peanut gallery."

So that's how it was going to be. Warren had assumed the worst. The worst was happening.

Goodpaster resumed: "Did you give Mr. Quintana any severance pay?"

"A week's wages. One hundred and ten dollars, my records show."

"And did you have words with him?"

"He seemed upset, and I got the impression—"

"No," Goodpaster interrupted, "don't give us your impressions. Just tell us what you said to him and what he said to you."

Warren could see that the jury reacted favorably. Goodpaster was being tough on her own witnesses. A nice touch. She was good.

Mr. Nguyen, a subtle gentleman, appeared to be annoyed at the rebuke. He obviously preferred to convey impressions. He wrinkled his forehead and stroked his tie with a pointed fingernail.

"I said to him, 'I'm so sorry, but I must let you go,' and I gave him the money. And he said, 'That's not fair.' I believe I then repeated that I was sorry."

"And what did Mr. Quintana do?"

"He became angry and spoke in an intimidating manner. Then, just before he left, he cursed at me."

"You understood he was cursing at you?"

"It was very clear."

"Thank you, Mr. Nguyen. Pass the witness."

Warren conferred in whispers for a minute with Hector before he rose. This was the part some lawyers reveled in. Tear the witness a new asshole, they said. Warren's general idea was somewhat less brutal: plant a slim needle of doubt in the witness's credibility, and keep doing it with each witness until the accumulated effect created a painful suspicion in the jurors that something was awry, that the prosecution had somehow been carried away with the passion to prosecute for prosecution's sake. It was not altruism on Warren's part, it was a belief that at the outset of a trial jurors tended to identify with civilian witnesses; they could quickly form a resentment against a belligerent defense attorney.

On Hector's behalf, however, he decided to bare his claws at least halfway. He stepped forward into the well of the courtroom, at a midpoint between the counsel tables and the judge's bench.

"Mr. Nguyen, you mentioned that the previous owner told you Hector was a good worker, but he drank now and then on the job. No—a couple of times he'd been 'perhaps intoxicated,' that's what you said. Nevertheless, the previous owner thought enough of him as an employee not to fire him, isn't that so?"

"It would seem so," Mr. Nguyen said carefully.

"Sir, before you moved here, where did you live?"

"In Singapore. And before that, Saigon."

"How many languages do you speak?"

"Five, to different degrees of fluency. Vietnamese, of course—English, French, and Thai. And some Chinese, the Mandarin dialect." He offered a modest smile.

"But you don't speak Spanish, isn't that so?"

"I have not had the opportunity to learn."

"And when Mr. Quintana supposedly cursed at you, it was in Spanish, isn't that so?"

Mr. Nguyen frowned. "As I said, it was clear."

"Sir, excuse me, but I didn't ask you if it was clear or not, did I?"

"No, but—"

"Please, Mr. Nguyen! I asked you if Mr. Quintana cursed at you in Spanish, didn't I?"

"Yes, I suppose you did."

"You know the answer to that question, don't you?"

"Yes." Nguyen twisted in the witness chair and glanced up at the judge.

Warren said, "Would you do the jurors and me the courtesy of looking at me, not at the judge, and answering the question that was put to you? Did Mr. Quintana curse at you in Spanish?"

"I seem to recall that was so."

Warren's voice rose angrily. "Did you understand one word Mr. Quintana said?"

"Some few words," Nguyen said, trying to save face.

"Oh?" Warren gambled. "Repeat them to the jury, please."

"I do not remember them," Nguyen said.

"No further questions, your honor."

The next witness, Rona M. Morrison—a pale, nervous woman in her late forties—was sworn in. She seemed to project: why am I here? I didn't do anything wrong.

Prompted by Nancy Goodpaster, she related that at about a quarter past eight on the night of May 19 she had delivered some skirts and cotton sweaters to the dry-cleaning establishment on Wesleyan, and on the way back to her car had "just kind of peeked into this station wagon was settin' there." And there was a man on the seat who "looked real dead."

"What did you do then?" Goodpaster asked.

"Yelled, I s'pose. Then this lady came out of the dry cleaners."

Goodpaster had some crime scene photographs stamped by the clerk and formally introduced into evidence, and then handed them to the witness.

"Is this what you saw, Ms. Morrison?"

Rona Morrison nodded, then began to leak tears.

Warren scowled. A weeper was always a bonanza for the prosecution.

"Ms. Morrison," Judge Parker said, stabbing out her cigarette in a big green glass ashtray, "my court reporter doesn't have a nod button. So would you kindly compose yourself and then answer yes or no."

Yes, that's what Morrison had seen. Goodpaster passed the photographs to the jury. Let them dwell on the face painted with blood, the staring eyes.

Warren took over for cross-examination. There was

nothing of value he could learn, but it was an opportunity to get the jury to understand that he wasn't out to savage truthful witnesses.

"Ms. Morrison, this is painful for you, isn't it?"

She said it was. She'd had nightmares.

"I can understand that. Did you see anyone else in that parking lot that evening?"

No one that she could recall.

"You didn't see *this* man, did you?" He put his hand on Hector's shoulder and squeezed it.

"No, I didn't see him."

"Thank you, Ms. Morrison. No more questions."

Goodpaster called the crime scene photographer to nail down the fact that the photographs shown to the jury were indeed photographs of the body of Dan Ho Trunh. A Fire Department emergency medical technician testified that he had arrived at the Wesleyan Terrace parking lot at 8:27 P.M. on May 19 and checked for a carotid pulse before pronouncing Trunh dead. Then the Harris County assistant medical examiner took the stand to tell the jury that the cause of death, in lay terms, was a .32-caliber bullet lodged in the brain.

It was tedious and painstaking business, but in theory a jury arrived collectively virgin, knowing nothing about either crime or victim. You had to prove to them that crime and victim in fact existed.

Warren waived cross-examination for those three witnesses. From the corner of an eye, he saw Judge Parker nod. Good fellow, she seemed to indicate. That's the way to get on with it.

"The state calls Sergeant Hollis Thiel."

Wearing the customary ill-fitting brown suit of a Homicide detective, Thiel settled into the witness chair. Pink-faced, with eyes like hard little brown buttons, he was at ease. He had been here before. He was a master of cop jargon: "Sergeant Douglas and I received the assignment at twenty-hundred-twenty-five hours on 19 May 1989. We arrived at the seven thousand block of Wesleyan at approximately twenty-hundred-fifty hours. The complainant was in a reclining position in the front seat of a 1983 Ford Fairlane station wagon. . . ."

Goodpaster asked him what he had found when he searched the vehicle.

"Registration papers for the vehicle, which led us to a positive identification of the complainant as Dan Ho Trunh. A box with various electrician's tools. Some dirty shirts and a couple of balled-up jackets."

No weapon of any kind, Thiel replied, when asked. No wallet, no money.

"As an experienced homicide investigator, did you detect any signs of a struggle that preceded Mr. Trunh's being shot and killed?"

"No, ma'am."

"Pass the witness."

Warren stepped in front of the defense table.

"Sergeant Thiel, isn't it a fact that in Harris County more than two out of three homicides involve a victim and a murderer who are either friends or blood relatives?"

That was indeed a fact, Thiel said, before Goodpaster got to her feet to object on the grounds of relevance. Judge Parker sustained the objection.

"Your honor—"

"Don't argue with me, Mr. Blackburn. I've ruled."

Warren tried another tack. "Sergeant Thiel, your expertise in homicide investigations has been established by Ms. Goodpaster. So let's follow through. When you reached the crime scene, the window on the driver's side of the victim's car was open, is that correct?"

"Yes."

"And the driver's door was unlocked, wasn't it?"

"Yes."

"You found no wallet on the victim or in the car?"

"None."

"If Mr. Trunh had a wallet, someone took it before your arrival?"

"That's correct."

"And there's no telling, is there, who took that wallet? It didn't have to be the person who shot him, did it?"

"Objection!" Goodpaster barked. "Calls for speculation."

"Sustained."

"But, your honor—"

"Sustained. Get on with it, Mr. Blackburn."

Warren seethed a moment, then calmed down.

"Let me put it this way, Sergeant. All anybody had to do—anybody who came along—was to open the door the way you did, and see a dead man and take his wallet. Isn't that true?"

"Objection!"

"Don't answer, Sergeant!" the judge cried. "Mr. Blackburn, that's enough! I'll see both counsel in chambers!"

Two rebukes from the bench on the first morning. Juries invariably followed the judge's leaning, if the judge leaned. And Lou Parker leaned hard. I'm getting killed, Warren thought. In chambers, seated at her desk, the judge coughed for a minute, lit another cigarette, then pointed that familiar finger at Warren's chest. "Now listen here!" Her voice was phlegmy from smoking. "When I rule, that's *it*. You want to appeal to a higher court and claim error, be my guest. But don't try to get in the back door when the front door's slammed in your face, or I'll hold you in contempt! This is *my* courtroom. You follow?"

Warren considered his options. He could placate her, he could argue the point on its merits, he could shut up and let her roll over him, or he could take a stand. He felt he had come a long way since he had lied for Virgil Freer, a long way even since J. J. Gillis. He was tired of being stepped on by this woman.

Warren said, "No, Judge, this is not your courtroom.

Your only function is to help the two of us"—he waved to include Nancy Goodpaster—"present a true case to the jury. You can rule, and you may be right more often than wrong. But you've got to rule without prejudicing the jury against me and my client. Because until that jury comes in with a verdict, it's Quintana's courtroom. He faces death. I'm not going to hurry this case along so you can get a better suntan in Hawaii."

Seated next to him, Nancy Goodpaster bowed her head.

Lou Parker had been looking at him, openmouthed. She had clenched a fist and her jaw now moved open and shut a few times in a vacant way. Warren believed she wasn't aware of it.

"Don't say another word," she stammered. "I'm not prejudicing anybody, you hear? You'll follow my rulings! Right or wrong, I'm the judge! Now get out! The next time you give me lip like you just did, you'll find yourself sleeping in jail!"

She had backed off. He wasn't in jail, and if she put him there she couldn't keep him there. A lawyer cited for contempt was entitled automatically to a release on a personal recognizance bond. If not, the judges could always threaten the lawyers: I'll put you in jail if you don't do what I say.

And she had stammered. Maybe she'd lay off from now on, not just back off.

In the hallway, en route to the courtroom, he stopped at the water cooler. When he straightened up, Nancy Goodpaster was looking at him. Tight-lipped, sad-eyed, she shook her head back and forth. He realized again that she didn't have it in for Hector Quintana; she was just doing her job. And you're killing Hector, her eyes said.

Goodpaster called Paul Stimac, a thin, sandy-haired man who looked as if the sun had never touched his face.

"Where do you work, Mr. Stimac?"

"In the Circle K, corner of Bissonet and Harding. I'm the night cashier."

On the evening of May 19, Stimac related in a high-pitched voice, a man had come into the store and pointed a gun at him. Yes, the man was in the courtroom. He identified Hector Quintana.

"Were you frightened for your life, Mr. Stimac?"

Warren calmly objected.

The judge glared down. "On what grounds, Mr. Blackburn?"

"Irrelevant, and calculated to inflame the jury against my client."

"The question goes to his state of mind, not the facts," Goodpaster countered.

"That's still irrelevant," Warren said.

"I don't think so." The judge shook her head. "The man was there and he had a gun pointed at him. I think it's relevant how he felt. Objection overruled."

"Judge!" Warren said sharply. "The state of mind of this witness may be relevant to the alleged attempted robbery but not to the crime my client's charged with."

"Overruled. I *said,* overruled!"

"Well, I'd been stuck up twice before," Stimac answered. "I wasn't too scared. I knew what to do." He had pressed a button on the floor that would summon the police, then stalled. He handed over the money. The police came.

Warren took over on cross. "Mr. Quintana never threatened you, did he?"

Goodpaster objected. "Calls for a conclusion on the part of the witness."

"Sustained," Parker said.

Warren shrugged lightly. "I'll rephrase. Did he ever say anything to you like, 'If you don't hand over the money, I'm gonna blow your brains out'? Anything at all like that?"

"No," Stimac said, "he just ast for the money. He looked more scared than I was."

"Would it surprise you, sir, to learn that the pistol Mr. Quintana pointed at you had no bullets in it?"

"Objection," Goodpaster cut in—"there's no predicate."

She meant that you couldn't ask a question implying a fact that had not yet been established as a fact. The gun wasn't loaded, but no witness had as yet testified that it wasn't. As Warren well knew. But the jury didn't, yet, and they would wonder.

"Sustained," Judge Parker rumbled. She seemed to be saying: Do your worst, counselor, but I'm still going to win. I'm the judge and it's my court.

In the afternoon, after lunch, Officer L. E. Manley took the stand. A young, athletic-looking black man, he testified that he and his partner had raced over from the North Shepherd substation and apprehended the defendant as he trotted out of the Circle K, pistol in hand. Naturally they took the pistol away from him.

"Yes, this is the same weapon," he said, after Goodpaster had it entered into evidence and placed it in his hands. "A .32-caliber Diamondback Colt. This particular one has a distinctive ivory-inlaid butt. Lightweight, very little recoil. And it's had some work done on the hammer and recoil spring. Makes it real easy to fire. Just a little tug on the trigger will do the trick."

Warren scribbled some notes. New information. Thank you, Officer Manley.

Goodpaster asked Manley, "And were there any bullets in the pistol when you took it away from Mr. Quintana?"

She wanted to defuse the issue raised when Stimac was on the stand. You see, jury, we have nothing to hide. *I'm* letting you find out it wasn't loaded.

"No, ma'am."

"Pass the witness."

In any felony case, the defense always works with a theory to impress upon the jury, a theory that will build and counter the prosecution's contention that the defendant is guilty. The theory of defense may be right or wrong, valid or invalid; it has only to be coherent, logically acceptable, and to plant in the minds of the jurors a reasonable doubt as to guilt. In this case Warren had a rare advantage. He knew that his theory was completely valid. Hector Quintana had not been there in the parking lot on Wesleyan. Warren had known before he cross-examined Hollis Thiel that Hector had not taken Trunh's wallet. And now, with Officer Manley on the stand, Warren knew exactly why work had been done on the Diamondback Colt's hammer and recoil spring to make it "real easy to fire."

With Manley's help he established that Hector had carried no bullets on his person, and none had been found inside or outside the Circle K.

"Do you get many robbers who use an unloaded gun?" Warren asked.

"Only the dumb ones," Manley said, chuckling, and the jury chuckled too.

"Move to strike," Goodpaster said. "Irrelevant."

"Motion granted." Judge Parker instructed the jury to disregard the answer.

Warren persisted: "How many robbers with an unloaded gun have you run across in all the years you've been a police officer—none, right?"

"Mr. Blackburn!" the judge thundered.

"Your honor," Warren said calmly, "it was an entirely different question."

Judge Parker ordered: "Don't answer, Manley! And you, Mr. Blackburn, I am *warning* you—move along!"

Warren asked, "Tell us this, Officer Manley. This particular gun—you said it had an ivory handle, and the hammer and recoil spring were fixed to make it an easy trigger pull. Have I got that right?"

"That's about it."

"In your experience, it's not the sort of gun a man would carry, is it?"

Manley glanced at Goodpaster. Swiftly, Warren cried, "No, don't look to her for help! Just tell the truth."

"No, it's not," Manley said.

"You would say, wouldn't you, that it's a woman's gun?"

"Objection!"

"Sustained," the judge declared.

But the point was made to the jury, if anyone on it was listening and cared.

"No further questions."

On redirect, Goodpaster asked, "Is there anything about this gun that prevents a man from using it?"

"No, ma'am."

"And the defendant was carrying it that night, wasn't he?"

"Yes, he was."

On recross, Warren hammered away. "He was carrying it, but didn't it occur to you at the time that it wasn't his gun?"

"Objection. Calls for speculation."

"Sustained."

"Can you think of any reason, Officer Manley, why a homeless and dirt-poor illegal Mexican alien would be carrying a gun that not only was unloaded but was, by your own admission, the sort of gun that men don't carry?"

"Objection! Calls for speculation, and there's no predicate that he was 'dirt-poor.' "

"You can answer, Manley," Judge Parker said, surprising Warren. Then she added, to the prosecutor, "Or else he'll just rephrase and worm it out of him some other way."

Manley shrugged. "It might have been the only weapon he could get hold of. He might have borrowed it. He might have found it somewhere. Anything's possible."

"Pass the witness."

But that was all for Manley. He was told to step down.

The expert from HPD Ballistics then identified the Diamond-back Colt as the tagged weapon that had been handed to him on the night of May 19 by Officer Manley and afterward matched against various bullets used in unsolved crimes. It wasn't until late the next afternoon that the bullet retrieved from Dan Ho Trunh's brain was brought into the lab. There was an immediate match.

It was after three o'clock. Time for one more witness if they didn't take a break, and that was Judge Parker's intention. Sergeant Craig Douglas was sworn in, and he explained to the jury that on the morning of May 21, in the offices of HPD Homicide, he had rearrested Hector Quintana for capital murder. He had read the defendant his rights and asked him if he wished to make a statement. The defendant had declined the opportunity. Before Warren could object, Douglas volunteered, "He pretended he didn't know what I was talking about."

"Sergeant Douglas," Warren began on cross, "you said Mr. Quintana pretended he didn't know what you were talking about. Did you have some special method of getting inside his mind to reach that conclusion?"

"No," Douglas said.

"No further questions."

Judge Parker rapped her black oak gavel, then dismissed the jury until nine o'clock the next morning.

When they had gone, the bailiff and another deputy put the handcuffs back on Hector's wrists. They stepped aside for a minute to let the defense attorney and his client confer. Hector looked worn-out and pale.

Warren said, "Listen, it went well. And tomorrow will be even better."

Hector nodded with terrifying politeness, but his face was almost womanly with quiet woe. *He knows,* Warren realized, *knows I'm pecking away at a steel wall.*

"Your turn will come," Warren said, a little desperately.

Hector shook his head. "They will not believe me. I will die." His voice was like an axe falling.

"No. Listen! You have to believe in me."

But Hector turned his back and nodded to the bailiff, who led him away.

Johnnie Faye Boudreau entered the courtroom a few minutes after 9 A.M. on the second day of the trial, just after the *Quintana* jury had filed in from the jury room and taken their places on the black Naugahyde swivel chairs in the jury box. Warren's eye fell on her immediately.

That was not difficult. She was an advertisement of blazing red and white, like two thirds of the American flag which the Supreme Court had so recently decided might be burned without offense to the law of the land. She wore a cherry-red double-breasted linen suit over a white camisole, Mexican silver bracelets on both wrists, a red leather shoulder bag, red high heels to match the suit, and atop it all a large-brimmed white straw hat. Her tight skirt was well above the knees. She had on silver eye shadow and too much rouge. Warren remembered an old saw that he had heard either in a song or from one of his father's cronies: *The devil is a woman in a short red dress.*

The courtroom was not crowded. The same friends and members of the Trunh family were there from the day before, plus a handful of the retired elderly groupies who could always be counted on for a capital murder trial.

Johnnie Faye took a seat in a back row and smiled across the room at Warren. He nodded back at her coolly just as Judge Parker entered, the bailiff demanded order, and the state called Mai Thi Trunh as its first witness for the day.

Dan Ho Trunh's young widow wore black. She was a composed witness who spoke slowly and simply, her grief not flaunted but clearly there. Warren was moved by her. When you murder a man, you strike the worse blow not so much at the man as at those who loved him. He wondered if Johnnie Faye ever thought about that. Yes, and pigs could fly.

He had a powerful and almost calamitous urge to clasp Hector Quintana by the arm, turn him in his chair and say, "That woman in red is the one who murdered the man you're accused of murdering. Go to her, Hector. Ask her how she can live with it."

Instead he scrawled rapid notes on his legal pad. Mrs. Trunh was on the stand for two purposes: to elicit sympathy and to help prove that her late husband was in possession of his wallet on the morning of his death.

Under Nancy Goodpaster's patient questioning, the jury learned a great deal about the Trunh family before the day of Dan Ho's death. All of it irrelevant, but Warren did not object. When a bereaved witness testified, a defense counsel had to take it up the *culo,* as Warren was fond of saying. In most cases, you or your client deserved it. Not in this one. But there was nothing he could do.

Goodpaster's merciful "Pass the witness" occurred only a few minutes before noon. The jury was led away by the bailiff, who would escort them to a nearby restaurant and feed them courtesy of the state. Hector Quintana was led away by the deputy sheriff to a holding cell in the courthouse basement, to be fed a meal brought over in a steam tray through the underground tunnel from the Harris County Jail.

Warren walked slowly to the rear of the courtroom where Johnnie Faye Boudreau waited for him in her cherry-red suit and white hat. She had just finished touching up her lipstick.

"That was boring," she said.

"I suppose so. What are you doing here?"

"You're my lawyer, I came to watch you at work. When do you get to strut your stuff?"

"After lunch. You'll be disappointed."

"That remains to be seen. Let's go."

"Where?"

"Lunch."

"No thanks."

"That's dumb," Johnnie Faye said. "A lady and a client offers to take you to lunch, you should do it. I know you're not exactly crazy about me, but we're going to see a lot of each other. It won't hurt you to be civil. Besides, I want to find out how you're doing with your wife. And I want to talk about the case. *My* case."

"I'm on this case now. When I want to talk to you about yours, I'll call you and we'll meet in my office."

"You *are* mean," she said, touching his arm. Her lips made a little pouting motion, a moue. She was flirting with him, he realized. He could hardly believe it. His bile rose; he was ready to hit her.

"You're insane," he said.

Before he turned his back and walked away, he saw a quick and exacting look in her eye, the look that Clyde Ott may have seen more than once, or that she may have cast from a distance at Sharon Ott and then from more intimate quarters at her useful boyfriend, Dink. She could easily kill me. She's capable of it, he realized. Like them, I know too much. Then the expression vanished and her eye was as flat as stone. Her blue-gray eye.

She was back in her seat at the rear of the courtroom for his cross of the widow Trunh.

Warren was aware of time pressure, as if he were in a chess match and had squandered most of his allotted minutes with the opening moves. After voir dire he and Nancy Goodpaster had discussed the trial sequence. "I'll finish by Tuesday," Goodpaster promised, "so you've got until Thursday lunch break for your witnesses. The judge will charge the jury the minute you're done, and they'll start to deliberate right away. She'll keep them here as late as necessary on Thursday evening until they reach a verdict." Friday, the jury would decide on the punishment: life or death. On Friday evening Judge Parker would fly to Hawaii.

Warren shook his head in disgust. "You're assuming they'll come in with a guilty verdict."

Goodpaster nodded soberly. "Yes, I am."

With all that in mind, and more, Warren stood and faced Mai Thi Trunh.

The theft of Dan Ho's wallet was what turned simple murder into capital murder. The key to the widow's testimony was her statement that her husband had taken the wallet with him on the morning of his death. She hadn't seen him pick it up from the bureau and put it in his back pocket. "But he always did," she said, during Goodpaster's direct examination.

Circumstantial evidence, a leap of logic leading to: if the wallet wasn't discovered at home, Dan Ho must have had it with him when he was murdered. But perhaps during the course of the day he had been pickpocketed, or inadvertently dropped it in the street. Who could prove otherwise? And perhaps Mrs. Trunh was mistaken. The wallet might still be in the house, under a pile of shirts or in a hiding place she didn't know of. She couldn't swear under oath that there was no such hiding place. Warren might move the widow to say, several times, "I don't know," or, "Yes, that is possible." On cross-examination you were permitted to lead a witness and seize control.

But Dan Ho Trunh did take the wallet, Warren believed. Mrs. Trunh wasn't mistaken.

"The defense has no questions," he said.

"You may step down," Judge Parker said to Mrs. Trunh. She threw a brief smile in Warren's direction. Smart lawyering, counselor. And I'll make my plane.

Nancy Goodpaster rose eagerly. "The state calls its last witness—Mrs. Siva Singh."

Behind her eyeglasses the Indian woman looked nervous. That wouldn't hurt her, Warren thought. The jury could identify with nervous witnesses who were decent people and had become involved with a crime through no fault of their own. Goodpaster gave her some time to develop a rapport with the jurors, asking about her background and her family and her job. She had been born in Jaipur; she was forty-one years old and had two children. She and her husband had emigrated to the United States twelve years ago. They spent three years in Burlington, Vermont—"it was jolly cold indeed"—then moved to Texas. They owned the dry cleaners on Wesleyan. Her husband worked in the back. He also did tailoring. "Very fine work," she said, "at reasonable prices."

Some jurors laughed.

Pleased, Goodpaster got down to business. "Mrs. Singh, please tell us where you were on the evening of May 19."

In the Wesleyan Laundry & Dry Cleaners. Her husband was there too, doing some rush orders for dry cleaning.

"On that evening, did a Mrs. Rona Morrison enter your store?"

Siva Singh described how Rona Morrison—"a satisfied customer for many years"—had come in to drop off her dry cleaning, exited, and a minute later, in the parking lot, screamed. Singh had hurried outside to find Mrs. Morrison on her knees by the side of a parked station wagon. After she had seen the bleeding body of a man inside the car, she had brought Mrs. Morrison inside and called the police.

"Now let's back up a bit," Goodpaster said. "Did anything unusual happen *prior* to Mrs. Morrison's scream and your discovery of the body?"

"Yes indeed. I was working in the back of the Wesleyan Laundry & Dry Cleaners when there was a noise, which I later understood had been a gunshot. I returned to the front of the store."

"From behind the counter you had a clear view of the parking lot?" Goodpaster asked.

"Quite clear."

"Please tell the jury what you saw."

"A man stood by the station wagon—"

"The same station wagon in which you and Mrs. Morrison later found the body?"

"The same. He was perhaps thirty or forty feet away from my point of observation. He seemed to be leaning in the window, or perhaps he had already leaned in the window and was just, how shall I say, straightening up from doing so. I am not precisely sure. Then he turned and ran away. Rather rapidly, if I may say so."

"You may say whatever you please, Mrs. Singh, provided it's an accurate recollection." Goodpaster looked at her soberly, then asked, "When the man turned to run, did he turn toward you, or away from you?"

"Most definitely toward me, so that I was given the opportunity to see his face."

"You saw it clearly?"

"Quite clearly."

"Can you describe him to us, Mrs. Singh?"

"He was about five feet nine or five feet ten inches tall, with long dark hair, and wore just a pair of trousers with a shirt. He wore no jacket. He looked to be poor and homeless. He was white, not black. He seemed most certainly to be Hispanic."

Goodpaster hesitated a moment, and Warren wrote a note on his pad. He wondered again: who was the man in the parking lot? Weeks ago in the early evening he had made the rounds of all the shops in the mall, asking if anyone had seen such a man on the night in question. No one could recall anyone. Did anyone habitually hang around the mall at night? Just an occasional wino. None of the clerks or store owners remembered any one of them in particular.

Siva Singh had seen someone, he didn't doubt it, but not Hector Quintana. Johnnie Faye had been in her car, and even if she had stepped out of it for a moment, there was no way she could be mistaken for a man. Some passerby, he decided, who had seen the body, become frightened, then bolted. Still, that didn't account for the missing wallet.

"When the police came," Goodpaster asked, "what did you tell them?"

"Precisely what I have told you. I narrated these events. I described the man I had seen running away so rapidly."

"The following day, Mrs. Singh, when you were asked to appear at the Harris County Jail, please tell us what happened."

Siva Singh described the police lineup. Six men were paraded before her. She saw them full face and in profile for several minutes. She identified one of them as the man whom she had seen running away the night before.

"You were certain it was the same man?"

"Quite certain."

"I have just one more question. Do you see that man in this courtroom today?"

"I do indeed."

"Point to him and describe him, please."

She pointed toward the defense table. "He is wearing a white shirt and blue single-breasted suit."

Goodpaster smiled in embarrassment, and said firmly, "Mrs. Singh, there are *two* men at the defense table wearing white shirts and single-breasted blue suits. Can you be more specific as to which one you saw in the parking lot?"

The jury began to titter. From the back of the courtroom, Johnnie Faye Boudreau brayed a laugh. Judge Parker raised her eyes comically toward the ceiling.

Warren, the second man in the blue suit, had almost laughed too, but he clamped his lips shut to stifle it. Siva Singh and Hector Quintana were the only ones who neither laughed nor smiled.

Mrs. Singh threw a hand to her open mouth and rose slightly in the witness chair. Then she tore her hand away and stabbed it toward Hector. "I am mortified! It is he! The man in the blue tie! I do not know the man wearing the yellow paisley."

The jurors' laughter surged back for a moment, then ebbed away. The judge tapped her gavel.

"Let the record reflect," Goodpaster said gravely, "that the witness has identified the defendant, Hector Quintana."

"Let the record so reflect," said Judge Parker, nodding at the court reporter.

Laughter can kill too, Warren thought.

He rose to face Siva Singh. At first he kept a good distance away, stationing himself on the other side of the courtroom from the jury so that Singh, if she focused on her interrogator, would not be able to look directly at them.

The key to any cross-examination was control. In direct examination of a friendly witness, a good attorney would efface himself and ask questions that allowed long answers. He wanted the witness to be in control, to elaborate, to mesmerize the jury and make them believe. Cross was more of a duel. One or the other, attorney or witness, would dominate. The most difficult witness to dominate was a sincere witness. You could too easily be embarrassed by that sincerity and appear to be a bully.

Softly, softly, catchee monkey . . .

He introduced himself to Mrs. Singh, even though he had already done so during his aborted interview at the Wesleyan Laundry & Dry Cleaners. "Please forgive me," he said pleasantly, "for confusing you today by wearing the same color suit as my client."

"It is I who ask your forgiveness," Siva Singh said, blushing.

"And you have it, ma'am."

Singh smiled in gratitude. He saw that she had been frightened of him. And that was no longer true.

"This isn't the first time we've met, is it?" Warren asked.

"No."

"I came to talk to you some weeks ago at your place of business, isn't that so?"

"Yes, that is true," Singh said unhappily. She lifted her eyeglasses and scratched her nose.

"I wanted to discuss this case, do you remember?"

"At the time, that is what I presumed."

"And you wouldn't discuss it with me, because you were under the mistaken impression that Ms. Goodpaster, the prosecutor, had forbidden you to do so. Isn't that true?"

"That is so. I apologize, sir."

"No, Mrs. Singh, again it's I who should apologize. I should have got Ms. Goodpaster to call you and explain that you were at liberty to talk to me. And then I should have gone to talk to you. But I was very busy. Please forgive me."

Singh showed white and perfect teeth. Her dark brown eyes glittered.

"Your eyeglasses are for distance, aren't they?" Warren asked, remembering how she had taken them off to reach into her pocketbook for Goodpaster's business card.

"Oh, yes. And with them, if I may say so, I can see perfectly."

"Can you see at a distance without them?"

"Quite well."

Warren frowned. "Were you wearing them on the night of May 19 when you saw the man leaning into the station wagon and then running away into the darkness?"

"Indeed, yes, I was wearing them," Singh said gravely, "or I would not have seen him as clearly as I did."

Warren thought for a moment, then moved a few feet closer to her.

"Ma'am, what is your native language?"

"Hindi," Singh said, a little surprised, and suddenly wary. "But of course as a child in Jaipur I learned English."

"In school?"

"Yes."

"And you speak it perfectly. English English, not American English, correct?"

The wariness vanished. "Indeed, yes," Singh said, smiling.

"If you'd indulge me, ma'am, I'd like you to shut your eyes for a moment and then answer a question."

Obediently, Siva Singh shut her eyes.

Warren said, "As best you recall, how tall am I?"

"Objection!" Goodpaster cried.

Before the judge could rule, Siva Singh's eyes flew open.

"Withdraw the question," Warren said.

He began to move about the room, pacing. The eyes of the jurors followed him. He halted when he was close to the jury box.

"Mrs. Singh, before the police arrived to talk to you on the evening of May 19, did you tell either your husband or Mrs. Morrison that you'd seen a man running away from that station wagon in the darkness?"

"Indeed, I told my husband. My customer Mrs. Morrison was much too upset to talk to. I would describe her as hysterical."

"I would appreciate it," Warren said gently, "if you would just answer my questions without adding your impressions. If the question calls for a yes or no answer, just answer yes or no."

"Forgive me," the Indian woman said.

"Nothing to forgive, ma'am. It's a common mistake. Now, before the police came, you told your husband you had seen the man running away. Did you at that time describe the man to your husband?"

"No, not then. Later I told him that—" She stopped, biting her lip; she had almost done it again. Warren gave her a reassuring look.

"Did you describe him to your husband later, after the police had gone?"

"Yes."

"In detail?"

"Yes, I believe so."

"Do you recall what words you used when you described him to your husband? Just answer yes or no, ma'am."

"Yes."

"Please tell the jury what you said to your husband, Mrs. Singh."

Thankful not to have to respond yes or no, she thought a moment, then looked at the nearest juror and said: "I told my husband that the man was perhaps five feet nine inches tall. That he had long dark hair. That he wore just a pair of trousers with a shirt. That he did not wear a jacket. That he appeared to be a poor and homeless fellow. That he was white, not black. That he was most certainly Hispanic, and that I had never seen him before in my life."

Warren waited as long as he dared for it to register.

Then he said, "Mrs. Singh, aren't those just about the exact words, with the phrases in exactly the same order, that you used to describe this man to the police when they arrived?"

"Perhaps. That may be so," Mrs. Singh said.

"I can ask the court to provide you with a copy of your statement to the police. It may refresh your memory. Would you like me to do that, Mrs. Singh?"

"That is not necessary," she replied.

"Are they just about the same words and the exact order of phrases?"

"Most probably," Singh managed.

"And in this courtroom today, when the prosecutor asked you to describe the man you saw running away from the car in the darkness, didn't you use the exact same words and order of phrases that the police copied down as your sworn statement?"

"Most probably," Singh said again.

"Do you have a copy, either here or at home, of your sworn statement to the police?"

"Yes."

"Have you memorized it? Word for word? Phrase for

phrase, in the right order, so that there would be no discrepancies?"

"I don't understand," Singh said helplessly.

"Would you like the court reporter to read back my question?"

"No."

"Then please answer it, ma'am. If you can."

"I cannot," Singh said.

"Why not?"

"I did not memorize it, sir. But I studied it."

He had got away with that last one, he realized, breaking the cardinal rule of never asking a hostile witness a question that began with *why*. But no matter how she answered, she had still memorized. That she was a hostile witness Warren had never doubted. The creed of all courtroom combat was: if you are not for me, you are against me.

He moved to the other side of the courtroom, next to Hector Quintana. The jurors' eyes followed him carefully.

"Mrs. Singh, when you talked to the police and described the man whom you saw running away, you said: 'I thought he *might* have been Hispanic'—isn't that so? Just yes or no, please."

"Yes."

"And then to my colleague, Ms. Goodpaster, earlier today in this courtroom, didn't you say: 'He seemed most certainly to be Hispanic'?"

"Yes."

"And a few moments ago, when you were relating to the jury what you told your husband, you said: 'He *was* most certainly Hispanic.' Didn't you, Mrs. Singh?"

"I may have done so."

"Isn't it a fact that with each description, as time moves on, you grow more positive?"

"Objection," Goodpaster called out sharply, a little desperately. "Badgering the witness!"

"Overruled," Judge Parker said, to Warren's surprise. "You may answer, Mrs. Singh."

"I do not know the correct answer," Singh said.

"Isn't it a fact," Warren said quietly, "that when you saw the defendant sitting in this courtroom today, that was the precise moment you decided that the man you saw running away from the car was definitely a Hispanic?"

"That is not actually a fact," she said, glowering.

"What is a Hispanic, Mrs. Singh?"

"A person from Latin America, sir."

"How would you describe such a person physically?"

"They are usually dark. Not very tall."

"You are dark too, Mrs. Singh, and not very tall," Warren said, in his quietest audible voice. "I suspect your husband is also dark. Is either of you Hispanic?"

"Most definitely not," she replied.

"Do you have anything against Hispanics?"

"Not in any particular way."

Warren pounced: "You have something against them in a *general* way, is that what you're telling us?"

"It is just that I have noticed that many of the unemployed and homeless men in our city are of Latin origin."

"Just one thing more, Mrs. Singh." He saw her relax. "At 8 P.M. the parking lot outside your dry cleaners is relatively dark, isn't it?"

"There are lights."

"Are they bright?"

"Yes."

"Was the station wagon parked directly under one of them?"

"Not precisely. But it was not too far away."

"Yes or no, Mrs. Singh. Was it parked directly under one of them?"

"No."

"Do you know how far apart those lights are spaced in the parking area?"

"Goodness, not really."

"Would you say they're placed more than a hundred feet apart?"

"I'm not sure."

"Isn't it a fact, Mrs. Singh, that they're approximately one hundred and twenty feet apart from one another along the outer perimeter of the parking area?"

"I do not know."

"Do you know how far the nearest light is from where you sat in the front of your store?"

"It is not far."

"How far is 'not far,' Mrs. Singh?"

"I am not exactly sure."

"Isn't it true, Mrs. Singh, that the nearest light is approximately forty-five feet from where you sat?"

"That may well be."

"And isn't it true, Mrs. Singh, that the station wagon was parked at least twenty feet from the base of the nearest lamp?"

"That also may be."

"You came from the back of the laundry a minute or two after you heard the gunshot?"

"Yes."

"Your husband was operating the dry cleaning machines in the back?"

"Yes."

"And it was hot and steamy back there?"

"Oh, yes, near the presses, always."

"Did you wipe your glasses, Mrs. Singh, to get the fog off them, before you looked out into the parking lot and saw the man running away?"

"I do not remember."

"The man who was running away, you saw him clearly?"

"Quite clearly."

"Mrs. Singh, in the Queen's English, which you learned in Jaipur and still speak, does the word 'quite' mean *very*, or does it mean *sort of*?"

"I beg your pardon?"

"When I asked you if you could see well at a distance without your glasses, you answered, 'Quite well.' And yet your glasses are to help you see things at a distance, aren't they?"

"Yes, exactly."

"So what you meant when you said 'Quite well' was really 'Fairly well'—isn't that so, ma'am?"

"That is possible."

"When Ms. Goodpaster asked if you saw the man's face when he turned toward you, and you replied, 'Quite clearly'—you actually meant 'fairly clearly.' Isn't that true, ma'am?"

"I could see him," Singh said. "He was dark and scruffy-looking."

"A Hispanic."

"Well, I am not sure of that now."

Warren took a shaky breath and paused to let that register with the jurors.

"And then later, when Ms. Goodpaster asked if you were certain that the man you picked out of the police lineup was the same man whom you saw 'quite clearly' in the parking lot, you replied that you were 'quite certain.' You meant *fairly* certain, didn't you, Mrs. Singh?"

"He was quite similar," Siva Singh replied softly, "if he is not the same man. And if he is not, then I am so terribly sorry. I will not forgive myself."

"Do you think *he* will forgive you?" Warren asked.

Mrs. Singh did not answer.

He was torn between ending right there and going on. There were other areas to cover, but he was afraid now that they would prove anticlimactic. He glanced at the jury. They were with him. They would not forget.

Just a little bit more, he told himself. He wanted to show the jury that Dan Ho Trunh could easily have been followed to the dry-cleaning establishment by someone who knew his habits. A red herring, but he needed it. There was

the matter of the murder weapon in Hector's possession, a
fact that he could not cast doubt upon the way he had cast
doubt upon Siva Singh's positive identification.

"Mrs. Singh, was Dan Ho Trunh also a regular customer, like Mrs. Morrison?"

The witness brightened. The ordeal seemed to be over.

"Yes, he came once a week. He picked up and delivered
his things at the same time. A very neat man indeed. He
was also a most satisfied customer, as Mrs. Morrison is."

None of the jurors smiled at that now.

"Mr. Trunh came always on the same day?" Warren
asked.

"That is correct. On Friday evening."

"Let's say between 5 and 8 P.M.?"

"That is correct."

"And May 19 was a Friday?"

"I believe that is correct."

Thiel had testified that some dirty shirts had been found
in the back of the station wagon. Warren was not quite
sure where to head from here; he decided to amble along a
little while until it came to him. If it did.

"Do you know what he was going to deliver to you that
evening, Mrs. Singh?"

"No, sir—how could I know that?"

"Which laundry or dry cleaning of his was in your store,
that he was going to pick up? If you remember."

"Ah, I do indeed remember," she said happily. "Five
white button-down shirts, a gray suit, and a gentleman's
green cotton sweater. He had left them with us the week
before. They were picked up and paid for on Monday."

Warren said, "I'm confused. Do you mean the Monday
before the murder?"

"No, sir. The Monday following."

Warren frowned, still a little puzzled. "You mean they
were picked up by Mrs. Trunh, or one of her family?"

"It was most definitely not Mrs. Trunh or one of her
family," Singh said. "But he had the proper ticket."

Warren said, "I won't keep you much longer. Now, going back to Mrs. Morrison when you found her kneeling beside the car—" He stopped.

"Wait a minute. *Who* had the proper ticket, Mrs. Singh? Who picked up the shirts and suits and sweaters?"

"I had never seen him before," Singh said.

"Describe him!" Warren demanded.

Siva Singh looked distinctly uncomfortable.

"Do your best," Warren begged.

"I should say he was of medium height. Poorly dressed. He smelled dreadfully of alcohol."

"Was he Hispanic?"

She hesitated. "I cannot say with certainty."

"Was he Asian?"

"Most definitely not."

"Was he black?"

"No." She looked down into Warren's hot eyes. A little frightened by what she saw, she drew back a few inches into the safety of the witness chair. "He had the proper ticket," she bravely explained. "He paid."

Warren wanted to hug her and kiss her. He wanted to dance around the courtroom and click his heels in the air.

But he calmed himself. He said, "Thank you, Mrs. Singh. I have no further questions right now—" He turned swiftly to look up at Judge Parker. "But I ask that this witness remain on call today in the courthouse. And I would like a conference, your honor, in chambers."

Light-headed, his mind spinning through the possibilities, Warren paced the floor of Judge Parker's chambers, moving in and out of dusty blocks of light that beamed through the high windows. The smell of fresh coffee, provided by the bailiff, filled the room.

Warren halted and said emphatically, "I want to take Dan Ho Trunh's widow on a short voir dire, out of hearing of the jury. I'll ask her just one question. Did she or any member of her family ever have the dry cleaning ticket in their possession? If the answer is no, and I believe it will be no, then this is not a capital murder case. Some unknown white man stole Dan Ho Trunh's wallet, probably from his dead body, and three days later that same unknown man picked up the clothing. And he probably saw the murder take place."

"What makes you think *that*?" Goodpaster asked. From a corner of the room, leaning against the bookcase, she was frowning. Warren suddenly understood why. His unspoken assumptions revealed that he knew something that no one else in the room knew.

"Because Siva Singh heard the gunshot. A minute or two later she went to the front of the store, and there was the man leaning into or out of the car window. The woman's a lousy eyewitness, but she ain't completely blind. So whatever this guy was or wasn't doing, he was *there*. I mean, he was in the parking lot when Trunh was shot."

Guardedly, the prosecutor said, "Let's assume for the moment that's all true. Why aren't you suggesting to us that this unknown man shot and killed Trunh?"

"Well, he may have. Maybe he did." Warren had difficulty looking Nancy Goodpaster in the eye.

"And why couldn't Quintana have shot Trunh and thrown the wallet away after he took the money out of it? Somebody else could have picked it up and made off with the laundry ticket."

"There are a lot of possibilities," Warren said, "but only one set of facts." He turned to the judge, who sat behind her desk, still in her robes, chain-smoking. "However it turns out, if the widow never had possession of the dry cleaning ticket, I've got to find this man. I'll need a continuance. At least a week." He cracked his knuckles and flexed the muscles in his back. "I start trial this Monday in the Ott case. I'll need whatever time it takes to finish up in the 342nd."

The judge tapped a blunt finger on her calendar book. "You expect me to tell this jury to go home and spin their wheels for two weeks?"

"If that's what it takes," Warren said, "yes, I surely do."

"You've got a hell of a nerve. I'm going to think on this," the judge said calmly. "Meanwhile, you take the Trunh woman on voir dire and ask your question. Maybe you won't hear the answer you want to hear and that'll put an end to this ruckus. Is she still in the courtroom?"

"She'd better be," Warren said.

The bailiff provided a fresh pot of coffee for the jury, sequestered now in the jury room next to the court coordinator's office. In the courtroom, Mai Thi Trunh settled once more in the witness chair. Warren reminded her that she was still under oath even though the jury was not present.

No, she said quietly, she had never seen the dry-cleaning ticket. She had forgotten all about it. Normally her husband carried such things in his wallet.

"Permission to approach the bench!" Warren headed there, Goodpaster close behind.

"Let's keep this off the record," Judge Parker said, waving away the court reporter who normally hovered nearby, her stenograph on a high tripod. The judge, the prosecutor, and counsel for the defense formed a tight huddle.

Warren declared, "Your honor, based on the existence of a vital witness, I request a continuance until I finish the Boudreau trial."

"No, I can't allow that," Judge Parker said.

"I beg your pardon. What did you say?"

"You're not deaf, counselor. If you want to halt this trial to produce a new witness, you've first got to show me that his testimony is relevant, material, and necessary. You can't do that. You don't know what this man will say, or if he even exists. And you have to show me a reasonable expectation that you can find him. How are you going to do that? You don't know his name, where he lives or what he looks like. He could have left town."

With cold fury Warren said, "I know he's white and resembles Hector Quintana. He's probably a bum, so he won't leave town. I know he's got the victim's clothes and might be wearing them. I know that a man's life may depend on my finding him. And I *will* find him."

"Maybe you will, maybe you won't. I have to balance your chances against the problem of letting this jury stew for ten days or more and forgetting every damn word they've heard. I might have to pick a whole new jury. Aside from that, when I get back from vacation, my docket is full."

With a new jury, Warren realized, he would lose all that he had gained. Goodpaster would explain to Siva Singh the error of memorizing a description. He would have a new witness on the stand.

Trying to bridle his rage, Warren gripped the edge of the bench. "The jury won't forget. As for your docket, your honor, that's your problem. You'll have to rearrange things."

"No chance of that," Parker said. "I've ruled, and that's final. Let's get on with this trial."

Warren said sharply, "I want the rest of this on the

record." He beckoned to the court reporter, who obediently moved forward, fingers poised on the keys of her machine. "Your honor, I'm formally asking you to recuse yourself on this case. Step down. I want a new trial with a new judge."

The judge bared her teeth. She took a few quick little breaths, like a sprinter in the blocks. "On what grounds?"

"On the grounds of prejudice from the bench."

"Because I overruled most of your damn fool objections? Because I won't let you hunt for a phantom witness? Wake up and smell the coffee, counselor. You're out of line again!"

They were no longer whispering. The entire courtroom could hear.

"Because of all that," Warren lashed back, "and a lot more. Because the first time we met to talk about my taking this case, you told me not to waste your court time. Hurry it up and plead it out, it's a whale in a barrel for the state—your exact words. You weren't supposed to know the facts of the case, but you weren't deaf or blind. And you repeated that in front of me and the prosecutor three weeks later. You thought we had our signals straight. Forty years pen time was a good deal for a man who claimed he was innocent! You threatened that if I went to trial with Quintana, I'd never get an appointment in your court again. *You* were out of line then. That's a clear violation of judicial canons. That's what you get away with, day in and day out, but not with me. I refuse to continue in this courtroom. I'm walking out."

Quietly and coldly, Judge Parker said, "I can hold you in contempt now. Your reputation stinks. A contempt citation would stand up."

"Try it. I have a witness right here." He flicked a finger at Nancy Goodpaster. "She remembers."

Confidently, Judge Parker turned to her chief prosecutor. "You don't remember any of that, do you, Nancy?"

Goodpaster took an unsteady breath, and said, "Yes, I do."

The judge's face turned a mottled pink. "I said what he says I did? You claim you heard that?"

"Yes," Goodpaster said. "You said it all, your honor."

The judge spun on the court reporter. "Get out of here! This is off the record. *All* of it was off the record."

The court reporter retreated in haste.

Warren said quietly, "If you won't recuse yourself voluntarily, I'll file a motion in another court for your recusal. Right now, this afternoon. We'll have an open hearing. I've never been disrespectful to a judge, but there's a first time for everything. I'll nail your ass to the wall."

"Fuck you, counselor," Judge Parker whispered. Her eyes were the color of smoking charcoal. She adjusted her robes. She drummed her fingers again on the court calendar. Warren glanced up at the wall clock behind the bench. It said nine minutes to three. In steady, silent jerks, the second hand worked its way around the white face. A minute passed.

Judge Parker said, "Look for your witness. The law requires you to exercise due diligence. If you can't find him before your other trial's finished, that's it. We resume. Same jury."

"Thank you, your honor," Warren said cordially.

When he left the courtroom at a quarter to four, Johnnie Faye was waiting for him in the corridor by the water fountain. She looked tired, he thought. Her lipstick was fresh but some of the makeup had faded. Her broad white hat was slightly askew.

Warren asked, "You were there?"

"I heard it all. You were real good with that Indian lady. And you've got guts—I heard you blast that judge too. I picked the right lawyer."

"Thank you," he said flatly.

"Can we go have a cup of coffee and talk?"

"Not now. I have work to do."

"When *are* we going to talk about my case, counselor?"

"Monday morning at eight o'clock in Bingham's court-room. We'll be picking the jury and we'll want your help."

"You're going out now to hunt for this guy that Mrs. Mahatma Gandhi says was in the parking lot?"

"Yes."

"Good luck," she said. "Oh, by the way," she asked innocently, "how should I dress on Monday for court?"

Warren looked her up and down. If she wore what she was wearing now, any jury would give her sixty years without parole. "Wear what you'd wear for church," he said.

That evening, after he had changed into jeans and poured a drink, he saw in the bathroom mirror the bleary, red-eyed look of a lawyer on trial. I need time out, he decided. A little injection of good energy before I start hiking around town in search of a man who might not be there. There were five full days before jury selection began. He punched out Maria Hahn's number. Ten minutes later, with Oobie curled in the back seat gnawing on a tennis ball, he drove out to Maria's condo near River Oaks. On the way he stopped off to buy a bottle of decent zinfandel.

Maria cooked lasagna. She wore old jeans and a blue cotton cowboy shirt with nothing underneath it except flesh. When she got up from the kitchen table to bend over and check the oven, he found himself staring like an ado-lescent at the globes of her buttocks pressed against the worn jeans. There, or at least in the vicinity, he thought, is Nirvana and Lethe all in one package. Could life be that simple?

"How did it go for you today?" she asked while they ate.

"Good." He gave her a synopsis.

"So now you have to find this guy."

He waited until he finished chewing a mouthful of lasagna. "But not tonight."

"You have a plan?"

He knew that she loved plans. "I'll come up with one," he promised.

"You need help? Like a wheel man?"

"The last time you were my wheel man it didn't work out so well. Next time I might get killed."

"Well, now we're experienced. We learn from mistakes. That's what it's all about, isn't it? Randy's away and it's a dead week for me."

"Let me think about it. How was your day?" Warren asked.

She told him in detail; he hadn't realized a court reporter paid that much attention. "You never can predict what a jury will do—this afternoon a guy and a gal got ten years probation for seventy pounds of marijuana. That just cracked me up. Of course they'll be revoked within six months and they'll do the time. They'll skip to Ohio, where they come from, then get caught lighting up a joint on some street corner and the computer will ship them back to Texas. I never make any money on these probation cases—no one ever asks for the record. I told Judge Bingham I want a cocaine bust or a sexual assault."

"And I'll bet he let you put that in the record."

She smiled with approval. "He's a sweetheart. I'll miss him."

Warren looked at his watch. It was nearly ten o'clock. "Let's put the dishes in the machine and go to bed."

"I thought you'd never ask," Maria said. "Never mind the dishes."

In bed she was a startled animal. When Warren next looked at his watch it was midnight.

"No sophomore jinx," Maria said, looking down from where she straddled him.

"Get off me, Hahn. I need some sleep."

"You got what you need, Blackburn."

Grinning, she rolled off him and switched off the lamp. In the darkness, with her curly brown hair pressed against his neck, he traced the length of her own long neck with an unseen fingertip. He felt her heartbeat against his stomach. He was exhausted but he knew he would sleep as he had when he was a boy, before he had married the law. I could get used to this, he thought, just before his eyes closed.

On Monday, July 24, five days after Judge Parker had granted a continuance of trial in the *Quintana* case, the two lawyers defending Johnnie Faye Boudreau met for breakfast in Rick Levine's suite of offices in the Old Cotton Exchange Building on Travis Street. They drank black coffee and ate prune Danish. An hour later, through the blue-gray shade of oak trees, they walked past the Old Market Square and the civil courthouse. The criminal courthouse was only a few blocks away.

Warren lagged behind. "Now that I see you in daylight," Rick said, turning, "I have to tell you that you look like one of my nags after they've finished last in a six-furlong race. Did you know that a horse needs four days to recover from a race? Never mind their legs, they wear their hearts out. It's a cruel sport, like lawyering. I thought you had a few days off. What the hell have you been doing?"

He had been hunting for a man who wasn't there.

For five days and nights, with and without Maria, he had prowled the streets of downtown Houston and the Third Ward, talking to every bum and homeless man he met. On that last afternoon in Judge Parker's court, Siva Singh had provided little more in the way of description. A white man of medium height and average build, poorly dressed, scruffy-looking, dark-complected or suntanned more than fair: that was all Warren had to go on, plus the possibility, courtesy of Mai Thi Trunh, that he might be wearing a gray suit or a green cotton sweater. The widow had looked through her late husband's clothes and confirmed Siva Singh's memory; those seemed to be missing. All his shirts that went to the dry cleaners were white button-down oxfords. He wore no other kind.

Warren had gone to all the missions and soup kitchens, the parks, the crummy bars in Montrose and the Heights, the ice-houses, the Greyhound and Amtrak stations where derelict men and women slept on wooden benches. He had cruised past the Wesleyan Terrace Shopping Center three times a day. He had tried the city's hospitals and the jail. Without luck.

There was nothing more he could do except do it all over again.

"Okay," Rick said, "I understand. And now, if it's not too much trouble, try to concentrate on Madame La Farge, our worried client."

"Why is she worried? We've prepped her till she's sick of it. We've got a great case."

"Because you've been neglecting her. She called *me* on Friday to chat. She must have been real desperate. I told her you were thinking about her night and day."

"I am," Warren said.

In Judge Bingham's baronial wood-paneled courtroom, the first row of public benches was set aside for the media. Outside, in the crowded hallway, the halogen lights above the TV cameras glared brightly. Reporters thrust microphones at opposing counsel. Johnnie Faye Boudreau, outfitted in the gray shantung suit that she had bought at Neiman-Marcus on the day she had murdered Dan Ho Trunh, assumed a modest position between and just behind her lawyers.

"Mr. Levine and I expect a short trial, and a verdict of not guilty for the murder of Dr. Ott," Warren said into the microphones.

"Will Ms. Boudreau testify on her own behalf?"

"When the time comes, Mr. Levine and I will confer with our client and make the proper decision. Now, if you'll excuse us . . ."

The reporters turned to Bob Altschuler, in a flawless black double-breasted suit that hid his growing girth.

Headed for a political campaign leading to a judgeship, he was always happy to talk to reporters.

"I don't represent the state so much as I do the victims and the grieving families of the victims. That's a concept we tend to forget about in this day and age. Now, in this particular case . . ."

On the way into the courtroom, Johnnie Faye tugged at Warren's arm. "You know, you could have done that with a little more enthusiasm. You could have said *you* believed I wasn't guilty."

"That's what we hope the jury will say," Warren replied.

"Am I going to testify or not?"

"If it's necessary."

"So why have you been working my ass off and telling me what to say when I get up there?"

"Wait." Warren stopped to face her, and made sure Rick heard his words. "I never told you what to say, only how to say it. I told you, if you testify, to tell the truth. Remember that."

Voir dire began. This was not capital murder: the prospective jurors could be interrogated en bloc in a single panel of sixty.

Johnnie Faye helped the defense team make their picks. "I don't like that woman in chartreuse, the nurse. She looked at me in a kind of nasty way." And: "That guy in the black windbreaker—he's sympathetic. I can tell. Pick him."

Rick in each instance argued with her. The nurse was divorced, and nurses dealt with battered women; she would be a fine defense-oriented juror. The man in the windbreaker was a Lutheran; they believed in an eye for an eye.

Warren said, "Let her have her way. She has good instincts."

For this trial Bob Altschuler had chosen to work with two young assistant district attorneys, one man and one woman, whom he was grooming for other courts. Both had close-cropped hair and wore glasses, and neither one ever smiled except at each other. "They look mean," Johnnie Faye whispered.

"They *are* mean," Rick said. "It's a prerequisite for the job."

Maria Hahn recorded the proceedings. Whenever she caught Warren's eye, she smiled decorously.

The jury was chosen by two o'clock the next afternoon, and Judge Bingham then called chief counsel to the bench. On the shelf just below the judge's fingertips, Warren could glimpse stacks of various court documents, a book on how to enlarge your vocabulary, a copy of Fowler's *Modern English Usage,* and a slim pamphlet on the care and growing of zinnias.

The judge said, "We can begin now if you like. Get through the opening statements. Or do it tomorrow morning. You two gentlemen decide."

Altschuler shrugged. "The state is ready."

"The defense is ready," Warren said.

That evening he and Maria drove in her car to Tranquility Park. Some homeless men were camped there, sleeping or cooking meager meals under the magnolia trees. Some were gaunt, some seemed well fed. Most had beards and looked like unwashed loggers. Shopping carts were parked under several trees.

None of them wore any of Dan Ho Trunh's clothing. Warren talked to each man: none had been in the Wesleyan Terrace parking lot in late May when a shot was fired, or at least none admitted to it. Warren watched their eyes carefully as they responded, and he also held a folded ten-dollar bill between two fingers.

"Let's try Hermann Park," he suggested.

In the car, Maria said, "You made a good opening speech today. Short and sweet."

"Did I? I just stated the facts and what we intend to prove."

"That's what an opening's meant to be. Bob went on forever, nearly put the jury to sleep. He sounded more like he was giving final argument."

"He's Harris County's answer to the neutron bomb," Warren said. "All the buildings remain standing, but all the people succumb to his commentary."

"Why didn't you object?"

"Our case will speak for itself." He thought for a while. "Which reminds me—what ever happened between you and Bob?"

"I shouldn't tell you."

"Then don't."

"But I will."

Bob Altschuler had been assigned as chief prosecutor in Judge Bingham's court three years ago, when Maria's son Randy was five. Randy's father was a Dallas homicide detective who had come to Houston to testify in some case. "I hopped into the sack with him a few times," she said, "and woke up pregnant. I was really pissed off. I didn't want this guy as a husband—he was a hunk, nothing more. But I decided I wanted to have the baby. I was thirty-one years old, the timing was right. I'd gone through an awful abortion when I was nineteen. So I had Randy. No regrets. I love that kid."

With Bob Altschuler it was a sweet affair because it was dangerous; he was top gun in the 342nd and he was married. She was in love with his mind, he with her body.

Warren could easily understand that.

"The thing is, he wanted to leave his wife and kids and marry me. He has three daughters, teenagers, very difficult young ladies. Apparently it's hell at home—Hysteria City, rock and roll, locked bathrooms. And the wife's in and out of therapy. I was tempted, because Bob was crazy about me and he really liked Randy. I kept telling him that Randy would get to be a teenager too, but he said boys are different. Anyway, in the end, I wouldn't do it. An affair is one thing, but I didn't really love him and it was breaking up a home. I believe in that stuff. You can't keep trading off. So we broke up. He took it a little hard."

"That's apparent."

"Yeah, I guess so. I still like him. He's a terrific lawyer, tough to beat in trial. Now you tell me what happened with you and your wife."

As best he could, Warren told her.

Maria said, "I don't get it. She must be nuts. You're a wonderful man."

"Thank you. Most of the time I don't get it either. Maybe I wasn't always so wonderful."

"Well, shit happens."

Was that it? Warren wondered. Lately Charm had invaded his mind only at random moments. He wasn't getting over the hurt of her abandonment, but scar tissue was beginning to form. Knowing Maria had certainly helped. He had spent every other night with her after the night she had cooked the lasagna. They had hunted together for the man who wasn't there. When it had grown too boring or discouraging, he had made a U-turn and driven her home to bed. Once they had gone to a movie, bought popcorn, held hands. Her hands were slender and unusually cool. So shit happens. A simple view of events. Maybe, in the long run, wise. He saw Maria as a simple person, not extraordinary, as he had once seen Charm to be extraordinary. But maybe extraordinary people are too difficult to deal with, certainly to mate with. Too much drama and anxiety along with the stimulation. He didn't view himself as extraordinary; he was just a hardworking lawyer. One day he would have kids, new walls on which to hang his photographs, a new lawn to mow. Maybe he needed an ordinary woman who wanted to please him and whom he could please without doing emotional headstands. He wanted harmony, ease. In court he had his full share of drama, worry, self-torture. Maybe simplicity was the answer.

He pulled the car into a parking space near the stables in Hermann Park, where he had found and lost Pedro. It was a warm evening but not warm enough to sweat. The lights of the city glimmered through the trees, and he could see the glow of Johnnie Faye's high-rise, the lit windows spaced out at this distance like instrument panels of a jet.

"You see anyone?" Maria asked.

"No, but we'll poke around."

"Speaking of poke, have you ever done it on the grass under a tree at night?"

"Are you serious?"

"That's a subject I never joke about. Well, rarely."

"Have you?"

"No, but I always wanted to. I've got a beach blanket in the trunk."

"Can we look for my man first? So I won't be thinking of other things?"

Maria sighed. "Okay."

The shed behind the stables was empty, but Warren, using his flashlight, noticed some empty beer bottles and a rolled-up bundle of dirty clothing. The door to the stables was locked. He heard hoofs moving about in straw. Following the beam of the light, he walked across the springy dark grass toward the dressage ring.

Maria touched his arm. "Someone's there. Two guys, it looks like."

Warren raised the beam until it outlined two men leaning in repose against the wooden fence surrounding the ring. They were smoking and talking softly. Smoking a joint, he realized, from the sucking sound. As he and Maria drew closer, the tiny red tip vanished behind one of the men's backs.

A voice said, *"Qué pasó?"*

He shone the beam into one of the faces. A Mexican. Then into the other face.

"Pedro?"

"Quién es?"

"Me. The lawyer! The lawyer you ran away from, you

bastard! Hector's lawyer! I gave you forty bucks, remember?"

"Oh, yeah." Pedro turned to his companion. *"Es el pinche abogado de Hector. Me quería ir al juez para ayudarle, recuerdes?"*

—Hector's fucking lawyer, who wanted me to go to court to help him.

"This is your friend Armando?" Warren asked, trying to be a little friendlier now.

"This is Armando. He don't speak English."

"So what happened to you, Pedro? I came back to look for you and you were gone."

"Lost my job, man. Had to go. They feed you at the mission. But I doan like the mission. I come back."

"Let's get out of here," Warren said. "I'll buy you both a beer."

He drove them all to a nearby bar and bought a pitcher of Michelob on tap. "Listen, Pedro, and you too, Armando. I need you guys. More important, Hector needs you. His trial's still on. Next week I get to put on my witnesses. My turn, you understand? I get a chance to try and save your friend's life. I need you to get up there and swear that Hector didn't own a pistol. Will you do it? And don't bullshit me. Yes or no."

They kept looking calmly at Maria's breasts. She was drinking a beer with one arm wrapped around Warren's shoulder. It was chilly in the bar and her nipples were prominent under her white T-shirt.

"We get in trouble," Pedro said finally.

Warren said, "You'll get in trouble if you don't stop eyeballing my girlfriend's tits."

They stopped immediately.

Warren thought it over. "You mean trouble because you have no papers."

"That's it."

"I told you before, they can't ask you about that. I'll

protect you. You swear that Hector had no pistol, then you go."

For a while the two men talked rapidly in Spanish, arguing. Warren waited impatiently.

"Okay," Pedro said. He nodded at Armando: "But he doan speak English so good as me."

"If he testifies, the court will provide an interpreter. Where are you guys sleeping these days?"

Pedro shrugged. "Where we can."

"If you know a cheap hotel, I'll put you up there for a week. Or, wait—I've got a better idea. You can stay at my place. A nice apartment. Food, beer, all on me. Free. All you have to do is take care of my dog."

Again they talked rapidly together for a minute. Pedro turned back to Warren.

"You got a TV?"

"With cable. Movies day and night. Two Spanish-speaking channels."

"VCR?"

"That too. You can rent *Viva Zapata,* triple-X rated movies just down the block. Whatever you like. I pay."

"And we doan get arrested? Doan get kick out?"

"You have my word. *Mi palabra de honor.*"

Armando spoke again. Pedro said, "He wants to know if your dog bites."

"Not unless I tell her to," Warren said.

Back at his apartment in Ravendale, he said, "Don't use the telephone to call Mexico, I can't afford that." He figured they might do it anyway, but this way they would keep the calls to under ten minutes. And they would probably enjoy getting away with something that hadn't been offered.

"Hey, you bein' good to us," Pedro said. "We doan fuck with you now."

He sounded sincere, and Warren changed his mind. "You can call once a day."

"No telephone where we come from," Pedro explained.

Maria looked up from her nail-filing. "Why don't you ask them if they've seen the guy you're looking for?"

Warren gave a description of the man.

"Lotta guys look like that," Pedro said.

Warren described the clothes that had been taken from the dry cleaners. Pedro turned to Armando and chattered in his musical Spanish. Armando chattered back. Pedro said, "We know him. We seen him at the mission. Green sweater, gray suit. Sure. He's a fuckin' wino. Name is Jim something. Everyone laugh when he tell his whole name, but I doan get it. Few nights ago he get drunk and somebody steal all his new clothes."

"When did you see Jim last?" Warren said excitedly, leaning forward across the kitchen table. "Is he there now? Is he at the mission?"

"No, he come and go. He there one night, then he gone for a long time. Then he come back. Then he go. He sleep all over town. I see him maybe two nights ago."

"But you know him? You could recognize him?"

Pedro nodded.

"Listen," Warren said, "I've got a job for you guys. I'm in court all day on another trial, another case. At night I have to work on it too. I'll pay you to look for this Jim. You find him, you bring him to me—or you hold him and call me and I'll come get him." He stopped for a moment to consider: incentive was the key. "You find him by the weekend I'll give you a hundred bucks each. Find him in the next few days, I'll give you more."

Above the crash of gunfire and squealing of tires that came from the TV, Pedro spoke to Armando. Looking immensely pleased with herself, Maria went into the little kitchen to mix a drink.

"Okay," Pedro said.

They shook hands. The Mexicans' palms were hard, but they shook hands softly, unaggressively, in their fashion.

A little while later, Pedro asked, "Where we sleep here? You got only one bed."

"It's a big bed. You can share it, or one of you can bunk down on the couch."

"Where you sleep?"

"Don't worry about me," Warren said.

"Pinche cabrón," Pedro said, winking. He was calling Warren a fucking billygoat. Warren wanted to protest, but it hardly seemed worth it.

In the car on the way back to her house, Maria hugged his arm. "See? Shit happens. But sometimes good things happen."

He laughed happily. The sound seemed to echo in her car, or perhaps in his mind. A long time since he had heard it.

The next day he started the second trial.

Reporters and television cameramen thronged the corridor outside Judge Bingham's courtroom. The state was ready to present its case against Johnnie Faye Boudreau for the murder of Dr. Clyde Ott.

"Are you satisfied with the jury, Mr. Blackburn? . . . Do you still anticipate a verdict of not guilty? . . . Will Ms. Boudreau testify on her own behalf?"

The questions came from all directions. Warren thought, a year ago I would have given blood for this kind of attention.

"Neither I nor my client have anything to say at this early stage of the trial. But I'm sure you can manage to squeeze a few words out of the prosecutor."

Bob Altschuler, in a stylish blue blazer and regimental tie, stepped forward to the microphones. Warren pulled Johnnie Faye into the courtroom.

The prosecution began its case in the usual manner, with the Harris County chief medical examiner establishing the cause of death: one .22-caliber bullet entering through the superciliar arch of the frontal lobe and exiting via the occipital lobe of the brain; a second bullet lodging in the middle lobe of the right lung. Death was instantaneous. The shots appeared to have been fired from a position directly in front of the complainant at a distance of approximately four to six feet.

Altschuler then asked if the medical examiner could determine whether or not Dr. Ott had been moving, or standing, or lying down when the bullets struck him. A lengthy technical explanation of angles and probable order of wounds followed.

"Can you boil that down for us, sir, and come to a conclusion that we laypersons who haven't been to medical school can understand?"

"In my considered opinion, when he was killed, Dr. Ott was standing still."

"Pass the witness."

Warren remembered all too well: *"He was running at you when you shot him?" "Yes." "He never hesitated? He never stopped?" "No."* That was Johnnie Faye's story, what she would testify to. If Clyde was standing still, it meant there was considerably less reason to shoot him. And it also meant she had lied to her lawyers.

Warren took the medical examiner on cross, but the doctor, who was not only a forensic pathologist but an attorney, refused to budge.

"Sir, your opinion that Dr. Ott was standing still when the bullets struck him—that's not necessarily a fact, is it?"

"In this instance, yes, it is. He was almost certainly standing still."

" '*Almost* certainly' doesn't mean 'certainly,' does it?"

"Well, I'll amend that. There's no doubt in my mind."

The more Warren nagged at him, the firmer the medical examiner became.

"Have you ever been proved wrong in such an opinion, sir?"

"Not that I'm aware of, except insofar as a jury's verdict of not guilty can be considered proof of error."

"What you mean, sir, is that in another case you testified to a set of facts or probabilities and the jury didn't believe you, isn't that right?"

"Objection," Altschuler said, rising. "He has no idea what another jury believed or didn't believe."

Warren turned to Judge Bingham. "Your honor, this is an expert witness—he's allowed to answer any way he pleases."

"It's close," the judge said, "but I don't think I can allow it. Objection sustained."

"No more questions," Warren said, sitting down, where he began to chew on the end of a pencil. Johnnie Faye threw him a dark, questioning look. Rick's eyes were hidden by a raised hand.

Photographs of the body were introduced into evidence, and then Tommy Ruiz, the homicide sergeant, told of his arrival at River Oaks. He had found the defendant waiting at the front door. She had flipped a cigarette onto the lawn before stepping out to meet him. Referring to his notes as transcribed into the HPD offense report, Ruiz quoted Johnnie Faye as saying: "When we got downstairs I tried to get out of the house, but Clyde was in the hallway and blocked the way. . . . I picked up a poker to defend myself and he grabbed it away from me. . . . I didn't mean to kill him, but he was coming at me like an old grizzly bear, waving that poker over his head." A poker had indeed been discovered about eighteen inches in front of a white leather sofa in the living room, Ruiz testified. Dr. Ott's body was half on the sofa, half on the floor.

Using a schoolteacher's pointer and a large three-colored architectural chart propped against an easel, Ruiz described the Ott house in detail. Altschuler had him dwell on the huge dimensions of the living room ("about thirty-two feet by nearly forty-five feet, plus an alcove for the piano and one for the bookcase and a sofa"), the placement of the furniture, the broad marble staircase ascending from the vestibule to the second floor, and the spaciousness of the archway leading from the living room to that vestibule and the front door.

Altschuler said, "Would it be difficult, Sergeant Ruiz, if a person was standing in either the archway or the vestibule, for another person to run past him—that is to say, run *around* him? I mean, was it too narrow for one person to dodge another person?"

Rick Levine objected. "Calls for speculation."

He and Warren had agreed that Rick would do the cross-examination of Sgt. Ruiz; only the lawyer scheduled to do cross could make objections during direct examination of the witness.

"Sustained," Judge Bingham said, after a little thought. "You can rephrase, Mr. Bob."

Altschuler asked, "Approximately how many people of average size, standing side by side, could fit across that archway, Sergeant Ruiz?"

"Ten or twelve," Ruiz replied.

"Was there any furniture or anything in that archway that might impede easy passage?"

"No, sir. Nothing."

"And how many square feet was the vestibule?"

"It was eighteen by eighteen. So I guess that's over three hundred square feet."

"Does three hundred and twenty-four square feet sound accurate?"

"Yes, it does."

"About the size of a large bedroom?"

"You could say that."

"Any furniture in the vestibule that could impede entrance or exit in any direction?"

"A couple of fancy wooden chairs, but they were against the wall. Two small carved tables with Tiffany lamps, but they were also against the wall on each side of the door. Basically, it was a large, empty space."

"When you arrived at Dr. Ott's house, how much time had elapsed since Ms. Boudreau's telephone call to the HPD dispatcher?"

"About twenty minutes."

"Did Ms. Boudreau seem drunk or sober?"

"Objection," Rick said swiftly. "They didn't run any tests on her. Calls for the witness to speculate."

"Sustained," the judge said.

"One more question. The white leather sofa in the living room—about how far was that from the bottom of the marble staircase?"

Ruiz looked carefully at his notes and then up at the architectural chart. "I'd say about sixty-five feet."

Altschuler passed the witness and Rick took him on cross. Unfortunately for the defense, Tommy Ruiz was not a cop who lied or fudged. Rick stayed away from the subject of the theoretical exit from the living room and concentrated on the distraught state of the defendant when the police arrived.

Altschuler asked for redirect. "Sergeant Ruiz, you just stated that soon after Ms. Boudreau met you at the front door smoking a cigarette, tears appeared in her eyes and she seemed very upset. Were you standing close to her, or were you at a distance?"

"Close. A few feet away."

"Did you smell alcohol on her breath?"

"No, sir."

"Did she appear to know what she was doing?"

Rick objected again.

In his reverberating baritone, Altschuler exclaimed, "*They* opened the door to speculation in this area, your honor! *They* asked the sergeant for his opinion of Ms. Boudreau's condition when he first arrived. I didn't object. Now I'm just following through."

Judge Bingham said, "I'm sorry, Mr. Levine. Mr. Altschuler is right. I have to overrule you." He turned to Ruiz. "You may answer."

"She seemed to know exactly what she was doing," Ruiz said.

"Did she then or later slur her words or make any movements or say anything that led you to believe she was at all drunk?"

"No," Ruiz said. "She seemed completely sober and in control."

In the street, with Johnnie Faye a few steps ahead of them, Rick looked thoughtfully into Warren's calm eyes. "This is going to be a little tougher than we thought it would be."

"Altschuler prepares," Warren observed.

At lunch with her lawyers, in the same garden restaurant where Warren had talked to Judge Bingham, Johnnie Faye's eyes were cloudy.

"I don't get it. What was that last part all about? What's the big deal about drunk or sober?"

Bob Altschuler, Warren explained, was mounting a double-barreled attack both on her credibility and her duty to retreat. In a few days, despite what had been said in front of the TV cameras, Johnnie Faye would take the witness stand. "And on cross," Warren said, "Altschuler will try to prove that you could have got out of the house, meaning there was no reason for you to shoot Clyde. If you were still a little drunk, as you claim you were, you might not have been able to get out so easily, and it helps to explain why you couldn't control the trigger. Being drunk doesn't negate a crime but it doesn't work against you. But Ruiz says you weren't drunk."

"Well, maybe when *he* got there I wasn't. But I was drunk when Clyde and I got back to the house. I told you that."

"Yes, you told us that."

"So what should I say about it?" Johnnie Faye looked worried. "Was I drunk or not? And what about that coroner? What about that standing-still bullshit?"

The lawyers were silent. Rick coughed. Warren sipped his iced tea. The medical examiner's testimony devastated her current version of self-defense.

Johnnie Faye's silver eye shadow glittered in reflected sunlight. "You guys told me I had nothing to worry about, that we'd win in a walk. You sons of bitches lied to me."

"I told you we had a good case if you were telling the truth," Warren said coolly. "If you always tell the truth, as my mother used to say to me when I lied about spilling Kool-Aid on the rug, then you can never forget what you said. So that's what you'd better do."

* * *

After lunch the state called Sgt. Jay Kulik, the HPD fingerprint expert. In his late thirties, Kulik was a curly-haired man with a handlebar mustache and a modest professional demeanor. After he had lectured at some length on the technicalities of fingerprint analysis, and it was established that both Clyde Ott's and Johnnie Faye Boudreau's prints were found on the thirty-two-inch-long, three-pound poker, Altschuler asked Kulik to describe in lay terms the exact placement of those prints.

"Her prints were all over it," Kulik said. "At the bottom, at the top, and in the middle. Both palm and fingertips."

"And Dr. Ott's prints?"

"One set only, at the bottom—the handle part. No palm prints. Just fingertips of both hands."

Altschuler produced the poker with its police I.D. tags, and had it entered into evidence. He asked permission from the judge to approach the witness.

"Please stand up, Sergeant. Pick up this poker in such a way that your palms don't touch it. In other words, just with your fingers."

Kulik did so. Obviously, an awkward grip.

Altschuler took a step backward. Turning to face Johnnie Faye, he fixed her with a stern look that blazed with reproach. With his back to the witness, he said loudly, "Sergeant, see if you can raise the poker over your head, holding it only with your fingertips. Can you do that?"

"It's not easy," Kulik said.

"You can't do it?"

"I can, but I wouldn't. It's not natural."

Altschuler turned to him again. "Now, Sergeant, grip the poker in a natural way and raise it over your head. You can swing it a little if you like."

Kulik drew it back and took a short swing, as if he were about to bunt.

"If that poker were taken from you now, Sergeant, and your office examined it, what would you find?"

"My fingerprints and palm prints."

"And there were none of Dr. Ott's palm prints on that poker, were there, when you examined it in your lab the day after his murder?"

"No, sir. None. Just prints of his fingertips."

"Does that lead you to believe, Sergeant Kulik, that Dr. Ott in fact *ever* held that poker up above the level of his shoulders?"

"No, sir, it doesn't."

"What does it suggest, Sergeant Kulik?"

"Objection," Warren called loudly. "Calls for sheer speculation."

"Sustained," said the judge.

Altschuler looked carefully at the jurors to assess whether or not they had understood. Satisfied, he said, "Pass the witness."

Warren asked for a ten-minute recess. Ignoring Johnnie Faye, he drew Rick into the hallway around the corner. He was pale. "The poker story," he said, "is a fucking fairy tale. She planted it. She put Clyde's prints on it after she shot him."

"You think the jury figured that out?" Rick asked.

"If any of them didn't, Altschuler will make it clear enough in final argument."

"I know this guy Kulik. He's an honest guy, a solid witness. You can't shake him."

"But I've got to do *something*. I just can't figure out *what*."

"Save it for final argument," Rick suggested. "Point out that Clyde's palm prints could easily have been smudged and unrecognizable. But don't do it now because Kulik will say it's highly unlikely. Just pass the witness, like it's not important what he said."

Warren shook his head gloomily. "What else are we going to find out that we don't know?"

"Maybe the truth," Rick said.

* * *

The next witness was Lorna Gerard. Plump and suntanned, with a nervous twitch at the corner of her mouth, Lorna Gerard was Sharon Underhill's much-divorced daughter. She had been asleep in the house on the night of the murder. Had seen nothing, heard nothing. She had taken some sleeping pills, and the house was so huge.

Altschuler asked if she had known the defendant, Johnnie Faye Boudreau.

"Yes, in connection with my stepfather. She was his mistress. I was with them on several occasions, sorry to say."

"Tell us about those occasions, if you will, Mrs. Gerard."

At the defense table, Johnnie Faye whispered sharply in Warren's ear. *"Object! It's none of her fucking business."*

Smiling crookedly, Warren whispered back, "That's not a proper objection."

"Just do it!"

Warren whispered, "Keep quiet, will you? I want to listen."

Lorna Gerard said that a month after Sharon's death, Clyde had brought Ms. Boudreau to Dallas, where they'd all had dinner at a French restaurant in the Anatole Hotel. The woman had said, "Clyde and I are going to get married." Clyde had said, "Maybe." The woman called him a "chickenshit motherfucker" and walked out in a rage. Clyde then said to his stepdaughter, "I'm getting rid of her as soon as I can, I promise you. Just let me handle it my way."

On another occasion, without Ms. Boudreau present, he said, "I'm frightened of her." Lorna Gerard had asked why, but Clyde declined to explain.

Judge Bingham overruled Warren's objection.

Johnnie Faye scribbled a note and shoved it at Warren. Rick, sitting on her other side, reached over and snatched it. The note read: *That's all hearsay! Object again!! Fight for me!!!*

Rick whispered, "It goes to the relationship between the parties, and to motive."

"Fuck the parties!" Johnnie Faye whispered back.

Rick said softly, "One's dead and male, and the other's not my type."

A week before Clyde's death, Lorna Gerard continued, she came down to visit old friends in Houston. Staying at the house in River Oaks, she heard the Boudreau woman arguing with Clyde in other rooms. She couldn't make out what they were saying. At one point when they were sitting in the gardens watching Clyde play tennis with a friend, Johnnie Faye tried to find out from Lorna how much allowance Clyde was giving her. Lorna wouldn't say. "I love your stepdaddy to death," Johnnie Faye told Lorna, "but he can be crazy. Sometimes I lose my temper."

"And did she say anything else about your stepfather?" Altschuler prodded.

"Yes, she certainly did. A few days before she shot Clyde, she was rattling on one afternoon while I was trying to watch TV, and she said to me, 'When your stepdaddy gets mean and drunk and passes out, I could cut his throat in his sleep.' Those very words. And there may have been more, but I put my hands over my ears."

Despite himself, Warren glanced quickly at Rick, who was blinking. Johnnie Faye had never told them of this incident or of the argument in the Dallas restaurant. They had asked her if there had been any such moments; she had denied it.

Altschuler asked Lorna Gerard, "You took Ms. Boudreau seriously?"

"I didn't think it was a joke."

"Did you ever see your late stepfather strike Ms. Boudreau, or hear him threaten her in any way with bodily harm?"

"No, he just wanted to get rid of her. But he didn't

know how. She had a hold on him of some kind. I can guess what it was."

"Move to strike!" Warren said sharply.

The judge solemnly instructed the jury to disregard all that Lorna Gerard had just said other than her answer in the negative.

"Your mother died in 1987, didn't she, Mrs. Gerard?"

"Yes."

"Under what circumstances?" Altschuler asked.

"She was murdered."

"Did Dr. Clyde Ott ever tell you who he thought had done it?"

"Objection," Warren snapped.

"Sustained. Don't answer, madam."

"Pass the witness," Altschuler said.

Warren took her on cross.

"How much allowance did your stepfather give you, Mrs. Gerard?"

"A hundred thousand dollars a year."

"And you also have an income of your own, don't you," Warren asked, "from your mother's estate?"

"Yes, I do."

"Did you love your stepfather?"

"Not really. I didn't know him well."

"Did you know Ms. Boudreau as well as your stepfather?"

"Of course not."

"You mean you knew her hardly at all—isn't that what you're saying?"

"I suppose so."

"And it's a fact, isn't it, that you didn't know her well enough to know when she was serious or when she was exaggerating?"

"Well, if you're referring to what she said about Clyde that night in front of the TV—"

Warren interrupted: "Mrs. Gerard, I didn't refer to anything. Just answer the question that I asked you."

"I knew her well enough for *that.*"

Clearing his throat, Warren said, "Mrs. Gerard, you must have heard people say things like that many times. Do you always take them seriously?"

"I took *her* seriously. You should have seen the look in her eyes."

Warren could have asked the judge to instruct her to be responsive and stop commenting, but he sensed that her prejudice against Johnnie Faye favored the defense.

"When Ms. Boudreau made the remark you attributed to her, about cutting Dr. Ott's throat in his sleep, you were downstairs watching TV?"

"Yes."

"Do you recall what program you were watching?"

"A movie, I think."

"You don't remember which one?"

"No."

"You were enjoying it?"

"Well, I was *trying* to."

"Where was Ms. Boudreau standing?"

"Behind me. Near me. I don't remember exactly."

"You were seated and she was standing, isn't that correct?"

"Yes, I guess so."

"Don't guess. Tell us if she was seated and you were standing."

"All right. Yes, that's how it was."

"Can you look in two directions at once, Mrs. Gerard?"

"No, of course not."

"Isn't it a fact that if you were watching a movie and Ms. Boudreau was standing behind you, you couldn't possibly see what you describe as 'the look in her eyes' when she made the remark you say she made? Just tell us yes or no, please."

"Well, I *saw* it. Don't ask me how. I *did.*"

"And then, after the alleged remark, you say you covered up your ears so that you wouldn't hear any more?"

"It wasn't an alleged remark. She said it."

"I didn't ask you that, Mrs. Gerard. I asked if you covered up your ears so you wouldn't hear any more."

"Yes, I did."

"Did you hear anything more that she said?"

"No. I didn't want to."

"So that if Ms. Boudreau said anything else, such as 'I was just joking' or 'I didn't mean it,' you wouldn't have heard her—isn't that right?"

"She didn't say anything like that."

Warren smiled. "No further questions."

"Nice work," Rick said when Warren returned to the defense table, just as the judge called a break so that Maria could stretch and flex her hands from the stenograph.

Johnnie Faye pulled her lawyers to a secluded spot down the corridor. Crimson spots burned on her cheeks. "I don't like the way this is going."

"You should have told us about that stuff," Warren said.

"Well, it's all a lie."

"You didn't have that discussion in the Anatole in Dallas?"

"No fucking way."

"You didn't say anything about Clyde when Lorna was watching television?"

"You think I'm nuts? Listen, that Lorna is a paranoid schizophrenic. You know what that is? She hates my guts! She's making the whole thing up!"

Neither Warren nor Rick said anything. Johnnie Faye fled to the bathroom down the hall.

"Our client's in deep shit," Rick said.

"Richly deserved. It's a lie from beginning to end. We should have expected it."

"What made us think this was an easy case?"

"Yeah, my dog could win this case, you said."

"Your dog *could* have won it if our client was telling the truth."

"Truth," said Warren, "is not her strong suit."

"Don't panic. You may have it in for her because of Quintana, but you've got to help her."

"I'm doing all I can," Warren said angrily.

After the coffee break, Kenneth Underhill testified. He was Sharon's dissolute son, a man in his late thirties, unemployed and unemployable, as he readily admitted. He had a drug habit; he was in treatment. He stated that twice he had witnessed angry arguments between Clyde Ott and Ms. Boudreau. One had been at dinner in the Anatole with his sister present, and he recounted it much as Lorna Gerard had done. The other had been at River Oaks; he couldn't remember exactly what had been said, but Ms. Boudreau had definitely been abusive.

When Altschuler passed the witness, Warren said, "No questions."

Johnnie Faye kicked him under the table in the ankle, and Warren gasped in pain. Just loudly enough for the judge and jury to hear, she hissed, "He's lying! What's *with* you?"

Clenching his teeth, bending to rub his sore ankle with one hand, Warren said quietly, "Don't *ever* do that again. Now listen to me. We may have to live with this, but the arguments cut two ways. Clyde provoked you. You provoked him. Get it?"

"And you provoke me. Get it?"

Warren smiled for the jury to see. "Now shut the fuck up. And if you kick me again, I'm walking out of the courtroom."

With the afternoon waning, Dr. Gordon Butterfield took the stand for the prosecution. Altschuler's aim was to defuse the issue of Clyde's threat made at the Houston Racquet Club.

". . . so, after the drink had been thrown by Ms. Boudreau, when Dr. Ott said, 'You bitch, I could happily kill you for that,' your firm impression was that he didn't mean it literally?"

"Absolutely not, and my wife had exactly the same impression. Clyde calmed down right away."

"Dr. Butterfield, how would you characterize Dr. Ott?"

"A hardworking, hard-living, gregarious man. Loyal, generous, and amusing. Quick-tempered but also very forgiving."

Altschuler passed the witness.

"Just one or two questions," Warren said casually. "Dr. Butterfield—hard-living, among other things, means hard-drinking?"

"Yes, to an extent."

"Partying?"

"Yes, I suppose so."

"Sexually promiscuous?"

"It might mean that."

"Quick-tempered means he lost his temper easily, isn't that right?"

"Yes, but—"

Warren cut him off: "You've answered. And losing one's temper means unreasonable anger and shouting, doesn't it?"

"I suppose so."

"Did Dr. Ott habitually use cocaine, to your knowledge?"

Butterfield glared and his cheeks flushed a rosy red. "You know the answer to that. I told you when you came to our house. He was a *doctor*."

"You're telling us, Dr. Butterfield, that it's impossible for a doctor to ever use cocaine?"

"It's *very* rare."

"No more questions."

Judge Bingham rapped his gavel and announced that the court would adjourn until nine o'clock the following morning. As they all rose while the jury left the courtroom, Rick turned to Warren and said, "You done good."

Johnnie Faye looked with a dignified curiosity at each

member of the retreating jury. When she turned on her lawyers the expression was replaced by a glare of rage.

"What a bunch of happy horseshit. You know that Clyde sniffed cocaine and you're just not smart enough to get that tightassed doctor pal of his to admit it. You let Ken—a goddam druggie!—say whatever he wanted to." She sneered: " 'Pass the fucking witness.' I could have any lawyer in town in a big case like this and I wind up with a pair of douche bags like you guys. Two cupcakes! One of them goes off to the racetrack every chance he gets, and the other slobbers in his beer because his wife left him, which I now fully understand. You didn't even ask that peckerhead fingerprint guy any questions! Did you guys make a deal with the prosecutor? This isn't a trial, it's a farce—a fucking kangaroo court! I think I have to talk to the judge."

"I'm not sure he'd be willing to listen," Rick said. "Now try to calm down."

"Calm down? I'm calm! I'm just shit-scared!"

"You don't have to be," Warren said. "We haven't told our side of the story yet. We have you to testify. How can we lose?"

After Johnnie Faye and Rick had gone, Warren trudged through the tunnel to the jail to visit Hector Quintana. He brought with him a Spanish-language newspaper and a paperback book of stories by García Márquez.

"I don't want you to think I've forgotten you," he said.

Hector, behind the steel mesh, looked listless and weary. He was having trouble sleeping, he said. The bed was lumpy, bowed in the middle. His back ached. One of his two friends in the jail, a man from Matamoros, had just pled out to twenty years in a drug-smuggling rap and been transferred up to Huntsville to do his time. The other friend, from Mexico City, who was awaiting sentencing on a guilty plea of manslaughter and who worked with him as a dishwasher, was always bringing Hector gifts: toothpaste, a new bar of Ivory soap, cigarettes. He was always asking questions about Hector's case.

"You think he's a snitch?" Warren asked.

"I doan know. I thought he was my fren'. Now I doan know." Hector looked as if he wanted to cry.

"Don't talk to him. I know that's tough, but it's the only way. Have you heard from your wife?"

Not lately. He hadn't written Francisca that he was in trouble. He didn't want her to worry.

"Is there anything I can do for you?" Warren asked.

Hector shook his head.

"I found your amigos, Pedro and Armando. They can't visit you, they'd have to show I.D. and they're afraid they'd get busted by Immigration. But they send you a hug, a big *abrazo*. They're going to testify for you. Say that you had no pistol."

He didn't tell him that they were also out hunting for the man called Jim. If indeed they were.

"I been thinking," Hector said. "I talk to my fren' from Mexico City, and some other guys. They say it's bad to have a trial. The jury kill you. I think maybe that happen. They look at me in a bad way. My fren' say TDC so crowded that in a few years they going to cut everyone's time down to *una tercera*." A third. "So maybe I should do what you say before."

"Do what, Hector?"

"Say I did it. Go for forty years, to jail. Get out in *una tercera*."

Warren knew that Hector had understood little of what had gone down in the courtroom with Siva Singh. He had been watching the jury. And listening to jailhouse lawyers.

"Hector, the choice is always yours. It's never too late until the jury leaves the courtroom to make up its mind. But don't be frightened. We can win. You can go home to El Palmito."

"I am frightened," Hector said.

As well he should be, Warren thought. It was his life at

risk, his years in jeopardy. There was the problem of the possession of the gun, the murder weapon. Nothing would erase that from the mind of the jury. Warren's heart felt weak. He summoned up all his courage and said, "Don't worry. Have faith in me."

He left the jail in a chastened mood. For Hector, he realized, I would do anything and I'm always asking myself: Am I doing *enough*? But not for Johnnie Faye. Rummaging in memory, he saw himself standing before Judge Parker after the Freer fiasco. "We're supposed to do all we can to help our clients," he had said then, "even if they've sold cocaine to children."

"I'm doing the best I can," he had said to Rick. But was that really true? He wanted to fulfill his obligation, triumph, win the case. Losing would not ruin his life, but it would put him right back where he had started from. But a powerful unreasoning part of him wanted her to be found guilty. Now he believed that the plea of self-defense was a sham; either she had coolly planned the murder of Clyde Ott or shot him in a rage and then, with equal cunning, calculated the best way to wear the cloak of innocence. She was guilty, Warren believed. She should pay the price. Go to prison for life. Rot, you fucking barracuda. If she walks out of that courtroom a free woman, and if Hector dies, I'll gladly kill her. He felt shipwrecked on an island of doubt. Yet he had willed it. He had chosen. Crazy, he thought again. Crazy. Like a shipwrecked sailor staring up at a copper sun, going blind.

If I'm so divided, if I loathe her as much as I do, how can I do my best? But that's what it means to be a lawyer.

The morning papers headlined the previous day's events in court: WITNESS IN DR. OTT'S MURDER TRIAL DETAILS ACCUSED'S THREAT AGAINST VICTIM. Under that was a photograph of Johnnie Faye leaving the courtroom with her lawyers. Chic in her gray shantung suit, she was beaming at the camera as if the jury had just rendered a verdict of not guilty.

The night before, in his apartment at Ravendale, Warren had watched the news on the local CBS affiliate. Then he switched over to Channel 26 for the independent news, catching the end of the trial report. Smiling again, Johnnie Faye's head was slightly bowed, as if in modest victory. The expression on his own face, as he brushed past the reporters' microphones, was one of stolid acceptance. Rick was no more sanguine. *We both look like we took it up the culo,* he thought. *And we did.*

Voice-over, Charm said coolly: "The prosecution, led by Assistant District Attorney Robert Altschuler, will continue presenting its case tomorrow, and then the defense will have its day in court, or as many days as it needs. Johnnie Faye Boudreau's chief counsel, Warren Blackburn, still has refused to comment on whether or not his client will testify—" Her face appeared against the familiar skyline backdrop. Looking well, Warren thought. "But attorneys around the courthouse say that Johnnie Faye Boudreau must take the stand if her plea is self-defense. We'll have an up-to-date report tomorrow at five o'clock on Independent Action News. . . ."

At eleven o'clock Pedro and Armando thrust open the door; Warren had given them his spare key. They'd hung around the mission since late afternoon, Pedro reported.

The man they knew as Jim hadn't showed up. They were hungry. What was to eat?

Warren said, "Look in the fridge, or run around the corner to the chicken place." He handed Pedro a twenty-dollar bill. "And tomorrow, do me a favor and go to the mission in the morning. Stay there until midnight. Later, if you have to. *Find* this guy. Call me in the late afternoon and leave a message on my machine—I want to know if anything's happening."

"No buses after midnight," Pedro explained.

"Take a taxi back. I'll pay for it."

The apartment was a mess. The ashtrays were full. There were dishes in the sink, wet towels crumpled on the bathroom floor, two empty six-packs of Carta Blanca on the coffee table and a pile of videotapes atop the TV.

"And keep this fucking place clean," Warren growled.

He left for Maria Hahn's condo.

"The State of Texas calls José Hurtado."

Warren consulted his copy of the witness list and the state's required order of proof, where three Hispanic names appeared next to the mailing address of the Hacienda restaurant. Hurtado was the maitre d' and another one, Daniel Villareal, the waiter. The third, Luis Sanchez, was no doubt one of the musicians.

Hurtado set the scene for the jury: a candlelight dinner, mariachi music, an arguing couple, and frozen margaritas. Many margaritas. Four margaritas before dinner, at the bar. Six more during dinner. He produced the check and Altschuler had it entered into evidence.

"Strong drinks, would you say?" the prosecutor asked.

"A margarita is strong. It is not meant for a child."

"Pass the witness."

"No questions," Warren said.

Luis Sanchez took the oath and settled into the wooden chair. He was not one of the two musicians Warren had talked to on his visit to the Hacienda. He was a thin, grave, pockmarked man of forty. I missed this one, Warren realized grimly. Shit happens.

Sanchez, as it turned out, was the barman. He remembered Dr. Ott, who seemed already drunk when he walked into the restaurant and consumed three of the four margaritas the barman had served. The doctor and the lady with him had argued. She had cursed at the doctor.

"Do you remember what words she used?" Altschuler asked.

"I cannot repeat them here."

"You can, Mr. Sanchez. It's allowed. We're all adults, this is a court of law, and we want the truth."

" 'Cocksucker,' " the barman said. " 'Stupid fucking son of a bitch.' "

"Is that all?" Altschuler asked mildly.

"She kept saying to the man, 'You lied to me.' She was very angry."

"Lied about what? Did she say?"

"I didn't hear."

"And were you abusive to him?" Warren had asked Johnnie Faye. *"No, I just shut up and listened."*

His turn came. He was not at all prepared, but the course was clear. "Mr. Sanchez," Warren asked, "were you the only barman at the bar that evening when Dr. Ott and Ms. Boudreau were waiting for a table?"

"Yes."

"Are you an experienced barman?"

"Yes." Sanchez smiled for the first time.

"You know how to mix all those fancy drinks? Frozen margaritas, whiskey sours, piña coladas, and so forth?"

"Of course," Sanchez said, raising his chin a little.

"How many people were at the bar, let's say between nine and nine-thirty, when Dr. Ott and Ms. Boudreau were there?"

"Many people. Ten, twelve. I cannot remember exactly."

"You mixed and served every different drink for those ten or twelve people?"

"Of course."

"You're really able to do that?"

"Of course."

"And you have to move back and forth between your different customers, don't you, to take new orders and mix drinks?"

"Yes."

"So you weren't watching Dr. Ott and Ms. Boudreau all the time, were you?"

"No."

"Do you listen to all your customers' private conversations?"

"Of course not."

"You're too busy, isn't that true?"

"That is true."

"And you certainly weren't listening to Dr. Ott and Ms. Boudreau *all* the time they talked, isn't that true?"

"Yes, that is true."

"However, you did hear an argument between them?"

"Yes."

"But you didn't hear every single word of that argument, did you?"

"I cannot say. The bar is noisy."

"So that if Dr. Ott had cursed at Ms. Boudreau, or insulted her before she cursed at him, you might not have heard it—isn't that a fact?"

"That is possible," Sanchez said.

"Have you heard many arguments at your bar in your long experience as barman?"

"Many."

"Did you ever hear one person argue with himself or herself?"

"I don't understand."

"Strike the question. How many people does it take to argue?"

"Two," Sanchez said.

"No further questions."

Daniel Villareal, the table waiter, took the stand. He had served six margaritas at the table, he told Altschuler: three to the gentleman and three to the lady. The lady had ordered them. The lady, he noticed, only drank one of hers. She pushed the others across the table to the gentleman.

"And he drank them?"

"I didn't see him drinking all of them, but all the empty glasses were in front of him."

"What did the lady drink during all that time?"

"A lot of water. I had to fill her glass twice."

Warren looked at the jury and for the first time understood how clever Altschuler had been in selecting them. The women jurors all had a certain prim look. They would assume that seven or eight margaritas would put a man under the table, at least make his head reel. Certainly render him incapable of halting the exit through an eighteen-foot-wide vestibule of a woman ten years younger, a hundred pounds lighter, and in control of her faculties.

Johnnie Faye's face at the defense table was as wooden as the plank on which she rested her elbows. Rick whispered in Warren's ear, "We're getting killed. Don't do any cross on this guy either. It'll only get worse."

"I've got to try," Warren said.

He asked the waiter, "Please describe Dr. Ott."

"A big man. Lot of hair, going gray. Red cheeks."

"Did he tip well?"

"Oh, yes."

"Then you had waited on him before?"

"Yes."

"He always drank a lot, didn't he?"

"Yes."

"Did he ever fall down or stumble?"

"No."

"Did he become incoherent? Did he talk in a way that you couldn't understand him?"

"No."

"Have you noticed that big men who are regular heavy drinkers have a greater capacity for alcohol than is normal?"

"Objection," Altschuler interrupted. "Calls for an opinion."

"Sustained."

"No further questions," Warren said.

Altschuler called the last witness for the state: Harry T. Morse. A middle-aged man with thinning hair and a beaked nose, Morse identified himself as the assistant manager of Western America, a pistol and rifle practice range seven miles north of the city. They also sold guns and ammunition.

Morse carried a bundle of papers wrapped in rubber bands, and Warren wondered what they were.

"Do you see anyone in this courtroom who ever came to Western America, Mr. Morse? Besides myself to interview you, that is."

"Yes, two people. That woman in the gray suit is one— the woman sitting over there." He pointed to Johnnie Faye Boudreau. "And the judge is the other."

Judge Bingham clapped a hand to his lined brown forehead. He carried a .38 Saturday Night Special in his waistband. He had been threatened several times by convicted felons, and someone had once pulled a knife on him in front of his church.

"Never mind the judge," Altschuler said, smiling. "We'll concentrate on the lady in the gray suit. Why are you so sure it's she whom you saw at Western America?"

"Object as to relevance," Warren said desperately. He remembered asking Johnnie Faye if she had ever practiced with the pistol. *Once, five years ago, when I bought it. I don't even think I hit the target more than two or three times.* He had a feeling that was about to be contradicted.

"Overruled. You can answer, sir."

"Good-looking lady," Morse said. "Kind of memorable."

Morse said that he had seen her practice at least twice at the pistol firing range.

"Did you observe what kind of pistol she used?"

"She had three. A .32-caliber Diamondback Colt, an ivory-handled Colt .45, and what looked like a .22-caliber semiautomatic."

Warren's heart beat a little faster in his breast. He leaned forward intently, resisting the urge to look at Johnnie Faye.

"Three?" Altschuler's mouth gaped in feigned surprise.

"Yes, sir."

"How are you able to identify those three guns so positively, Mr. Morse?"

"She laid them down on the counter when she registered to shoot. I noticed them. We don't get that many ladies, and I never saw one bring three pistols before."

"When did all this take place?"

"The first time, maybe a year or so ago. The last time, not so long ago."

"Can you be more specific about the last time?"

"Wish I could. April or May's my best guess."

"Don't guess. Think about it. When was the last time?"

"Late April. Maybe early May."

Johnnie Faye pushed a note at Warren. *Do something!!*

Without taking his eyes from the jury, he wrote under her words: *Nothing to do—yet.*

Altschuler said, "Mr. Morse, do you have your registration sheets for the last eighteen months with you today in court? I'm referring to the names and addresses the people give to you when they come to practice at Western America."

Morse offered the thick bundle of papers wrapped in rubber bands, and they were entered into evidence for the state.

"Have you and I studied those registration sheets together, Mr. Morse? On two separate occasions?"

"Sure have," Morse said.

"Does the name Johnnie Faye Boudreau appear anywhere on those sheets?"

"No, sir. And we looked hard for it."

"Can you account for that, Mr. Morse?"

"Well, I saw her sign in each time. So she must have used a fake name."

Warren objected as to relevance; he was overruled.

"Just a few more questions, Mr. Morse, and then you can go back to Western America." Altschuler walked over to the jury box, where, one hand on the railing, he paused for dramatic effect. "Did you ever watch the lady in the gray suit—the lady sitting over there, who is the defendant in this murder case—shoot with her three pistols at the targets on your range?"

"Both times. I was interested."

"And what did you observe?"

"She hit that bull's-eye a lot. Almost always hit the target."

"Was she equally skilled with each weapon?"

"She had trouble with the .45. It has a lot of kick. It's an army weapon."

"You saw her fire the semiautomatic .22?"

"Yeah, but it wasn't semiautomatic. Probably had the sear filed down. You pull the trigger and don't let go, it goes right on shooting."

"In your opinion, based on your eyewitness expert observation, was she comfortable with that .22? Did it look like she was aware of its automatic capability?"

"She was aware. She looked comfortable, like she knew what she was doing. Bang bang bang. Like it was fun."

"Pass the witness," Altschuler said, glaring at Johnnie Faye Boudreau.

Hopeless, Warren thought. He had a client who never told him the truth. But he strode forward with confidence into the well of the courtroom, halting a fair distance before Harry T. Morse.

"Sir. You just said that Ms. Boudreau fired the pistol like it was fun. You did say that, didn't you?"

"I may have."

"Did you or didn't you? I can have the record read back to you if you're confused."

"I said it," Morse replied, glowering a little. "I'm not confused."

"What's your definition of fun, sir?"

"Having a good time, I guess."

"Do you equate having a good time with serious intent?"

"Not usually."

Warren glanced at the jury. Their faces were like stone.

"You do have people who come to Western America just to have a good time, don't you?"

"Sure."

"You wouldn't characterize your customers as potential murderers, would you?"

"Hell, no," Morse said.

"You wouldn't characterize Judge Dwight Bingham as a potential murderer, just because he goes to your firing range to practice with his pistol?"

"Absolutely not," Morse said. "The people have a right to bear arms. Says so in the Constitution. Can't bear arms safely unless you know how to use them."

"Thank you, Mr. Morse. No more questions."

Altschuler stood and said gravely, yet with an air of triumph: "The state rests its case."

The clouds were low-lying, the sky elephant-gray. A tornado danced along the western regions of the county. At five o'clock Warren and Rick ducked into a small Greek restaurant near the courthouse, where Warren ordered a Greek salad and an espresso. He had not eaten lunch and he was hungry. Rick drank a double scotch on the rocks.

"Look, here's the problem," Rick said. "Despite all the shit that got thrown at us today, our case hinges on whether or not the jury will believe the dragon lady when she gets up there to testify. She says Clyde threatened her life, and now it turns out she threatened *his* life. She says she was drunk and had no way to get out of the house—the restaurant people say she was sober and kept shoving drinks across the table at Clyde, and Tommy Ruiz swears you could have driven a Mack truck on either side of the good drunken doctor through that hallway. She says Clyde was coming at her with the poker—the medical examiner claims he was shot standing still. Worse, Kulik says there should be palm prints. Then this last guy gets up there and paints Miss Corpus Christi as a cross between Annie Oakley and a moll from Murder Incorporated. And we still haven't got to that funny little business of the poker winding up on the wrong side of the sofa. What I'm saying is, the black widow is headed for life in the penitentiary. If we want to win this case, you have to talk to her. You *do* want to win it, don't you?"

Warren had no idea how to answer with any full measure of truth. Rick was an energetic man who always did his best. And yet he was no moralist. A younger lawyer in his office had once asked him, "Do your clients call you Rick or Mr. Levine?" Rick had replied, "Depends on the size of the fee. If it's high enough, they can call me asshole."

In the restaurant Warren put down his espresso and asked, "Do you remember when we first started out? When we passed the bar and took the oath? Do you remember how we felt?"

"I was scared," Rick said.

"So was I, but that's not what I mean. I felt I was on the side of the angels, a regular little Don Quixote. We were going to help people and have a good life at the same time. Be proud. We used to talk about the philosophy of justice, remember? I felt I was going to do so much. You did too."

"Yes," Rick said, "I remember that."

"And now we deal with scumbags, we help scumbags stay out of jail. Because it pays. Because it's a job."

"Your client, this Hector, doesn't sound like a scumbag—"

"He's not. He tried to rob a Circle K with an unloaded gun, but he's a decent man. Of course, I thought that about Virgil Freer. I'm older now. Maybe I make better distinctions."

"That's the answer." Rick nodded sagely. "Grow older. Make better distinctions."

Warren said, "I wish that I owned a shoe store like my grandfather. The worst you can do is pinch someone's bunions."

"No, you don't wish that. You love what you do, just like me, even when you hate it. Keeps you off the streets. You just wish life was simple black and white. But it's not. Never will be." Rick allowed himself the whisper of a sigh. "I know what you mean, but if you think about it too much, you go nuts. Do your job, enjoy your life. Like they say, this isn't a dress rehearsal. It's all we've got. Don't go nuts on me, boychik."

Warren nodded, trying in his mind to separate the concepts of what was ethical, what was practical, and what a man needed to do in order to preserve sanity and self-respect.

"Let me remind you of something," Rick said. "A lawyer's client in trial can't be guilty until a jury says so. Guilt is a technical, legal concept. A lawyer says to his client, 'I'm instructing you to tell the truth. But you testify however you think you should.' "

Warren still said nothing; his mind still churned.

"Jesus Christ!" Rick, in alarm, watched Warren's face reflect his thoughts. "You're not going to sell her down the river, are you?"

"No. I want to win. I'll talk to her."

"Then get her ready." Rick raised an eyebrow. He said quietly, "There are ways."

"I know there are."

"You want me to handle it?"

Warren shook his head emphatically. "I said I'll do it."

On his way to the jail to see Hector again, the pillar of rain beat mercilessly on Warren's head. He kept thinking of Harry T. Morse, who had casually mentioned that he had seen Johnnie Faye fire the gun that had killed Dan Ho Trunh. For a moment Warren had been thrilled, could think of nothing else. But if he brought Morse into Parker's court to try to identify the Diamond-back Colt, at some point he would have to admit his own knowledge. He could not do that.

"This can't be happening," he said aloud, in the rain. "This is fucking *insane.*"

Later, from Maria's bedroom, he called his apartment for messages. Pedro picked up the telephone.

"What the hell are you doing there?" Warren said angrily. "It's not even ten o'clock!"

"Take it easy, *patrón.*"

The mission had been closed since early morning, Pedro explained. Full of *policía.* Late last night some bum was shot to death in the toilet. Blown away, man. No one knew why. Two other men sitting in the open stalls saw it happen, had even seen the man who killed him. Another bum, they thought, but they didn't know him, had never seen him before. The cops had been asking questions of everybody all day.

Warren drew in a deep breath. He listened to the rain, still slapping against the roof and pouring through its gutters. He heard far-off thunder. He asked, "It wasn't Jim, was it?"

"No," Pedro said, "I tole you, they never seen him before."

"I mean the man who was shot and killed."

That wasn't Jim either. Pedro had thought of that. Lot of people knew Jim and no one had seen him for days. Might have left town. He did that sometimes, one guy said. Went south toward the border, had a common-law wife down there. No one knew which town.

"Did this guy you spoke to know Jim's last name?" Warren asked.

"Jus' his nickname. They all call him Jim Dandy. Suppose to mean something, but I doan know what."

They promised to go back the next day, if the cops were gone. "And your wife call you here, little time ago," Pedro said, with an understanding leer in his voice. "Say for you to call her."

"My wife? Are you sure? Did she give her name?"

"No, she just say, 'Ask him to call his wife.' "

Warren hung up. Another murder. Too much death, too many lies. A man wasn't meant to deal with this shit all his life. He was meant to plant his seed and mow his lawn and work at something that gave him pleasure. Wondering if that would ever happen, he walked into the living room, where Maria was watching television. He wondered also what Charm had wanted, then realized he didn't care.

The rain ended, the storm veered northward, and on Thursday morning the city sweltered under the pressure of ninety-degree wet air. It pressed a clammy hand against Warren's forehead. Sweat slid down his cheeks. Rick waited for him on the fifth floor of the courthouse outside the walnut-paneled halls of the 342nd.

"Did you talk to her?"

"Not yet," Warren said impatiently. "But I will. Give me a break, will you?"

Cool air blew. The sweat dried slowly, leaving a sticky film on his face and the small of his back. His jockey shorts surrounded him like a coat of mail.

The first witness Warren called for the defense was Dr. George Swayze, the intern who had treated Johnnie Faye the previous December at Hermann Hospital. In a clear voice Swayze read a copy of his diagnosis and treatment for the broken cheekbone, and then, under questioning, said, "She told me that her boyfriend had done it to her."

"Did she describe the boyfriend?" Warren asked.

"She said he was a big man. And he'd been drinking."

On cross, Altschuler asked the doctor, "Did she say which of her several boyfriends had hit her?"

Warren objected to *several boyfriends*.

"Please rephrase, Mr. Bob," the judge said.

When Altschuler did, the doctor answered, "No, she never named the man."

The next witness was Cathy Lewis, former waitress at the Grand Hotel. Rick had finally tracked her down through the Department of Motor Vehicles; he took her on direct examination. Over Altschuler's constant objections that they were trying Johnnie Faye Boudreau for murder and not Dr. Clyde Ott for past indiscretions, Cathy Lewis told the tale of her affair with Clyde, and his swatting her in the mouth "with his big hairy paw," so loosening three front teeth that she had to have them replaced.

Cathy Lewis said that Clyde had paid the dentist's bill, and had also given her $25,000 in cash.

"For what?" Rick asked.

"Kiss-off money, and so I'd shut up."

Bob Altschuler said to the judge, "Your honor, I'd like to approach the witness. I'd like to see her teeth close up."

When he looked into her open mouth, he said, "They look terrific! Would you do me a favor and go over to the jury box and show each and every one of the jurors what a fine job that dentist did?"

Red-faced, Cathy Lewis did as she was asked. When she was again seated in the witness chair, Altschuler asked, "Do you have a receipt for that $25,000 in cash that Dr. Ott supposedly gave you, Ms. Lewis?"

"No, sir."

"So we have to take your word for it, right?"

"Yes, sir."

"You've been a cocktail waitress for most of your adult life, isn't that right?"

"Yes, sir."

"Ever do it topless?"

"For a while."

"Ever go to bed with men for money?"

"Not really," she said, before Rick had a chance to spring up and shout an objection. Altschuler's booming laugh echoed in the big courtroom.

"You never fired a gun at Dr. Ott, did you?"

"No."

"Do you carry a gun?"

"No."

He passed the witness. On redirect, Rick got her to say that a few of the men she had slept with, including Clyde, had given her gifts, paid some bills. Sometimes the gifts were cash. But there was no direct equation between the gifts and sex.

A witness on cross-examination, Warren had long ago realized, is like the target in a knife-throwing act, except in the courtroom the one who throws the knives is a stranger.

"That Altschuler is some clown," Rick said during lunch. "He treats this like a circus."

"It is," Warren said.

After lunch Warren put on a man who owned a gun store in southwest Houston. Qualifying as a weapons expert, the witness was shown the old .22-caliber pistol that had ended Clyde Ott's life. Difficult to handle, he said, in the sense that continued pressure on the trigger could do a great deal of damage. Yes, you could fire it without cocking the action, although it would fire more quickly if you cocked it. And yes, of course you could fire single rounds from it if you immediately released the trigger after each round.

The last two witnesses of the day were former patients of Dr. Clyde Ott. Before the first could be sworn in, Altschuler sprang from his chair to demand an offer of proof: a debate without the jury present. "The only possible reason these two women can be here," he complained, "is to cast slurs on a dead man. But a dead man's not on trial!"

The judge called both lawyers to the bench for sidebar. Warren argued quietly that it was a major issue before the jury whether or not Clyde Ott was violent.

"Are these women going to say he beat them up?" Altschuler demanded.

"We'll find that out, won't we?" the judge said. "I'll allow them to testify, Warren, as long as you stick to what's relevant. We'll take the objections as they come, Bob."

Patricia Gurian—a shapely blond woman of forty, married, a social worker—took the stand. Normally, she said, she would see a gynecologist twice a year for checkups. On her second visit to Dr. Ott, the nurse left the room to take a telephone call. Dr. Ott began to fondle Mrs. Gurian's clitoris, asked if it was sensitive.

"Objection!" Altschuler yelled. "It's not only irrelevant, it's prurient!"

Warren said, "Your honor, it's a line of questioning leading to show the character of Dr. Ott relative to the defendant. It also explains what happens next. Absolutely necessary."

The judge sighed. "All right, but get to it quickly."

Did Mrs. Gurian think Dr. Ott was out of line?

"Absolutely," she said.

Had it ever happened with a previous gynecologist?

"Never."

Warren moved close to the jury box, and stood next to one of the prim woman jurors in the first row. "What did you do when that happened, Mrs. Gurian?"

"I decided to leave."

"Did Dr. Ott try to stop you?"

"Yes, he did."

"How?"

"He blocked my path. Put his hands on my arms."

"Were you frightened?"

"Not really, I knew I could call for the nurse. And I had Mace in my handbag."

"Did he strike you?"

"No."

"Did he threaten you physically?"

"No."

"Pass the witness," Warren said.

"Sidebar!" Altschuler cried, and drew Warren with him to the bench for another private conference. "Judge," he gasped, "that was crazy! The woman didn't claim violence! So where's the relevance?"

"You should be glad she didn't claim it," Warren said.

Altschuler said in a harsh whisper, "He did that just to get in that crap about playing around with her snatch. Judge, that's outrageous! You can't let him put the second patient on the stand. I won't hear of it!"

That seemed to miff Judge Bingham. "Bob, you won't hear of it, but I may." He turned to Warren. "Will this be relevant, young man?"

"I'm not clairvoyant, your honor, but I can promise relevance."

The judge said, "Nice word, almost as good as prurient. All right, put her on."

Maria had been standing nearby, taking it all down on her stenograph. From the corner of his eye, Warren saw her trying to hold back laughter.

Judith Tarr—redheaded and in her mid-thirties, a divorcée who ran a catering service—took the oath. She was also attractive and outspoken. She had been a patient of Dr. Ott's several years ago. They had had an affair.

"How did it begin?" Warren asked.

"I was on his table, in the stirrups, and he started to play around with me down there—"

"Objection!" Altschuler yelled, and was overruled.

"—and then Dr. Ott said to me, 'Do you mind? Do you like that? You've got one of the prettiest pussies I've ever seen.'" Ms. Tarr shrugged. "I was lonely at the time. I like doctors. So I said, 'No, I don't mind, and thank you.' And that's how it started."

Warren glanced at the jury. There had been some quick intakes of breath and two of the women were frowning. The only laughter came from the reporters' bench.

"Was Dr. Ott married at the time?" he asked.

"Yes, it was about half a year before his wife was killed."

"How long did your affair last?"

"Four months or so."

"Was he ever violent with you?"

"He was a rough man. He drank a lot and took cocaine

in my presence. I didn't like that. But no, he was never actually violent. I mean, he never hit me."

"Pass the witness," Warren said.

Altschuler, steaming, asked for a ten-minute break. He grabbed Warren by the elbow and steered him to the hallway that led to Judge Bingham's chambers. He was almost hopping up and down in his black cordovans. "What kind of shit was that?" he snapped. "You're not clairvoyant, but you 'can promise relevance.' What kind of schoolboy stuff are you trying to pull?"

"It worked, didn't it?"

"It was damn close to unethical!"

"Fuck you too," Warren said quietly.

He went back to the defense table. Johnnie Faye reached up and squeezed his hand. "Counselor," she said, "you're in high gear. I've got faith again."

Finished for the day, he sat with Johnnie Faye in her car in the San Jacinto Street parking lot. She was driving a rented Chevrolet. Where the Mercedes was, Warren had no idea. Repainted and sold, he guessed. He made no comment.

"Tomorrow morning I put you on the witness stand," he said, "so listen to me now. Dress conservatively, and go easy on the eye makeup. You may be nervous, but I won't ask any serious questions for the first five minutes until you get used to being up there. You can talk at length, if you care to, on anything that seems important and in your favor. Look at the jury from time to time but don't smile at them like you're trying to win friends. You can repeat anything that Clyde said to you. That's not hearsay. If I ask you what someone said, give it word for word, as best you can. Say, 'He said . . .' and then go on to quote him, or her. That always impresses a jury. And give details. Don't skimp. If you mention a TV set, don't just say 'a TV set.' Say 'a forty-inch Mitsubishi TV,' or whatever it is. That way the jury will learn to trust your memory for details. You understand?"

"I'm with you, counselor."

"When it comes time for cross, Altschuler will try to pull your chain. Don't get trapped into arguing with him. Be calm. Look him in the eye, and if it's an important answer and you're feeling particularly confident, speak directly to the jury. Don't ever look to me for help—the jury will notice and mark it against you. Keep your hands in your lap. Hold your handbag if you have to. If you don't know the answer to a question, don't guess. Say so. Most of his questions will force you to say yes or no and you've got to do it. But if he asks something like 'Do you still beat your dog?'—you've got a right to say, 'I never beat my dog.' If you're not sure whether the answer is yes or no, say something like, 'I don't think I can give an honest yes or no answer to that, sir.' If you don't understand a question, ask him to repeat it. If you think I should object and I don't, there's a good reason. Trust me. If I do get up to object, don't answer the question unless the judge tells you to. Is all that clear?"

"Like crystal."

"Do you have any questions?"

"I got about a hundred," Johnnie Faye said. "I've been listening to all those witnesses, same as you. What about this missing palm print—how do I account for that? What about those lies Lorna Gerard told about how I threatened Clyde? What do I say about whether or not Clyde was coming at me across that living room, like he *was*? What about after I came downstairs, my trying to get past him and out of the house, when I couldn't? And that bullshit about my being such a hotshot with that teeny .22? What do I *say*?"

"I keep telling you and you don't listen," Warren said. "You just tell the truth . . ."

He omitted the second part of Rick's dictum to witnesses: ". . . but you testify however you think you should." Warren made distinctions. He had to live with

himself when this case was over and he returned to save
Hector Quintana's life, if he could.

He went back to Ravendale at seven o'clock. Except for his
dog lying on the sofa with a tennis ball gripped in her
teeth, the apartment was empty. He took Oobie for a run
along the bayou, fed her, washed the dishes in the sink,
scrubbed the ashtrays, put out the garbage and straightened up the mess around the TV. He noticed a new cigarette burn in the sofa. The message light on his answering
machine was blinking.

The first voice on the machine was Pedro's.

"Callin' in, like you say to do. We talk to a guy knows
this Jim. He says he almost for sure left town. Gone home.
Some place called Beaver. Call you later. *Viva México,
patrón.*"

The second message was from Charm. She said in a
calm tone, "Please call me at home or at the station, Warren. I need to talk to you. I called yesterday too, left a
message with one of the handymen. Thanks."

Maria's voice came on the tape. She hadn't had a chance
to talk to him in court. "You were great today. Bob's nose
was really out of joint, you should have heard him carrying
on afterward with the judge. Are you coming here for dinner? No rush, but let me know. See you around, counselor."

Warren dug his old Rand-McNally Road Atlas out of a
carton and paged through to the back, to the list of Texas
cities and towns. There was no place called Beaver, or
anything that sounded like it. There were Beeville and
Bellville. He turned to the map and traced the coordinates
for Bellville. It was far to the north near the Louisiana
border. Beeville he knew: about two hundred miles southwest from Houston on Route 59, the road to Laredo and
the border.

He called Maria to tell her he would be at her apartment
between eight and eight-thirty. He would shop on the way,

broil some swordfish steaks. He set the phone down, drumming his fingers lightly on the tabletop. The last time he had spoken to Charm had been weeks ago, sitting on the hood of Johnnie Faye's Mercedes. He had expected to hear from her after his visit to Arthur Franklin, but what followed was silence. No word or papers from Franklin. Now she had called him twice.

Whatever it is, I don't need it. Let Franklin tell it to me.

He showered and changed his clothes, set out a fresh suit and other things for tomorrow to take to Maria's. Every morning between seven and eight he drove Oobie from Maria's house to his apartment and let her in the door without waking his Mexican guests. "You can leave her here," Maria said. "I can feed her if you get back late." He explained that Oobie was used to running along the bayou in the evenings. It was his way of maintaining a measure of independence. Not too much domesticity, not yet. These were his thoughts, not things he explained. But he knew that Maria understood. At least she never argued or commented.

"What's with you and Tall Maria?" Rick had asked yesterday.

"How do you mean?"

"I've got eyes. And not just me. Someone who lives near her saw you guys together a couple of times. Word gets around."

Warren didn't define what was happening with him and Tall Maria. He wasn't quite sure. Didn't want to speculate. Or know.

He was ready to leave the apartment, about to gather up the clothes neatly laid on the back of a chair by the front door. He hesitated. Charm had called on two successive days. If I don't call back I'm going to think about it and wonder. I'm going to feel guilty. She still has that power. Ridiculous, but true.

He tapped out the familiar number. The line was busy. For a few minutes he threw the tennis ball, and Oobie compulsively chased it across the carpet, retrieving it, dropping it at Warren's feet, panting and wagging her tail. He tried the number again. Still busy. He left the apartment.

"**H**ow old are you, Ms. Boudreau?" Warren asked pleasantly.

"Exactly forty. I'll be forty-one next month, on the fourteenth of August." She looked directly at a woman of approximately her own age sitting in the first row of the jury box, and smiled.

"And where were you born and brought up?"

"Odem, Texas, down near Corpus Christi. Just a little town. Cotton, goober, scrub oak country. My daddy had a gas station, an Exxon. My mama helped him run it. I worked there for a while pumping gas. I can change the oil on a car. Daddy was a part-time preacher too—taught me scripture. Passed away about five years back."

"You have brothers and sisters?"

"Two brothers, but they got killed in Vietnam. I guess they were what you'd call unsung heroes. One sister, and she still lives back in Odem near my mama. I visit every chance I get."

"Tell us what happened to you after you left Odem."

Altschuler objected: "Your honor, we're not here to listen to a paperback romance. The defendant is accused of willful murder."

"Yes, and so let's hear her," Judge Bingham said.

Johnnie Faye, wearing a simple dark-blue high-collared silk dress, told the story of her life to the jury and the packed courtroom. An early mistake in marriage. Struggles to educate herself, although she was basically a working gal. A wonderful experience at the age of twenty-one, when she was lucky enough to win a beauty contest. She'd been proud to represent Corpus Christi in the Miss Texas Pageant.

She talked about coming to Houston, a frightened country girl. She had to support herself so she danced for a living. Sent money back to her mama, who had a heart condition. Made another mistake in marriage. She shifted her gaze to the jury. "My fault. Chose wrong. I haven't been lucky with men."

No children. That was an ache inside her. She wished she'd had them but now it was too late. Finally, a good break: a chance to run a nightclub. Which she still did. It was hard work, the hours were strange, you met weird people. But life was full of compromises, God hadn't made a perfect world.

"How did you meet Dr. Clyde Ott?"

He had come to her club about four years ago. He had a girlfriend who danced there. He had introduced himself to Johnnie Faye. They had become friends.

"At first you were just friends?"

"Oh, yes. I wasn't a kid anymore. I didn't want to rush into things. And I knew he was married."

"But then you became intimate?"

"After a while. Yes, very intimate."

"How did you feel about the fact that Dr. Ott was married?"

"I felt bad, but he told me he was very unhappy with his wife. I was always a sucker for a sad story. I fell in love with him. I couldn't help myself."

"Love is a powerful emotion," Warren said. "Tell us, if you will, what your relationship with Dr. Ott was like."

Sharon had died so tragically. Johnnie Faye helped Clyde get through that. But he drank a lot, and smoked marijuana and sniffed cocaine, both of which she hated because drugs had killed one of her brothers. She advised Clyde on his investments and his health: sent him to an herbologist for a series of colonic irrigations, put him on rolled oats and alfalfa sprouts, begged him to slow down his ingestion of the flesh of dead cows and pigs. Tried to persuade him to stop smoking dope and sniffing the white powder. To little avail.

Clyde wanted to marry her. But she wasn't sure it was the right thing to do. He had a violent side to him. Once, in front of mutual friends, he threatened to kill her. Several times when he was drunk, he hit her. She begged him to go on the wagon. He tried once or twice but couldn't stick to it. Go to AA, she said. He refused, called it Mickey Mouse stuff. And then last December he struck her again, breaking her cheekbone. He was starting to accuse her of looking at other men, of actual involvement with them, and none of that was true. But he became even more jealous and threatening. That's when she realized the love affair was doomed.

But Clyde relied on her for so much. Let him down easy, she thought. Let's be friends, she told him. She wanted to help him get over her.

"And so you kept seeing him?"

"From time to time, if he promised to stay sober."

"Did he always keep his promise?"

"No, but I cared for him, so I saw him."

"Did you still sleep with him?"

"Now and then. I was weak, I guess. And he was very dominating."

"What were his relations like with his stepchildren, as far as you were able to observe?"

"He dominated them too. He said, 'Lorna's a lush, worse than me, and Ken's a middle-aged junkie.' At a restaurant in Dallas we had this big argument. Clyde told them he wanted to marry me, and that got Lorna all worked up. He was afraid she was going to embarrass us all at the dinner table, so he backed off and said, 'Well, maybe we won't get married. We'll see.' I got angry, and I cursed at him and walked out of the restaurant. That was dumb. I regretted it right away."

So she had come to terms with that, Warren thought, and decided to admit it—with a twist. Johnnie Faye's voice

was sincere. Delicately, Warren smiled. Not a smile of en-
couragement but one of acknowledgment. He hadn't had
to tell her what to do.

Time to test her.

"In Lorna Gerard's presence, Ms. Boudreau, did you
ever say anything like, 'When Clyde gets mean and drunk
and passes out, I'd like to cut his throat in his sleep'?"

Johnnie Faye blushed. "I did say that," she said calmly.
"One afternoon Lorna was watching TV downstairs in
Clyde's house, sitting in front of that big forty-inch Mitsubishi TV set, drinking about her sixth scotch on the rocks.
She was usually drunk before noon. Chivas Regal, as I
recall, in a crystal glass. I needed someone to talk to, because Clyde had walloped me again the night before, just
before he passed out. Lorna was real involved in her TV
program and wouldn't listen to me. So I had to grab her
attention somehow, and that's all I could think of saying.
Imagine, my saying such a thing in front of a man's stepdaughter! I tried right away to tell her I didn't mean it, but
she put her hands over her ears, wouldn't listen. I was so
ashamed afterward I cried. Just felt awful. I told Clyde
about it later that day when he was sober and he said,
'Lorna hates you 'cause she's got this weird idea you're
trying to convince me not to keep giving her money. Now
you've given her another reason to hate you.' "

Neat, Warren thought. Again a nice twist. She must
have been up half the night working all this out.

"Did you ever apologize to Mrs. Gerard?"

"Of course I did. But she was still upset and wouldn't
listen. I didn't blame her."

You vicious bitch, you would have cut *her* throat in her
sleep if you could have got away with it.

Warren moved forward to the evening of May 7, to dinner at the Hacienda restaurant. He asked if the dinner had
any particular purpose.

Johnnie Faye said, "From my point of view it was a
goodbye dinner. I just couldn't take it anymore. I figured,

we go to a public place I can tell him we're through—too many people around for him to haul off at me like he usually did. But it didn't work out that way."

Warren remembered the transcript of Johnnie Faye's tapes with Scoot: *"I wanted to marry him, but he kept stalling, and it goddam upset me. . . ."*

Well, she lied then—or was lying now. Or lying both times. No matter what Warren actually believed, there was no basis in fact for him to conclude she was perjuring herself. She was under oath now, and she hadn't been with any of her lawyers. It was not unethical for Warren to let her keep talking.

He reminded himself of that as he asked, "In the Hacienda, were you drunk too?"

"A little bit."

"Did you argue at the bar in the restaurant before you sat down to eat?"

"Yes, I was upset because Clyde told me he'd been snorting cocaine again. So I yelled, 'You lied to me!' Because he'd promised he wouldn't do that anymore. And I cursed at him too. I've got a foul mouth sometimes. Comes from running a nightclub—once in a while you have to deal with some mean people."

"At the bar of the Hacienda, and at the dinner table, did you try to get Clyde drunk?"

"He kept telling me to order new rounds of drinks. I said, 'I don't want to drink anymore.' He said, 'Just do what I say, woman.' So I did—I didn't want to get him any angrier than he was. When the drinks came he'd finish his real quick, then he'd say, 'If you're not drinking that, hand it over.' He could drink all night and not fall down."

"What happened after you left the restaurant?"

"I'd meant to take a taxi back to his place, on my own, because I had to pick up my car. But I figured if he drove he'd kill himself. So I drove him in his Porsche. And when we got to his house he said, 'Come on in, let's talk some more.' "

"Did you talk?"

"Well, we went upstairs for a while. Then he disappeared into the bathroom. He was in there maybe five minutes. When he came out I could see he was crazy. What he did in there, I don't know, but his eyes were red and he was sweating. And he was yelling again. He slapped me in the face. I ran downstairs and he followed me."

"To where?"

"To the living room."

"What did he do in the living room?"

She described how Clyde had screamed and cursed at her, how she had picked up the poker from the fireplace to keep him at bay, how he had twisted it away from her and raised it above his head.

"Please wait a moment, Ms. Boudreau," Warren said, holding up his hand. "Sergeant Ruiz has told this jury that when he arrived at River Oaks, you stated to him that you tried to get out of the house but Dr. Ott blocked your path." Warren waited a few moments, until she nodded. "Did that happen?"

"Oh, yes," Johnnie Faye said, "that happened *before.* I mean, when we first arrived. I wanted to leave then, and Clyde blocked the way. Of course I could have got round him—*then.* Sergeant Ruiz is absolutely right, it's a huge hallway. But Clyde wasn't going crazy *then.* He was begging me to stay and talk to him. I felt sorry for him, so I gave in. That's when we went upstairs."

Warren looked at her steadily. "You're saying that Dr. Ott didn't block your path *after* you both came downstairs, when you picked up the poker and he took it out of your hand?"

"That's right. Long before. I think I may have confused Sergeant Ruiz when I spoke to him later that night, because of course I was emotionally upset, to put it mildly."

"Then why, when you came downstairs *later,* knowing Dr. Ott was already angry and aggressive and, as you put it, 'crazy'—why didn't you then go straight out the door to the safety of your car?"

A spark showed in Johnnie Faye's eyes. A little coal of fury. But it was gone instantly after it glowed. Warren didn't think the jury had seen it.

"Because I'd left my handbag on the sofa in the living room," she explained. "My car was in the front driveway and the keys to my car—my Mercedes—were in my handbag. My brown handbag which I left on the white leather sofa before I went upstairs."

Details, Warren had told her. The Mitsubishi TV. The brown handbag, the white sofa. She was remembering, even if the details were part of a new fiction.

"I see." He took a moment to readjust, then moved closer to the jury box. He could feel the intensity of the jurors' concentration. "Ms. Boudreau," he said, having no idea what she would answer, "please tell us where you were after you came downstairs, where Dr. Ott was, what happened, and in what order."

Johnnie Faye obliged. She had come down the stairs and picked up her handbag from the sofa. Clyde yelled at her that he was going to beat the shit out of her. She picked up the poker to defend herself. He was a big, powerful man. He grabbed the poker from her and gave her a shove that sent her across the room, tumbling backward onto the sofa. Then he said, "Now I'll kill you, you bitch. You're just asking for it."

More new information. A new order of events. A creative mind at work.

Warren asked, "And then what did Dr. Ott do?"

"He rushed across the room toward me, and while he did that, I reached into my handbag—on the spur of the moment, you might say—and I took out my little pistol. That was just pure reaction, because I never intended to use it. My heart was beating *so* fast. Then he stopped, kind of skidded to a halt on the carpet, and stood still. He was maybe six feet away from me. I said, 'Don't come any closer, Clyde, or I'll shoot.' But I was just bluffing then.''

"You were still sitting on the sofa?"

"Yes."

"And he was standing still, not charging at you?"

"That's correct. But then I managed to stand up. And he lifted the poker to swing it at my head. I knew he'd kill me or at least beat me senseless. You've seen that poker— it's big and heavy. So I pulled the trigger of my pistol. I didn't mean to kill him, just maybe scare him or wound him and put him out of action so I could get away safely. But the pistol kept firing. I didn't mean for that to happen, I couldn't control my finger. I guess I was panicked or something.''

Clyde fell forward onto the sofa. She just barely managed to duck out of the way. The poker fell to the carpet.

"And how did you feel at that moment, Ms. Boudreau?"

"Terrified. Horrified at what I'd done. Awful." Johnnie Faye put her head in her hands. She rocked a little in the witness chair, to simulate grief.

Judge Bingham asked Warren, "Would you like to take a five-minute break, so that the witness can compose herself?"

"No, thank you, your honor. If it please the court, when Ms. Boudreau recovers, we'll go right on."

The judge glanced at his court reporter. Maria nodded; she was fine.

Johnnie Faye reached into her handbag, not for a .22 this time, but for a Kleenex. She blew her nose.

"I can go on now," she said softly. She turned to the judge. "Thank you for your concern, your honor."

"Ms. Boudreau—" Warren leaned forward. "After the shooting, did you call a doctor or an ambulance?"

"No, sir. I started to, but there was so much blood that I suspected the worst. I felt Clyde's pulse. None at all. I realized he was dead. Then I did a stupid thing." She hesitated, lowering her head.

Now Warren had no idea at all what was coming. But he asked, "What did you do, Ms. Boudreau?"

"I picked up the poker from the carpet where Clyde had dropped it. I don't know why I did that. I guess I was frightened and a little hysterical. I kept working the handle of the poker around in my hands. Maybe I just needed something to hold on to. I almost put it back against the fireplace, but then I thought, no, that's even more stupid. I kept telling myself, you did a terrible thing but it wasn't wrong—you *had* to do it. So then I dropped the poker back on the carpet just about where Clyde had dropped it."

Warren almost smiled in appreciation of her arrogance. All the bases were covered, including the missing palm prints. If the jury believed her. He looked Johnnie Faye in the eye. Her head was raised now and her glance was unwavering.

"Please tell the jury: before Dr. Ott raised the poker over his head, did you threaten or provoke him in any way?"

"No, sir."

"When Dr. Ott raised the poker over his head, did you fear for your life?"

"Yes. I was frightened out of my wits."

"Where were you at that moment?"

"I was sitting on the sofa, where he'd thrown me. Then I stood up."

"Did you have anywhere to retreat?"

"No, sir. The sofa was very close against a bookcase. I didn't have anyplace to go."

"Did his actions happen quickly or slowly?"

"Very quickly."

"Did you mean to kill Dr. Ott?"

"That was the last thing on my mind."

"You were sober or drunk when you pulled the trigger?"

"Sober by then. On the drive home I sobered up."

"Ms. Boudreau, you were sitting in this courtroom

when Mr. Harry Morse of Western America testified that you visited his pistol range and used a name other than your own. Why did you do that?"

"I value my privacy," she said. "And I didn't think there was any law against using a different name if you weren't out to cheat somebody. I didn't cheat Mr. Morse. I paid for my time and ammunition."

"Did you own as many as three pistols at that time?"

"I did then. One got stolen afterward, and the other, the .45, I keep at my club, in the office, in a desk drawer under lock and key. I'm the only one has a key."

"Did you have legal registration for all three pistols?"

"For the .45 and the .22, yes. Not the other one. Someone gave it to me as a gift. I forgot to register it."

"What did you need those pistols for?"

"Protection. We were held up about five or six years ago. And, like I told you, some weird people come to nightclubs. Someone followed me home once and tried to rape me. After that I carried a pistol in my car. That's the one that got stolen, the one that wasn't registered."

Not stolen. Thrown into a Dumpster, after you'd killed a man with it.

"One more thing, Ms. Boudreau. Mr. Morse also testified that when you were practicing at his pistol range, he observed you shooting. He said you were a good shot. Is that true?"

"Yes," she said, "I'm a very good shot."

"Then tell us, please, how you account for the fact that you meant only to wound Dr. Ott, and yet two of the three bullets you fired hit him in vital places and killed him?"

The coal didn't glow this time. She was in control of herself, prepared.

"I think he may have moved, just slightly. And I was in a panic. I had been thrown violently to the sofa. I was in fear of my life. My hands were shaking. It happened so quickly."

Warren had had enough. He said, "Pass the witness."

"We'll stop here," Judge Bingham said. "After lunch, Mr. Altschuler, if you care to, you can take the defendant on cross-examination."

Striding back to the defense table, from the corner of his eye Warren noticed a slender blond woman with high cheekbones sitting at the rear of the courtroom. Interesting-looking. She reminded him of Charm, except she was thinner, bonier. I should try to call Charm this evening, he thought.

"Good work," Rick said.

"What the hell are you talking about?" Warren shook his head angrily. "You think I told her to say all that shit?" He began to gather up his papers and stuff them into his briefcase, when someone tapped him lightly on the arm from behind. He turned—it was the blond woman who looked like Charm. Only he had made a slight mistake: it *was* Charm.

He was appalled to think that he hadn't recognized her. His wife had become a stranger.

The weight she had lost caused the bones of her face to be more clearly outlined. It made her seem older, but it was becoming, as if the last generalized fat of youth had finally worn away to reveal the specific woman. She shook his hand with a gentleness and gravity that were unfamiliar.

"I called twice and left messages. You didn't call back. I needed to talk to you."

He didn't protest that he had called and the line had been busy. That seemed so flimsy.

"This is a bad time, Charm."

"I know that," she said softly. "I'm sorry, but I thought we might grab a quick lunch. I have to get back to the station in an hour. Can you do it?"

Warren hesitated. He had said to Johnnie Faye all that he intended to say. In the afternoon she would undergo cross-examination; he wanted time to ponder the holes in her story, to figure out where Altschuler might gain entry to rip apart the whole fabric. It was definitely the wrong time for a visit, an unnerving chat. Part of him wanted to say to Charm, "Go away." Part of him wanted to say exactly the opposite. And he owed her a thank-you—it was she who had pointed out the blue dent on Johnnie Faye's Mercedes—although there was no way he could pay it.

On the other side of the defense table, Rick cleared his throat. "I'll go with our client. No problem."

Johnnie Faye smiled at him. "I'm fine. Take your wife to lunch."

As they left the courtroom the reporters moved in like a platoon of infantry veterans occupying a conquered village. But Warren brushed past them almost roughly, murmuring over his shoulder, "No comment now. When the trial is over, I'll talk." Steering Charm by the elbow, he fled with her through the welcome closing door of a down elevator. The bone of her elbow was hard enough but in the gloom of the elevator, descending, he felt that he was with a ghost.

Warren knew he had been weak. He should have said no. He didn't want to hear any more accusations or details of her affair or enter into further debate on the division of property. She could have written him a letter; she could have had Arthur Franklin contact him.

The feeling that he had succumbed to pressure was an odd one, a new one. No, he realized—old. It was the feeling he had lived with for those three years since Virgil Freer. But during that time he had denied it, tamped it down into deeper parts of his being, where it had festered. He had convinced himself and Charm that it was otherwise. Again he amended that. *Not* convinced Charm, not in the end. She had seen through his denial, his confusion, his ennui. But she hadn't been able to help him, and he surely hadn't been able to help himself, or hadn't wanted to with sufficient vigor. How odd, to see that so clearly now. Under the same skin was new resolve, new perception. He was not even the person he had been before Virgil Freer. The old person had assumed that there was logic to human events, that if you did *a*, then *b* would follow. If you worked diligently and imaginatively at something that gave you pleasure, you would succeed. If you married for love and were kind, you would be happy. If you raised children with discipline and loving guidance, they would turn out well and make you proud. Life was not like that. He had been naive, a child in a lawyer's gray suit. Life was an ongoing war against unseen and usually undefined enemies. Your own naivete was one of those enemies. You had to battle it, and improvise, and guard your back. See things clearly even if it made you scream.

He took Charm to the little Greek restaurant. There was

better food in other places near the courthouse, but those restaurants were always crowded, noisy with lawyers and court personnel, not places to bring your wife who was divorcing you and wanted to talk. On the way over he spoke succinctly about the case, and at his side Charm listened, apparently interested but for the most part silent. The Greek place had plastic tablecloths and thin, bent forks. The table was wobbly until Warren stuffed a folded paper napkin under one leg. He ordered a Coke and a salad, and Charm ordered something he couldn't pronounce. Warren leaned back in his chair.

"So? What's up?"

Charm said, "I've split up with Jack. That's the name of the man I was seeing. Jack Gordon. About two weeks ago."

Good, Warren thought. At the same time a part of him thought, not good at all. Not good for her and probably not good for me.

"I told you he was married, had three kids, and he was in the process of divorcing. That was all true. But maybe it wasn't as clear-cut as he made it sound. I mean, he's divorcing, but he still has a lot of ambivalent feelings about his wife—her name is Emily—and certainly about his children. He's Jewish. He feels a lot of guilt."

Warren cocked his head and asked, "Do you have to be Jewish to feel guilty about divorcing your wife and giving up your children?"

"No, but it adds a certain dimension to the process." Charm managed the pained shadow of a smile.

I like the way she puts things, Warren thought. I always did. Suddenly he felt in all his parts the enormous weight of loss.

"Anyway," she resumed, "I'm not into ambivalence. We had it out, and he cried, and I wasn't exactly dry-eyed, and I finally said, 'You're a grown man, go back to New York, see Emily. Get your act together.' So he did, but then I went through a lot of soul-searching, the result of which was that I decided all this was a little too complicated for me, and maybe I hadn't been thinking all that clearly. Maybe my feelings for him were ambivalent too. I mean, I cared for him, but I wasn't up for all that Sturm und Drang. And then there was you. Jack was always jealous of my feelings there. I told Jack a lot about you."

"Oh?" Warren felt uncomfortable. And yet he was curious.

"He wound up thinking you were a pretty nice guy, even though you threatened to stomp him with your cowboy boots. He couldn't quite figure out why I'd left you."

Warren said nothing.

"So I called him in New York about ten days ago," Charm related, "and told him it was all over. I suspect in some way he was relieved. It had all happened too soon for him. I mean, too soon after his marriage ended."

"Well," Warren said, "life doesn't always work on a convenient timetable"—aware that he was skirting the deeper issue. He busied himself with his salad, picking out the last bits of feta cheese.

He looked up and saw that Charm was disconsolate. She lowered her head and raised one hand to press against her temples. She had hardly touched her food.

"I feel so shitty," she murmured.

"Because Jack's gone."

"Partly. Mostly because I walked out on you the way I did. Or kicked you out, as the case may be. I made a mistake. Now I'm paying for it."

She had said this without his being able to see her eyes. When finally she lowered her hand, he saw that her eyes were filmed with tears. He ground his teeth as some of her pain invaded him.

"I apologize," she said. She still was not looking directly at him; her eyes were lowered like a penitent's. She was sniffling. "For then, and for now. I shouldn't come to you like this and snivel like a schoolgirl. But I had to tell you."

"I don't know what to say, Charm." And that was true.

"You don't have to say anything. Well, maybe you do. Do you hate me, Warren?"

"No."

"*Did* you hate me?"

"Hate is the wrong word. I was angry. I was hurt. You can understand that, can't you?"

"Did you find another woman?"

"Yes, there is someone else."

"Shit," Charm said. She reached into her handbag and blew her nose sharply in a tissue. "Well, that's the way it goes, I guess. Is it serious?"

Warren said, "It's still in the fun stage."

Charm began stuffing things back into her handbag. "I'm going to let you pay for lunch. I'm leaving." She spoke nervously, softly. "I'm so ashamed of the way I acted with you. I didn't stop loving you, I just got fed up with our life. I came here to tell you that, and that other stuff, and to ask you if . . ." She choked a little and the echo of her voice crowded the air with melancholy. "And to ask if you'd come home. Not today, but when you were ready. Don't answer now. I know what you'd answer. I can see it in your eyes. And don't pity me. I'll be okay."

He wanted to say something, although he had no idea what words would come from his mouth. His mind was jammed, the circuitry overloaded with contradictory thoughts and emotions: pity and anger and tenderness, a burst of affection followed by a stab of disgust, even a flash-flood memory of what he had once called love. But he had no chance to voice any of them. He felt his lungs were filled with sorrow, not air. She fled from the restaurant.

Rising from his chair, Warren watched her reach the door and shove it open, vanish into the hot street. What a good-looking woman, he thought—what great legs, what a gorgeous ass. What heart, what soul. What a quick mouth. What a fool she was. And I don't want her back.

There it was, not to be denied. He looked at his watch.

He had ten minutes to pay the bill and get to the courthouse for the cross-examination of his client.

Glancing at his notes, Bob Altschuler leaned back lazily in his chair at the prosecutor's table. He said, "Ms. Boudreau, I remind you that you're still under oath to tell the truth."

Johnnie Faye's hands were on her handbag in her lap. She met Altschuler's distant hard gaze without wavering.

"We'll start at the beginning, work our way gradually up to the night of the murder, just as your attorney did. Does that suit you?"

"That's up to you, sir," Johnnie Faye said.

Altschuler raised an eyebrow, then studied the yellow legal pad. "All right . . . I recall that you said drugs had killed one of your brothers. Did you say that?"

"Yes, I did."

"But you also said, earlier in your testimony, that both of your brothers had been killed in Vietnam. Which is it, Ms. Boudreau? Drugs or bullets?"

A mistake, Warren thought. She'll only get more sympathy from the jury. But he knew where Altschuler was headed.

Patiently, and in detail, Johnnie Faye explained what had happened to Clinton and then Garrett. She spoke directly to the jurors. Then she turned back to the prosecutor. "So what I meant was that Garrett was killed *by* Vietnam, even though he wasn't actually killed *in* Vietnam."

"In other words, when you were testifying you said one thing and meant another—is that a fair way to put it?"

"In a way. But about my brother Garrett, I didn't think that was important."

"It's only important insofar as this jury can see how your mind works, Ms. Boudreau, when you're asked to state the truth under oath."

Before Warren could object, she said, "I *was* telling the truth. I said later that my brother died of an overdose."

Two minutes into cross, Warren thought, and she's already being drawn into arguing with Altschuler. She'll get ripped apart. Warren stood, shaking his head sadly. "Your honor, the prosecutor is meant to ask questions of the witness, not badger her or lecture to the jury. Would the court be kind enough to remind him of that?"

"Is that an objection, Mr. Blackburn?" Judge Bingham asked.

"It is, your honor."

"Sustained. Don't do that anymore, Mr. Altschuler."

Warren glanced sharply at Johnnie Faye, hoping the message had got through. But she was leaning slightly forward in the witness chair, clutching her handbag. Her eyes were focused completely on Bob Altschuler.

Altschuler said, "Ms. Boudreau, you told the jury, didn't you, that back in 1970 you were proud to have represented Corpus Christi in the Miss Texas Pageant?"

"Yes, sir, I was."

Consulting his notes, Altschuler said, "Isn't it a fact that you made a speech at the Miss Texas Pageant, in front of television cameras, denouncing the pageant as a 'stupid and demeaning charade'? Aren't those your words, Ms. Boudreau?"

"They may have been, but that had nothing to do with how I felt about going there to represent my hometown."

Altschuler turned to Judge Bingham. "Your honor, would you please instruct the witness to answer yes or no if a yes or no answer is called for."

Judge Bingham nodded. "Please try to do that, madam."

Johnnie Faye said, "Your honor, I can't do that if he's going to twist the facts."

Warren's eyes rolled in their sockets. Now she was arguing with the judge!

Bingham ignored her and said, "Continue, Mr. Bob."

"Didn't you also say to the press at the Miss Texas Pageant: 'Virginal meat is the only kind the male chauvinist pigs will let you show off in this circus'? Aren't those your words?"

Johnnie Faye's fingers dug even deeper into the leather of her handbag.

"Yes, sir, I said that."

"Were those words meant to demonstrate how proud you were to represent your hometown?"

"That's not true."

"Excuse me, are you answering yes or no?"

"I'm trying to say that one thing had nothing to do with the other."

"Does that mean yes or no?"

"No," she said angrily. "Or yes. I don't even remember your stupid question."

Altschuler nodded, as if he had learned something of great moment. "Strike the stupid question," he said. "Now, Ms. Boudreau, in deploring the difficulties of your work at your nightclub, you said that God hadn't made a perfect world. Do you believe in God?"

"Yes, sir."

"Do you go to church regularly?"

"Objection," Warren said. "Irrelevant."

"She opened the door," Altschuler explained, "when she brought up God."

"She opened the door to whether or not she believed in God," Warren argued to the bench. "She didn't open the door to her churchgoing habits."

"He's just splitting hairs," Altschuler snapped.

"I don't think so," said Bingham. "I won't allow it. Objection sustained."

Altschuler growled, "If counsel for the defense doesn't want the jury to know his client's so-called 'churchgoing habits,' I won't ask." He shook his head in apparent disgust.

If Altschuler was going to play the role of gunfighter, then Warren would play sheriff. Instantly he was back on his feet—"Your honor, I object. And I'm sure the jury can do without all these melodramatic facial gestures."

"Nonsense!" Altschuler barked. "We're looking for the truth! I think we have a right to know if we're dealing with a truth-teller or a hypocrite!"

With fervor that waltzed perilously close to gallantry, Warren turned to the judge and said, "Your honor, please! These are just speeches and innuendos." He might not have been so protective, he knew, if Altschuler hadn't been so personally aggressive. *Lawyering is acting. If a lawyer gets a jury to trust him more than the other son of a bitch, he's home free.*

The judge banged his gavel. "Stop this horseplay, both of you! Mr. Warren, your objection is sustained. Mr. Bob, go on with your cross-examination."

Calming himself, Altschuler asked, "Your nightclub, which I gather isn't part of God's perfect world, is that a topless nightclub?"

"Yes, sir, it is."

"Young women dance naked from the waist up?"

"Yes, sir."

"They sometimes approach as close as six inches to the customers and shake their breasts in the customers' faces?"

"Sometimes, yes."

"And do they ever perform any sexual services for the customers?"

"Not that I know of," Johnnie Faye said.

She was in control again. With his objections, Warren had bought her time. She had figured it out.

"You said, speaking of Dr. Ott's wife, 'Sharon had died so tragically.' Tell the jury, if you will—how did Mrs. Ott die?"

"I believe she was shot down outside an aerobics center back in 1987."

"Did you have any personal knowledge of those events, Ms. Boudreau?"

"No, I did not. Just what I read in the papers and what Clyde told me."

"Weren't you extremely friendly with a man named David Inkman, known as Dink, whom the police suspected of murdering Mrs. Ott?"

"Objection!" Warren cried. "No predicate, and it's irrelevant, and there's an outrageous implication!"

"Sustained," Judge Bingham said. "The jury will disregard the question and any implication. Get off that, Mr. Bob."

Disregard, but think about it.

"Ms. Boudreau, you owned three guns at one time, isn't that correct?"

"Yes."

"And one of them, a .32-caliber Colt, was unregistered?"

"Yes."

"Are you aware that's illegal?"

"Yes."

"That gun was given to you as a gift?"

"Yes."

"By whom?"

"David Inkman."

"A gift from a dead man." Altschuler sniggered. "Tell us," he said, veering again, trying to confuse her, "after the first time Dr. Ott allegedly struck you, were you concerned for your personal safety?"

"Yes," Johnnie Faye said.

"And didn't you begin carrying a .22-caliber pistol in your handbag so that if Dr. Ott threatened to strike you, you could protect yourself?"

"No, I always carried that pistol. It had nothing to do with Clyde. I believe I mentioned that someone once tried to rape me."

"Did you report that attempted rape to the police?"

"No."

Warren paid close attention. She was in trouble, but she was bearing up. Her hands were steady on the handbag.

"How many drinks did you have at the Hacienda on the night of May 7, Ms. Boudreau?"

"Two or three."

"And so Dr. Ott had at least seven drinks, and possibly eight?"

"Yes."

"Didn't you plan to drink just enough so that you'd stay sober, and didn't you encourage Dr. Ott to drink heavily?"

"No, I didn't do that at all."

"You admit to having a foul mouth, don't you?"

"Sometimes."

"But you have a quick memory?"

"I have a good memory, yes."

"Tell this jury the words you used at the Hacienda bar when you cursed Dr. Ott."

"I don't like to use those words in public, sir."

"Your honor, please instruct the witness to be responsive."

"You can answer, madam," Judge Bingham said.

"I called Clyde a cocksucker and a lying son of a bitch, because he'd told me he wouldn't use any more cocaine."

"Don't you yourself use cocaine and marijuana, Ms. Boudreau?"

"I have in the distant past used small amounts of marijuana. There's a lot of stress in my job. I've never used cocaine."

Altschuler's eyes were inky and threatening like those of a deep-water fish. "Don't you distribute and even sell cocaine to some of your personal friends at your topless nightclub, Ecstasy?"

"No, I don't do that."

"What time was it exactly when you came back to Dr. Ott's house from the Hacienda on the night of May 7?"

"Let's see . . . we must have left the restaurant around eleven. So call it close to eleven-thirty."

"You went upstairs with Dr. Ott?"

"Yes."

"You had sex with him then, didn't you?"

"Yes. He insisted."

"You mean you didn't want to have sex with him?"

"No. I mean that's right—I didn't want it."

"He insisted, and you didn't want it. He was drunk and under the influence of cocaine, and you were sober. Are you telling us, in those circumstances, he was able to force you to have sex?"

"Yes, that's right."

"Did he threaten you with bodily harm if you wouldn't do it with him?"

"No. He just shoved me down on the bed."

"But you knew, didn't you, when you went upstairs with him, that he wanted to have sex with you?"

"No, I didn't."

"You thought he just wanted you to tuck him into bed?"

"I thought he wanted to talk."

"You couldn't talk downstairs in the living room?"

"I'm sure we could have. But he wanted to go up. I was feeling sorry for him." Suddenly, amazingly, tears flooded Johnnie Faye's eyes. "Sir, I shouldn't have gone up and gone to bed with him to have sex." Her voice choked. "I'm ashamed that I did that, but I'm not perfect. People don't always do the right thing every hour of the day and night."

Altschuler hesitated. With a witness like Johnnie Faye Boudreau he would normally slash at her character, impeach her believability, approaching the task with the distaste of a man forced to clean out a blocked sewer. But now she bent with every blow like a pliant branch. Yes, her girls shoved their breasts into men's faces; yes, she had smoked marijuana; yes, she had called Clyde a cocksucker; yes, she had gone to bed with him. And now there were tears.

"So that night," Altschuler asked, "you had sex with him completely against your will? He *raped* you?"

"No, he couldn't do it. That's what got him so angry."

"He couldn't perform, and that made him angry?"

"Yes, sir."

"He slapped you in the face?"

"Yes."

"Were you frightened when he got angry and slapped you?"

"A little."

"And so you rushed downstairs to get your pistol out of your handbag?"

"No, sir."

"You did rush downstairs to get your handbag, didn't you?"

"I got dressed and walked down in a hurry. I needed my handbag because my car keys were in it. I wanted to leave."

"You had left your handbag on the living room sofa, is that what you claim?"

"Yes."

"You knew your pistol was also in your handbag, didn't you?"

"I didn't think of that at the time."

"You always carried that pistol in your handbag, didn't you?"

"Yes."

"Are you telling us that on the night of May 7 you didn't know your pistol was in your handbag?"

Jesus, Warren thought, he's good.

"I'm not saying that—"

"Stop. Is the answer yes or no, Ms. Boudreau?"

Johnnie Faye wiped her eyes and turned to Judge Bingham. "Your honor, that's like asking me, 'Do you still beat your dog?' I can't give a simple yes or no honest answer. I want to answer truthfully, but he won't let me."

"Answer as best you can," the judge said.

"My answer is: I knew it was in my handbag, but I wasn't *thinking* about it being there."

And she's good too, Warren thought. It was a contest worth watching. But he was not sure whom he was rooting for.

"She's answered," the judge said. "Move along, Mr. Bob."

"When you went downstairs to the living room and picked up your handbag with the pistol in it, Ms. Boudreau, you say that Dr. Ott followed you. You could have left the house then, couldn't you?"

"He came downstairs before I'd got the handbag."

"You're telling us that you were sober, and you couldn't have picked up your bag and walked or run out the front door before a drunken man clambered out of bed and stumbled down a long flight of stairs?"

"He was right behind me."

"How far behind you?"

"I don't know, I didn't turn around. I heard his footsteps behind me, and I heard him shouting."

"And he blocked the front door so you couldn't leave?"

"No, he didn't do that then. That was long before."

"Ms. Boudreau, right after the murder, was your memory fresh as to what had happened?"

"Yes."

"Less than forty minutes after the murder, didn't you tell Sergeant Ruiz that Dr. Ott had blocked the front door *after* you and Dr. Ott had come downstairs?"

"Yes."

For half an hour Altschuler played the theme of her prior inconsistent statement to Ruiz. Johnnie Faye admitted that she might have said certain words to Ruiz, but the facts were incorrect. She had been confused. She might have thought her memory was fresh, but she was actually in shock.

"So," Altschuler said, "you picked up the poker from the fireplace to strike him?"

"No, sir."

"You didn't pick up the poker?"

"Yes, but I picked it up because he threatened me."

"You were going to defend yourself with the poker?"

"Yes."

"You meant to kill him with that heavy iron poker, didn't you, or inflict serious bodily harm?"

"No, sir. I meant to keep him away from me with it."

"And then he took the poker away from you?"

"Yes."

"He was drunk and stoned, and you were sober, and yet he was able to take the poker out of your grasp? You couldn't elude him?"

"Yes, he was able, and no, I couldn't elude him."

"And he blocked your path to the front door?"

"No, sir, not then. He threw me onto the sofa."

"And then you took the pistol from your handbag?"

"No, sir. Not until he raised the poker and said he was going to kill me with it."

"That's when he charged across the room at you, isn't it?"

"Yes, sir."

"And you shot him twice as he was charging at you, isn't that so?"

"No, sir. He stopped short, he stood still, and I said, 'Don't take another step, Clyde, or I'll shoot you.' "

"You had already cocked the action?"

"No, sir. I didn't cock it."

"But when you took the pistol out of your handbag, you released the safety catch so that it would fire, didn't you?"

"I must have done that without thinking."

"You said you were a very good shot, didn't you?"

"Yes, on a target range."

"What part of Dr. Ott's body did you aim for?"

"His shoulder."

"Left shoulder or right shoulder?"

"Left, I think."

"Show us how you held the gun. Just use your finger

and point it at me. You can stand up from the witness chair if you like."

After a pause—but no objection came—Johnnie Faye stood and raised her hand, fist clenched, index finger protruding. Her elbow was bent.

"Your arm wasn't level?"

"No, sir."

"Can't you shoot more accurately if your firing arm is level?"

"Yes, you can."

"On the firing range at Western America, don't you shoot with your arm level and extended in order to hit the target?"

"Yes."

"So with your arm bent, weren't you taking a grave risk that your shot, which you say was aimed at his left shoulder, might be off a few inches and hit him in the heart instead?"

"I didn't think about the risk. I was frightened."

"You knew that gun had its sear filed off illegally, making it fully automatic—you knew that, didn't you?"

"I knew about the sear. I didn't know that was illegal."

"You pulled the trigger three times, didn't you?"

"No, just once. But it kept on firing."

"You missed with the first shot?"

"I don't know."

"You mean you may have missed with the last shot? Shot him twice in the head and chest, and then fired another round to make it seem as if you'd just been shooting wildly?"

"No, sir, I don't mean that. I mean that I didn't know then and don't know now which two of the three shots hit him."

"Ms. Boudreau, isn't it a fact that you could have run around him and made your way to the front door and the safety of your car?"

"No, sir, I was on the sofa."

"Isn't it a fact that you could have used your pistol to keep him at bay while you ran or walked past him?"

"No, sir. Even if I could have done that, he could have used that poker to brain me when I ran by."

"You didn't think it was worth a man's life to take that risk?"

"I wasn't thinking that clearly."

"You thought it was better to kill him and be done with it?"

"No, sir."

"Isn't it a fact that he never picked up the poker?"

"No, sir, he did pick it up."

"Isn't it a fact that the reason his palm prints weren't on the poker was because after you shot him you picked up the poker yourself and then pressed a dead man's finger-prints onto it?"

"No, sir, that's absolutely not a fact."

"Come on, Ms. Boudreau—didn't you decide to kill Dr. Ott because you were in a rage that he wouldn't marry you?"

"No, that's not true either."

"What *is* true, Ms. Boudreau?"

"That I shot him in self-defense. That if I hadn't done it, he might have killed me. *Would* have killed me."

"Ah, but which is it? Might have or would have? You're not at all certain, are you?"

"I was certain then," Johnnie Faye said, "that he *would* have killed me."

"I take it you're no longer so certain."

"Yes, I still am. He would have done it."

"But a moment ago you used the words *might have,* didn't you?"

"Yes, I did."

"So there *is* a doubt in your mind!"

Johnnie Faye took a deep breath. "Sir, ever since this happened on the night of May 7 I've been in agony over it. I've hardly slept. I didn't hate Clyde. Taking a person's life is the worst thing a human being can do, and if you take the life of someone you once loved, even if you didn't mean to do it, you live in hell forever. So, yes, there have been doubts in my mind—lots of them. Terrible moments. I cry all night long sometimes. But I believe with all my heart— unless I wanted to take the chance that he would kill me— that I had no choice."

From the blotch of dark pink color that spread across Bob Altschuler's face, Warren gathered that the prosecutor knew the jury had been sold some snake oil. But there was little he could do anymore, not until final argument. Glaring stonily at the defense lawyer, he passed the witness.

For the better part of two hours the state and the defense tossed Johnnie Faye back and forth between them, Warren working to patch the leaks in her fabricated story and Altschuler seeking to punch out new holes. Then, with Altschuler's final derisive "Pass the witness" and Warren's confident cry of "The defense rests!"—it was over.

Just after five-thirty in the afternoon, a weary Judge Bingham tapped his gavel on the walnut bench. "On Monday morning," he said, for the benefit of the jurors and the media, "I will charge the jury. Then we'll have final argument by both attorneys. Defense goes first. The state last, because they have the burden of proof." He turned to the twelve jurors and the two alternates. "Don't read the newspapers over the weekend. If you feel you must read the foreign news and the sports pages, or *Peanuts* and *Garfield,* have someone in your family clip out anything that's been written in the paper about this trial. Please try not to watch the news on television. And don't discuss the case with your family or friends. You'll begin deliberating on Monday afternoon. Since no one can predict how long that will take, I suggest you bring your overnight kit in case you have to spend the night here. Not *here*"— he smiled— "we're not quite as inhuman as all that. I mean in a hotel. Now y'all have a nice weekend."

The jury filed out. The courtroom smelled of stale air

and sweat. Warren, even before he and Rick rose from the counsel table, saw the media people beckoning or bearing down upon them. He raised a hand to keep them at bay. "Don't move," he ordered Johnnie Faye. He drew Rick forward to the empty jury box. He had instructed him to watch the jurors the whole time during both direct and cross, to pick up reactions.

"She did well," Rick said. "She's a real pistol. She's a one-woman argument for gun control law."

"Are we ahead or are we behind?"

Rick meditated a moment, then brightened. "I'd say it's a tie late in the fourth quarter. They've got the ball deep in their own territory. It's up to us to stop them. Dee-fense," Rick chanted.

"Thanks. Just tell me—do they believe her or not?"

"Some do, some don't. The women looked the most skeptical. When you do final argument, pitch it to the women. I've made a lot of notes. You want to meet tomorrow and work on it?"

"Make it Sunday," Warren said. "Tomorrow I'm going out of town."

"Attaboy," Rick said. "Take a holiday. Go to the beach. Stick your head in the sand. Clear your mind."

Heat waves rippled above the highway. The land spread flat and brown in every direction. A wit had once said, "Texas is a place where you can look farther and see less than anywhere else on earth." Warren's head ached. The trial of Johnnie Faye Boudreau, wherein he believed his client was guilty but was obliged to fight for her freedom, was about to come to an end. After that the trial of Hector Quintana, wherein he knew his client was innocent but couldn't prove it, would resume. His estranged wife, who had left him for another man, had changed her mind and wanted to come back to him. Now, on Saturday morning, Maria Hahn sat at his side in the BMW, fiddling with the tape deck. What I would like to do next week, Warren thought, is get on a plane to Bali. Alone.

He tried to banish Charm to the back of his mind. Don't think about her. Don't think about an elephant.

He had been to see Hector early that morning. Abiding misery had made the Mexican's face a little grayer than on the previous visit; there were purple blotches on his cheeks. Warren wanted to say, "I'm working for you, I'm doing all I can. Don't give up"—but the words forming in his mind seemed powdery and without substance. "How are you?" he asked.

"I can't sleep good," Hector said.

"They keep you awake?"

"No. Me. I do it."

"Not much longer," Warren promised. "Maybe next week."

"I want to tell you something," Hector said. "On my mind a long time. I lie to you."

"What about?" Warren asked, his heartbeat perceptibly quickening.

"The shopping cart. You ask me a long time ago if I steal it. I say I found it." Hector shook his head. "That's the only lie I ever tole you."

Warren thought, My heart will break if this man goes to prison.

He promised to come by on Sunday and bring a newspaper.

Maria put on a tape that she had brought with her for the trip: a caterwauling black soul singer, with a heavy bass beat.

"Do me a favor," Warren said. "Look in the glove compartment. I think there's some Vivaldi there."

A sign flashed by. VICTORIA: 10. BEEVILLE: 56.

Vivaldi soothed him for a while with part of The Contest of Harmony and Invention—*Le Quattro Stagióni,* the four seasons of the year. The four seasons of life. Childhood, often called youth. Manhood. Decay. Dying. Was dying a season? Sometimes it seemed that way.

He was a forgiving man. His nature suffused his profession. A lawyer more than most men had to learn to forgive. To forget was more difficult. But that could be done too. Life moved on like a river, and water could not long remember the bruise it had received from a rock upstream. The final question was: what do I want?

Not to punish her, Warren thought. That would be coarse. I do love her. Whatever that means. *Partners and companions. Substance, richness, longevity.* When Charm had told him she was in love with another man and might abandon her marriage, Warren's mind had used those words. He had not spoken them; in his mind they were far more than words. His mind, struggling for coherence in the midst of such crippling confusion, told him they were poor ways to say that in the eyes of the universe a life is a pitifully brief chemical event, but it can have continuity. Continuity can have shape, structure. Shape and structure is all we have to keep the demons of nothingness at bay, to pass through the years feeling decent, timidly proud. You can't throw away eight years if you have the chance to retrieve them and build on them.

But I'm young, Warren thought. I can make fresh starts. I can find continuity even if my life is broken into chapters. There are chapters in a book, but the book still forms a whole. There are seasons, wickedly different, but they are linked.

He was fond of Maria, enjoyed her—he was not in love with her. Did not love her yet, but could. And with time, if he chose to invest it, would. He saw that clearly.

GOLIAD: 8. BEEVILLE: 38.

"You okay?" Maria asked, shifting in her seat to pick up a thermos that she had filled with Gatorade.

"Fine," Warren said.

"How's your headache?"

"Almost gone."

"Want a sip of Gatorade, honey?"

"No, thanks." He smiled.

The little conversations that break up our thoughts, keep us sane and make us feel loved. I wish I could tell her everything, take her into my heart and mind. But we never can. Can only hint. Can share but can never be one.

Not just Maria. He didn't fault Maria, or himself. We are so fucking alone.

Honey, she had called him. She was affectionate, needed affection but asked little else so far. She didn't mind that he was separate. Charm minded. I could be happy with Maria, he thought. Alone and happy. But happy is for adolescents, pop songs and idiots. Call it content. I could grow old with her and we would never know anything about each other except what each of us wanted the other to know. There would be hints for the receptors to grasp but no knowledge. And perhaps that's best. I could do my work, raise her son, have a kid of my own with her. Grow old with ease. The river would flow. There would be rocks and eddies but it would be navigable. I'd have to listen to a lot of riddles, but she'd have to listen to a lot of snores. And I wouldn't have to buy another camera.

His mind was coming down off the high. Beeville was not far ahead.

"You worried about the case?" Maria asked.

Yes, I'm worried that my client will be found not guilty. Not just worried. Crazed.

"It's complicated," he said.

She asked no more questions. Warren was grateful. Thanks, honey.

Outside the courtroom, late yesterday afternoon, Johnnie Faye had caught him by the arm. "How'd I do?"

"We'll see," he answered cruelly. "Maybe they'll believe you."

Her eyes had narrowed. "You better make a good speech for me."

"Maybe Rick will do final argument."

"No. I want you. I trust you."

Yes. That was his obligation, one way or the other. He nodded his agreement.

Now on Saturday morning he was driving to Beeville to hunt for a man with a nickname. The man might not be there. He might have been and gone. Without him, Warren believed, the *Quintana* jury would come in with a guilty verdict. A pile of circumstantial evidence, but circumstantial evidence was often the most compelling. A shaky eyewitness stood at the core of it, but there was the matter of the pistol gripped in Hector's hand. The pistol wouldn't go away.

They reached Beeville at eleven o'clock in the morning. It was an old cattle town north of the King Ranch. Not too far from Odem and Corpus Christi, where Johnnie Faye had been bred to be a monster. Warren wondered about Mama, to whom she was still loyal, and Daddy, who had run the Exxon and preached hellfire and brimstone on Sunday mornings. What were they really like? What had they done to her? Or not done? What had gone askew in her mind? He would never know.

He slid the car off the bypass road and drove down the main street. They passed a motel, a supermarket, a bowling alley. No parking meters, no high-rises. Pecan and oak trees drooped in the dust in front of small brick houses with picket fences and parched lawns. Warren spotted a pool hall and a Mobil station.

"Pool hall's probably the best bet," he said to Maria, "so I'll try the Mobil first." He had done the same thing as a boy, eating his vegetable and baked potato first, saving the rib-eye steak for last.

Outside the car the heat struck a mean blow. A young black man was pumping gas, and a white man of about fifty sat at the cash register in front of the rattly air-conditioning unit, working on credit card receipts.

Warren, in boots and worn jeans and shirtsleeves, stuck a toothpick between his teeth and said, "Mornin'."

"Mornin' to you."

"Hot day."

"Sure is."

"Man in this town, some folks up in Houston call him Jim Dandy. He around?"

The man behind the cash register grinned, showing yellow teeth. "You the law?"

Warren felt like Gary Cooper or Jimmy Stewart in an old western. The setting was right. The dialogue was hoary.

"Shoot, no," he said. "I'm a lawyer. Tryin' to help Jim out."

"Well, Jim Dandy's around. Was, anyway."

Warren took a twenty-dollar bill from his shirt pocket and lifted a map of Mexico from the rack next to the cash register. "I guess I can use one of these. Keep the change, friend."

The station owner took the twenty, opened the cash register, and gave Warren eighteen dollars change. "This ain't

Houston," he said. "Jim Dandy's up at Kitty Marie's. You know Kitty Marie too?"

"No, sir," Warren said.

"Little house on DeKalb Street. Go back up a few blocks past Walgreen's and turn right. Next to last house on the block, got a beat-up black Chevy pickup in front of it. Kitty Marie's shift at McDonald's don't start until late afternoon, so she's likely to be home."

"What's his real name?" Warren asked.

"Who?"

"Jim Dandy."

"That's his real name. His name is Jim Dandy. That's the name he was born with, that's what we call him."

Warren laughed quietly. "Like you guessed, I never met him. Anything I need to know?"

"Well, Jim Dandy's so poor he'd have to borrow money to buy water to cry with. And Kitty Marie's so ugly she'd run a dog off a meat wagon. So if you were a religious man you might say that God did them both a favor by uniting them. Other than that, what else you need to know?"

"Nothing," Warren said. "Thank you."

"You're welcome, son. Nice car you got out there. Get good mileage?"

Warren discussed the BMW for about three minutes, and then walked through the heat again and got into it.

Two minutes later he knocked on the door of the next-to-last house on DeKalb Street. The rear bumper of the black pickup truck, above a dragging tail pipe, had a sticker that said: HONK IF YOU LOVE JESUS. The house looked as if it would fall down if you kicked hard at any one of its rotting gray boards. A woman in her late thirties, with pink rubber haircurlers and buck teeth and a black hair growing from the tip of her nose, opened a screen door. It groaned on its hinges; the screws were pulling away from the wall. Warren handed her his business card and the eighteen dollars change from the map of Mexico, and asked for Jim Dandy. That old drunken dog was still in bed, she said, but it seemed she couldn't move fast enough to get him out of it.

Jim Dandy sat at the kitchen table drinking a cold long-neck, the second of a six-pack that Maria had provided after a dash to the nearest supermarket. Now Maria was outside with Kitty Marie in the brush, explaining how tomatoes and lettuce might grow. Boots up on a kitchen chair, gripping his own longneck, Warren sat opposite Jim Dandy at the rickety table.

Jim Dandy fit Siva Singh's description, as many men would: closing in on forty, dissolute, long-haired, and pot-bellied. He hadn't shaved in several days. The flesh beneath the stubble had the liveliness of linoleum. He smelled of yesterday's beer and last week's body odor. He wore an army fatigue jacket with the insignia removed, and a pair of jeans with so many holes they would have been fashionable in Beverly Hills. Warren knew they would be just about his only clothes, except for a week's supply of white socks—maybe two pair.

"I'll tell you again, pardner," Warren said, planting his boots on the floor, "while you're still sober enough to hang on to it. You're not going to get in trouble. No one cares you took the wallet. But you have to admit you did it and say what you saw. All of it."

"Don't sit well," Jim Dandy said.

"What's your problem? You can tell me."

"I spent the money."

" 'Course you did. You ain't got no savings account in the bank, so you spent it. No one gives a flying fuck. Unless of course you don't come up to Houston."

Jim Dandy kept rubbing his hands as if to warm them. He kept throwing quick random glances at Warren and then out the window at the women in the yard. "I can't do it," he said.

"Then you're in the deep weeds, pardner. Then the law might want to know what you did with the money."

"How's the law gonna find out I ever had it?"

"I'd tell them," Warren said.

"You'd do a rotten thing like that, hoss?"

"I might. I've got a man facing the death penalty."

"How'm I gonna get up to Houston?" Jim Dandy asked.

Warren laughed. "With me, today. And I run a kind of little hotel up there. Got a couple of amigos bunked down there already. You're invited, free of charge. Free beer until the day you testify, free eats as long as you stay."

Jim Dandy looked Warren up and down, frowning. "I won't eat nothin' that jumps, crawls, or climbs trees. And I won't put nothin' in my mouth that I can't identify."

"Supermarket's right around the corner. You can shop. I pay."

"What about Kitty Marie?"

"She'll be here when you get back. She ain't going anywhere, is she?"

"Well . . . I done 'bout lived myself to death down here, and you seem like a fair man. Okay."

Warren rose immediately from his chair. "Getcha tail up, kiss that woman goodbye, tuck the rest of that beer under your arm, and let's go party."

On the drive north to Houston, with Jim Dandy in the back seat and the windows open to release some of his body odor, Warren asked him, "Why'd you go back to the dry cleaners and pick up those clothes?"

"Got drunk," Jim Dandy said. "Seemed like a good idea at the time."

"They fit?"

"Sort of. Little small."

"Got stolen from you, I heard."

"Hell, no. I sold 'em for ten bucks," Jim Dandy said. "They was too fancy for me, and I allow they was bad luck clothes. Fella that bought 'em from me got shot full of holes. Killed real dead right there in the mission. I done a lot of things in my life I guess I shouldn't have did, and most of 'em I was so drunk I can't even remember. I figured old fate was catchin' up, maybe somebody'd been lookin' for *me*. That's why I left town and come back to Beeville."

At a few minutes past eight o'clock on Monday morning, July 31, Warren stood before Melissa Bourne-Smith's desk in the 299th District Court. "We're doing final argument today in the 342nd," he told the court coordinator. "Will you please tell Nancy Goodpaster and Judge Parker that as soon as the jury reaches a verdict, I'm ready to pick up where we left off in *Quintana*. The judge may want to get word to the jurors. And to Mrs. Singh."

"The judge is in chambers," Bourne-Smith said. "You can tell her yourself."

"I haven't got time now. Ask her to leave a message on my machine. Her Worship have a nice vacation?"

"Says she did." Bourne-Smith couldn't help laughing.

Warren found an empty courtroom on the seventh floor and spent forty-five minutes going over the notes he had made on Sunday. Then he stuffed them into his briefcase; he would not refer to them again. At nine o'clock sharp he appeared in the 342nd. Judge Bingham nodded his appreciation. Everyone rose in the huge courtroom as the jury filed in to take their seats.

Judge Bingham read the charge. Johnnie Faye Boudreau stood indicted with the offense of murder. "Under our law a person commits the offense of murder if he, or she in this case, intentionally or knowingly causes the death of an individual. Ms. Boudreau has admitted to causing the death of Dr. Clyde Ott and has pled not guilty by reason of self-defense. An accused cannot be found guilty of any offense if she engaged in the proscribed conduct because she was compelled to do so by the threat of imminent death or serious bodily injury, provided that she did not provoke the victim into so threatening or attacking. Our law, in addition, requires that anyone who feels she is facing such a threat has a duty to retreat, if retreat is possible, before taking action against the threatening person. If you find beyond a reasonable doubt that Ms. Boudreau provoked the attack, or that she had the opportunity to retreat and did not do so, and willfully caused the death of Dr. Clyde Ott, you will return a verdict of guilty. If you find that she exercised her duty to retreat, or found it impossible to do so, and did not willfully cause the death of Dr. Ott, you will acquit the defendant and return a verdict of not guilty."

The judge ended by telling the jury that after they retired they were to select a foreperson, and during their deliberations they were to communicate with the court only in writing, which they would give to the bailiff.

He said, "Mr. Blackburn, you may open for the defense."

Stepping forward, Warren thanked the jurors for their patience and attention during testimony. "I want to remind you," he said, "what Judge Bingham told you during voir dire. Under our law, the state has the burden of proof. Johnnie Faye Boudreau was not required to prove to you that she was not guilty in the death of Dr. Clyde Ott. She was not even required to prove to you that she pulled the trigger in self-defense—although she did, of her own free will, swear under oath and give unflinching detail in the face of vigorous cross-examination that in fact she did so. The state was required to prove to you that she was guilty of willful murder. And they must prove it to you beyond a reasonable doubt. You would abandon your oath as jurors if you didn't keep that in mind all the while during your deliberation."

Briefly he summarized the facts from the defendant's point of view: a stormy relationship between lovers, a history of abuse by the victim—"a man whose death some may indeed mourn but whose way of life certainly doesn't seem worthy of praise. Cathy Lewis, one of his girlfriends, told you he knocked out her teeth and gave her $25,000 as hush money. Mrs. Patricia Gurian told you that he tried to take advantage of her sexually in his office and then, when she wanted to leave, tried to detain her. Judith Tarr, another patient, told you that he did the same thing, and she was forthright enough to admit that she succumbed. Johnnie Faye Boudreau herself has told you of beatings and hospital treatment. Dr. Ott was not a kind man, as we hope and pray our physicians will be, and as they usually are. He was a brute."

And the son of a bitch needed killing.

"As for the defendant, she is a worldly woman—make no mistake about that. She runs a topless nightclub. But I remind you she is not on trial for that. By her own admission, she is capable of what she calls 'a foul mouth'—but she is not on trial for that either. She owned three handguns. That is not a crime. She practiced with them at a pistol range. That is not a crime. All of us, even if we don't have personal knowledge, understand what it means to be an attractive single woman in a major city where crime threatens every citizen. And even Mr. Morse, a witness brought to you by the prosecution, said that you can't bear arms safely unless you know how to use them.

"Mrs. Lorna Gerard, a subsidized stepdaughter of Dr. Ott, quoted Ms. Boudreau as having said, after yet another volatile argument, 'When he gets mean and drunk, I could cut his throat in his sleep.' Are we meant to take that seriously?" Warren smiled with a certain delicate intimacy and pointed an idle forefinger back and forth among the jurors. "How many of us have used the words, 'I could kill him for that'? Did we really mean them? Have any of us killed?" He waited a moment for the concept to register in the jurors' minds. "Dr. Butterfield admitted that his friend Clyde Ott said to the defendant, after she had thrown a drink at him, 'You bitch, I could happily kill you for that.' He also told you that Clyde Ott had a quick temper. But

Dr. Butterfield took great pains to point out that of course his friend didn't mean his remark literally. Well, which is it? Do we take such angry statements at face value, or do we accept them as part of human frailty? I think you know the answer."

He stopped in midflow and moved from the well of the courtroom back to the defense table, close to Johnnie Faye Boudreau, who wore gray.

"Beyond that, you have listened to the defendant under oath. You have listened to a brave and independent woman, and a sad woman. She loved Clyde Ott. Not wisely, perhaps, but for a long time. She tried to get him to cut down on alcohol, whose excessive intake reduced the doctor to the level of a rabid cur. Tried to get him off drugs, which surely were destroying his mind. Clyde Ott was rich, but Johnnie Faye Boudreau had a job and she paid her own rent. She never took advantage of Dr. Ott's considerable wealth. Whether or not she wanted to marry him and *he* was reluctant, or he wanted to marry her and *she* was reluctant . . . who cares? Your experience should tell you that these areas are never cut-and-dried. The fact is, she lived as an independent single woman. I think that takes a certain amount of guts, even in this age where women are struggling for rights and status equal to that of men.

"And so we come to the tragic events on the night of May 7. And they are tragic—Ms. Boudreau doesn't believe otherwise. She is sorrowing. You could see it. She did not mean to kill Clyde Ott. She meant to defend herself and keep him from killing her or inflicting grave bodily harm. She has told you what happened. That is the truth. She did not threaten deadly force. There is no other truth. The state has provided not a single witness to say otherwise. They have provided a fingerprint expert who testified that there were no palm prints on the poker with which Clyde Ott threatened the defendant. But the defendant herself has admitted that she picked up the poker after Clyde Ott was dead and, no doubt, in what we can clearly understand was a semi-hysterical state, inadvertently destroyed some of the prints on that poker. Destroyed evidence that would have completely exonerated her! Can she be blamed for that? Blamed for her actions at a moment that would have made you, or me, or anybody, a victim of genuine shock and horror? I point out to you that if she were guilty of murder, ladies and gentlemen, she didn't have to tell us *anything* about the poker! If indeed she were guilty of murder, she could have wiped that poker clean, because her prints were on it. But she didn't do that! She told us the full story!"

He moved back to the jury box.

"You have heard from Judge Bingham about what our law calls 'the duty to retreat.' I will ask the men among you: if a raging, two-hundred-and-twenty-pound drunken man came at you with a heavy iron poker, and said quite clearly that he was going to kill you with it—what would *you* do? You might try to get away. Would any of you do that? I doubt it. You might try to reason with him, although we all know what it's like to reason with an angry drunk—you'd be risking your life on a bad bet. You might try to grapple with him, strike him with your fists, wrestle him to the ground. Some of you might be brave enough to do just that. Some might not. Or, if you had a pistol in your possession, you might do what Johnnie Faye Boudreau did."

Warren paused before the jury, studying the intent faces.

"And now I will ask the women among you: would *you,* because you are women, beg for mercy? Would you have tried to run away? Ms. Boudreau couldn't. The archway and the vestibule were wide—God knows the prosecutor has given us their dimensions until we've got them memorized. But the reason she can't get through that wide space, ladies, is that she is on the sofa, backed against a wall! There could have been a football field behind Clyde Ott— he could have been standing in front of Tiananmen Square in Beijing and it wouldn't have made any difference to Ms. Boudreau's ability to get away. So, under those circumstances, I ask you: would you fight back with your woman's body? I don't think any of us believes that Ms. Boudreau could have done that. Would you, because you're 'only a woman,' try to reason with him and pray to God that the man with the poker wouldn't splatter your brains on the carpet or leave you a blank-eyed idiot for the rest of your life?" Warren's voice rose in volume. "Because that's the only kind of retreat that was possible! Take the beating or fight back! That's all she could do!"

You have no duty to retreat.

"Johnnie Faye Boudreau fought back. She shot him, and the shots killed him. She didn't mean to, but that's what happened. And so I ask you men and women on this jury if the state has taken up its proper burden and proved beyond a reasonable doubt that willful murder took place. I ask you if we, as Texas men and women, are meant to grovel and beg or accept death or probable disfigurement when we are flatly threatened. And as a reply to those two questions, I ask you to find Ms. Boudreau not guilty by reason of self-defense."

Warren sat down.

That was my best, he thought. I did it. I had to do it.

Occasionally, at various law schools in south Texas, Bob Altschuler taught classes in trial theory and practice. "By the time you get to final argument," he lectured, "the jury's sat through an awful lot of boring shit. Now they want drama. Give 'em what they crave for."

In practice, during final argument, at least once or twice he would bellow with the sort of anger associated with drill sergeants facing recruits on the parade ground. He was a big man and the jury tended to be impressed. Forty-nine times in a row such stagecraft had been the prelude to victory.

Today he snapped and scolded from the moment he got

to his feet and faced the jury. "Today," he bawled, "there's one important man who isn't in this courtroom! One man we need to hear from, and we can't, because he's dead! Shot twice—once between the eyes, and once right here!" Altschuler placed his right hand in the region of his heart. "Clyde Ott—*Dr.* Clyde Ott, a medical man and healer, no matter what ludicrous tales we've heard in this courtroom —is a man from whom we could learn a great deal of fact. Folks, you must be sick and tired of the way that doctor's memory has been scorned and defiled!" He pointed a rigid finger at Johnnie Faye Boudreau. "This woman who runs a topless nightclub shot him down in cold blood! Don't you know that? Don't you feel it in your heart of hearts?"

His body grew still. He shook his head, as if deeply perplexed. "Let's go through the evidence together."

He focused instantly on Johnnie Faye's statement to Sgt. Ruiz less than an hour after the murder. But here in court, Ruiz had testified and shown that statement to be an unlikely tale.

"So the defendant, under oath, changed her story! Told us that Dr. Ott had blocked the doorway *before* the two of them went upstairs, *before* he supposedly threatened her and picked up a poker. Well, folks, who do you believe? Sergeant Ruiz is a trained police officer. He told us the defendant wasn't agitated when he arrived at the house— she was waiting for him at the front door, smoking a cigarette. Why should she tell one story then and a different story now? Don't you know why? Because it suited her! She'd realized that if she didn't change the details of her story, she'd be in violation of her duty to retreat!"

Sighing, he shook his head again. "On the night of May 7 she told Sergeant Ruiz that Dr. Ott was coming at her 'like an old grizzly bear, waving that poker over his head.' Her own words. *Coming at her.* But then a few days ago the county medical examiner testified that Dr. Ott was shot *while he was standing still*! So what did Johnnie Faye Boudreau do after she heard that? *Changed her story!* Now she says Dr. Ott ran at her with the poker and then stopped, and that's when she shot him. Didn't you realize, folks, what she was doing? Didn't you realize what she was doing after Sergeant Kulik testified that Dr. Ott's palm prints should have been on the poker—*and weren't*? Until her testimony here, Johnnie Faye Boudreau never said a word to any authority about having picked up the poker after she'd killed Dr. Ott, and in the process possibly damaging his set of palm prints. She made that up! *This woman will say anything!*"

Warren had to tense the muscles in his neck; he had been on the verge of nodding in agreement.

"Now," the prosecutor continued, "let's consider all these various threats that the witnesses have told us about. Some were not idle threats, as counsel for the defense would have you naively believe. At the Houston Racquet Club, after Johnnie Faye Boudreau had thrown a drink at him, Dr. Ott said to her, 'I could kill you for that.' But he *didn't* kill her, did he? On the other hand, Johnnie Faye Boudreau, in front of Mrs. Gerard, said of Dr. Ott, 'I could kill him.' *And she did.* There's a big difference, don't you agree?"

Altschuler pointed a thick finger at Warren. "The defense attorney makes light of the venom that spewed from Johnnie Faye Boudreau's mouth at the Hacienda restaurant just prior to the murder. I don't make light of it—I think it shows us a predisposition to violence. Please remember that Dr. Ott also said to his stepdaughter, speaking of the defendant, *'I'm frightened of her.'* In her testimony, Johnnie Faye Boudreau didn't refer to that, and her counsel didn't ask her about it. Think about that! Why was Dr. Ott frightened? Why didn't Johnnie Faye Boudreau care to explain that to us?

"The defense also makes light of the fact that no more than a few weeks prior to the actual murder, Johnnie Faye Boudreau practiced at a pistol range with the murder weapon. All sorts of fun-loving people do that. Even the judge does it. Surely you see past that double-talk! Other people may practice with their pistols, and even this judge may practice, but the judge and those other people do not murder someone immediately afterward! Johnnie Faye Boudreau used a false name, just in case any inquiry was made. And indeed an inquiry was made, but unfortunately for Johnnie Faye Boudreau, Mr. Morse remembered her. She is indeed memorable."

He raised a finger and said, with solemn import, "And she is a very good shot."

Altschuler grew angry again. Warren was fascinated. Go for it, Bob. Do her in.

"Ladies and gentlemen of the jury, do you believe that she put a bullet into Dr. Ott just a few inches from his heart, *and didn't mean to kill him*? Do you believe she just meant to wound him, teach him a lesson? *'Naughty Clyde! I'll put a tiny little bullet in your lung, so you'll behave.'* And do you believe that she didn't know all along that the pistol was in her handbag? After she'd practiced with that illegal weapon twice on a pistol range, do you believe she didn't know to release her finger from the trigger if she didn't want to fire more than one shot? Do you believe Dr. Ott *'moved slightly,'* as Johnnie Faye Boudreau claims, and that's why the other bullet hit him *between the eyes*? Are we here to have the wool pulled over *our* eyes by a murder-ess?"

Altschuler gripped his head with both hands as if it might explode, as if all he had said was so beyond comprehension that belief in it might render him insane.

Then he became terribly calm.

"The state does not have to prove motive. The state is only required to prove that she caused the death of Clyde Ott intentionally or knowingly. But still, let's think about motive. The defense makes light of the question of who wanted to get married and who shied away from it. I don't. I think—based on the testimony of the stepchildren, Mrs. Lorna Gerard and Mr. Kenneth Underhill—that Johnnie

Faye Boudreau wanted to marry Clyde Ott and was in the process of bullying him into it. But then he backed down in front of his stepchildren, and as time passed his resolve hardened. That infuriated Johnnie Faye Boudreau. She may have given him an ultimatum that night at the Hacienda restaurant, and again he said no. So they went back to his house. She took him upstairs to bed, to see if a little sex would sway him. He was drunk. What exactly happened then, we'll never know. The only person who can tell us the truth is dead. What we do know is that they both went downstairs, where she shot him between the eyes while he was standing still."

Again Warren almost nodded. Despite the histrionics, Altschuler was a thinking man. He had figured it all out.

The prosecutor said, "You have to use your common sense, folks. You have to decide, based on the many self-serving contradictions in Johnnie Faye Boudreau's testimony, whether you can trust her word. Did Dr. Ott threaten to kill her with a poker? Of course not!" Altschuler trumpeted. "The whole poker story was fabricated! She put his fingerprints on it when he was dead! Only she didn't realize she had to put *palm* prints on it too!"

His forehead had begun to sparkle with sweat. "And now let's talk about the duty to retreat." He paused for a few moments, giving the jurors time to consolidate, anticipate. "Johnnie Faye Boudreau claims Dr. Ott had struck her several times before the night of May 7. When he was drunk, she says, he was capable of violence. Yet when she got to the house that night, she went inside. She could have left, but she didn't. She didn't have to go upstairs with him, but she did. He was drunk. Wasn't she frightened?" Altschuler threw his hands into the air. "No, of course she wasn't frightened! Why should she be frightened? She had a gun in her handbag!"

He smiled knowledgeably. He raised one finger.

"But wait. You're probably recalling, as I am, that Johnnie Faye Boudreau said she left her handbag on the sofa downstairs, which is what led to her later being placed in that position where, she claims, she couldn't retreat. Folks, you've seen the diagram of the Ott residence. You know where the living room sofa was in relation to the route from the front door to the staircase. *It was sixty-five feet out of the way.* Now I ask you—particularly the ladies—does a woman walk into a house that's not her own, and go upstairs with a man to his bedroom, and first march sixty-five feet out of her way to leave her handbag on the sofa in the downstairs living room? Think about what's in that handbag! Never mind her pistol—I'm talking about her makeup, her keys, her private and precious little things! No! *She takes the handbag with her!*"

He waited a full five seconds.

"And if she does that, ladies and gentlemen, when she goes downstairs again, trying to flee a man who's yelling at her and threatening her, *why doesn't she just go out the front door and drive home?*"

Altschuler went up to full throttle: "Even if you buy her fictitious story about the poker, she didn't retreat! She was egging him on!" With a harsh thrust of his hand, the prosecutor indicated Johnnie Faye, who sat immobile and without expression. "There sits a true monster! A woman without honor and without scruples! Deceitful! Cunning! Wicked! Manipulative! She's a cold-blooded killer, and I ask you, on behalf of the State of Texas and in the name of justice, to find her guilty of murder. Not murder by reason of self-defense—*willful* murder."

Warren wanted to applaud. Amen, he thought. Don't say any more, Bob. You've got her every way. Just sit down.

And Bob Altschuler did.

Judge Bingham nodded at the bailiff, and the bailiff nodded at the jury. Obediently the jurors rose and followed the bailiff through the back door of the courtroom to the jury room.

Shrugging his shoulders under his blue suit, Rick looked

at Warren with bleak eyes. Warren turned toward Johnnie Faye, whose face was icy. She was staring at Bob Altschuler, thumping into his seat and sipping a glass of water a few feet away at the prosecution's table.

"That son of a bitch," she murmured. "I'd like to put one between *his* eyes." She focused finally on Warren. "Well, counselor, good buddy, what do we do now?"

"We wait," he said coolly.

The charged hum of conversation gave the air-conditioned courtroom the feel of an airline terminal. The media and the spectators, the lawyers and the witnesses, had all paid for their tickets with one form of currency or another. They would all wait. At 1:30 P.M. the bailiff left the courtroom to buy sandwiches and soft drinks and coffee for the jurors.

"What about lunch for us?" Johnnie Faye asked Warren.

"I'm not hungry. You can go to the cafeteria in the basement if you like. Don't leave the courthouse."

"What does it mean if the jury takes a long time?"

"There's no rule for it."

"And when they come back in, if they look me in the eye, that's good, isn't it?"

"No rule for that either. They may look you in the eye and send you to prison for life. They may come in with their heads bowed because they're ashamed they reached a verdict of not guilty."

"And fuck you too," Johnnie Faye said. "What if they find me guilty? Do they let me go home and get my things in order?"

"You should have done that already," Warren said. "They'll cuff you and take you away."

Her lip trembled. "And what about an appeal?"

"You can hire a lawyer to do that for you."

"Will you do it? You know the facts."

Bizarre. She knows how I loathe her, but she depends on

me. Somewhere inside this monster is a child. An evil, macabre child, but no less a child.

"Yes, I know the facts. And that's why I won't do it. But plenty of other lawyers will. There'll always be somebody hungry enough, or someone you can con."

He got up and walked through the back door of the courtroom to a telephone reserved for lawyers and reporters. The door to the jury room was about ten feet away. He could hear the jurors' voices raised in argument but he couldn't make out the words. Maria Hahn came up to him and squeezed his arm. "What do you think, honey?" she asked quietly.

"I can't tell. Can you?"

"I told you—you can never predict."

"Bob was good," Warren said.

"He always is. Want to come into my office for a quickie? My door double-locks."

"And then the jury would reach a verdict just about the same time as you and I were reaching something else. I'll take a rain check. Tonight."

"Tonight," Maria said, laughing.

He called his office to pick up the messages. Charm spoke briefly, asking him to call back. A lawyer had checked in with a referral for a case, and one man had called directly from the jail, begging to see him as soon as possible about a drug bust.

So he would be working again. *I should feel a lot better about it than I do,* Warren decided.

He went through the courtroom and outside into the corridor to use the public telephone, which was more private, and called Charm at Channel 26.

"Warren!"—almost breathlessly, as if he had surprised her by returning the call. "How did it go? Are you done?"

He told her the jury was out and it had gone as well as could be expected.

"I have to talk fast," she said. "Just listen to me a minute. I didn't say everything I had to say the other day at lunch. I felt so awful, I was so tongue-tied. Can we meet to talk again?"

He tried to think that through.

"Don't cut me out of your life, Warren. Please."

He saw some TV cameramen moving rapidly outside the door to the courtroom. "I have to go. The jury may be coming in. All right. When?"

"Whenever you can make it. Tonight?"

"Not tonight. Lunch tomorrow, if that suits you."

She would be in Bingham's courtroom at noon. Before he could make other arrangements, she hung up. Warren hurried back to the courtroom and pushed open the swinging door. The TV cameramen were taping Bob Altschuler.

When they were finished, Altschuler grasped Warren's elbow and moved him firmly to an empty back bench. Altschuler's snapping dark eyes were flecked with pink and the lines seemed more deeply engraved from his nose to the corners of his mouth. Close up, Warren could see that his striped shirt was damp with sweat.

"Your client is guilty as sin," Altschuler said. "She hired Dink to kill Sharon Underhill. She hired a guy named Ronzini to kill Dink. We think a corpse that washed up on Galveston Island last month is what's left of Ronzini. And she got Clyde Ott drunk and shot him in cold blood. You know that, for Christ's sake, don't you?"

Warren thought for a moment or two. "Off the record?"

"Whatever you say. Whatever you like."

"I know it."

"Well, you didn't have any choice," Altschuler said, sighing. "I just wish you hadn't done such a fucking good job of defending her."

"You were pretty good too. I think you've nailed her."

Altschuler extended his big hand. Warren suddenly wondered, Why have I always believed I was better than he is? He thinks he's a righteous man helping to keep order in the universe—he sends guilty people to prison for as long as the law allows. I think I'm righteous because I keep them out for as long as the law allows. He's usually right, I'm usually wrong.

He took Bob Altschuler's hand and shook it.

At four o'clock the jury still had not reached a verdict. Judge Bingham sent a message through the bailiff: if they wished to continue deliberating, he would remain in the courtroom until 8 P.M. After that they would be escorted to a hotel where they would have dinner and spend the night. Then they would resume at 9 A.M. the following morning. Or, if they wished, they could quit at 6 P.M. and be taken at that time to dinner and the hotel.

A cryptic note came back from the jury foreman: "We will continue deliberating, your honor."

At half past four Warren conferred in whispers with Rick, then took the elevator up to the seventh floor and the 299th. Judge Parker's courtroom was empty except for the judge and Nancy Goodpaster, huddled at the bench, working on the court calendar. Goodpaster smiled quickly at Warren and mouthed a hello.

The judge was suntanned and looked as if she had gained a few pounds. "Well, if it ain't my friend Mr. Blackburn."

"How are you, Judge?"

"Just fine. And you, counselor?"

"Just fine."

"Jury still out in *Boudreau*?"

He nodded. "But the smart money says they'll reach a decision before eight o'clock this evening. Tomorrow morning at the latest. I've got my witness ready for *Quintana*. When can we do it?"

"Tomorrow and the next day are pretty free—anyway, I can bump a few people around. Thursday on, my docket's full. So you get going by tomorrow after lunch or I dismiss the jury and we pick a new one in September. That's it."

A new jury in September would cancel out all his advantage, and he would have to keep Jim Dandy on ice for at least a month. Warren looked gloomily into the judge's unfathomable eyes. Just then the telephone rang on the bailiff's desk.

Nancy Goodpaster walked over, picked it up and listened for a moment. "Yes," she said, "I'll tell him." She hung up and turned to Warren. "Your partner wants you in the 342nd. The *Boudreau* jury's coming in."

"All rise!" the bailiff called, and the jury filed in and took their seats. Johnnie Faye Boudreau stood between Rick and Warren at the defense table. Bob Altschuler stood at the prosecutor's table, slightly hunched, fingers tapping a light tattoo on the walnut. The jurors as they took their seats looked across at Johnnie Faye and met her questioning gaze. But there seemed to be no emotion in their eyes.

Judge Bingham asked if they had reached a verdict, and the foreman, the man in the black windbreaker whom Johnnie Faye had insisted be on the jury, said yes, they had. He handed a slip of paper to the deputy clerk.

"You may read the verdict," Judge Bingham said.

The deputy clerk read aloud in a calm voice: "We the jury find the defendant, Johnnie Faye Boudreau, not guilty by reason of self-defense."

The blood fled from Warren's face. Johnnie Faye let out a whoop. She threw her arms around Rick and hugged him. Then she wheeled with outstretched arms to hug Warren. But Warren was not there.

He strode, almost ran, out of the courtroom. Reporters trotted after him, plucked at his sleeve, shouting questions. For a moment he was trapped, could not evade them without shoving them aside. The microphones were nearly in his teeth. A tumult of galvanic anger rocketed through him from head to toe. "The jury has spoken," he replied, "for better or for worse. Ms. Boudreau is free. That's all that matters. I have nothing more to say."

But he couldn't get away. They were blocking him, clutching at his sleeve. "Mr. Blackburn, what do you mean *'for better or for worse'*? Are you casting doubt on the justice of the verdict?"

"The jury is always right," Warren said, quoting himself to his former client, "whether they're right or not."

Amid the clamor and shrieks of disbelief, he brushed past the reporters and cameramen. To every other shouted question he murmured, "No comment." He headed for the stairwell.

The door slammed behind him. Warren rested his forehead against the cool of the flaking drywall. His hands felt clammy, his stomach heaved and twisted. Altschuler knew the truth, and it didn't matter. You had no choice, Altschuler had said. But I did, Warren thought, and I made it. If I had real guts I would have grabbed those microphones and said, "She's free—free to lie, free to murder again, free to celebrate our complicity. If there's justice, it's only by accident. The system stinks. Ask a man named Hector Quintana, who may die for a murder he didn't commit: *She did.*"

He wanted to howl with frustration, and all he could manage was a pitiful groan to the four walls. But what could I have done that would have worked? Nothing. And what can I do now? Nothing yet. But so help me God, I'll find a way.

Above Rick Levine's massive desk in the old Cotton Exchange Building was a blue neon sign that said LAWYER. In one corner of the room stood wooden replicas of a medieval rack and an iron maiden. ("To help you remember more accurately," Rick would say to his clients.) In another corner on the parquet floor was a red bubble gum machine. Digging into a jar of coins, Rick fed two nickels into the machine and offered Warren one of the pink-wrapped pieces of bubble gum that popped out.

Warren shook his head. In front of him, on a corner of the desk, Bernadette Loo set down a mug of steaming fragrant black coffee.

After the verdict, Rick had talked to several of the *Boudreau* jurors. "You know," he said now to Warren, "it never ceases to flabbergast me how people take on new personalities. The rest of their lives can be all fucked up, they may cheat on their taxes and their spouses, and be real couch potatoes and dorks, but when they get to be jurors, man, suddenly they're conscientious Americans and professors of logic. They respect the law, they want to do the right thing. Gives me faith in the system."

"That makes one of us," Warren said impatiently. "So tell me what happened."

"They took the first vote right after they got to the jury room. Eight not guilty, two guilty, and two couldn't make up their minds. Right after lunch it looked like they were going to hang up. The foreman—the guy in the black windbreaker who owns a TV appliance store, the one our client insisted on having—was the last holdout. He says, 'I hated her guts, I just didn't believe half of what she said.' But this other juror, the shriveled-up secretary with the oil company, really got on his case. She kept telling him, 'You can't convict a woman because you don't like her. I want to vote guilty too, because I have doubts that she's innocent, but they're on the emotional level. And the judge told us that the state has the burden of proof.' You figure that one out," Rick said to Warren.

"Anyway, they kept arguing. That sourpuss in the first row says, 'I feel so sorry for Ms. Boudreau. Maybe she's guilty, but I think she really loved that awful doctor, and he took advantage of her and wouldn't marry her. She was brave, just like Mr. Blackburn said.'—Does that make you happy, boychik?—And then the clothing store executive, with the sideburns, the one who always wore a red tie?" Rick broadened his western accent: "He says, 'If a guy came at me with a poker, y'all better b'lieve I'd put *six* bullets between his eyes.' So black-windbreaker yells, 'What about the business of her making the detour to drop off her handbag?' And red-tie looks baffled and says, '*What* detour?' " Rick cackled like a rooster. "Another woman juror tells black-windbreaker, '*I* would have taken my handbag upstairs, but maybe Johnnie Faye was confused. I think that's why she wiped the palm prints off the poker. It's so hard to remember what you did and why you did it.' And black-windbreaker throws up his hands and says, 'I give up. Not guilty.' "

"And you still think they're conscientious?" Warren asked.

"Sure I do," Rick said. "It's a matter of definition and perspective. You have to remember that people are basically nuts."

Warren understood that his former partner, sitting behind his desk, wore the light air of triumph. They had won a big case. The newspapers had headlined the verdict and there were photographs of Clyde Ott and of a confident Johnnie Faye Boudreau entering the courthouse between her two lawyers. In a boxed sidebar below the headline, a bold subhead read: *"Defense Attorney Not Enthusiastic over*

Triumph; Casts Doubt on Verdict." All the late-night TV news reports led off with Warren in the hallway and moved from there to a clip of Bob Altschuler in the same hallway, stating that "No, I don't know what Mr. Blackburn meant. The basis of our adversary system in this country is that a defense counsel, no matter what his private beliefs, is required to make his best effort on behalf of an accused client. And Mr. Blackburn certainly did that. . . . Yes, he was skating awfully close to the line, but there are no penalties for such statements. . . ."

Even as he reached his office at nine o'clock on the morning after the verdict, Warren's telephone had been ringing. The red message light was blinking; the tape was full. He unplugged everything. At eleven o'clock he drove downtown to Rick's office near the courthouse.

Bernadette Loo flew into the office just as Warren set down his empty coffee mug. "She's here."

"Who?"

"The one who loves Chinks and gooks so much."

Rick turned to Warren. "She called me last night at home. She is seriously pissed off." He turned back to Bernadette. "So what did you tell her?"

"That you were with a client."

Rick swung back to Warren. "What do you want me to do?"

"Let her in. But frisk her first."

Rick laughed uneasily. A few seconds later, wearing the same cherry-red suit and white hat that she had worn to the trial of Hector Quintana, Johnnie Faye surged into the room, a hand planted on a wide hip, cheeks white, lips drained of blood.

She pointed a finger at Warren. "I want to talk to *him.* Alone."

Warren nodded. Rick went out the door with Bernadette Loo. A little too eagerly, Warren thought.

"Now listen," Johnnie Faye Boudreau said, her body quivering. "You shot your mouth off, you had your fun.

'For better or for worse . . . the jury is right whether they're right or not.' You greased your lousy little conscience. But let's get something straight—*you* didn't win that trial for me! I saved my *own* neck!"

"I'd say for the most part that's true," Warren replied calmly.

"You bet it is. And you came about one inch from getting disbarred for those cutesy remarks. Counselor, I want to remind you of the law. Whatever I told you is still privileged, unless you care to wind up pumping gas, which is what you'd be doing right now if my case hadn't come along to save your ass. Doesn't matter a fuck that you're not my lawyer anymore. Privilege is privilege. Is that clear?"

"That's always been clear," Warren said.

"And if I see your face one more time on TV talking about my case, or any similar shit—just watch out!"

Warren rose from his chair. "Are you threatening me?"

"A word to the wise," Johnnie Faye shot back.

Reaching past a pile of Rick's papers, Warren flipped the switch on the desk tape recorder. The green light blinked on. "Let me point out one thing to you," he said, "because it's my obligation to do so. Any admissions you make now don't fall under the cloak of privilege. Anything I find out that doesn't derive from what you told me when I was your lawyer, I can use against you. And I will. Now, you crazy bitch, keep talking."

Johnnie Faye Boudreau raised the middle finger of her right hand and jabbed it twice toward the ceiling. Then she wheeled around to the door. Hips gyrating, heels clicking on the parquet floor, she swung out of the office.

Warren shut off the tape recorder and picked up his briefcase. A moment later Rick came back in, shutting the door behind him.

"I heard some of that. You want my advice? Be careful.

That lady has a history of doing nasty things to anyone who stands in her way."

"I'm going to put her away for life," Warren said.

As they had agreed, Charm was waiting for him at noon outside the 342nd District Court, Judge Dwight Bingham's courtroom. Just after Warren said hello and Charm kissed him on the cheek to congratulate him on the verdict, the courtroom door swung open and Maria Hahn stepped out with Judge Bingham. They were laughing. Recognizing the caliber of the hilarity, Warren guessed that Maria must have just told him a new joke. The judge, halting, thrust out his hand. "Mr. Warren! I see by the papers you've been a bad boy." He inclined his bald head toward Charm. "Can't you control your husband, Mrs. Blackburn? Get him to keep his big mouth shut?"

But he was smiling. He had enjoyed the case. You could never suffer a reversal on an acquittal.

Maria Hahn wasn't smiling.

Warren exchanged a few more words with the judge and then said, "Goodbye, your honor. Goodbye, Maria. See you later."

"Join us for lunch," the judge suggested. "I can learn from your beautiful wife what's going on outside this courthouse."

"Thanks. Can't today," Warren said, suffering. "Some other time."

Again he took Charm to the Greek restaurant. She looked pale and even thinner than before. On the way, she said, "That's the woman you've been seeing, isn't it?"

"Which one?"

"Come off it, Warren. The tall one with the big boobs and great legs. The one who was giggling with the judge."

Warren was mildly amazed. "How could you tell?"

"The way she looked at you. And you at her." Charm clamped her lips shut.

In the restaurant, her eyes moist, hands trembling, she

said, "Give me a chance, Warren. Don't throw away our marriage for someone you hardly know."

"Whatever wrong I did, I never quit," he said. "You threw the marriage away, Charm."

"I almost did, and it would have been the worst mistake of my life."

He considered that she had her tenses mixed up but decided not to comment on it. He had no urge to argue, only to clarify. "Anyway," he said, "Maria doesn't enter into it."

"Of course she does." Charm spoke rapidly, with certainty. "I know what a relationship is like in the early stages. It's new, it's exciting, it's captivating. Best foot forward, all that stuff. You're a catch, Warren—you're a man of some substance. She'll work hard to land you, even if she's not aware what she's doing. Later it becomes real. Real is different." She clenched her fists. "We had real. And real is what matters."

Was that true, or were words and concepts just obedient servants to intent? He would have to think about what she said. He nodded, admiring her verve, liking her but still wary.

Charm flew on: "She must know you just can't excise a marriage the way you do a tumor. And she won't want you on the rebound. That never works, or it works for a time, and then it crumbles apart. I've been there. Our marriage wasn't perfect and it will never be perfect. Marriages never are. Don't think of the bad times, the craziness—that's the trap I fell into. Think of the good things we had. We can still help each other to grow up. Let me back into your life, Warren."

He realized she was something more than sincere. She knew what she wanted and she was fighting for it; but she was also trying to shed light into his life. She was an adult woman, complex, loving, fallible. And there was a tenderness underlying her words, a tenderness that he remembered, but suffused with a new emotion born of loss.

"Why me, Charm? What's so special? Aren't all men pretty much alike in the end?" He was not fishing for compliments. He needed to know.

"I'm not qualified on that score," she said. "I haven't known that many. But I know you, and you do the best you can with people and things, and I have a feeling your best is getting better all the time. I love you for having achieved that. What's special is *us*. Not unique, but special. Because we have a history. We created something. I know we can put it back together again if we're kind to each other. We were partners, and we can be partners again."

Those had been his thoughts, the thoughts that he had been unable to speak. That she echoed him moved him. Her words and the way she looked at him, sorrowfully, holding back the tears, a child asking for a forbidden sweet, grazed his heart and then forced an entry. He felt a change take place in him. He had mourned her going, he had been bitter. That was ending.

"I want children with you, Warren. I'm ready. I don't want anyone else's children but yours."

"That's a new tune," he said. He remembered his pain of more than a year ago.

"I know," she said, flushing. "But you were floundering, and I was an idiot. I didn't know how to help you and that made me feel a failure too. Please forgive me for that."

"I do," Warren said. "Charm, I need time. I can't be rushed. And I can't promise you a damn thing."

"The more time you spend with her," Charm said, "the less chance I have. That's the equation. I'll give you time, you know I will. But I can't hang around forever. I think I have a job in Boston with PBS."

"Oh?" He saw how the thought energized her. "Do you want to take it?"

"If we're not back together, yes. If we can be together, probably not. Your life is here."

"I have to go now," Warren said, after he had looked at

his watch. "I'm in trial in the 299th, and I have to meet someone in front of the courthouse. I can't be late."

"Do you love me at all, Warren?"

"Yes. I can't help that."

Color flowed into her cheeks that had been so pale. She looked grateful and, for a moment, happy. Her eyes glistened. "Call me," she said.

He stood in front of the courthouse, sweating even in the shade, tie unknotted, hands stuffed into his trouser pockets. He counted on their showing up, but a part of him knew that anything was possible. The management at Ravendale had already complained, one of the assistant managers knocking on his door to inform him that this was not a flophouse for homeless bums. Warren had gone to Janice at the front desk to explain: "These are witnesses in a capital murder case. They're being sequestered here. Please help me if you can." Janice said, "Leave it to me," and he heard no more complaints.

Warren had put Jim Dandy in Pedro's hands. "Whatever happens, don't let him drink tomorrow morning. Not even a beer. You and Armando sit on him if you have to. Get him under a shower. I want him wearing a shirt and pants, no army jacket. And be there at one o'clock sharp— American time, not Mexican time. If you don't show up, you could kill your friend Hector."

"Trust me, amigo," Pedro said.

Warren had called Ravendale twice this morning, once from his office and once from Rick's.

"It's fine," Pedro said, both times. "We be there. One o'clock sharp, gringo time."

At twenty past one a taxi drew up with Pedro and Jim Dandy in it. Grinning, Pedro raised his fist with one thumb up. Twenty minutes late, Warren thought. Not bad. He had allowed for half an hour.

* * *

He drew Nancy Goodpaster with him into her office and shut the door.

"Nancy, what you did that day at the bench, when you backed me up about what the judge said in chambers—that was brave. I think you're a terrific lawyer. I don't think you want to prosecute an innocent man."

Goodpaster said, "I promise you, that's the last thing on earth I want to do."

"I've got a witness who'll testify that he took Dan Ho Trunh's wallet. That's only part of what he'll say, but he won't even take the stand if he doesn't get immunity on the theft charge. I'm going to make a motion for that immunity. Go along with it. You won't regret it."

Nancy Goodpaster considered. "All right," she said. "I trust you."

Those were among the sweetest words that Warren had ever heard. He wanted to kiss her on the cheek, but he thought that might be unprofessional, and women lawyers these days tended to resent such gestures. Instead he said, "Thank you, Nancy. You ever quit this job and want to go into private practice, give me a ring."

"I might just take you up on that," Nancy Goodpaster said, "one of these days."

With the jury in place and Hector Quintana by his side at the defense table, Warren stood. "The defense is ready, your honor, and calls James Thurgood Dandy."

Jim Dandy slouched in the witness chair. He kept running a callused hand through his dark hair. He was almost as nervous as Warren. "Your honor," Warren said, "before testimony, the defense will make a motion *in limine.*"

He was already on his way to the bench, with Nancy Goodpaster following close behind. *In limine* meant "on the threshold." Warren said quietly, "Judge, this witness will testify, among other things, to having approached the car of the victim, Dan Ho Trunh, and taking a wallet and its contents from the dead man's hand. But this witness won't testify if his sworn statements prejudice his liberty. I request immunity for the witness on all felony charges of theft, on the grounds of an overriding need to have the facts clarified in a case of capital murder, which takes precedence."

Judge Parker said, "Counselor, a proper motion *in limine* is meant to keep facts out of evidence so that the jury won't be prejudiced against the witness. You want to put them *into* evidence. You sure you know what you're doing?"

"Yes, your honor."

Judge Parker looked to Nancy Goodpaster. "State has no objection," Goodpaster said.

For the benefit of the hovering court reporter, the judge intoned: "Immunity is granted the witness James Thurgood Dandy, limited to the felony charge of theft."

Jim Dandy was sworn in by the deputy clerk.

Warren could barely wait; he felt the surge of blood from heart to brain. He went through the customary business of asking name, address, age, and profession.

"Jim Dandy is what they call me."—"DeKalb Street, Beeville. Down south a ways."—"About thirty-eight."— "Don't have no profession."

"Sir, what do you do for a living?"

No one had ever called Jim Dandy "sir" before. He looked pleased. Warren could see his nervousness begin to ebb.

"I do whatever I can to make a dollar or two. Stuff like that."

Warren let it go and plunged in like a swimmer from a high board. "Do you recall where you were on May 19 of this year, at about 8 P.M.?"

"Well, I don't know that it was exactly May 19, but it was about then, and I know what you're talkin' about. I was sittin' against a wall, drunk."

"Where, sir?"

"Here in town. Some shoppin' center, guess you'd call it.

I bought a pint of Thunderbird there. Set me down to enjoy it."

"Did anything unusual happen while you were sitting against the wall in that shopping center?"

"Well, I had this natural need to relieve myself, you could say. So I did it, then and there. Couldn't wait. And while I was doin' that, I heard a yell and then a shot. Scared the dickens out of me."

"How do you know it was a shot, Mr. Dandy?"

"I'm comin' to that. Let me tell it my way, okay, hoss?"

"Okay," Warren said.

"It was a shot 'cause that's what it was. Couldn't a been nothin' else. I know what a shot is. I may be a drunk, but I ain't stupid."

"And so what did you do?"

"I turned my head around—I was still scared, but I was worried someone might be aimin' to shoot *me*—and there was these two cars there. A wagon, and the other was a nice big car. Can't tell if they're foreign or not anymore. But it was kinda new. Engine was runnin'. They was parked side by side. They was sorta facin' me."

"How far away from you?"

"Can't say. Not far, not close. Close enough to see."

"And what did you see, sir?"

"Didn't see anyone in the wagon. Saw a woman in the car."

Warren didn't bother looking at the jury: they were not the object of this exercise. He glanced at Nancy Goodpaster. She was hunched at the prosecutor's table, one hand grasping her chin, listening intently. That was how Warren had listened on the drive up from Beeville.

"Mr. Dandy, you saw a woman in the car that was parked next to the station wagon? A *woman*? You're positive?"

"That's right. Besides, I told you I heard a yell before I heard the shot? That was a woman's yell, what y'all might call a scream."

"Was there anyone else in the parking lot, either on foot or in a car?"

"Not that I noticed."

"The woman in the car was alone?"

"Didn't see no one else with her. Didn't get much of a chance to look, 'cause she sure tore outa there."

"Can you describe the woman in the car?"

"Sure can't. I saw long woman's hair and some red lipstick, and that's about all. Then she was gone."

"Did she give you any indication that she had seen you?"

"No, sir."

"Can you describe the car? The make? The model?"

"Not really, 'cept it was big and looked new."

"Before the woman in the car tore out of there, Mr. Dandy, did you notice if she had anything in her hand?"

"Looked to me like a gun."

"Can you describe the gun?"

"Can't do that. Was just a gun."

"Big or small?"

"It wasn't nothin' gigantic."

A great witness, Warren thought. He never speculated, never embroidered, and he told the truth. Warren looked again at Nancy Goodpaster. He saw in her face an intense concentration masking a growing amazement. But he also saw belief.

"What did you do then, Mr. Dandy?"

"Walked over to the wagon and looked inside. Man was dead in there." Jim Dandy sighed. "I took his wallet. He wasn't gonna need it no more."

Warren nodded. "Did you hang around to see what was in the wallet?"

"No, I skedaddled. I already seen there was money in it. Looked to see how much when I got round the corner."

"Besides money, was there anything else in the wallet?"

"A laundry ticket."

"Did you take that out of the wallet?"

"Put it in my pocket."

"What did you do with the wallet?"

"Threw it in a sewer."

"What did you do with the laundry ticket?"

"Well, a few days later, I figured, heck, dead fella don't need the clothes either. I still had some of the money left, so I went back there to the laundry and got 'em. Paid for 'em and took 'em away."

"Do you remember who waited on you in the laundry and gave you the clothes?"

"Indian lady."

"Can you describe the clothes you got from her at the laundry?"

"Nice gray suit. White shirts. Nice green sweater. Didn't fit too good—little tight. So I sold 'em down at the mission."

Warren elected not to pursue that now; that would come later, and not in this court. His voice rising, he said, "Mr. Dandy, have you ever in your life seen the man sitting beside me?" He put a hand—a hand that almost trembled —on Hector Quintana's shoulder.

Jim Dandy peered across the courtroom at Hector. "Not that I can recollect. Looks like a Messkin. I ain't got nothin' against 'em, but I can't always tell 'em apart."

"You didn't see this man in the parking lot outside the laundry that night, or in the car that the woman with the gun was driving, or anywhere around the vicinity of the shopping mall?"

"Nope."

"Did you see anyone that night who might have even looked like this man?"

"Nope."

"Thank you, sir," Warren said. "Pass the witness."

Nancy Goodpaster took Jim Dandy on cross for only fifteen minutes. She made him repeat most of his story; she focused mostly on the time frame, to make sure it was the night of May 19, and his certainty that it was a woman in the car. Warren never raised an objection. But Jim Dandy was certain. A person with long hair and lipstick was not a man. "I was drunk," he said, "and times have changed, but, ma'am, I ain't never *that* drunk I can't tell a man from a woman."

Goodpaster hesitated, bit her lip, then said, "No further questions."

To hammer in the final nail of innocence, Warren called Siva Singh as a witness for the defense. She quickly identified Jim Dandy as the man who had picked up Dan Ho Trunh's dry cleaning.

"And could Mr. Dandy be the same man you saw running away from the car and out of the parking lot?"

"That is possible," Singh said quietly.

After Goodpaster declined cross-examination, Warren said, "May it please the court . . ." and called for a ten-minute break for counsel to confer.

Goodpaster led Warren back to her office. She sat down behind her desk and said, "Give me a couple of minutes to work this damn thing out."

Warren waited while she stared out the window at the heat bouncing off a distant white building. Finally she faced him. "I have one problem. How do we know that it wasn't your witness, this guy Dandy, who murdered Trunh? He had motive—the money. He had opportunity. How do we know his whole story isn't a cover-up?"

"Then why would he be dumb enough to show up in court," Warren asked, "and take the risk you'd figure that out and nail his ass to the wall?"

"I have no idea," she admitted.

"He didn't do it, Nancy. I'm not guessing."

Goodpaster frowned. "You know something about this case that I don't know. You always did. Now let's stop fooling around. What is it?"

"I know that the woman in the car murdered Trunh. She threw the gun away in a Dumpster at Ravendale. Quintana was foraging there and he found it."

"And there's more than that. I can tell. Spit it out."

After a few moments, Warren said, "I know who the woman is."

"You mean you *think* you know."

"No." Again Warren hesitated. "She's admitted it to me."

"Jesus Christ! Then stop playing games! Who is it?"

"I can't tell you—it falls under privilege. When it's possible, you'll know. When you become my partner." He smiled briefly, exhausted. "And now let's wrap up *Quintana*. You're chief prosecutor in this court. You have the power. Will the state drop charges?"

Goodpaster sighed. "I guess we have no choice."

Warren said, "You always have a choice, Nancy. Don't sigh. Just be glad you're able to make the right one."

"Believe me, I am." With her sleeve Goodpaster wiped a light sheen of sweat from her forehead. "This could have been my worst nightmare come true. That jury could have given your client the needle. I was sure he was guilty."

"Don't feel badly about that," Warren said. "For a long time, so was I."

Goodpaster laid a slim hand on his shoulder. "I want to tell you something, Warren. You're a hell of a lawyer, and I've been here five years and I've seen a lot. I never saw anyone fight so hard for a client. And I never saw anyone stand up to Her Worship the way you did. You made my week. My year."

What she had said about fighting for his client made him feel that he had reached the zenith of his profession.

"You must feel awfully good," Goodpaster said.

"I do," Warren admitted. "But I'm damn tired." He suddenly felt he might cry. He had to turn away.

The law required a certain procedure. The facts would have to be presented formally to the Office of the District Attorney and the indictment quashed. Back in Judge Parker's courtroom, Goodpaster requested a continuance pending prosecutorial decision. "The state," she said, "is also willing to accept defense counsel's motion for bail on defendant's personal recognizance bond, if the defense so moves."

"Defense so moves," Warren said.

"Granted," said the judge, shaking her head in near disbelief. She rapped her gavel. "And will y'all go now, so I can dismiss this jury and get on with my docket?"

Warren walked over to Hector Quintana at the defense table. "You can go."

"Go where?" Hector said.

"Anywhere you like. You're free, Hector. It's all over."

Warren explained a few things, but he was not sure Hector understood them all. Hector murmured some phrases in Spanish, and then tears glittered in his eyes. He hugged his lawyer fiercely. "Thank you," he said. *"Diós te pagará."*

God will reward you.

Warren couldn't remember ever having been so glad. He cried and he laughed and he hugged and pummeled his client Hector Quintana at the same time.

"I have no money," Hector said, when they had both recovered sufficiently to deal with practical matters. "Where should I go?"

"I know just the place," Warren said. "And don't worry about money. Tomorrow I'll give you the money to get back to Mexico or to stay here, whatever you like. My pleasure. But do me a favor and come on along with me now. I have something to do. Something that can't wait."

"I owe you one," Warren said, "and I'm here to pay. But first you have to indulge me and answer a few questions."

Bob Altschuler's spacious sixth-floor office in the district attorney's building on Fannin was furnished in maple with imitation French provincial chairs. On his desk were photographs of his wife and three daughters, and Altschuler reclined in the kind of tall swivel chair that was usually the prerogative of judges and board chairmen. Hector Quintana was waiting outside in an anteroom.

Altschuler nodded coolly. "Go ahead."

"There was a murder in the mission about four or five nights ago," Warren said. "A bum, shot to death in the toilet. As far as I know, no one's been indicted—HPD probably doesn't even have a suspect. I don't represent anyone involved, and I haven't talked to anyone who's involved. But I think I know who did it. Before I tell you, I need a look at the offense report. Or else I need to talk to whoever's handling it at Homicide."

Altshuler frowned. "One bum iced some other bum. What's the big deal? It's a nothing case."

"I don't think so," Warren said. "I think it'll make you happy."

For a moment or two Altschuler fixed him with an astute dark look. Then he reached for his telephone. Ten minutes later Sgt. Hollis Thiel sat in one of the French provincial chairs next to Warren, hands resting on the paunch under his brown suit.

"Tell me what happened," Warren said.

Thiel's eyes in his porcine face were narrowed and suspicious. He glanced over at Altschuler.

"Tell him," Altschuler said.

"Four o'clock in the morning," Thiel said. "It's a real zoo over at the mission. Guys come in and out all night, sleep a little, booze it up, smoke, shoot smack. There's no night and day. So around four o'clock this guy goes into the toilet. His name is Jerry Mahoney. Guy about thirty-five or so, comes from Galveston. A kind of classy bum. Little fuck sells dope when he can get hold of it, and plenty of guys have a hard-on for him. He's at the trough taking a piss when another guy walks in. Other guy stands next to him for a minute at the trough, looks Mahoney up and down. Mahoney starts to wriggle his dick around before he zips up, this other guy whips out a piece, puts two bullets in the unsuspecting bastard, checks Mahoney's pulse, then beats it. One head shot, one body shot, both through and throughs. Mahoney's dead by the time the ambulance arrives. Never says a word."

"What was Mahoney wearing when he was killed?" Warren asked.

Thiel checked his notes. "Green cotton sweater, white button-down shirt, no tie, gray pants, brown shoes with holes in both soles. Kind of preppy. I told you, he's a classy bum."

"And there were witnesses," Warren said.

"Yeah. The toilets don't have doors, which is supposed to stop guys from giving blow jobs to each other in the stalls, if they're that way inclined. Two bums are taking a crap when Mahoney is killed." Thiel looked at his notes again. "One black dude named Fred Polson, one illegal alien named Raul Fernandez. They see it all. Scares them shitless." Thiel chuckled. "Literally."

"They give you a description of the killer? Don't tell me what they said. Just tell me if they gave one to you."

"Yeah, but they don't know who he is. They never saw him before."

"Let me guess," Warren said. "About thirty years old. Fair hair. Wore a black T-shirt and chinos. Tattoos on both arms. One's a dragon, the other says 'Rosie.' Tough-looking guy, with muscles."

That was the pattern. The new boyfriend did the dirty work. Johnnie Faye had been in court on the day that Siva Singh testified to a man having probably witnessed the murder. A bum with a laundry ticket for a green sweater and gray suit. The dirty work needed to be done.

Thiel's eyes narrowed to slits. Rustling his papers, he glanced up at Altschuler, who nodded his approval again. Thiel looked back at Warren.

"Close, counselor. One tattoo on one arm is what they saw. Polson says the guy was about thirty-two. Fernandez isn't sure. Maybe older. They both saw the muscles. Black T-shirt is correct. Guy wore a hat so they couldn't see his hair."

"You don't know who he is, right? No clue."

"Not yet, but I got a feeling one's coming."

"And you found the bullets in the walls," Warren said, "and the hulls were on the floor, probably behind and to the right. A .45 ejects behind and to the right."

"I didn't say it was a .45," Thiel said slowly.

"But it was."

"Yeah," Thiel said, "it was."

"Polson and Fernandez still around?"

"They're around."

"Why don't you pick them up this morning," Warren said, "so that they're sober and straight for the rest of the day. Then this evening you can take them to visit a few nightclubs." Warren handed Thiel a slip of yellow paper torn from a legal pad. "Here's a list of clubs. Tear it up before I leave this office. Look really carefully in the third one on the list. If you find the guy you're looking for, you have cause to search the premises. Bob will review the transcript of *Boudreau*—my direct examination of the defendant—and tell you where to look. The .45 may be there, or it may not. But the guy you find will know where it is, and he'll know who gave it to him and told him to ice a man in a green sweater and white button-down shirt. He's a tough little fucker—you may have to sweat him. But if you offer him the right deal for the right name, you're home free."

Warren turned to Bob Altschuler. "I just tried a case in the 299th. Interesting case. You'd like it. If the state's not completely broke, you should pay for the court reporter to transcribe the trial. Talk to Nancy. Pay attention to two prosecution witnesses—Mai Thi Trunh and Siva Singh—and one defense witness—James Thurgood Dandy. You read carefully, they'll tell you why Mahoney was wearing a green sweater and gray pants." Warren spelled the names, while Altschuler diligently wrote in block capitals on a yellow legal pad.

"Since you know so much," Altschuler asked, when he had finished, "why don't you just lay it all out on the table instead of making me jump through hoops and invest my valuable time?"

"Because this way," Warren said, "you'll have a greater sense of accomplishment. And then you can leave me out of it. You never talked to me. I'm just another scumbag defense lawyer. I'm not a witness. I'm not a source. Can you live with that?"

"Ah well." Altschuler smiled gently. "If things work out—why not?"

That evening Warren dipped into his wallet and said good-bye to Pedro and Armando and Jim Dandy. He settled Hector Quintana, his new guest, onto the living room couch at Ravendale. After Warren put fresh sheets on his king-size bed and ran along the bayou with Oobie, he showered, made sure Hector had everything he needed, and then drove to Maria Hahn's house. He had called her earlier to set the hour.

Maria's son, Randy, was home from Austin. Warren was glad. Maria fed Randy a veal roast and, while the boy ate, Warren discussed with him the plight of the second-place

Astros. When Randy had rinsed and stacked his dishes, Maria sent him into his room to watch the ball game on television.

She mixed two vodka tonics, then tucked her long legs beneath her skirt and curled into an easy chair. Her usually cheerful blue eyes were melancholy. Warren stood in the center of the living room, lifting his glass to inhale the aroma of grain and lemon.

He said, "Good kid, Randy."

"Yes, he is."

Tangled lives, Warren thought. No deceit, but no less tangled.

"How are you?" Maria asked tonelessly.

"I won two cases in two days. I feel great. But I didn't like bumping into you that way. Yesterday, outside the courtroom."

"So what happened with your wife?"

Warren told her everything. He was a good lawyer, he had good recall. It took a while.

"And what will you do?"

"I don't know," he said. "I told her I needed time."

Maria bit her lip. "I'm not happy about it, and I don't think you're doing the right thing, but I guess I understand."

"I'm not *doing* anything."

He remembered Johnnie Faye Boudreau's words: *"The good Lord hates a muddle the way a judge hates a hung jury. . . . 'Mr. Man, Mr. Lawyer, you can walk, you can run, you can lie down, but don't ever wobble.' "* The irony of taking advice from that quarter did not escape him. And so he struggled against it.

"We never made any promises to each other," Maria said. "No declarations of love. And shit happens."

"It wasn't shit. It *isn't* shit."

"Sure. You know how I talk. That's just an expression."

Warren wanted to hold her and comfort her, but he knew it wouldn't help. He felt a sadness of incipient loss.

Not overpowering, but it was there. So must she feel it too. There was only one right thing to do.

"Listen, I didn't come here to say goodbye. I came here to tell you I have a problem, that's all. I want to keep things clear. I don't want to hide anything. But I don't want to paint myself into a corner where I say something that I don't mean and that I'll regret. You follow? Probably not. I'm going," he said gruffly, angry at himself, setting his drink down on the glass coffee table in front of the couch where he had first kissed her. For a moment she bent her head, clasping slim ankles with slim hands. Then she looked up at him. Her eyes were cool.

"Are you moving back in with your wife?"

"That is exactly what I am *not* doing. Give me a break, Maria. Give me a merit badge for honesty. Maybe honesty is stupid in this kind of situation, but I like to think not. I'll call you, I'll let you know what's happening. And I promise you, for whatever it's worth, I won't play games. If I ever come back here, I'll be a free man." He paused at the door, turning. "You know something? You saved my sanity. You're a loyal friend."

"I'm good at that," she said. "See you around, counselor."

He went out the front door to his car, got in, and shut his eyes for a long minute. He had not meant to sweep her out of his life with a single blow like that of a leopard's paw. Yet it seemed that had happened. He felt stunned, pained—a little corrupt. He drove back to Ravendale.

He found Hector watching television and drinking a beer. Warren mixed a strong vodka tonic and sat down with him. They talked about life in Mexico and life in the United States and they kept drinking. "Are you going back to El Palmito?" Warren asked.

Hector said, "I miss my wife and children, but if I go back there I'll always be poor. I don't want to be poor." He shrugged. "Who knows?" He had told Warren the Mexicans had an answer to many difficult questions. That

answer was "Maybe yes, maybe no. But most probably
. . . who knows?"

After a while there was little to talk about except the
case, and Warren was tired of that. It was always that way
with clients after trial: you had been bound together like
shipmates on a storm-ravaged raft, and then with rescue—
or drowning—it was over. A lawyer learned to live with
loss even if he won. He had saved Hector's life but they
had little else in common.

On Monday, when Hector had made up his mind, Warren put him on a bus for McAllen, on the border, with
enough money in his pocket for a bus from McAllen to
San Luis Potosí, and from there to El Palmito, and something more to tide him over until he found work. Hector
thanked him quietly. "You will come visit me one day?"

"Maybe," Warren said. "Who knows?"

Hector smiled at that.

"Don't come back," he said to Hector at the bus station.
"Poor is not good, but I don't think this is better."

During the early part of the week he signed on three
new clients: a cocaine-smuggling case, an alleged rape of a
sixteen-year-old girl by the son of a prominent department
store owner, and a court-appointed capital murder that
another judge asked him to handle. Still working for
sleazeballs, he thought. But you never knew when another
Hector Quintana might come along, and you had to be
ready.

On Thursday he received a referral from a lawyer hospi-
talized with a kidney stone; the defendant, the owner of a
restaurant supply company, had been indicted for feloni-
ous assault. Warren read the file. The client, now out on
bail, was accused of battering his wife and stabbing her six
times in the arm and breasts with a toenail scissors. He
arrived in Warren's office.

"What's your version of the events?" Warren asked the
client.

"Shit, I was drunk, hardly knew what I was doing. But I want to tell you something—she deserved it."

"And I want to tell you something too—" Warren tossed the file across the desk. "I hope they put you away for twenty fucking years. Get another lawyer."

There are limits, he thought. For me, anyway.

The rape case fell into Dwight Bingham's court, which made Warren a little uneasy: he would see Maria Hahn every day. Well, he would deal with it. He was a civilized man. Nothing works out quite the way it's planned. He was beginning to grasp the human equation: to be intelligently alive means to cherish what you've got, fight for what you want, spurn what you don't want, and forget about what you can't have.

On Friday morning he called Charm at the station and said, "What are you doing tomorrow night? Would you like to have dinner?"

They went to an Italian restaurant, where they ate saltimbocca and drank a bottle of chianti. He took her back to Ravendale to show her where he had been living, and they were both nervous but nevertheless they went to bed. Warren was surprised that it was both so familiar and so exciting. At first she was shy, but the shyness left. In the night she clung to him.

On Sunday she invited him to the house. He stripped to the waist and mowed the lawn while Oobie ran in circles on the grass, fetching a dead tennis ball that Charm threw. Charm cooked blueberry pancakes and made a pitcher of Bloody Marys. In bed again, after brunch, she said, "There's something I haven't told you."

"And what might that be?"

"Bluestein, that agent I hired? He got me the job in Boston. I said yes."

"Well, that's good, Charm," Warren said easily, although he knew he had cause to be irked. "That's what you want. When did that happen?"

"Last week."

"And when do you start?"

"Right after Labor Day. Only—"

"Yes?"

"—I don't know how you feel about it."

"I feel," he said, "that it's dead right for you. If you mean do I feel like starting a law practice in Boston, or commuting to Boston for the occasional weekend in order to sustain a marriage, the answer is no."

"Are you angry?"

"No. Things will work out. You'll see." He was relieved. He was surprised by the feeling and kept it to himself.

On Monday morning, when he stopped by Bob Altschuler's office to discuss the rape case and hear the state's inevitable offer of a deal, Altschuler shut the door, grinned and said, "Before we get to that, I have news for you. Off the record?"

"Naturally."

"I read *Quintana*. You did a great job. We picked up a guy named Frank Sawyer last week at Ecstasy—positive I.D. by the two witnesses that he was the one burned this bum Jerry Mahoney. Couldn't find any weapon, but Thiel and Douglas sweated him. Douglas is particularly good at that. So finally Sawyer's lawyer says, 'What kind of a deal can we cut?' To make a long story short, we cut the deal and Sawyer says: 'This woman made me do it, see? She's my drug connection, and she knew some things about me that she threatened to tell to the law if I didn't play ball. I had no choice, see? She sends me down to the mission to find some guy in a green sweater and gray suit, some guy that might have I.D.'d her when she offed a fucking slope. So I did it. I didn't want to, but I had to. I threw the gun away in Buffalo Bayou, but I can show y'all where. And it's her gun.' "

Altschuler rubbed his big hands together vigorously. "So we got the underwater boys to dredge the bayou and they found the gun. An ivory-handled Colt .45. And it's hers, registered and all. Like she said under oath: 'It's in my desk, and I'm the only one who has a key.' Which means we have the necessary corroborating evidence to back up the accomplice-witness. We arrested her on Saturday night, right at the club. Boy, she screamed like a hog with a hornet up its ass, she cursed me like I was Satan come up from the pit. You would have loved it, Warren."

"I love it now, Bob. What kind of a deal did you make with Sawyer?"

"Thirty-five years. He's out in twelve, the little prick."

"You like the case?" Warren asked.

"I like the case," Altschuler said warmly. "You did the right thing."

"Close," Warren said, "but I haven't lost any sleep over it. And I would have done it anyway," he added, without even a hint of doubt. "Now tell me what lucky lawyer gets to defend my former client."

"Myron Moore." The prosecutor boomed a wicked laugh. "Doctor Doom! I don't know what idiot recommended him, but she went for it. I'm meeting Myron in half an hour. He wants to cut a deal too, but he can kiss my rosy-red bunions. If I can tie this one into Trunh, and I think I can, that's multiple murder—it becomes a capital. Whichever way, believe me, I'll take this case to a jury and if she doesn't get the needle, the cunt will do life without parole."

Altschuler extended his hand. Warren shook it, a little uneasily, and was at least pleased that this time he could extricate himself before his hand turned blue. But the sudden camaraderie bothered him. In six months, he knew, when Altschuler became a judge, he would have a friend on the bench. And to hell with that, he thought. I didn't need that before and I don't need it now.

He looked at the calendar on the prosecutor's desk. It was August 14, 1989. The date jogged his memory. "Bob," he said, "do me a favor?"

"Anything," Altschuler said.

"Ask Myron to give his new client a message from me."

"Sure," Altschuler said, puzzled, "but you'd better be careful. What's the message?"

"Just tell her 'Happy Birthday.' "

"Is it really? Delighted! Boy, I really had you figured wrong. You are some nasty bastard."

"No," Warren said, "not like you. But I have my moments."

When he finished their business on the rape case he hurried through the heat to the courthouse, reaching the fifth floor and the domain of the 342nd District Court a few minutes after noon. In the cool well of the empty courtroom Maria Hahn still sat at the court reporter's table, back turned to the door. She was alone in the room, gathering up papers, and Warren sensed she was about to rise from her chair and leave. Moving catlike with some speed, he bent behind her chair, put his cheek next to hers above the pulse of the white neck, took a quick breath to try and smother the aberrant beat of his heart, and said, "I have a riddle for you."

She didn't turn her head. Quietly she reminded him, "You said no games. And you made me a promise."

"I'm well aware of that," Warren said. "Here's the riddle. What is a criminal lawyer?"

"I know that one. *Redundant.* I've got a better one: why are they starting to use lawyers in laboratory experiments instead of white rats?"

"Tell me the answer this evening at dinner . . . if you're free. And I'll tell you everything that's happened to me."

Maria raised an eyebrow. "Everything?"

"Yes."

Late that night, after he had unburdened, he said, "So what's the answer?"

Maria softly sighed. Leading him to her bedroom, bending close as if offering a rare confidence, she said, "Because there are more lawyers than white rats. Lawyers clean up their messes faster than white rats do. If you have any sense, you don't get personally attached to lawyers. But mostly," she added, with a smile he would treasure, "because there are some things that white rats just won't do."

ABOUT THE AUTHOR

Clifford Irving was born in New York, educated at Cornell University and in Europe, and now lives in the mountains of Mexico with his wife, writer Maureen Earl. Together they have five children scattered over four continents.

Mr. Irving is currently at work on a novel about the death penalty.